THE VAGABOND VISCOUNT

Home is where the heart is

THE DUKE OF STRATHMORE

❧

SASHA COTTMAN

Chapter One

January 1817
    Bramshaw House
    London, England

A bolt of white-hot pain tore through his left hand, and Flynn shot to his feet. "Blast!" He danced about on the spot for a minute, muttering a long string of foul curses.

Falling off a horse hurt. Taking a blow to the head at Gentleman Jackson's boxing academy caused a certain degree of discomfort. But nothing in this world compared to the soul-deep agony of sticking a sharp sewing needle into the tender flesh of a finger. Especially when it was the little one.

"Ow, that hurts," he muttered.

Flynn shook the injured hand. Why that should make the slightest difference, he had no idea. Then again, the laws of logic weren't something that had ever really worked for him. Because if the world were in its right order, he shouldn't have to repair his own clothes in the first place. And he most certainly would have more than a paltry two good shirts to his name.

He was Viscount Cadnam; one day he would be Earl Bramshaw. Flynn would bet the few shillings in his jacket pocket that, at this very minute, no other noble in London was sitting in his bedroom repairing a shirt.

No, that particular torture was his alone.

As the pain subsided into a dull throb, Flynn picked the garment up and resumed his seat. He had no choice. If he was going to make it to the party tonight, he had to repair the torn seam. No one else in Bramshaw House was going to do it. The servants were all under strict instructions as to the modicum of service they were permitted to provide him. None of the household were foolish enough to tempt incurring his father's wrath by offering Flynn more.

Stabbing the needle back into the cream linen fabric, he consoled himself with the thought that Lady Augusta Kembal was going to be at this evening's ball. The Duke of Mowbray's eldest daughter was the one bright light in his cursed existence.

If I could just find a way for us to be together and then get out from under my father's repressive regime, my life would be grand.

He had lived with that hope for many years. Prayed that as soon as he was able, he could be away from his father. But Earl Bramshaw was a man determined to make his son's life a misery.

When he was done with his repairs, Flynn put the shirt on and finished dressing. He stopped and checked himself in the mirror. At first glance he appeared to be the same as most other men of London high society—well-turned out and privileged. It was only when he looked closer that he caught sight of the tiny repairs to his clothing. The threadbare and faded state of his unfashionable waistcoat held his gaze for a brief but disappointing moment. He could only hope it would be the same for the rest of the *haut ton* this evening. Heaven forbid anyone bothered to look down and take stock of his scruffy black boots. Leather polish could only hide so much wear and tear.

"You really do look like the Vagabond Viscount," he whispered to his reflection.

At a recent Christmas party, Flynn had bent to pick up a dropped handkerchief, but as he lowered himself to the floor, the unmistakable sound of fabric ripping had reached his ears. The ass of his trousers had finally given way. After that embarrassing moment, the London newspapers had bestowed upon him the title of Vagabond Viscount, and of course, it had stuck. Whenever he attended a function, the whispers of his new moniker followed.

Fortunately, he was made of stronger stuff, and like the rest of his life's trials, Flynn quickly learned not to take the taunt to heart.

Collecting his coat, he headed for the door and the staircase which led to the ground floor of Bramshaw House. He had made it most of the way to the front door when a familiar voice disturbed the night.

"Off to charm the ladies with your dashing good looks?"

Flynn stopped and slowly turned. At the top of the stairs stood his father, Earl Bramshaw, with his beloved greyhounds standing attentively either side of him.

His gaze took in the broad, solid form of the earl. Flynn's sire was gifted with powerful shoulders and legs as thick as tree trunks. His back remained untouched by the passing years. And while he was a man who spent his life indulging in the most fiendish of pursuits, Earl Bramshaw's health remained ruddy and strong.

The same could not, however, be said for his brindle-hued pets. Neither were in such fine fettle. One could only describe the dogs as being unhealthily overweight. An unkinder soul would simply suggest they were fat.

Did the dogs get the good roast beef tonight? I wasn't even offered the bone. The remains of fish from two nights ago were all I had for my measly supper.

He was tempted to ask his father what the dogs had eaten this evening, but Flynn had learned long ago that any sort of defiance would cost him dearly. His gaze drifted to the earl's sizeable right hand. It was clenched in a fist.

I have to get out of here before he decides I need a dose of his fatherly punishment.

"I am going to a ball to see some friends, my lord," replied Flynn. He addressed his father the same as all the household servants did—with fearful respect.

"Friends. Who would count you as a friend?" sneered his father.

The gray-haired earl made his way down the stairs with the chubby animals trailing in his wake. When he reached Flynn, his father's disapproving gaze took in his attire.

"Look at you. You are a bloody disgrace. It's a wonder people don't mistake you for a rag-and-bone picker. Well, you had better hurry up and land yourself a filly with a good dowry, because those clothes won't survive another season."

My poor attire is down to your tight purse strings. My lord.

He would dearly love to say that to his father, but he wasn't a fool.

"I am as eager to find the future Countess Bramshaw as you are, my lord. If you could perhaps see your way clear to paying for a new suit, I am sure that would help with my efforts to secure the hand of a suitable young lady," replied Flynn.

He had a monthly allowance from his late mother's marriage settlements, but it was barely enough to keep Flynn going. The state of his boots reflected his need to save money.

He walked most places rather than indulging in the extravagance of hiring a hackney cab. The Bramshaw carriage was reserved for the personal use of the earl and no one else. Genteel poverty might have a nice ring to it, but it wasn't a pleasant way to live.

"I bought you a new suit three years ago. I am not made of money," snapped the earl.

Money was tight in the Cadnam household, but Flynn suspected that was purely down to the gambling habits of his sire rather than the actual earnings from the family estate. Bramshaw Hall in Southampton ran a fine head of sheep, and its wool was of an excellent quality. Only the very best of London's tailors used it to make their garments.

There was no point in continuing the discussion. Any moment now his father would start in on him about how unworthy a son he was—how much of a disappointment he was to the Cadnam name. The customary tirade of insults would soon be followed by the wailings of the earl's self-pity.

It was when Earl Bramshaw eventually tired of feeling sorry for himself that things often turned dark. Flynn couldn't face that tonight. He had to see Augusta, and he didn't want to have to hide the telltale cuts and bruises from her.

"I am grateful for all that you do for me, my lord." Flynn bowed low to his father.

Please let me get out of here.

When one of the dogs began to fuss, Earl Bramshaw bent and gave it a tender rub behind the ear. It gave Flynn a moment's pause. Affection wasn't something he had ever received from his father.

Stirring from his musings, he made ready to make his escape.

"I shall bid you a good night, my lord."

He hurried toward the front door.

"Make sure she has plenty of money and a father who will indulge her. You can bed the wench while I work over her papa's purse. And don't do anything foolish like thinking you might marry for love." His father's words followed him into the street.

Once safely out in Cavendish Square, Flynn stopped and took the time to button up his coat and lift the collar. Anything to protect himself from the chilly January winter wind. From his pocket, he pulled a thin woolen scarf and wrapped it about his neck. It was a fifteen-minute walk to the party in Green Street, and if he kept up a steady pace, he would be nice and warm by the time he arrived.

He gave the front door a quick glance, then shook his head. As with a good many things, his father had it all wrong. Flynn hadn't the slightest intention of entering into a marriage of convenience to a woman whose dowry his father would then seek to raid.

I shall never do that.

Flynn yearned for a union based on mutual affection. For him to have a wife who loved him as much as he loved her. He wanted nothing like what the late countess and her husband had shared.

His parent's ugly connection had been a cold, hard lesson in what could go wrong. From what Flynn had gathered over the years, while the earl had been enamored with his stunning bride when they were first married, the countess could barely tolerate being in the same room as her husband. Flynn had been the first and only child of their ill-fated union.

His father had made it plain to him over the years that he held Flynn to blame for the breakdown of his marriage. And while he had never bothered to furnish his son with any particular reason for holding him to such an account, it was clear that the mere presence of Flynn was often more than enough to stir the earl's wrath.

That is not what I want for Augusta and myself.

He had to find a way for them to be together but not have her share his miserable home life. There were many things he had learned to endure privately, but Flynn would never subject Augusta to the tyranny of his father.

I must keep G away from him and his grubby fingers off her dowry.

But getting in-between Earl Bramshaw and money was always a risky proposition. Wealth was power.

He worried that if he did happen to marry the Duke of Mowbray's daughter, there was every chance that Earl Bramshaw would be waiting at the front door of the church, hand extended, seeking to claim Augusta's bridal settlement the moment the newlyweds set foot outside. It was one of the reasons why he dared not propose to her.

If only I could tell Augusta the truth as to why I hold her at bay. Of the shameful family secret I have had to keep hidden all these years.

He was a grown man, fit and healthy. But he was still no match for the brute strength of his sire.

Flynn would gladly hand over every last shilling he had if it meant keeping Augusta safe. But the bitter years of his own experience had taught him that Earl Bramshaw was a man who had no interest in seeing other people happy. He thrived on misery. Especially Flynn's.

The thought of his father wielding any sort of power over the woman he loved meant he couldn't offer for Augusta. He wouldn't knowingly put her in harm's way. He shuddered at the thought of his father and his unyielding fists.

I have endured because I've had to, but I'd rather die than let him get a hold of my beloved G.

But time waited for no man or, in this case, woman, and even the ever-patient Lady Augusta Kembal would eventually tire of waiting for Flynn to offer for her hand. And if he didn't, it was inevitable that she would, in time, look elsewhere. The thought of her being with someone else filled him with soul-deep despair.

I have to find a way out of this situation. I can't bear the thought of losing her.

Before crossing the street, Flynn stuffed his hands into the warm pockets of his coat. He might well be set to handle the cold of the night, but he was still struggling with the thorny problem of how he could marry Augusta while at the same time keeping her safe from his father.

There was one thing of which he was certain—if Earl Bramshaw dared lay a finger on the woman he loved, Flynn would kill him. Even if it cost him his own life.

Chapter Two

Augusta couldn't help herself. No matter how hard she tried, her gaze kept returning to the front door. If she wasn't looking, she was listening, taking in every name as guests arriving at the party were announced. But one face was yet to appear. One name was yet to be called. Viscount Cadnam.

You promised you would be here tonight. Where are you?

When the sharp elbow of her sister, Lady Victoria, dug firmly into Augusta's ribs, she quickly turned. "What?"

Victoria huffed in annoyance. "Gideon said that Flynn was coming tonight, so would you kindly cease with the love-struck glances at the front door. If you don't, people are sure to eventually notice. Besides, it's not that late. Give the poor man a chance to dress and make a proper entrance."

The idea of Flynn making any sort of grand entrance filled Augusta with a mixture of both joy and sadness. She would be happy to see him, but knowing that heads always turned whenever the Vagabond Viscount appeared at a social event made Augusta heartsick. It wasn't Flynn's fault that he lived with so few coins to his name. She hated the horrible nickname that the man she loved had been saddled with by London society. People could be so cruel. Especially Earl Bramshaw.

The members of the *haut ton* were more than content to judge a man on his manner of dress. Still, no one wanted to deal with the uncomfortable subject of just why a nobleman was forced to mend his own clothes and get about the city streets in tattered boots.

If only I could openly give him my love. Let the world know that he is mine.

Then she would be well within her rights to defend him publicly. To call to account those who whispered spiteful remarks. To confront his odious, penny-pinching sire. One day, she would do just that. She would give Flynn's father a piece of her mind.

Until then, she would remain nothing more than the sister of Flynn's best friend, Gideon. It was a role she constantly chaffed against. She wanted to be his everything.

Like the rest of her siblings, Augusta had been raised to speak her mind—and her heart. To seek love and claim it. The Kembal family was one where passion was not suppressed. Her parents had a fiery marriage, but secretly she envied them. They had blistering rows and were known to tear at one another. They were also madly in love.

Her cheeks burned at the sudden memory of wandering the woods near Mowbray Park the previous summer and stumbling upon the Duke and Duchess of Mowbray in the middle of marital congress. Her father had her mother backed up against a tree, with Lady Anne's legs wrapped around her husband's hips. From their grunts and sighs, there could be no mistaking their occupation. Her brother Lord Richard Kembal had dragged Augusta away with all due haste and made her swear never to tell a soul what she had seen.

That was a love she could understand. A union of two

people who had decided they wanted to be together and build a life based on their mutual desire. They were united as one.

I want that love. That life, with Flynn.

Her gaze drifted once more to the front door of the town house and the next guests whose arrival was being announced by the head butler. But she didn't take notice of them. Rather, her eyes settled on the man who had just taken his place at the back of the receiving line.

He is here.

Relief. Her pulse raced at the mere sight of Flynn. An aching need clenched in her core. Under her evening gown, her nipples turned to hardened buds.

He'd had this effect on her for as long as she could remember. Over the years, her girlish infatuation had matured into the wants and needs of a woman. To her heart's delight, her long-held prayers had been answered when, last summer, Flynn had finally let down his guard and confessed his feelings for her. Since that day, they had met in secret at every opportunity.

Flynn's declaration should have been the end of her problems, not the beginning. Any other young couple would have been able to go through the normal process of a public courtship leading to marriage. But Flynn's situation was anything but normal.

Augusta had never thought herself capable of hating someone, but what she felt toward Earl Bramshaw came close.

"It looks like someone has decided to save money on flowers this evening."

That voice had Augusta stirring from her private, forbidden thoughts of the viscount. She put her social mask firmly in place, then turned to face her cousin.

Lady Catrin Shale moved and came to stand alongside Augusta. The Earl of Shale's younger sister pointed at the nearest floral arrangement and gave a haughty sniff of disapproval. "I hear the hostess is working to a strict budget this evening, and it was either a room full of gorgeous roses or a quality orchestra. From the paucity of blooms, I would say that the music appears to have won out."

The fair-haired Catrin was a breathtaking beauty, a true diamond of the first water, but she was also an unashamed gossip. If there was anything of note happening within the ranks of the unwed misses in London society, she would without doubt be in the thick of it.

Until that moment, Augusta hadn't taken in much of the room. Her attention had been fixed on the front door and the other guests as they arrived. The details of this evening's decorations had evaded her notice. But as her cousin pointed to the small vases with white roses which were dotted around the room, it dawned on Augusta just how little money had been spent.

Red and white silk sashes had been draped over the frames of various paintings on the walls, but the frayed edges of several pieces marked them as not being new.

"Yes, well it makes sense to work within a budget. Flowers die so quickly, and silk is expensive," replied Augusta.

At this time of the year, roses were a costly indulgence. Even her own mother, the Duchess of Mowbray, drew the line on paying for hot-house flowers in January.

Lady Catrin eyed Augusta and Victoria slowly up and down. Augusta gritted her teeth. Her cousin was taking stock of their attire. Silently passing judgment on their gowns, jewelry, and hair. "And didn't they have two daughters married this past year? That would have cost a pretty sum," added Victoria.

"Well, one shouldn't host parties if one's purse is too thin," huffed Catrin.

It was nothing new. Augusta mirrored her sister's response

to their cousin's rude behavior and adopted a carefully managed air of disinterest.

One day you will be on the receiving end of someone else's judgment, and I can guarantee you will not like it.

Victoria caught Augusta's eye and shook her head. There would be plenty of time to discuss relatives and their lack of manners once they got home.

"I do so love your gown, Catrin. Is it new?" asked Victoria.

Catrin was dressed in a pale pink gown with a dark pink velvet-trimmed bodice. In her hair glittered a silver tiara. The headpiece matched perfectly with the pearl drop necklace and earring set she also wore. The earl's sister could have easily passed the dress standard for attending a formal function at Buckingham Palace rather than just a simple party in central London. Augusta imagined that Catrin had rarely heard the word understated. And if she had, she didn't care for it.

Victoria's question was, of course, a foolish one. There could be no doubt that Lady Catrin's gown was new. She wouldn't be caught dead wearing the same gown twice. Her brother Bartholomew, Earl Shale, had in Augusta's opinion, an unfortunate habit of indulging all his siblings. She had long suspected it was due to him having a lingering sense of guilt over not being present when his father had suddenly taken ill and died. Bat, as he was known, rarely said no to Catrin.

In reply to Victoria's question, Catrin simply gave a regal nod. "So, what were you two sweet things discussing earlier? I noticed you were staring at the receiving line. Was there a particular person you were waiting for?" she asked.

She loved her cousin dearly, but Augusta's tolerance for Lady Catrin Shale's need to poke her nose into everyone else's business only went so far. It stopped well before it reached the subject of Viscount Flynn Cadnam. The last thing she wanted was for Catrin to put two and two together and start a rumor.

The day you find out about Flynn and me is when the wedding invitation arrives at your mother's door. And not a minute sooner.

"Actually, we were having a small wager on the state of the supper offerings. G thinks they will be serving small cakes and sandwiches, whereas I believe they will be going for a full buffet effort," offered Victoria.

Thank you, Victoria.

Catrin raised an eyebrow, but if she had seen something, she wisely kept her silence. Anyone who had been watching the Kembal siblings closely would know full well they hadn't been discussing food. But while Catrin was quite happy to tell all manner of tales when the mood suited her, her cousins knew enough of her own wicked secrets to be certain that the Earl of Shale's sister wouldn't press them for more information.

"Yes, I was just going to pop into the supper room to settle our bet. Why don't you accompany me, cousin dearest? You are always such a good judge of these things," said Victoria.

Augusta could have kissed her sister for the suggestion of spiriting Catrin away. With her nosey cousin out of the way, she would have the perfect opportunity to slip unnoticed out of the main reception hall.

When a footman bearing a tray with glasses of wine and champagne stopped in front of them, a smiling Catrin picked up a small glass of champagne. Victoria gave the tray a quick once-over before selecting a glass of red wine. Augusta politely waved the footman away, saying, "Thank you, but not just now."

Victoria took a bemused-looking Catrin firmly by the arm. "Come, let's go and see what the catering has to offer this evening. I am keen to know if they have invested good coin in the food." She sniffed at the glass of wine and her brows furrowed. "Though, if this watered-down wine is any indication, I fear we might be in for an evening of disappointment."

It was testament to Victoria's skilled nose that she could tell that the wine had been diluted without even having to take a sip. When it came to food and drink, there were few who could hold their own against Lady Victoria Kembal.

The moment her sister and cousin disappeared, a much-relieved Augusta made a beeline for the nearest door. Her destination—the orangery.

Chapter Three

Flynn tracked Augusta's movements with a ravenous hunger. The way the bodice of her gown molded to her breasts had him touching his tongue to his lips. His belly might well be near empty, but he yearned for something else. For the brush of her sweet lips on his, and the sensation of his fingers on her firm, rose-colored nipples. Being with Augusta always filled the dark cavernous hole which held his soul.

She had stuck to their secret agreement and not met his gaze when he finally set foot inside the party. Instead, she had discreetly headed for the terrace doors and out into the night.

Good girl. You know what you have to do.

Over the past six months, they had met cloak-and-dagger in many hidden away places. Night gardens. Libraries. Flynn's particular favorite had been the back of a tea shop in Oxford Street, where a serendipitous encounter between him and Augusta had seen them slip away from her maid and younger sister, Coco, to experience a passionate ten-minute liaison that still had him lying awake at night remembering every wicked and delightful detail.

If anyone eventually discovered what he and the Duke of Mowbray's daughter had been getting up to, no doubt it would cause an outrageous scandal. And a hurried wedding. Flynn was at great pains for them not to be caught. When he and Augusta did eventually find a way to marry, it would be on their terms, and far away from the influence of his father.

Following in Augusta's wake, Flynn took the time to stop and greet other guests. His gaze roamed slyly over the room, seeking out his best friend. He was yet to lay eyes on the Marquis of Holwell, but if the loud peals of laughter which came from nearby were any indication, Flynn would hazard a guess that Gideon Kembal was in the main ballroom holding court. Augusta's brother loved a crowd.

Keep them laughing, my friend. I want to see your sister.

If Gideon was in full flight entertaining the other guests, it meant he wouldn't be looking for Augusta. That left Flynn open to spending time alone with her without being disturbed. The longer the Marquis of Holwell delighted the gathering, the better.

It was a frustrating ten minutes before he finally managed to make his way through the crowd. Keeping up the appearance of mingling rather than actually being on his way out of the building involved a certain level of skill. There were far too many watchful people at these sorts of events, and it would only take one slip-up for Flynn and Augusta's secret relationship to become public.

Flynn's heart was beating hard by the time he stepped out onto the terrace. He shivered as the cruel night wind bit through his thin evening jacket. And while London at night in January was bitterly cold, the chill did bring its own grace. No one else was out in the garden. There were no inquisitive gazes following him as he made his way down the side of the house and toward the glass orangery.

With one last glance over his shoulder, Flynn turned and

set his fingers to the handle of the greenhouse door. He slipped quickly inside. After closing the door behind him, he paused for a moment, waiting for his eyes to become accustomed to the darkened space.

"G," he whispered into the night.

The swish of her skirts announced Augusta's arrival. Her warm hand entwined with his, and Flynn let out a sigh of relief. "Gideon is playing court jester in the ballroom, so I think we have time."

She squeezed his fingers. "And Victoria is keeping my cousin Lady Catrin busy in the supper room. Hopefully, we have all margins for error covered."

The pale moonlight shining through the glass windows afforded Flynn a glimpse of the mischievous smile which sat on Augusta's lips.

I have been waiting for this moment all day.

He placed a hand gently about her waist and drew her into his embrace. Fire lit in Flynn's blood as Augusta offered her mouth to him and whispered, "Let us not waste a single minute."

She would never tire of the moment when his lips met hers. When Flynn claimed what she was willing to give. Augusta hoped that in time, he would take it all.

I am so ready for us to spend the rest of our lives together. You only have to ask.

As his tongue swept into her mouth, Augusta banished all thoughts of the future to the back of her mind. This was here and now, and she would be a fool not to seize this opportunity with Flynn and enjoy it for all it was worth. Nothing could come close to what these moments alone with him did to her body and soul.

The very first time he had touched her naked flesh, desire beyond Augusta's wildest imagination had flared to glorious life. These illicit encounters had given her a better understanding of the wicked looks her parents often exchanged when they thought no one else was watching. Looks which spoke of unsated lust.

The warmth of Flynn's lips against hers had the aching, heated need in Augusta's sex clenching. Her core pulsed with its demands. Of wanting to let him do with her as he pleased.

Touch me. Stroke me. Love me.

Flynn seemed to possess an almost primal instinct when it came to kissing her; every touch of his lips gave Augusta exactly what she desired. And as the kiss deepened and he held her close, she sensed he knew her body even better than she did. Here in his arms was heaven.

He clutched a firm hand to Augusta's rump and pulled her against him. She let out a groan at the first touch of his hardened manhood as it pressed into her abdomen. There could be nothing better than knowing what she did to him, of the carnal craving which now flared between them. If she could just be more certain of their future, she wouldn't hesitate to offer him her everything.

She had known Flynn for many years and was certain he wouldn't ever consider taking her virginity in a greenhouse. She could offer, but he would surely refuse.

Her hands drifted down from the lapels of his jacket, toward the top of his trousers. This was a dance Augusta had become quite skilled at over the months she and Flynn had been secret lovers.

He had taught her that there were other ways apart from intercourse in which they could be intimately connected. Ones which gave them both sexual pleasure, but which notionally still allowed Augusta to remain an innocent. Her fingers sought the first of these ways as she flicked open the

SASHA COTTMAN

top button on the front of Flynn's trousers. His body stiff-
ened, and she waited for the all too familiar words.

"Are you sure?" he asked, his voice gruff with lust.

The second button met the same fate as the first and as
the fabric fell away, Augusta reached eagerly for her prize.
"Absolutely," she purred, taking Flynn firmly in hand.

They moved slightly apart, and Augusta shifted her grip.
Flynn's hand settled on her left shoulder as she began to
stroke him.

The soft gasps which escaped his lips gave her all the
encouragement she needed. "You like this, don't you, my
love?"

He sucked in a tight breath, and Augusta softly chuckled.
She delighted in doing this to him, giving the man she had
loved for so long such intimate pleasure. When his grip on
her shoulder tightened, she sensed he was reaching the point
of no return. Without a moment's hesitation, she dropped to
her knees and took the length of him into her mouth. In the
ladies' retiring rooms at parties, she had heard plenty of
stories about this particular activity and how it quickly
brought a man under a woman's command.

Flynn uttered some strangled words which sounded like a
polite protest, but Augusta ignored them. He may well think
he should behave as a gentleman and not allow her to do this,
but she was set on her work.

His fingers speared into her soft chignon, leaving Augusta
to make a mental note to fix her locks before she returned to
the party. Those same fingers now fisted and tugged, lighting
up the nerve endings of each individual strand of her hair.
One day, she would tell Flynn what this did to her, how being
held while she pleasured him made her feel both powerful
and wanted.

She drew back fully on him, exalting in the low string of
curses Flynn was helpless to keep at bay. Holding the base of

20

his erection firmly in hand, Augusta ran her tongue along its length. Flynn shuddered, then muttered something else inaudible.

They had played this game enough times before for Augusta to know how close Flynn was to the edge. She licked the soft head of his cock, back and forth, teasing.

Beg for it.

He gave a halting plea. "Augusta. Please. Now."

Releasing him for just a brief moment, she glanced up at Flynn and smiled. In the dim light Augusta could make out the tight expression on his face. It was glorious. She had brought him to this desperate point, so it was only fair that she now rescued him from his torture.

Slowly she took his rigid length between her lips once more, working it into her mouth as far as she could, before hollowing out her cheeks and drawing back hard. He came with a shout, both hands landing on her shoulders as he slumped forward. Augusta continued to lavish her attention on his manhood as she gently brought Flynn back to the world.

"That was. You were. I..." he stammered.

She loved reducing him to this shattered mess, showing him just how much he meant to her.

Flynn bent and offered Augusta his hand before pulling her to her feet. They shared a moment of shy awkwardness as he set his trousers to right. He finally broke the silence with a husky. "Thank you."

As he ran his thumb down her cheek, Augusta bit her bottom lip. No matter how many times they had shared this sort of encounter, the anticipation of what he was about to do to her still had her quaking with desire. His fingers traced over her neck, across the naked flesh of her decolletage, before stopping at the top of her gown.

A thrill of lust coursed through Augusta as Flynn hooked

his finger in the top of her bodice and pulled her roughly to him. She loved it when he handled her this way. When he was in full rogue mode. "Lord Cadnam, how dare you," she playfully protested.

He smirked before capturing her lips with his and kissing her deeply. By the time Flynn eventually let her go, Augusta was panting. Her body thrummed with its heated demands.

"How dare I? Well then, perhaps I shouldn't do this. I shouldn't pull down the short sleeves of your gown and expose your naked flesh to the night air." His hands did exactly that.

Augusta swallowed deeply. The coin she had slipped to her maid had seen an end to the questions as to why Lady Augusta didn't wear any firm undergarments to parties and balls. The reason was standing right in front of her, staring at her hardened nipples like a cat about to lick the cream.

"And since I am not daring to do anything, it also means I won't be doing this..." He bent and drew her left nipple into his mouth. At the same time, his fingers pinched the right one, applying just the perfect amount of pressure. Augusta closed her eyes, her head falling back as a soft smile pulled at her lips. She reveled in the magnificent sensation of his mouth on her sensitive skin. Her core clenched as Flynn suckled. They may have only been sharing these secret moments for a matter of months, but their bodies had become well-tuned to what the other wanted. What they desired.

"How about we find somewhere a little more comfortable for you to sit so that I may continue *not* doing any of these wicked things to you?"

Augusta's brain was fuzzy with lust. Flynn could do whatever he wanted to her, just as long as he did it.

Flynn took her by the hand and led her over to a garden

bench deeper inside the orangery. Augusta sensed he wanted to be a little farther away from the front door just in case some other guests also decided that this was a good place for a private assignation. There would be hell to pay if they were caught *in flagrante delicto*.

He lifted her skirts as he sat her down. When she instinctively closed her legs, Flynn gave a disapproving "Tut, tut, Lady Augusta. You know how you have to sit for me."

Heat flushed her cheeks as Flynn pushed her knees apart. Kneeling before her, he ran his hands up her inner thighs, letting out a groan of male satisfaction when his gaze settled on the spot at the apex of her thighs. Augusta sighed. Her heart beat fast with anticipation.

I would give this man everything if he asked.

She barely had a second to become accustomed to this scandalous position before he slipped the thick tip of his thumb inside her sex. She was now little more than liquid heat. Augusta swallowed deeply, her head lolling forward and coming to rest against Flynn's chest as he stroked her hard and fast.

She whimpered as he teased her sensitive flesh, gasping when he shifted his thumb to stroke over her excited bud. When he thrust two fingers into her, Augusta's whole world shifted on its axis. At the same time, he pinched her nipple between his teeth.

"Oh, I love it when you bite," she sobbed. The pain was magnificent.

There were no words for what this did to her. Augusta was no longer in control of her own body. If Flynn asked, she would gladly offer up her soul.

Harder, deeper, he worked her until she shattered into a thousand shards of pleasure. Her desperate cries filled the quiet night air.

He continued to stroke her through the aftermath of her orgasm. His kisses and tender words of affection finally brought her back down to earth.

"I love it when you climax, G," he murmured.

"I love you."

Chapter Four

❧

Augusta avoided Flynn's gaze as she set her clothes to right. Her body still thrummed with pleasure, but her heart whispered its dark pain. These stolen moments were bliss, but they were still stolen. They were part of a secret affair. She would do anything to be able to take this forbidden love into the light and let it shine. To tell the world that she loved the Vagabond Viscount.

But no one else knew.

She hadn't even dared to share the depth of this illicit relationship with Victoria, her closest confidant. As far as her sister understood, tender kisses and sweet words were the furthest things had ever gone.

She considered her reasons for keeping Victoria in the dark to be based on sound logic. While Victoria was a romantic at heart, she was also a firm realist. If she had the slightest inkling that matters between Augusta and Flynn had progressed to this stage, Lady Victoria would demand that Augusta speak to their mother, who would, in turn, make certain that Flynn did the right thing and offered for her hand.

It would be so easy to do just that; casually let something slip and allow others to take command of the situation. The duchess would be on the doorstep of Bramshaw House the minute she discovered the truth. A wedding would soon follow.

That is what you want, so why not take the risk? End this cloak-and-dagger drama and finally become Flynn's wife.

Because Flynn had made it abundantly clear that a forced marriage was the last thing he wanted. If they were to ever wed, then it had to be a mutual decision. On their terms.

But what if this is all he and I will ever have? If Flynn won't take the next step?

Secret encounters were something that surely had a defined lifespan. The two of them couldn't go on meeting like this indefinitely. The London social season was looming large, and her parents would rightly expect Augusta to make a concerted effort to find herself a suitable husband this year. At one and twenty, she wasn't what one would consider to be on the shelf, but polite society had its rules and expectations. She had to marry.

Not only was she an attractive young woman, but she came with the added bonus of a substantial dowry. As the daughter of a duke, Augusta was by all accounts a prize catch. No doubt her name was already in the notebook of many a *ton* mother as a possible future bride for an eligible son.

But I don't want anyone else—I want Flynn.

This constant delay was beyond frustrating. It hurt. The fear that she may never get what her heart desired left Augusta feeling empty and dejected.

The time would surely come when they would have to face the reality of the situation. Hard choices and sacrifices lay ahead.

I have to be brave for the both of us.

She wanted them to take the next step. To confirm what really lay between them.

Augusta lifted her gaze to Flynn's and gave him a hopeful smile. At the same time, her fingers touched the edge of his jacket sleeve and gave a little tug. She didn't want to hear him say no, but she couldn't live without knowing. This uncertainty was slowly but surely killing her. "Have you given any further thought to us?" she asked.

Flynn nodded. "It's all I ever think about. But if you mean have I come up with a solution to my father's decree that you and I shall never marry? No I have not."

His words sent a stab of pain directly to Augusta's heart, and with it a little piece of hope broke off and died.

"I don't understand why he doesn't like me. I am sure that if my father spoke to him, they could overcome any sort of misgivings that the earl might have about me."

She hated the anguish and pleading in her voice but was powerless to do anything to stop it. What Earl Bramshaw had against her, Augusta couldn't fathom. She had met the man only once in her life, and that had been a brief polite encounter at her coming out ball several years prior. She and her potential father-in-law were all but strangers. Why didn't he want his son to marry her?

"You must know that you are not the problem, G, my love. I am. He is determined to be the one to choose my future wife and is therefore dead set against any woman who I might have in mind to wed."

Augusta put a hand over her heart and sighed dejectedly. "Then what you are saying is that we are doomed?" Her shoulders slumped. She was accepting defeat.

~

It wasn't a complete lie. His father likely wouldn't want them to marry. Not only was the Duke of Mowbray one of the few men in London society that Earl Bramshaw feared, but Augusta was a strong-minded young woman. She would stand her ground.

Flynn dared not reveal the full truth to Augusta. If he did, it would surely break her heart. Worse, she might decide that she could take the fight up to Earl Bramshaw. To defy him. The cost she would bear for her bravery would be too great. His father would do his all to destroy her. He would steal her light, and with it any hope that she and Flynn might ever have held for the two of them to find happiness. He could just imagine how much Earl Bramshaw would enjoy crushing the fighting spirit of the future Countess Bramshaw under his iron fist.

Until he could come up with a way for them to be together and safely out of his father's sphere of influence, he would have to continue to lie to the woman he loved. To the girl he couldn't imagine living without.

He reached for Augusta once more, intending to offer her a reassuring kiss, but she took a hurried step back and turned toward the door. "I think I might go and find Victoria. There is little point in me remaining here."

"You are angry with me, and I can understand why," he offered.

She shook her head. "I don't think you do, and that's the problem. You seem to think that we can go on like this forever. That these snippets of time when we are together could somehow be enough for me." Her voice trembled with emotion, and it was all Flynn could do not to offer up rash promises. Ones he wouldn't be able to keep.

"I will find a way. Don't give up on us. Please, Augusta."

He got a tired huff in response, and then she was gone, leaving him alone in the darkened orangery. For a moment,

Flynn simply stared at the door, struggling with the decision as to whether he should follow her quickly or remain here until Augusta had gone back inside. If he did trail in her wake, people would notice.

They were old family friends, and it was common for those sorts of people to marry within the *haut ton*—to embrace the understanding of friendship and comfort over the passion of love. The anguish and defeat he had seen on Augusta's face spoke of a deep longing, one which couldn't possibly be mistaken as that of mere friendship. She wore her heart on her sleeve. People would definitely notice.

Near the door, he stopped and picked a ripe orange off one of the small trees. The earl didn't have much of a taste for fresh fruit, so it was rare for such delicacies to be on offer at Bramshaw House. Flynn deftly peeled it and stuffed a couple of wedges into his mouth. It was good. Sweet and juicy. As he chewed on the fruit, he caught a glimpse of his reflection in the expansive and expensive glass windows of the orangery.

A world-weary young man stared back at him.

You look closer to thirty than barely five and twenty years of age.

He could well understand Augusta's ongoing frustration. She wanted him to declare their love to the world. And as much as his heart yearned to do just that, he didn't dare.

Any other young nobles would have been free to share their hearts and make plans for a future together. If his had been a normal existence, he would have already spoken to Clifford Kembal, the Duke of Mowbray. Heaven knew, with the liberties he had taken, he should have made an appointment to see Augusta's father many months ago. If he had, then he and Augusta would have been married well before Christmas and now be enjoying a life of wedded bliss.

"But he wouldn't ever want that," he muttered.

The very notion of Flynn finding happiness stood against

everything his father had ever done. Ronald Cadnam had made it clear—the only good marriage for his son and heir would be one just as miserable as his own had been.

If he did marry Augusta, he feared she would simply become another prisoner in his father's house. Made to live a life on the edge of poverty the same as him.

His father would do his utmost to get his hands on his daughter-in-law's dowry, and the moment he did, the reality of what she had married into would finally be revealed to the future Countess Bramshaw. She would be fleeing to the sanctuary of her family home, begging her father to find a way out of the nightmare. But there would be none—his mother's life had taught Flynn that harsh lesson.

"I can't do that to Augusta. Have her suffer the same as Mama did. I won't," he muttered.

He stuffed another piece of the orange into his mouth. The bitter taste of Augusta's pain threatened to overwhelm the sweetness of the fruit.

Right now, she was probably back in the ballroom, silently cursing him for his cowardice. For his indecision.

That he loved her was beyond doubt but finding a way for them to be together seemed near impossible. A better man would have bowed out. Let her down gently and spared both their hearts.

I love her. She is my world.

He couldn't remember a time when he didn't ache for the kisses of Augusta Kembal. There was something about the way she smiled that had him drawn to her like the proverbial moth to the flame.

Tossing the rest of the uneaten fruit into a nearby pot, Flynn left the orangery and made his way inside. It was a sin to waste food, but he had to find Augusta. He couldn't bear the thought of how they had left things. It would have been far simpler to go and collect his threadbare coat, take his leave, and walk home.

I need to see her. To let her know that this is not how we will end. I will find a way.

~

Back inside the party, Flynn went in search of Augusta. Passing the door of the supper room, his senses were filled with the enticing aroma of freshly baked pies. His stomach growled its insistent demand for food.

First, I need to find her, then I will think about feeding you.

Spying his quarry, his footsteps slowed. Across the main room, Augusta stood with her back to him, talking to her sister and cousin. Their disagreement had left him rattled. From the way Augusta was leaning in toward her sister, her fingers brushing against Victoria's deep purple gown, he sensed she was barely holding her emotions at bay. Whether she realized it or not, Augusta had an unusual tell. Whenever she was in distress, she sought the solace of Lady Victoria's hand.

Flynn came to a complete halt as the younger Kembal sibling reached out and gently took Augusta's hand in hers. As their fingers entwined, Augusta's stiff shoulders dropped a little. She had found comfort.

If he went to her now, he would only stir up the pain once more. It was better to let Augusta be, to do as he had always done retreat into the shadows.

He retrieved his coat and discreetly left the party.

Chapter Five

Augusta's frustrating encounters with Viscount Flynn Cadnam were so common that her pride had its own special little spot in the dark recesses of her mind, a place where it could go and lick its wounds. It had scurried into its familiar home the second she had left the orangery. It was still huddled in the corner by the time she got home.

Alone in their shared bedroom, Augusta and Victoria had taken up their usual spots on the loveseat by the window and were staring out into the night. They each held a glass of stolen brandy. If their father had figured out who the culprit was that helped themselves regularly to his best spirits from his study liquor cabinet, he was keeping his own counsel.

Augusta took a small sip of the strong drink. She didn't particularly like brandy but holding a glass of it somehow helped to make her feel more like a fully formed adult.

Seated next to Augusta, with her brandy glass resting on a voluminous book of curry recipes, Victoria gave a resigned sigh. "What are you going to do about Flynn? You can't keep waiting and hoping that he is going to suddenly offer for you."

There were times when Augusta felt she was stuck on a

miller's wheel, going round and round, never getting off nor making progress. How many nights had the two of them sat here and discussed her continued heartache over Viscount Cadnam?

She would dearly love to know the answer to that question. Nothing she had done so far seemed to move him an inch. Her greatest fear was that he was guilty of simply toying with her, and no matter what she did, nothing would ever come of their relationship.

He wouldn't ever use me so wickedly. I know he loves me.

The alternative was too awful to even contemplate. She had to hold fast to her hopes and dreams.

Augusta had already attended the weddings of several of her close female friends, girls who were her own age. She could name another dozen young women of her acquaintance who were betrothed. And the rest—well, they were actively on the hunt for a husband, for their forever mate.

Her problem wasn't so much in finding the right man. She was convinced she had already found him. Her problem lay in the deep-seated worry that he might not view her as being the one for him. That Flynn might well be hedging his bets.

Love was a two-way street, and she wouldn't ever settle for anything less than a full commitment from the man she married. As she gave over her heart to her husband, she would expect him to reciprocate and offer his own in return. For her to have and to hold.

I am not convinced that he is prepared to stand up to his father and fight for us.

And if Flynn wasn't going to go into battle with his ogre of a father and win his approval for his son to offer her marriage, then they were as good as finished. Her heart might well make its protests, but her pride wouldn't let her sit idly by while she wasted the best years of her life on a man who didn't have it in him to take that final step.

Her chest tightened painfully as that horrid notion settled in her mind. She had always thought a life without Flynn wasn't one worth living. That she must surely die if he up and married someone else. Now it seemed that she might just have to accept that as her fate.

And if it is, what can I do to avoid spending my life in silent regret?

As the future earl, Flynn had to marry. It was expected of him. No matter the strained relationship he had with his father, Viscount Cadnam would have to produce an heir. Earl Bramshaw might, by reputation, be a horrid man, but Augusta doubted he was a fool. Because only the most reck-lessly vindictive of men would allow his bloodline to die out just in order to spite his son.

"What am I going to do about the dear viscount? That is a very good question." Augusta fell silent for a moment as she struggled to put her thoughts into words. "I am thinking that perhaps it is time I took a different path in life. Flynn won't confront his father about us, which means the earl won't ever approve our marriage. The way things currently stand, we are both condemned to purgatory."

Just saying the words brought hot stinging tears to her eyes. She blinked hard, hoping they would go away, but more followed. Her free hand wiped at her face as Augusta tried to stop the quiver in her lip and her jagged inhale of breath, but it was no use. She covered her face and sobbed. Her heart was breaking.

"Oh, G, I am so sorry," said Victoria, resting her fingers gently on Augusta's shoulder and giving her a comforting pat.

She would surely fall to pieces if her sister offered her a hug.

"You might be right in looking elsewhere for happiness. I know that sounds cold, but it may just be what you have to do. You can't waste your life pining over someone who shows no sign of ever making you an offer of marriage. You love him, but I fear it is not enough."

There was a hard reality in the situation between her and the viscount. Flynn may, as he had so often claimed, truly want her, but at the same time, he wasn't prepared to make a major sacrifice and go against his father. And while Augusta was more than prepared to elope to Scotland and marry Flynn at Gretna Green, he wouldn't ever do such a thing.

He hadn't even bothered to seek her out after their disagreement in the orangery tonight. Instead, she had seen him head toward the front door, collect his coat, and disappear into the night.

I am finished with waiting for him to grow a spine.

"It does sound cold, but I fear that my looking elsewhere for a husband is the inevitable direction in which my connection with Flynn is headed. Only a deluded fool would continue to cling to hope when there isn't any. If I don't do something, I run the very real risk of waking up one day old and alone."

Not even for Flynn and the love she held for him would Augusta do that, nor would her parents let her.

Continually dashing herself against the granite obstinance of Earl Bramshaw was a fool's endeavor. The more she thought about it, the more it made sense for her to let Flynn go.

"My head says one thing, but my heart cries another," added Augusta.

She reached for a handkerchief. It was late, and she was heartsore.

I don't want to talk about Flynn anymore tonight. I can't handle the agony.

Augusta pointed at the cookbook in her sister's lap. "That looks interesting. Are you going to ask cook to try something new?"

Victoria softly smiled. They both knew what the Mowbray House head cook would say if she was asked to attempt a curry. Good old English roasts and plain meals were her forte, and she didn't hold a favorable view of other cuisines.

"Well, I am game to try this new Indian curry. Apparently, it is all the rage. But, no, I wouldn't be so stupid as to ask cook to make any of it," announced Victoria.

Augusta couldn't care less about food. She just wanted the comfort of being close to her sibling. "Remember when Serafina stayed with us, and she wanted cook to make pasta?"

"Yes, it was almost as bad as when Mama insisted Serafina drink orgeat. I have nightmares about watching her face as she downed her first glass. Poor girl. All she really wanted was a glass of red wine," said Victoria with an overdramatic shudder.

Augusta's dark mood broke as she burst into laughter. Her Italian friend, Serafina de Luca, had been a guest of the Kembal family the previous year, and her Roman tastebuds had been assaulted by British cuisine. Her pleas for fresh pasta or any sort of Italian food had fallen on the cook's deliberately deaf ears. "Yes, poor Serafina, she kept trying to tell Mama that at home she was allowed to drink wine, but instead she was forced to drink orgeat."

The lovely Serafina had spent her entire two-week stay at Mowbray House being fed a steady diet of hearty roasts and potatoes.

Victoria held her brandy glass to Augusta's. "Here's a toast to special friends whom we miss, and to other friends who may just end up being that."

Augusta quietly studied her drink. Her sister's words held a great deal of truth. Serafina had gone home to Rome, leaving a hole in Augusta's life that her friend's occasional letters couldn't possibly fill. And as for her other friend, she was coming to the conclusion that she may well have to set the relationship with Flynn back to what it had once been, simply friendship.

I have to stop meeting him in secret. I am only making this harder on myself.

"I expect you are right about Flynn. I can't see a way that would have him go against his father."

Victoria set her drink aside and turned to Augusta. "Hear me out on this would you? How do you think Viscount Cadnam would react if he saw you dancing with other men? With potential suitors. Would jealousy help to push him into finally doing something about confronting his father and demanding more money so he can offer for you?"

Augusta flinched, shocked at the very thought of manipulating Flynn in such a cruel manner. There were plenty of other young women in London society who wouldn't hesitate to use such tactics to force a reluctant beau into offering marriage, but Augusta wasn't one of them. Nor would she lower herself to begging.

She took a sip of the brandy and stared at the glass once more. The gold liquor was tart and bitter to the taste. "After tonight, we need to start stealing other bottles from Papa's study. I can't drink this—it's awful. I think I might even prefer orgeat."

Victoria took hold of Augusta's hand. "It seems a night for making decisions."

"Yes, I think it is. But while I won't miss the brandy, I might need time to grieve over the other loss."

The crack in her heart grew wider. And in the days ahead, it would likely break. As painful as it would be, Augusta sensed it was the only thing she could do. Let it happen, then allow grief to find a way for things to slowly mend.

Only then could Flynn Cadnam go back to being what he

had been to her when they first met all those years ago. Her brother's best friend, and nothing more.

"I think it is time for me to move on."

Victoria shook her head. "But not before you throw the dice one last time. I want to see what Viscount Cadnam does when he sees other men paying you special attention. If that doesn't force him to make a move, then as far as I am concerned, he doesn't deserve to be anything in your life. Not even a friend."

Could she cut Flynn out of her life completely? Until now, Augusta couldn't have imagined doing such a thing. But then again, she hadn't ever been at such a desperate point, one where she knew she had to do something.

"Alright, I am going to give him one last chance to save our love."

"Good. And if he fails, then he only has himself to blame."

Chapter Six

"Ah, Cadnam, just the chap I was looking for."

Flynn had had enough experience with his father's insistent creditors to know that those words were never good. Especially when he was in no position to be able to make a polite escape or pretend he hadn't heard his name being called.

Seated by the fire at White's club in St James's Street, he had nowhere to run. A gentleman couldn't just ignore another club member and make a dash for the door. It simply wasn't done.

I am certain there is a rule against collecting debts while on club premises.

And if there wasn't, then there damn well ought to be.

He lifted his gaze from scanning the gossip paragraphs of the *Morning Herald* and gave his fellow associate a wan smile. In his experience, it always paid not to give any sort of encouragement to people who sought him out.

"Good afternoon," said Flynn, his voice edged with suspicion.

To his surprise, the other man offered him a friendly grin.

SASHA COTTMAN

"I have some tickets to the theatre for tomorrow night, and I was wondering if you would like them. They come with entry to a private box, drinks, and a hot supper. Everything is included."

Flynn's eyebrows rose. No one ever offered him anything. It was always what he could do for others, which usually involved asking him to speak to his father and request that the earl make payment of an overdue account.

"How much?" Flynn replied.

The other gentleman put his hand into his coat pocket and pulled out a small cluster of papers. He handed them to Flynn. "They are free. Gratis. A friend has a play on at Covent Garden, and I am unable to attend. When I realized I wouldn't be able to use them, I immediately thought of you."

Wonderful. Now I am the charity case of the club.

His uncle Charles Cadnam paid for Flynn's annual club fees. It was the only birthday gift he ever got, and he made a point of using it to its fullest value. Without his favorite chair by the fire at White's, Flynn would be lost.

Free tickets to the theatre are too good to refuse. Beggars cannot be choosers.

He took the tickets and tucked them into his jacket. "Thank you, that is very generous of you. I appreciate your kindness."

"We chaps need to stick together. There are four tickets, so if you have some friends you would like to invite, that would be a great help." The other club patron gave him a pat on the shoulder and then moved away, calling out to some friends across the other side of the room.

Alone again, Flynn pulled the tickets out from his pocket and examined them. From the title, he assumed it was a comedy.

The Humorous Lieutenant
A play by Beaumont and Fletcher
Covent Garden
At 8pm, January 18, 1817

"I could do with a good laugh."

Treating friends out to a night of entertainment and food was something he had never been able to afford. This was a golden opportunity, one not to be wasted.

After folding up the newspaper, he tucked it under his arm and summoned a footman. "Could you please fetch me my coat?"

St James's Street to Berkeley Square was an easy five-minute walk. Flynn wrapped his scarf around his neck and stepped out into the brisk winter morning. He had a spring in his step as he made his way down Berkeley Street.

At Mowbray House, Flynn received a warm welcome from the head butler, after which he was ushered into an upstairs drawing room. He barely had time to take a seat by the fire before a large glass of whisky was handed to him.

The Kembal family and their servants had always shown him special kindness. Mowbray House was a precious refuge, one he was at pains not to abuse by visiting too often.

"Flynn Cadnam, always good to see you," said Gideon. The Marquis of Holwell entered the room with his usually cheery greeting. He pointed to the butler. "Has Lord Cadnam got a drink?"

The butler nodded. "Yes, my lord. And cook has been informed of his arrival."

Heat burned on his cheeks as Flynn turned his head away. No matter the time of day, whenever he arrived at the Duke of Mowbray's home, he was immediately offered a generous drink and food was hurriedly arranged.

Gideon dropped into the burgundy leather chair opposite to Flynn's. His face was also flushed, but unlike Flynn, his breathing was heavy.

"Are you alright?" asked Flynn.

The marquis chuckled. "Yes, I've been trying to get some exercise." He patted the front of his waistcoat. The buttons held, but they were clearly under strain. "I paid a visit to my Uncle Ewan and Aunt Caroline at Strathmore House late this morning, and instead of taking the carriage, I took a leaf out of your book and went on foot."

Flynn nodded his approval. "And how was the walk?"

Gideon's face screwed up in disgust. "Bloody cold. My hands and nose are freezing. I didn't realize how far it was until I was halfway there. Then because I am a stubborn ass, I walked all the way back here just to be sure I hated the whole experience. I won't be doing it again anytime soon."

How many times had Flynn had to endure long walks because he didn't have any other choice? At least Gideon was doing it through free will. He had a carriage and coins at his disposal.

"I'm sorry I missed you the other night at the ball. Something came up, and I had to leave in a hurry," said Flynn, changing the subject.

"Yes, I was wondering where you had got to. Victoria said you had arrived, but then you disappeared," replied Gideon.

Augusta didn't mention me. I hope she isn't still angry. Not that I can blame her if she is, I made a mess of things.

The other night. What a disaster that had been. Flynn still didn't know what he should do. Augusta had been furious when she stormed out of the orangery. The memory of the anguish on her face as she brushed past him sat etched in his mind. She had called him out on his dithering. On his refusal to speak to his father.

Can you blame her?

Of course, he couldn't. It wasn't her fault that he wasn't able to tell her the truth of his situation. That he didn't dare offer for her hand. His lie had finally borne fruit, and it was a bitter harvest.

How can I tell her that I am a coward who lives in fear of his own father?

"The truth is, I was feeling a little unwell, so I took myself off home. Didn't want to be around other people if I was coming down with something."

Another coward's lie.

One day, some day, he would stand up to Earl Bramshaw. And damn the consequences.

What would be left of him afterward, Flynn dreaded to think.

Chapter Seven

Flynn slipped out of Bramshaw House early Saturday morning. The theatre wouldn't be open until eight, but he didn't want to be around the house while his father was at home.

Just after dawn, Earl Bramshaw had started yelling at the servants and in Flynn's experience that was never a good sign. Taking his temper out on the staff would only last for so long. In his bitter understanding, it was often a prelude to the main event. Dishing out verbal and physical abuse was what his father seemed to live for when it came to dealing with Flynn.

It was far safer for him to be out the house and wandering the streets of London rather than lingering at home waiting for the moment when the hammer might fall.

He had a well-used list of places where he could go in the meantime. On Saturdays, his usual haunt was a coffee house just off Oxford Street. A discreet place whose owner didn't mind that Flynn lingered long after his coffee and small breakfast had been eaten. The kindness of strangers, who had, over the years, become friends, was a rare gift in his life.

The rest of the day was spent wandering through various

shops and haunting places where the store owner never complained if he didn't actually buy anything.

By the time he did reach Covent Garden late that day, Flynn was tired. He could also admit to being a bundle of nerves. His relief at Gideon's immediate acceptance of the invitation to tonight's play had been dampened somewhat with the discovery that while Augusta was attending, it was under noted sufferance. With Lord Matthew Kembal making up the fourth member of the party, Flynn could only hope he would add his customary light-heartedness to this evening's event and save it from being a complete disaster.

I just have to try and avoid upsetting Augusta as much as possible.

The Kembal siblings met him inside the elegant foyer of the theatre. Flynn shook hands with Gideon and Matthew, then bowed low to Lady Augusta.

He took in her pale lilac and white floral gown. Such an outfit might make another girl look washed out, but Augusta's long brown locks only served to highlight the delicate lace overlay to magnificent effect. Flynn longed to run his fingers through her soft tresses and place a tender kiss on her lips. To drop to his knees and offer up his heartfelt apology over the pain he continued to cause her.

You truly are a beauty. Any man would be honored to have you as his wife.

"Lady Augusta, you look wonderful," he said.

The soft smile and glint in her eye, which she normally greeted him with, was missing. Augusta gave him a brief, cursory nod. "Lord Cadnam. Thank you for inviting us this evening. The play should be interesting. I hear it is a new version of a previous one that didn't do so well."

Gideon, love him, gave Flynn a cheerful pat on the back. "Now then, Augusta, one should never look a gift horse in the mouth. Especially not when it comes with food and drink.

And I'm sure the playwrights have been hard at work ironing out any creases in the production."

Matthew chuckled. "We live in hope. But if it's a long-winded mess, then we shall just have to press on with making use of the wine and whisky."

His guests' words sent Flynn's hopes for the evening crashing around him. The play had already been dubbed a disaster. Of course, that was why he had been given the free vouchers. It was because no one wanted them.

Tickets gripped tightly in his hand, Flynn led his party of guests up the stairs and to the private box that had been reserved for them.

Please don't let this play be an utter shambles.

His prayers were not answered. Less than an hour later, Flynn was silently cursing the so-called friend who had gifted him the tickets. The play was, as Lord Matthew had described, a long-winded mess, and the songs were nothing short of awful. Patrons had begun to file out of the theatre long before the main intermission. The number of empty seats in the stalls was fast becoming an embarrassment.

From where he sat in the private box, Flynn was certain that for every person who rose from their seat and departed the theatre, the actors on the stage died just a little. People didn't go quietly either. Some were already shouting for their money to be refunded before they made it out into the foyer.

The only blessing was that Matthew had taken the seat next to Flynn, leaving Augusta placed on the other side with Gideon. He didn't want to face her, not after the ball and especially not after this travesty of a play.

As the curtains closed at the end of the first act, the small party rose from their seats. Flynn was beyond mortified.

I wouldn't blame them if they decide to leave.

He, however, would remain to the very end. It was too early to go home. His father would still be up.

Matthew clapped his hands together loudly and announced, "So, we made it through the first half. Well done, everyone. Hopefully, some food and a few stiff drinks will give us enough strength to soldier on to the finale."

Flynn caught the hard glare that Augusta shot her brother's way. "That was uncalled for, Matthew. Viscount Cadnam was gracious to invite us out this evening. It's not his fault that the playwright has not been able to produce an entertaining piece of work."

Gideon slung an arm around his younger brother's neck and gave his hair a good ruffle. Matthew screwed his face up at being manhandled, but wisely took his punishment.

"Yes, dear brother, don't be an ungracious wretch or I shall have to ask Mama to send you back to the schoolroom to learn some better manners. If you are out with the grown-ups, you have to behave like an adult. Now come with me, and let's go and find some champagne."

"But what about Augusta? Should we be leaving her with Flynn? I mean, is that allowed?" replied Matthew.

The younger Kembal sibling might be struggling with some forms of social grace, but he clearly knew enough about the rules regarding unmarried young ladies being left in the company of males, not from their family.

Augusta sighed. "I have known Lord Cadnam since I was a young girl. He is Gideon's best friend, so if I can trust any gentleman in London to behave with honor, it is him."

Gideon nodded. "Yes, I don't think they will be undertaking a moonlight flit to Gretna Green in the short time we are gone."

Flynn gave a tight smile to the jest. Gideon meant well, but he didn't understand how deep his remark bit. He, like the rest of the Kembal family, were still clueless about the complicated nature of the relationship between Augusta and himself.

With Matthew still held in his brotherly embrace, the Marquis of Holwell headed for the door. "No eloping, you two. We won't be long."

"There is little to no chance of that. I don't expect the Vagabond Viscount could even afford the price of two coach tickets to Scotland."

As he caught Matthew's quip, the social grin on Flynn's lips hardened.

Augusta was going to throttle her youngest brother. The play was awful. Bad but not so bad as to make it actually amusing to watch. Just diabolical. Whoever had decided to make changes had only succeeded in making it worse.

Things were awkward enough between her and Flynn without Matthew throwing his careless remarks about the place. She doubted that there was a single young person in the *haut ton* who didn't know that Viscount Cadnam barely had a farthing to his name. But only a hurtful, selfish cad would actually make mention of it.

The minute they were alone, she turned to Flynn. "I am so very sorry about Matthew. I am sure he meant no harm, but there are times when he doesn't think before he speaks. That comes from having a privileged background. He has never had to worry about where the next coin comes from. I apologize on behalf of Gideon, Matthew, and myself."

The look she got in response to her apology had her almost wishing she had kept her mouth shut. Flynn's expression all but said, please don't pity me.

"It's not as if it is a lie. Matthew shouldn't be punished for

speaking the truth. I couldn't afford one coach ticket to Scotland, let alone two."

She might well be frustrated with him and on the verge of
ending their relationship, but Augusta's heart still went out to
Flynn. Tonight, should have been a special treat. One where
he could feel proud. Instead, it had become yet another
reminder of his unfortunate situation.

Her chest tightened as Flynn drew closer. She had spent
the best part of the last few days doing her utmost not to
think about him and their encounter in the orangery. Of their
painful parting. And her decision to give him one last chance
before she moved on with her life.

"If anyone should be apologizing, it is me. I am sorry
about how things ended at the party. You were angry when
you left, and rightly so."

She pushed back her shoulders, forcing herself into a
stance which spoke of committed resolve. "The fact that I am
here under sufferance should be enough for you to know how
things stand between us. And speaking of us, Viscount
Cadnam, I think it is time we forget any of it ever happened
and put it all in the past."

Those words had sounded so perfect when she'd
rehearsed them in front of the mirror in her bedroom. But
when she actually said them to Flynn, it was clear they were
lacking in conviction.

*I wonder how many times I will have to say something like that
to him for either one of us to believe it.*

Empty though they were, they were the only thing
Augusta could say to him—her only weapon against the agony
of her heartache. He was the one who made her feel this way,
but he was also the one who was set on not publicly declaring
himself or his love.

If only he didn't hold such power over her heart.

If he loves me, he won't let me go. He will fight for us.

The unfulfilled longing which held her was a cold, hard master. Its claws were sunk deep into her skin.

Flynn stepped closer, and Augusta's breath caught in her throat. The hopes and dreams she had stuffed into the same corner as her pride now came rushing back out. They danced about in front of her like playful puppies, desperate for attention. It would be a foolish thing to pick them up and give them a little pat.

Foolish but so tempting.

I have to be strong and resist desire. There is no other way to get through this and survive. I must know if his love for me is strong enough.

Their hands brushed against one another, and Augusta screwed her eyes shut. She went to pull her hand away but couldn't summon the strength. "Please don't tease me anymore, Flynn. I beg of you. You have made your position clear. Your father will never agree to our union, which means you cannot offer for me. Whatever we had, whatever we were, it's over. It would be cruel of you to toy with me further, and I hope that you are not that sort of man." Her voice cracked with emotion. She wasn't nearly as strong as she hoped she might be. Her resolve was ready to crumble. And when it did, she had no doubt that she would throw herself into Flynn's embrace and beg him to kiss her.

Augusta was still wishing she was anywhere but here when their fingers twined into one another. A single tear snaked its way down her cheek as she stood gazing out at the half-empty theatre. They were silent for a time. Augusta still searched for the right words to say but knew nothing would help. If this course of action failed, then Flynn was lost to her.

I don't know how much more of this I can take.

"I wonder how many people will come back for the second act," he said.

A dejected sigh escaped Augusta's lips. Flynn had

retreated to the safety of small talk. Neutral ground. A place where neither of them had to risk their hearts. If she had any sense, she would take this as the opportunity to concede defeat.

And move on with her life.

"If the other patrons know what is good for them, they will eat the food and then go and seek entertainment elsewhere. The actors are quite good, but the material is a tissue of absurdity," replied Augusta.

I can't believe we are standing here holding hands and discussing the play.

Flynn's grip on her hand tightened. "I expect the poor theatre critic for *The Star* will have to spend his entire Sunday searching for the right words to describe what we have witnessed here tonight. I can think of a few choice words, but most would not be fit for publication."

Augusta pulled her fingers free of Flynn's grasp. As she did, her chest tightened, and her breathing grew labored. She could have sworn her heart had actually broken in two.

"It must be awful to have worked to create something and then have it fail," he added.

I know exactly how that feels.

At least her defeat was something she could suffer in private. The gossip columns of the London papers had only taken notice of Flynn because of his obvious lack of funds and poor attire. They had given him the title of Vagabond Viscount and then, fortunately, moved on. They hadn't noticed Augusta. She had been spared that humiliation.

She could just imagine what the newspapers would have had to say about the daughter of the Duke of Mowbray conducting a secret love affair with an impoverished noble. They would've run out of both ink and paper before they were done.

"Yes. Just because you hoped with all your heart that

something would work doesn't mean it ever will. But I am sure the writer of this doomed play will come up with something fresh very soon. They will put the disappointment behind them. Seek pastures new."

Flynn met her gaze. His lips opened, and Augusta steeled herself for his reply. But he said nothing. Instead, he moved away as the voices of her brothers drifted in from the hallway outside their box. Gideon and Matthew appeared through the heavy red curtains; both carried a glass of champagne in either hand.

"That was quick," noted Augusta.

"Yes. It would appear that few people are staying to sample the refreshments. The biggest crush is at the front door. Theatre patrons are flooding out into the street," replied Gideon, handing her a glass.

Matthew passed a drink to Flynn, then downed his own in quick fashion. "Drink up, everyone. We may as well enjoy the catering before the second act. There is no point in us trying to leave. I expect there will be carriages blocking the road outside for some time to come."

"Yes, and who knows, if we down a few more glasses of champagne, the play might well start to improve," added Gideon, offering Flynn a wry smile. Augusta could just imagine that her brother was feeling sorry for his friend, sharing in the viscount's embarrassment.

Augusta's gaze fixed on Matthew's empty glass. It would be so easy to do as her brothers had suggested and dull her pain with a glass or three of sparkling wine. She could pay the price and stay in bed tomorrow. Hiding under the blankets seemed the best place in the world to be right this very minute.

But she wouldn't.

You are Lady Augusta Kembal, and you will conduct yourself with all due decorum.

Her governess's teachings were well ingrained. A lady might suffer disappointment and heartache, but she kept those things private. Never allowed them to cloud her judgment. Emotions were to be carefully controlled. One might consider a spontaneous moment of indulgence, but a lady never acted upon that impulse.

I should have listened to my own counsel long ago and not let things get to where they did with Flynn. I knew I was treading on dangerous ground when I let him kiss me that first time. When I agreed to our secret affair. I was a fool.

But her heart had made its demands clear, ignoring all the risks. The moment Flynn had touched her, had taken her into his embrace, all sense and reason had been lost.

The harsh lesson of first love had been cruel, but Augusta had finally learned its teachings. She wouldn't make that same mistake again.

Augusta handed Gideon back the glass of champagne. "Thank you, but I seem to have lost my taste for such things."

Chapter Eight

The Star
Monday 20 January 1817

It is, from beginning to end, a tissue of bombast, silliness, and absurdity.
The curtain fell amid the hisses and groans of a great majority of the House.

Lord Matthew Kembal tossed the newspaper onto the breakfast table and clapped his hands together. "Well, if that isn't the worst review I have ever read, I am a horse's ass. At least the champagne and roast beef sandwiches they served at intermission were top-notch."

Augusta studied her eggs. The Monday morning review of the play they attended on Saturday night was bitingly accurate in its scorn. The audience had indeed shown its displeasure at the end of the evening. She doubted the writers would attempt another resurrection of something that should have been left to die in the first place.

She still held a sense of pity for Flynn over his clear mortification at having invited his friends to what should have been an entertaining evening, only to then discover the play was nothing short of terrible.

Gideon shook his head. "Poor Flynn. He was so excited when he told me he had been given free tickets to the theatre. Now we can all understand why his acquaintance at White's was so keen to be rid of them. Still, it was nice to be out with friends and family, so I don't consider the night to be a complete disaster."

Her eldest brother could always be relied upon to come up with something positive to say. He was a fierce defender of his friend.

"G said the catering was adequate. Though my own experience of Covent Garden is that things are rather bland, and dishes are left to go cold before they are served," offered Victoria.

If she didn't know better, Augusta would have sworn that Victoria had been born with a salt and pepper shaker in either hand. No silver rattle for her.

At least the conversation this morning revolved around the play. It helped to keep her thoughts away from the subject of Flynn, of her decision to finally put any hopes she might have held for them firmly in the past and move on.

She had set aside the plans to use other men in order to make Flynn jealous, deciding that if he wasn't prepared to offer for her of his own volition, then theirs wasn't a relationship worth fighting for. As he had held her hand at the theatre and made small talk, the truth of the situation had finally crystallized in her mind.

Flynn would never be hers.

Her heart still whispered otherwise. Still held onto hope. She could only pray that in time it, too, would get the message. There was not, and had never been, any real chance of her becoming Viscountess Cadnam.

She downed the last of her tea and rose from the table. "If you would please excuse me, I have some letters to write."

Augusta made her way upstairs to the main drawing room. This room overlooked Berkeley Square and was one of her favorite places in Mowbray House.

The morning sun shone weakly through the windows. London in January could be cold and dull, and she was grateful for any sort of bright warmth. She took a seat at the oak table close to the window, claiming her regular spot. If her day went as usual, by midmorning her sisters, Coco, and Victoria, would have joined her, and they would be working on their own correspondence.

In Victoria's case, her efforts would include writing her latest piece of advice on the best places to dine in London and then pasting it onto the pages of the newspaper. Some might view such a thing as being silly or trite, but Augusta had long shared the secret that her sister wanted nothing more than to have her measured comments published. For people to take both her and her love of food as seriously as she did.

The door of the drawing room opened a short time later, but instead of one of her sisters making an entrance, it was her mother. The Duchess of Mowbray swept into the room with all the elegance most other women reserved for formal events.

She headed toward the window, before coming to a halt just a foot or two away from the glass. It was the exact same place she stood most mornings. It was the perfect vantage point for her mother to see and, just as importantly, be seen.

The duchess was Berkeley Square's equivalent of an old town crier. If she was at the window of her drawing room at this hour of the day, then all was well with the world.

"Your father quoted the theatre critics' thoughts on the play you attended on Saturday night to me earlier this morning. Little wonder the three of you were home so soon after it was due to end. It sounded positively horrid."

Her daily ritual conducted, Lady Anne moved away from the window and came to join Augusta. She took a seat at the table. By the way her hands tapped gently on the highly polished surface, it was clear she was in the mood to talk. "My maid mentioned that your maid is worried about you, Augusta dear. Is there something you would like to discuss with me? You know you can trust in my complete confidence."

Her mother might well be a leader of the *ton*, but she had always made time for her children. Under most other circumstances, Augusta would have sought out Lady Anne and talked things over, but she had decided to keep the subject of Viscount Flynn Cadnam a private matter, only sharing her thoughts with Victoria. The duchess didn't need to be involved. With the relationship now over, any advice her mother might seek to offer was likely moot. "Thank you, Mama. I am well," replied Augusta.

The duchess shifted in her seat. When she clasped her hands in front of her, the message was clear. She wasn't going anywhere until Augusta shared her troubles.

I wish you weren't so stubborn. You don't need to fight my battles.

"If you don't wish to discuss specifics or even particular people, we could simply discuss the nature of your problem. Sometimes even general advice can help."

The duchess was not going to let the matter rest, which meant that Augusta had to find a way to confide in her mother without telling the truth or, worse—lying. Lady Anne was an intelligent woman, and she could spot a mistruth some way off.

Augusta took in a deep breath. Perhaps her mother was right. A problem shared could be a problem halved. Or at least it might be good to get some of her troubles off her chest.

"It's a matter of the heart. There was a particular gentleman who held my attention for quite some time. I have recently decided to end our connection. The problem being that whenever I thought he was about to do something regarding a possible future together, he took a step back."

It made Flynn sound so heartless and cruel.

He is not a bad man. Maybe I was just pinning my hopes to him when there was never any hope in the first place.

"I see. And this gentleman is not a rake nor one with a reputation for dallying with young women's affections?"

Augusta shook her head. "No, he is not." That wasn't the Flynn Cadnam, who Augusta knew. He had always been polite and considerate around women. If he was a rake of the highest order, then he was also a masterful magician who kept it well hidden.

"This man is, as far as I know, both honorable and a respecter of the female sex. If there is an issue in his life, it lies with his family. Or, in this case, their opinion as to my lack of suitability," replied Augusta.

The duchess's lips pursed, and a scowl appeared on her brow. "What do you mean your lack of suitability? You are the daughter of a duke. I couldn't think of a more suitable young lady in the entire city of London. Or, if I am being completely honest, the whole blessed country. Is that what the young man in question has told you?"

There was a definite chill in her mother's voice. The

duchess was clearly ready to go into battle with this unknown family who had dared to cast aspersions on her eldest daughter. Any moment now she would rise from her chair and be demanding that Augusta gave her a name.

But she couldn't do that, even if it meant defying her mother. Flynn had enough to contend with in his life without having the Duchess of Mowbray setting her vengeful sights on him.

"I don't think it is his entire family, just his sire who seems to have an issue with me. Truth be told, I have only ever met this young man's father once or twice, but he has apparently made his opinion of me clear. I am not good enough."

Her mother sat back in her chair and crossed her arms. "You may not wish to give me names, but I can guess at several families who might hold this foolish view. Rest assured, Augusta, it has absolutely nothing to do with you, but everything to do with how your father has structured your dowry."

The mention of her dowry suddenly made horrible sense to Augusta. Her bridal settlement was carefully worded. If any family sought to gain access to it through marriage, they would be in for a large dose of disappointment. And if Flynn's father was as hungry for wealth as Augusta suspected, then the reasons for him deeming her unsuitable could well be down to her marriage settlement. To his inability to touch it.

Oh God, is that why he won't offer for me? Because of money.

If that was the case, then the notion of throwing other men in Flynn's face wouldn't do anything—it would only serve to cause him undeserved pain.

She met her mother's gaze, and the duchess slowly nodded. "Your dowry is watertight. It is designed to protect you and your children in the event of something happening to your husband. No one can kick or kiss it out of you. Which means, if you are foolish enough to give your heart to a man who is unable to access his own money, then you, my dear, are signing up for a life of poverty. Your annual pin money allowance is generous but not enough for a couple or a young family to live on."

Lady Anne rose slowly from her chair and straightened her skirts. "And, of course, your father would never agree to such a union. Neither would I. You must have heard of the phrase, *marry in haste, and repent at leisure*. It exists to warn lovestruck people not to throw their lives away in the hope that the person or circumstances into which they marry will change. People don't. And aside from sudden tragic events, nor does life."

The duchess made it most of the way to the door before she stopped. She returned to the table, and it was then that Augusta caught the worried expression on her mother's face.

"We are still not naming names but let me say this, and I want you to take careful note. If you changed your mind and did decide to marry this mystery man, things could be difficult for the two of you for a very long time. And I mean years. If, for instance, he happens to be the heir to a title and he has a terrible, awful father, nothing will change until either his sire dies, or the young man in question grows a spine."

Augusta nodded. "So, what you are saying is that it might be best for all concerned for me to look elsewhere for a future life partner?"

Her mother softly sighed. "I know it hurts, sweetheart. But there is nothing romantic about being trapped in a marriage which you quickly come to regret. Being near penniless while trying to survive in London society would be one of the worst fates, I could ever imagine for any of my children. The likes of you and I have not been bred for that kind of existence. Has it occurred to you, Augusta, my dear, that this man might be holding back in order to protect you? If that is the case, then he truly does love you. And his love is strong enough that in accepting his inability to ensure your financial security, he is prepared to let you go and find it elsewhere."

The duchess's words of warning were still ringing loudly in Augusta's ears long after her mother had left the room.

Chapter Nine

Flynn watched Augusta from his vantage place a few yards across the other side of the ballroom. Dressed in a pale lemon creation which draped perfectly from her bustline all the way to the top of her matching silk slippers, she looked as she always did to him—positively radiant. On any other night, he would have found his way to her side, bowing low as he told her just how lovely she was in his eyes. Then they would steal away and find a secret place to share kisses and tender embraces.

But not tonight.

This was the closest he dared get. Her note thanking him for the evening at the theatre had been both polite and brief. The sort of thing one sent to a casual social contact, not a longtime friend. And most certainly not a man who had known her as intimately as he had. The true intent of her short missive had been received and understood. She was angry with him, and as punishment, he had been placed firmly into the brother's best friend box, and there he would stay.

The thought that she had indeed put an end to their love

affair burned like acid inside him, eating away at his soul. He wanted Augusta. Craved her touch. She was the perfect woman for his wife. For his viscountess and future countess. He had spent years thinking of her and imagining what she would look like when heavy with his child. A baby they would have created in a moment of passion and love.

And now she barely speaks to me. This is beyond awful.

He glanced at the left sleeve of his suit jacket, but instead of congratulating himself on the excellent handiwork of repairing the hole which one of his father's greyhounds had put in the cuff, he inwardly groaned.

I am a beggar amongst wealth and privilege. What can I dare to offer any woman?

For a brief moment, he found himself envying the footmen and maids who were serving the guests. They knew their place in the world and were able to live true to it. He was like a poor relative who spent their days living on the edge of poverty, dependent upon the good favor of others.

Tonight's party was like most others at this time of the year. London was slowly coming back to life after Christmas. People were returning from their estates and making ready for the opening of parliament on January 28th.

Flynn liked to sit through parliamentary sessions. He was genuinely interested in good government, and when he did eventually become Earl Bramshaw, he intended to take his place in the House of Lords and participate fully. A good deal more than his father did. The current earl rarely attended parliament as it would mean him having to get out of bed early after a long night at the card tables.

Augusta greeted some mutual friends, her elegant curtsy evidence of her privileged upbringing. Flynn's gaze went to the tall, dark-haired gentleman who stepped forward and took the hand of the duke's daughter, then bowed deeply to her. Anger sparked in his brain as the man, a wealthy noble, led a smiling Augusta out onto the dance floor.

Flynn gulped a large swig of his drink as the couple joined in a waltz. He savored the pain as the brandy burned his throat on its way down. Jealousy coursed hot through his veins.

Augusta was, as always, light of foot and graceful as she twirled around the dance floor. But Flynn's attention was fixed on her partner. He was far *too* good a dancer, in Flynn's twisted opinion. He was holding her *too* close. His hand was *too* low on her waist. It was all he could do to stop himself from marching across the floor and making his displeasure known to all and sundry. With his fists.

If he made a public display of his anger, questions would surely follow. None of which Flynn was in any sort of position to be able to offer up an evenhanded answer to if asked. But if he couldn't do something about Augusta and her liberty-taking beau, her brothers surely could.

Flynn's gaze tracked frantically over the crowd, searching. Where the devil was Gideon or any of the other Kembal males? Didn't they see what was happening? This scoundrel was making sweet music with their sister. They really ought to put a stop to this scandalous behavior.

He finally spotted Lord Richard Kembal in the gathering. Augusta's brother was watching the waltz, but to Flynn's disgust and abject horror, instead of him being outraged, he was smiling. Enjoying the sight of Augusta dancing with someone who wasn't Viscount Cadnam.

Has the world run mad?

The truth of things settled heavily on his shoulders. Richard was watching his sister dance with a perfectly accept-able noble bachelor, an eligible male who could make an offer of marriage to Augusta and deliver on his promise.

Bloody hell. What am I going to do?

He might be struggling, but it was clear Augusta was doing as she had promised she would. She was moving on with her life. And the man she was dancing with... he still had his hands far too low on her waist. Resting his fingers on her magnificent curves, the ones which, as far as Flynn was concerned, were by rights only his to touch. To caress.

It didn't matter that to a sane observer there was nothing out of place with this waltz. They moved well together, and if the smile on Augusta's face was any indication, she found her gentleman partner perfectly acceptable. From where Flynn stood, it appeared that he was the only person who found it to be an utter abomination.

Augusta's words from the night at the theatre came back to haunt him. To remind him of where the two of them now stood in her heart and mind.

Whatever we had, whatever we were, it's over.

She had to know he was watching. Was forcing him to endure the sight of her dancing with another man her way of making her position clear? They were finished. He had lost her.

Augusta was a strong girl, and no doubt in time, she would find a way to move past her heartbreak. She would marry someone else, while he would be left with a lifetime of remorse. Forever lingering at the edge of the dance floor while she smiled and waltzed, held in the arms of another man.

I am losing her.

The thought of the one bright light in his life no longer shining for him sent a sharp spear of pain to Flynn's chest. If she did find another to marry, he couldn't blame her. Apart from a shared existence of misery, there was little he could currently offer Augusta.

The waltz finally, mercifully, came to an end. When Augusta left the dance floor, Flynn followed her. She stopped a passing footman, who was bearing a tray of drinks, and reached out to take a glass of champagne.

Flynn stepped forward, scooping up the glass before Augusta had the chance to claim it. A flash of annoyance crossed her face. "I didn't think you drank champagne all that often, Lord Cadnam."

She was back to calling him by his title. Gone was the soft 'my love' or 'my heart' he had grown so accustomed to hearing from her sweet lips. Even *Flynn* would have been better than being subjected to the impersonal, formal way Augusta now addressed him.

He handed her the champagne before dipping into a low bow. "Lady Augusta. You look divine this evening. Pale lemon suits your complexion."

Augusta took the drink, but she wouldn't meet his gaze. "Thank you."

Flynn moved closer. They were in public, so he was at pains to make their encounter seem as casual as possible. Old friends simply catching up at a party, nothing more.

"I watched you dancing," he said.

He wasn't going to even name the lord Augusta had waltzed with. The mere thought of where that rogue's hand had been, was enough to have him fighting the urge to go and do damage to the man's face.

"Did you? I hadn't noted your presence. My dance teacher always taught me to focus on my footsteps while at the same time making sure I was smiling at my partner. That doesn't leave much opportunity to see who is standing on the edge of the dance floor." Augusta still refused to meet his eyes.

You knew damn well I was watching.

She was lying. And she most certainly would have known he would follow her when the waltz was over, and her dance partner had taken his leave.

Look at me now, G. Tell me the truth of your heart.

"Is this your way of punishing me? You ask me not to be cruel, and yet you throw another man in my face at the first opportunity you get."

She finally met his gaze. Her light brown eyes were cold and hard. Their usual warmth was sadly lacking. Her protective armor was firmly in place, set up to shield herself from him.

Augusta held the untouched glass of champagne out to Flynn, thrusting it toward him. "Take it or wear the contents. Your choice, Lord Cadnam. I don't care either way."

He reluctantly took the drink. "We have to talk, Augusta. I won't have you throwing yourself at the first eligible bachelor just in order to vex me. We are not done."

She let out a tortured gasp and quickly turned her head away. Flynn's heart sank at her obvious distress. "Augusta, my love," he murmured.

"Don't," she choked out.

What he would give to be able to take her in his arms and hold her right now. To let her know that he hadn't given up on them. To tell her he loved her, and always would.

Flynn was about to throw all caution aside when out of the corner of his eye, he spied Gideon making his way toward them. He offered Augusta the champagne once more. "Your brother is about to descend upon us, and I, for one, don't want to have to explain to him as to why I am holding your drink, and you are on the verge of tears."

To his relief, she took back the glass and made a hurried effort to compose herself.

"Good evening. I was wondering when I would catch up with the two of you," said Gideon.

The two of us. If only you knew the truth, Gideon.

Augusta offered up a tight smile to her brother, and if the Marquis of Holwell noticed the tears which glistened in his sister's eyes, he thankfully made an effort not to mention them.

"I was busy dancing the waltz while Flynn here was kindly minding my drink. How has your evening gone so far, Gideon?" replied Augusta.

His friend let out a huff. "Boring. I am so utterly over these parties. I have no idea how I am going to survive the coming social season. There had better be some fresh faces arriving in London, because I am tired of seeing the same people at the same parties, night after night."

If that were the extent of his own problems, Flynn would be more than happy. But Gideon did have a point. London society had a certain sameness to it, especially at this time of the year. People were slowly making their way back to town, but the wet and cold winter weather kept most social activities confined to indoors. There was a finite amount of dancing and making of small talk that a person could undertake before it all blended into one.

The only point of interest in all of this was Augusta. And now he was in grave danger of having to watch while she not only danced with someone else but went off and married them.

Ten years he had spent living with regret. First with the loss of his beloved mother, and then with the misery of life with his father. There wasn't a day that Flynn didn't wish he was back living at Bramshaw Park, far away from London and his hated sire. He couldn't ever find it in his heart to regret loving Augusta.

I am going to go and speak to my father, damn it. He has to see reason.

He wasn't going to let Augusta out of his life. She was his, and it was high time he took control. Claimed what they both wanted. Gave her the future she deserved. A future with him.

"I'm sorry, but I am going to have to take my leave of you. I need to go home and speak to my father," he announced.

A frown appeared on Gideon's face. His friend knew the truth of Flynn's home life. Of the terrible beatings he had endured at the hands of the earl. That only the gravest of occurrences would see Flynn making the effort to voluntarily speak to his sire.

"Would you like me to come with you?" offered Gideon, his voice edged with concern.

His friend's timely presence had saved Flynn from the violent hands of his father more times than he could remember, but this was one occasion where he couldn't help.

Flynn did his best to ignore the look of worried interest on Augusta's face, silently praying she wouldn't ask as to why her brother was offering to accompany him home. He was a grown man; he shouldn't need anyone to protect him.

One day you might know the truth. I just don't know how I could face you afterward.

"Thank you, no. Though I do appreciate the offer. There is an important matter I need to discuss with my father tonight." He turned and bowed to Augusta. "My apologies, Lady Augusta, I was hoping to share a dance with you later, but this pressing issue cannot wait."

He left the Kembal siblings and made for the door, stopping on his way out to grab a generous glass of whisky, which he downed in quick time. A stiff drink always came in handy for a shot of warmth before facing the bitter winds of a January night. A half-mile walk lay ahead of him from the party to his family home.

Who knows. Perhaps during that time, I might come up with something compelling to make the old swine see reason. He could agree to let us marry and live happily ever after.

He huffed at the insane futility of hoping Earl Bramshaw might grow a heart. Who was he trying to fool?

I have to do something. I can't lose her. But what?

~

Reaching Bramshaw House, he knocked on the front door. His father didn't consider him worthy of a key. The old butler had once confided in him that the earl took particular pleasure in making his son and heir linger outside in the street. Flynn was simply grateful that he didn't have to use the servants' entrance. He wouldn't put it past his father.

He waited the customary, infuriating ten minutes before someone finally opened the door. By the time he stepped inside Bramshaw House, Flynn's body had cooled, and he was shivering. It would take another good hour before he managed to get warm again. It was petty, little things like this that were the constant bane of his life.

"Lord Cadnam," said the footman. He didn't bow to Flynn.

It was just another mean-minded act from his father. The servants were given free rein to treat Flynn like an unwelcome guest. The spiteful ones took full advantage of this directive, while the wiser ones stuck closer to the rules of expected servant-master behavior.

Flynn kept a long list of the names of servants who would be leaving this place without references the day he became earl.

He found his father asleep, seated in a chair by the fire in the main sitting room upstairs. The two enormous greyhounds were lying in the prime position of warmth in front of the hearth. They looked well-fed. A juicy meat bone sat next to the larger of the two beasts.

We must have had beef this evening.

When he said we, he didn't include himself in that count.

He hadn't seen red meat on his plate in weeks. A thin vegetable broth had been the extent of his supper offerings earlier this evening. Flynn's stomach growled at the sight of the meat.

He didn't dare sneak food from below stairs. The one and only time he'd tried had seen him soundly beaten and the Bramshaw House cook summarily dismissed for not keeping the door to the kitchen locked.

The earl stirred and cracked open an eye. "Come skulking about, have you? Thinking to do me in while I am asleep— that would be right. A cowardly act to end my life," grumbled the earl.

Most other people would flinch at such a cutting remark, but Flynn was long past the point of being impervious to his father's bitter words of abuse. That should have been a good thing for him. But unfortunately, over the past few years, the earl had also come to the same realization and decided that what his son really needed was to feel the weight of a cane smashed across his back.

"I would never willingly seek to do you harm, my lord. I have come to ask for your consideration about me being able to take on a wife. And for you to grant me access to suitable funds to support a family."

The earl's top lip curled up in obvious disgust. "What woman would want you? Or is this your cock talking? Couldn't find a stray matron who would take pity on you and let you into her bed, eh?"

Flynn steadied himself. His gaze settled on the floor. He knew better than to meet his father's eye. "The title needs a legitimate heir. And in order for that to happen, I have to marry. My lord."

One of the slumbering dogs stirred and lifted its head. Flynn caught sight of his father's hand as he reached out and gave the animal a friendly rub behind the ears.

"Who is a good boy? You always love a good long nap after supper," said the earl.

His father picked up the beef bone, and the dog lazily licked at it before turning its head away. Its stomach was no doubt still full from the earlier meal.

He loves those dogs more than he cares for me.

Flynn wasn't naïve. The greyhounds had always come ahead of him.

"As I was saying. If I am to produce a legitimate heir, I need to marry. Which means I have to be able to provide for a wife."

The earl kept fussing with the dog, making Flynn wait. He finally dropped the bone to the floor before sitting back in his chair and letting out a tired sigh. "As with everything, I have to hand it to you on a platter."

"Pardon?"

"I have told you that I will find you a wife. One whose papa is rich and who will indulge his daughter when I press her for money. His purse can provide for the two of you."

Why can't you just let me choose my own wife?

Flynn cleared his throat, then paused. He knew enough of his sire's temper to sense when he was treading on dangerous ground. The cane was nowhere to be seen, but no doubt it was somewhere close at hand, ready for his father to put it to evil use.

"That is very gracious of you, my lord, but I am quite capable of finding a wife. I just need a little money."

"You will marry who I damn well tell you to," said the earl, his tone low and threatening.

"Please. That is unnecessarily cruel."

The earl rose from his chair, and Flynn took a hurried step back. The safety of the door beckoned.

"What is cruel is having to see your face every damn day. Haunting the halls of my home. Carrying my name."

Flynn's gaze shifted to the other side of the chair, where he spied the end of his father's weapon of punishment. Any minute now, it would be waved in his face.

"But why would you need to choose a wife for me? There are plenty of young ladies in high society who are perfectly acceptable," Flynn asked.

Augusta's name stuck in his throat. He was torn. Desperate to marry her, but still in fear of putting the woman he loved in harm's way.

The why was more important than the issue of who in this situation. Where his son was concerned, Earl Bramshaw never did anything without there being a way to inflict some measure of pain.

"The cards and horses have not been running my way for quite some time. The particular chit I have in mind has a sweet papa who will clear all my debts if you marry his daughter. With the lure of a title and social connections for his little girl, her father's purse will be open to me. Once you are wed, you will work your charms on your new wife and get money when I need it. Women tend to do what they are told if given the right sort of motivation."

Flynn shuddered at that last remark. It held all manner of distasteful notions. Earl Bramshaw viewed most people as a means to an end, so a daughter-in-law wouldn't pose any real problem for him. Which meant Flynn would struggle to protect her.

What was surprising about any of this to Flynn? Nothing. The debt-laden earl had solved his money problems and found his son a bride in the process. What Flynn thought of it likely didn't figure into his father's thoughts.

And I thought to ask you to let me marry Augusta. Perhaps she is better off marrying someone else. At least she would be out of your vile reach.

The pain of his father's rejection continued to stab at his

heart. After all these years, it really shouldn't, but it did. Flynn hated himself for craving just an ounce of affection from his sire. Even one kind word would have been better than the sun shining brightly on a cloudless day. But that was never going to happen.

"What do I get out of this?" he ventured.

The earl scoffed. "You get a roof over your head and a warm body in your bed. It's more than you deserve."

When the other greyhound made a noise in its sleep, the earl turned to the dog. He stepped away from his son, his muscular hands flexing as he moved closer to his favored pets. Flynn caught a second glimpse of the hateful cane poking out from behind the chair. A familiar ripple of fear raced down his back. It was a warning. If he remained in the room, there was every chance he was going to be on the receiving end of his father's wrath.

It was time to concede defeat and beat a hasty retreat. The earl was still fussing over the dogs as Flynn made his way to the door. As soon as he was outside in the hallway, he hastened his steps. He was at a half run when he rounded the corner, taking the stairs two at a time up to the next level of Bramshaw House.

Once inside his bedroom, Flynn locked the door. For a moment, he stood listening for any sign of his father having followed him. To his relief, there was only silence in the house.

He began to process the conversation he had just had with his father. Earl Bramshaw had chosen a bride for his son. A stranger whose father would not only settle the earl's debts, but who would one day become Flynn's countess.

The mere notion of marrying this unknown woman made him nauseous. How could he possibly share his future with someone he had never met?

I have to do something. I can't let this happen.

He was going to have to come up with a plan, and quickly. If he didn't, not only would Augusta be lost to him, but he would be saddled with some stranger as his wife. Flynn could just imagine that his father might already have the church and minister booked. And knowing how cunning the earl was, the first Flynn would know about it would be when the banns were being read in church on Sunday morning.

Augusta would suffer the same heartbreaking experience that he had felt watching her dance with another. The dance had ended, but marriage to another was for life.

No. I won't stand for it. He has gone too far.

It was time to finally throw off the shackles of his life. To strike a blow for the future he wanted, for both himself, and the woman he loved.

He was not going to give Augusta up, nor was he was going to let his father near her.

Chapter Ten

Flynn's feet pounded the pavement as he made his way from Bramshaw House to his uncle Charles's home the following morning. In his coat pocket were several pieces of paper covered in hastily scribbled notes. The fire of grim determination burned brightly in his heart.

Late last night he had roughed out a plan, but he needed someone to offer him strong counsel and confirm whether his thoughts made sense. His greatest fear was that he was deluding himself—that he was in real danger of throwing his life into the air, only to have the breeze pick it up and scatter it away to the four winds.

Charles Cadnam was the only man whose opinion Flynn fully trusted. He was also the one man who had a solid understanding of just how dire Flynn's situation had been over the past years. Not even Gideon knew the full extent of the earl's wicked ways.

He was shown into the upstairs drawing room of number five Mortimer Street, where he waited patiently for his father's younger brother to be informed of his nephew's unexpected arrival. An apology was on his lips the moment Charles stepped through the door.

"I am so sorry to disturb you, Uncle. But this is an urgent matter."

Charles Cadnam welcomed him with open arms. "You have nothing to apologize for, my lad. You are always welcome here. My home is your home."

If only it could be. He had tried to move to his uncle's house several times, but each time Earl Bramshaw had vowed to cause harm to his brother's wife and children if Flynn didn't immediately return home. The rest of the Cadnam family knew better than to treat those threats as idle ones.

His welcome was the same as it was when he visited Mowbray House—food and drink were quickly arranged. Charles offered Flynn a seat by the fire, but he politely declined. "I walked over here, and my feet still want to move." Impatience and worry coursed through his veins.

His uncle stood, hands clasped gently together, while Flynn paced back and forth across the room doing his best to burn off his nervous energy. It was only when a sense of calm began to finally descend that Flynn came to a halt. He paused, then took in a deep breath. His whole future hung on the outcome of this meeting.

His gaze landed on Charles. The facial similarities between him and Flynn's father were such that, for a moment, he hesitated; his mind was playing tricks and imagining that he was speaking to the earl.

"The earl informed me last night that he has decided I am to marry some young woman whose wealthy father will clear his gambling debts. What I think of this arrangement isn't important, but to say that I am in shock that he would actually do such a thing would be a gross understatement."

Charles screwed up his face in disgust. "Do you have any idea as to who she is?"

"No. It was one of those conversations where it wasn't wise to linger and ask too many questions," replied Flynn.

A brief, knowing nod was his uncle's response. There was no point in discussing the details of the previous evening. Both men had been on the receiving end of Earl Bramshaw's wrath. Of his fists, and his cane. Old wounds and shared experiences had never healed for either man.

Flynn hadn't slept. He had been tempted to go for a long night walk, but history had taught him the bitter lesson that the front door of his family home would remain closed to him if he arrived any time after midnight. It was better to suffer in the warmth of the house than freeze to death out on the street.

"What are you going to do?" asked Charles.

There wasn't a lot which Flynn could do—not unless he was prepared to risk a great deal. And that was the reason for his visit this morning. He needed someone to help weigh up the pros and cons of his fateful decision. "I could just buckle under and do as I was told. Give up the last shred of my pride and self-worth," said Flynn.

"You mean allow him to finally destroy you? I thought you were stronger than that," replied Charles.

Flynn closed his eyes and lowered his head. How many years had he been trying to remain strong? Withstanding all that his father had thrown at him. "I am tired. Sick to my heart with everything. But, yes, if I yield to his dictate, I may as well go and throw myself into the River Thames. Death might be the better option."

Charles moved quickly, taking Flynn into his embrace. He hugged him. "Don't think like that, please. I will do anything I can to help you. Just don't give up hope."

In the early hours, Flynn had come to a decision. His future life would be hard, but it would be one where he was in charge. He no longer cared about the title, nor keeping the family fortunes. Love was all that truly mattered. Without Augusta, life was not worth living.

"I am going to speak to the Duke of Mowbray and ask for his daughter Augusta's hand in marriage. What Earl Bramshaw thinks of that, I honestly don't care. I refuse to let him rule my life any longer."

When his uncle drew back, Flynn caught the deep worry lines on his face. He wasn't surprised. This was a radical shift in the way he usually dealt with his sire's decrees. Normally, he pushed down his pride and buckled under. But when it came to his and Augusta's future, he had decided he wasn't going to simply acquiesce; he was going to fight.

"Do I take it that you and Lady Augusta have an understanding?"

Flynn shook his head. That was another difficult situation he had to deal with, but one he sensed he could overcome. Augusta cared for him, and if she wanted them to share a life, then she would have to be by his side as he took on the world.

"There is…" He stopped, unsure of what else to say. Things that had made perfect sense at two o'clock this morning didn't quite hold their own in the cold light of day. "There is a romantic connection between us. One we have kept secret. I have tested Lady Augusta's patience to its very end, and she has asked that since I don't feel I can offer her marriage, that I let her go. I cannot do that and still live."

Those words sounded trite. They spoke of the mere whispers of starry-eyed lovers. Hopes and fanciful dreams. How could such wistful thinking hold out against the iron will of the Earl of Bramshaw?

"Are you here for my counsel?" asked Charles.

"Please. I have put my thoughts down on paper, but I need someone with a wise head to tell me if my plans are all in vain. You are the only person I can trust to be honest with me, Uncle."

A knock at the door interrupted their conversation. A footman and maid entered the room. One carried a platter of food. The other, a smaller tray with a pot of tea, cups, and saucers. Flynn silently stared at his fingernails, waiting with bated breath while the servants set the dishes on a side table, then withdrew.

As soon as the staff were gone, Charles motioned toward the food. "Come, eat, then let's talk."

Flynn stirred from his musings. For the first time that he could remember in a long time, he didn't want food. Instead, he crossed the floor and took a seat on the sofa which sat under the window. Pulling the papers out of his coat pocket, he set them on the small occasional table in front of the low couch. "I went through some calculations last night. Of what sort of money, I would need in order to move out of Bramshaw House and set up a home for my own family. Could you please take a look at the numbers and give me your considered opinion? I need to know if this plan has any sort of merit."

His uncle stopped in front of the sofa and bent, giving Flynn a pat on the shoulder. "Go and put some food on a plate, my lad, while I have a look at this." Charles was always at pains to make sure Flynn never left his home without his belly being full.

The tray of food was a welcome attempt at a distraction, but Flynn's gaze kept darting to the sofa where Charles sat, pouring over the notes.

He had just stuffed a small cucumber and cheese sandwich into his mouth when his uncle let out a huff and spoke. "This is a lot of money you are asking me for."

Flynn set the plate of food on the sideboard and returned to the sofa. Borrowing from his uncle was the only way he could move forward with his plans. "Yes, I know. I will repay it with good interest when the time comes."

The time in question being when he eventually became Earl Bramshaw. It went without saying that Charles could be waiting many years for his money.

Charles lifted his head, and his gaze went to the ceiling. He closed his eyes for a brief moment, and Flynn's heart sunk immediately to his stomach. His uncle didn't like his plan.

"Do you have any idea as to the amount of Lady Augusta Kembal's dowry?"

Flynn shook his head. "I put an estimate in, but no, I don't." He pointed at the sheet of paper where he had written down the number. "If her father is as wise as I suspect he is, he will no doubt have tight settlement clauses. A good deal of the money will be held in trust for her and our children. The rest will be remitted over a period of time. And while Augusta will have some pin money, it should be hers. Which is why I shall have to find paid employment."

He hoped the Duke of Mowbray had structured his daughter's dowry that way. Flynn couldn't bear the notion of something happening to him and his father then attempting to access the money, which was meant to keep a roof over Augusta's head.

The late Countess of Bramshaw had left Flynn a little money from her dowry. He had lost count of the number of times the earl had tried to get his hands on it. Knowing how moneygrubbing his father was, he had to make certain that any funds which Augusta brought to their marriage were kept safe.

But without his uncle's money, he wouldn't be in a position to set up a separate home for him and Augusta. The other option of moving into Mowbray House with her family would cause the sort of scandal for which his father would seek retribution.

"Am I asking too much of you?"

Charles shook his head. "No, the numbers all make sense.

There is, of course, a strong family obligation to support you. But even if that wasn't the case, I would still lend you the money. You have to get out from under my brother. This is your life, Flynn, and that of your future children."

The thought of his wife and their offspring had been the final deciding factor for Flynn. He couldn't in all good conscience bring children into the world, knowing that he was condemning them to a life under the harsh yoke of his father. The abuse had to end with him.

He wouldn't dare risk their physical safety, nor accept the possibility that, in time, his wife and family would come to hate him for trapping them in a life not of their choosing. His own suffering had shown him the dark path they would be forced to follow him on.

No. I won't do that, not for all the money in the world.

"My actions may cause a ripple or two in society, but I'm now at peace with that outcome. It's what the earl will do that concerns me more. I'm worried that my father will possibly seek revenge. The loan is only part of the reason why I am here today. I fear that he will lay the blame for my escape at your feet."

They had been here before, dealing with the threats from the earl when Flynn had attempted to leave home a few years previous.

Charles drew in a shaky breath, but Flynn caught the look of quiet determination on his uncle's face. "I will protect my wife and family. Christopher is no longer a child, and he knows enough about my brother to understand the risks. I don't think our family will come to a state of open war, especially not if you take the Duke of Mowbray's daughter to wife."

Not yet at war. Could now be the final peace before an open raging battle?

"If anyone can stand up against your father, it is Clifford

Kembal. He won't hold for anything untoward to happen to his eldest daughter."

Flynn nodded. He had considered that notion. "The Duke of Mowbray won't have to fight my battles. Since my father will have no ability to wield financial influence over us, he shouldn't have any reason to come near Augusta. Setting up our family and life away from him will keep my wife safe."

He was going to have to explain a lot of this to the duke before he asked for Augusta's hand in marriage. That was going to be a tricky conversation. But Flynn was set in his course of action. Even then, there was always the chance that the duke might not agree to the marriage.

Deal with that problem if and when it arises.

Flynn raked his fingers through his short brown hair. What he was going to tell Augusta was yet another thorny problem he would have to overcome. In an effort to protect her from the ugly truth about his father, he had lied to her about some things. She deserved to know what he had planned, and why. He couldn't allow the woman he loved to walk blindly into a marriage where, despite his best endeavors, her new family may eventually be set for bloody battle.

"I need to speak to Augusta before I talk to her father. I want her to understand that if we do marry, we won't be living at Bramshaw House. Nor do I intend to be using the title Viscount Cadnam for the foreseeable future. The break with my father has to be complete."

His sire couldn't disown him, but Flynn could refuse to use his courtesy title. He wouldn't be living under the same roof as the earl, something which wasn't unusual—married sons often set up separate households—but by refusing to be associated with his father's titles, he would be making a bold public statement. One which would no doubt have tongues wagging within the *haut ton*.

That had been a moment of inspiration in the early hours

of the morning. A preemptive strike against the earl to show him that he meant to keep his word and not return to Bramshaw House until the day he became Earl Bramshaw. He would go about town as Mister Flynn Cadnam.

"Ronald will not take that well," replied Charles.

It was strange to hear his father's Christian name. Flynn didn't use it, nor did he think of his sire in that way. To him, he was Earl Bramshaw, a stranger who just happened to live in the same house. A cruel man who he had met a mere handful of times before the countess's death.

"No, he won't. But it's time I made a stand. I'm under no illusion that when I finally do come into the title, he will have frittered away much of the family fortune. That most of the property, that which is not entailed, will likely be all gone."

His uncle had already done so much for him over the years. Paid for many things that society would have naturally assumed his father would have done. Flynn would forever be grateful to Charles.

And if he did go ahead, defy the earl, and marry Augusta, his father would double down on destroying his legacy. Flynn would inherit debts and a ruined estate. The price of freedom would be a heavy one.

But the woman I love, and our family will be free.

Charles rose from the sofa and made his way over to the sideboard. He picked up a small beef pie, then set it down. His shoulders sagged as he spun to face his nephew. "Your mother never wanted this for you. She did everything she could to protect you from him. I just wish she had lived a little longer."

"So, do I. I never realized that she was the one thing which stood between him and me."

The countess and her son had lived at Bramshaw Hall in Southampton for the first fifteen years of Flynn's life. They were not permitted to travel to London or have guests stay with them. The only respite he'd had from a life of seclusion had been the time spent away at school.

Flynn's first real encounter with his father had been on the day of his mother's funeral. It had been a brief and formal introduction, after which the earl had brought him back to London. Within days, the abuse had begun.

I won't let my children or wife be put in harm's way. This evil has to stop.

Silence hung in the room for a minute. The subject of the late countess was always one which brought pain.

"I can lend you the money but are you really serious about working for a living?" said Charles.

Borrowing from his uncle would see him and Augusta set up, but Flynn would have to work to provide for his family. The hard financial reality was that even though he was a future earl, he was going to have to secure paid employment.

"Yes, I am. There is no other way." In his coat pocket, Flynn had a list of things he was good at—a list he had put together when it became clear that the money, he had counted on borrowing from his uncle was not going to be enough.

"I will start making private inquiries of various connections about employment. London society knows I am always short of money, so it won't come as too much of a surprise when people learn that the former Vagabond Viscount has taken a job."

Charles flinched. "I hate that moniker. You shouldn't have to work outside the estate; from what I recall, it has always provided a good income. I could perhaps offer you some work with my company. It might only be a few days a week as I am training Christopher to take over the management from me, but it would give you something."

Flynn shook his head. He had considered that option but decided he didn't want to get in the way of his cousin.

Christopher Cadnam had his own life to live, and a right to his father's wealth. "No, I couldn't. But thank you. I have some ideas I might be able to put to good use. I will seek an occupation that allows me to earn a viable income for the foreseeable future."

Moving out of Bramshaw House was a crucial first step in his plan. If he then managed to establish financial independence from his father, the earl wouldn't be able to interfere in his marriage or his life.

"Where will you live?" asked Charles.

A shrug was the only answer Flynn could manage to that question. He had the beginnings of a plan, but some things would take time to arrange.

Today was a bright new world of questions and what-ifs. It had been many years since he had last known the simple joy of hope. Since before his mother had died.

His father had pushed him to this point, forced him to finally break free of his shackles. "It's an odd thing, but I am grateful for the earl having made this decision. He has taken his avariciousness one step too far. I am not going to yield to him any longer."

Flynn's heart was racing at a fast tempo, and his mouth was dry. Adrenaline was pumping through his body at a rate of knots. But so was determination.

When he did finally meet with the Duke of Mowbray, he intended to have a solid plan in place. One which would allow Clifford Kembal to overcome any lingering doubts he may have about Augusta becoming Flynn's wife. Failure was not an option.

Chapter Eleven

Over the next few days, Flynn successfully avoided his father. During that time, he spoke to a couple of friends who were in business, making subtle overtures about the need for him to find a job. To his relief, most of them were able to look past the fact that Flynn came from the nobility and shouldn't therefore have to work. By week's end he had several strong leads, and he was feeling positive about his future.

Now he just had to talk to Augusta and let her know that he was done with indecision. That when he soon made an appointment to speak to her father, it would be with a clear financial plan in place.

Private musical performances were not normally to Flynn's taste, but in order to see Augusta, he was prepared to suffer through an evening of them. After arriving at the function at a town house in Silver Street, he took a spot at the back of the room and settled in to wait.

When the supper interval arrived, he intended to approach Augusta, and hopefully over a cucumber sandwich or two, finally convince her that he was ready to have *that* talk. The one they should have had a long time ago.

He shifted across several seats as more guests arrived, finally ending up in the very far corner of the elegant drawing room. It was close to the fire, so Flynn wasn't going to complain. Hearing his father's angry grumbles as he stomped about in his study at Bramshaw House a short while earlier had seen him dash out of the house without his gloves or scarf.

The early warning signs of the earl embarking on one of his violent rampages had been rippling through Bramshaw House for the past two days. Flynn's well-developed sense of self-preservation had seen him do his utmost to keep out of his father's line of sight. The earl's temper had a tendency to escalate quickly, and he hadn't wanted to be in the house when things eventually did explode. He was privately worried that news of his life-changing plans had somehow got back to his father, and he might return home to find the door locked permanently against him.

From where Flynn sat at the back of the audience, he could just make out the top of Augusta's head. Fortunately, she wasn't following the horrid, feathered cap fashion trend which so many other women embraced, so it made spotting her beautiful brown locks all that much easier.

Tonight, she had gone with a soft chignon. He loved it when she wore her hair like that; it made his fingers itch thinking how easy it would be to slip the pins and ribbons from her tresses and have them tumble down.

Of course, in his imaginings Augusta would be naked when he teased her hair free. She would step into his embrace, offering her lips for his hungry kiss and sighing softly when he took one of her soft-peaked nipples between his thumb and forefinger and gave it a gentle tweak.

She loves it when I do that.

"Wine or brandy?"

Flynn stirred from his lustful daydream. A footman was standing to his right with a tray of drinks in his hand. "Brandy, thank you," he replied.

It was another hour of songs, musical pieces, and some dull poetry before the evening's host announced supper. To his relief, the performances had mostly been of a first-rate standard. Flynn, who considered himself accomplished with the piano, was delighted that several of the piano pieces were ones which he knew quite well.

If he had his way, he would practice the piano at home, but the earl was not one for having music in the house. The only chance Flynn did get to play was at the home of friends who politely indulged him from time to time.

As soon as everyone rose from their seats and began to mingle, Flynn sought Augusta out. She was talking to her sister Coco, the youngest of the Kembal offspring. As he approached, Lady Coco met his gaze and touched her sister's arm. She whispered something to Augusta, but Flynn didn't catch it.

To his disappointment, Augusta stayed where she was, her back turned toward him, her shoulders stiff. He could just imagine that she was composing herself, putting her social armor in place.

I have hurt you, and I am so sorry.

If there was any justice in the world, they would have been the first words he spoke to her. But in the middle of a crowded supper room, manners had to take precedence.

"Lady Coco. Lady Augusta. What a pleasure to see you both here this evening."

Augusta finally spun slowly on her heel to face him. She dipped into an elegant curtsy. "Lord Cadnam."

He caught the odd look of confusion on Coco's face, and it was clear her thoughts had gone to wondering why her sister was addressing an old family friend in such a formal manner.

Coco held out a hand. "Flynn. What brings you out to an evening of music?"

He gladly took the opening. "I played the piano and violin from an early age. I was even graced with the chance to learn the hammered dulcimer, which few in London high society can play."

Augusta lifted her head and gave him a tight smile. "You do play the piano quite well. And Mama has always said you would have made a fine professional musician if you had ever pursued such a career."

Talk about a stiff conversation. This was how strangers, newly acquainted people spoke, not friends who had shared many an afternoon laughing and playing parlor games. It was sad, but it served to strengthen his resolve.

If anyone could understand the need to protect oneself, it was Flynn. He was the master of the polite façade. Of hiding one's pain, both emotional and physical, from the world. Augusta was doing her best, but she couldn't hide her heartache. It was written all over her face.

She shouldn't have to be doing this, and after tonight he was determined, she wouldn't ever have to do it again.

I just need a moment alone to speak to her.

To confess his feelings and talk about his plans for their future.

Lady Coco looked from her sister to Flynn, her brows furrowing as she did. "Have the two of you had a fight? I heard the play at Covent Garden was terrible, but I don't see how that could be Flynn's fault."

The question was addressed to Augusta, who was now wearing a tight smile on her lips. If she smiled any harder, he was certain her face was going to crack.

Flynn stepped forward. "Could I trouble you for a word in private, Lady Augusta?"

At that moment, Lady Coco had the good sense and grace to move away. She gave a cheery wave to another guest and bid her sister and Flynn a quick. "I shall leave the two of you to resolve your disagreement."

His hand was on Augusta's arm before she had the chance to follow after her sister. "Please, Augusta, we need to talk. I have important things I must tell you."

~

She didn't want to talk—she wanted to crawl up into a ball and cry. Why was he doing this? Adding more pain to an already tortuous situation. But with his hand resting gently on her forearm, Augusta had little choice but to nod and agreed to Flynn's request.

If you think you are going to play games with me, you have another think coming. I am done with it all.

"Alright, Flynn. You can have five minutes, and not a minute more. Come with me. I know this house well, and it has several small rooms where we can retire to speak in private." She glanced down at his hand. "You can let go of my arm. I don't need you to steer me."

With Flynn following close behind, Augusta made her way out of the supper room and toward a long hallway. At the end, she turned right, then made a second and even sharper right turn into a small sitting room. It was one of those little nooks that could be so easily missed as you rounded the corner.

Flynn did miss the room. Out of the corner of her eye, Augusta caught a glimpse of him as he flashed by. A grunt of surprise, then a huff of "Right," finally had him joining her. He closed the door behind him.

Augusta marched over to the window. She wanted to

maintain a degree of distance between them. There was safety in remaining at least a foot or two away from Flynn. It had been hard enough for her to keep her composure when he touched her arm—she didn't need him to do that again.

"Now what do you want to say?" she said, turning to face him.

It came out as harsh as she intended. She was in agony over him. Why shouldn't he also feel some of her pain?

Flynn moved quickly across the floor, and before she had time to protest, he had swept Augusta into his embrace and his lips were on hers.

There was nothing tender or sweet about the kiss. It was powerful, commanding. A statement of claim. His tongue brushed past her teeth and at the first touch of it against her own tongue, Augusta let out a groan.

Her hands went to the sides of his jacket, and she clung to him tightly. If he thought to move away, she had him held fast. But as Flynn deepened the kiss, it was clear he had no intention of going anywhere.

She sighed as he cupped the nape of her neck, the warmth of his hands sending a shiver of lust down her spine.

I shouldn't be doing this—we are finished.

Her sensible self was crying 'no' but her heart spoke louder. *Yes. Yes.*

The kiss continued, and Flynn settled into a rhythm of working his lips over hers. Augusta was certain her bones had all but melted and she would fall to the floor if either of them dared to let go.

I can't live without him.

"Augusta. Forgive me. I was a fool. I am sorry. I never meant to hurt you. I am going to speak to your father."

He murmured these words in between kisses. She caught most of them, but her brain was too scattered to take much of them in. His actions were speaking louder than anything, and that was all she wanted. All she craved.

When he finally did release her from his kiss, Augusta stood panting, staring up at him through glazed eyes. "What happened. What made you change your mind?"

"I didn't change my mind; I've always wanted you. But I wasn't lying when I said my life was complicated. The only lie was me trying to convince myself that I could live without you. I don't care what my father does—I will give it all up in order to marry you. If you will have me."

"I love you, Flynn. And if you feel enough for me, then we can find a way for this to work. All I ask is that you are truthful with me. Why is your father so set against me? Is it because he won't be able to get his hands on my dowry?" Her gaze searched his, seeking an answer. "Because that is what my mother seems to think."

Flynn's expression turned dark. "Did you really speak to the duchess about us? Is that why you called things off?"

His words were an odd mixture of fearful interest. They didn't fill Augusta with a sense of hope. "In a way I did. I posed the question of why a noble family would not find me suitable. Apart from being outraged that anyone would think her daughter less than a prize catch, she suggested it wasn't me that was the issue but rather the terms of my marriage settlement."

"And that if your future husband's family tried to get their hands on a large portion of the money, they were going to be disappointed?"

"Exactly. Is that why your father is against us marrying? Please, Flynn, I have to know." She was done with half-truths. If he was serious about a future with her, she had to know everything. Starting with his father.

His hand settled easily about her waist, his thumb stroking up and down her spine. Flynn sighed. "My father loathes me. That is clear to anyone. What I have never told you is that he has made it his life's mission to make certain I am miserable. He controls everything. And if I marry, that will also go for my wife. He will do everything to seize my bride's dowry. But because of who you are and your family, he wouldn't be able to manage that so easily. You, Augusta my love, would be a sharp thorn in his side. One he couldn't seek to influence without having to make major concessions. The earl would hate that more than you can possibly imagine."

She sensed there was more to the story than just her dowry. Why, for instance, did he always refer to his father as 'the earl'? There was no love lost between Flynn and his sire, and she couldn't understand why. She was going to get to the heart of things before Flynn put a wedding ring on her finger.

I owe it to our future children. Children who cannot be raised in poverty.

"What are we going to do? If the earl controls your family purse strings, how are we to make a life together? We can't possibly live with him at Bramshaw House."

Sweet thoughts of happily ever after were swept aside as her mother's words of caution came back to mind. She wasn't meant for a life lacking in wealth. Nor for a man to control her life like Earl Bramshaw did with Flynn.

"I've some plans I am working through, and hopefully in the next day I should have a clearer idea as to how they will be accomplished. But no, we won't be living with the earlever."

"After that, will you speak to my father?"

The Duke of Mowbray was going to have a lot to say to anything that Flynn had in mind, especially when it came to the lack of funds. It was going to take more than some vague words of promise before Clifford Kembal agreed to let his daughter marry a near penniless noble.

Flynn nodded. "I will. Could you and I arrange to meet

tomorrow afternoon at Hyde Park? We can talk more fully then."

Their serendipitous meetings in the park had been going on for some time. Augusta and Victoria had taken to regularly strolling in Hyde Park in the late afternoon, just before the usual crowd of evening patrons descended. Viscount Cadnam had a fortunate habit of also walking in the park at that same time.

"Alright, let us talk tomorrow. But I want you to know that this is your last chance. I can't... I mean, I won't... live like this any longer." Augusta took hold of Flynn's sleeve. He was offering her his assurances of a future together, but it wasn't the first time he had done that, and then backed away from his promises.

This time she was determined that it was going to be different. If his promises came to naught, like they had so many other times, she was going to give Flynn his marching orders. Either tomorrow they would be committed to one another and ready to speak to her father, or they would be finished for good.

"I don't intend for us to have to endure this pain for one more day if I can help it. Augusta, my love, I just need you to believe in me."

Augusta softly sighed. "I do believe in you, Flynn. It's the machinations of others that I fear."

He bent and kissed her. "The earl won't win."

Chapter Twelve

F lynn's morning had been a particularly good one. To his
delighted surprise there was more than one person who
was keen to secure his services. People who genuinely wanted
to see the Vagabond Viscount living a life truer to his noble
origins. To actually be happy. When the time came that he
did become Earl Bramshaw, Flynn would remember those
friends and their valuable support.

He was in a joyful mood as he stuffed his gloved hands
into his coat pockets and marched in through the front gates
of Hyde Park. Being January, it was cold enough in the late
afternoon for there to still be a thin layer of predawn ice lying
about the ground under the trees. It might have been chilly,
but at least the lack of crowd made it easy to spot Augusta
and her sister Victoria walking arm in arm through the park.

There were times when he could have sworn the two
Kembal women were joined at the hip. Flynn's gaze drifted to
the Mowbray House footman in full livery, who trailed behind
at a respectable distance.

While Victoria gave him a cheery wave, Augusta seemed
less sure of her greeting. His grand declaration of the

previous evening hadn't quite been the success he had hoped it would be, and there was a decided air of uncertainty about the smile that Augusta finally offered him. Her kisses had been sure, but her words less so.

Of course, she is unsure of things. You have kept her waiting for long enough, and last night you only made more vague promises to her.

But she was here, and that was what really mattered. It was better than the precarious position he had been in with Augusta only a matter of days ago. Hope had returned, and with it, the prospect of them finally being able to reveal their love to the world.

If his change of luck held, Lady Victoria would do her usual trick and wander away to find something of interest while he spoke to her sister. A cluster of trees or a statue of some historic figure would suffice.

"Lady Augusta, Lady Victoria, what a pleasant surprise," he said, dipping into a low bow.

"Lord Cadnam, fancy meeting you here," replied Augusta.

His gaze went to Victoria, who slowly shook her head. He was still on shaky ground with Augusta's loyal sibling, but at least she had a smile on her face.

Victoria cleared her throat. "I might just go and have a look at that water thing," she said, waving her hand vaguely in the direction of the Serpentine. She moved away toward the lake, beckoning the footman to follow.

It left Flynn and Augusta alone. This was the moment he had been hoping for, when he could finally tell her of his plans and for them to agree on the way forward. Together.

Augusta had been in two minds all day as to whether to meet with Flynn. She had spent a good hour in her room quizzing Victoria over the possible reason for his sudden change of heart. One minute he was all very mysterious and telling her his life was complicated; the next, he was asking to speak to her father.

He had said everything she wanted to hear, but her mother's words of caution still sat front and center in her mind.

I am going to get to the bottom of things before he speaks to Papa.

She wanted to be certain of the decisions that loomed large in her future. No matter if her delaying matters caused Flynn a certain degree of frustration, she had to be doubly sure that she was making the right decision. Once they were married, there would be no going back. Besides, he'd made her wait long enough. Now it was his turn to cool his heels.

They wandered along the main path through the park, Victoria and the footman lagging well behind. Augusta glanced back over her shoulder, snorting when she caught sight of her sister giving the Mowbray House servant what appeared to be a lecture on how you should prepare roast vegetables. The footman had the good sense to at least appear somewhat interested.

As she turned away, Augusta caught Flynn's eye. He grinned at her. "Your sister is very passionate about her food. I wonder what sort of gentleman will be able to keep up with that when it comes time for her to look for a husband."

Augusta frowned. She hadn't truly given the subject much thought. Victoria herself had never made mention of being interested in anyone. Nor had she ever raised the subject of marriage.

"He had better like a variety of dishes is all I can say. I can't see Victoria being happy with someone who only likes plain English food," replied Augusta.

They strolled on for a time, just making small talk. All the while Augusta's head was full of questions. When she could stand it no longer, she stopped.

"Why? Why now have you decided that you are ready to

build a life with me? And how is it that you have suddenly come up with a plan to make it all work?"

Suspicion sat heavy in her mouth, and it was reflected in the tone of her voice. She might be in love with Flynn, but Augusta wasn't stupid. Something major had to have occurred in his life, and she needed to know exactly what that thing was. Her future happiness depended on it.

He let go of her arm, and his gaze dropped to the ground. The badly worn toe of his boot was further scuffed as he pawed at the dirt and stones. His nervous tics only served to heighten her concern.

"I have wasted too long. Spent years wondering how I could win your heart. Then when I realized you truly did love me..." His head lifted, and their gazes met. "Well, I didn't know what to do. I shouldn't have taken the liberties I have with you, but I couldn't help myself. I was still trying to figure things out when you told me you were done with waiting and that you would look elsewhere. Even then I didn't quite believe it. Not until I saw you dancing with another man. Smiling at him. That's when I realized I couldn't live without you. That for you I would risk everything."

She hated that it had taken an ultimatum on her part for Flynn to finally decide that he wanted her. It should never have come to that point.

"I need to know how we are going to deal with your father. I am sure that he won't take the news of us becoming betrothed all that well. Last night, you mentioned having plans." Out of the corner of her eye, Augusta caught sight of a small group of other park visitors heading their way. She moved to one side, making room for them to pass.

It was a relief to note that none of them were women she recognized from her acquaintance. She wouldn't have to exchange pleasantries or small talk with them. All she wanted to do was sort things out with Flynn.

But the group, which was led by a young woman dressed in a pale green gown with matching coat and feathered hat, kept on heading directly toward them. Augusta and Flynn both took a step back.

Hyde Park is big enough that you don't need to cut us down in your haste.

The woman and her small party of friends drew close. A collision was inevitable. When they finally got within a yard of where a perplexed Augusta and Flynn stood, the young woman hailed them. "There you are. I was beginning to think you had gone."

"Is she a friend of yours?" asked Flynn.

Augusta shook her head. "No, I have no idea who she is." From the way the young woman spoke, she wasn't from elegant London society. There was a definite hint of an East London accent in her voice.

"May I help you?" asked Augusta, trying her best to be polite, while praying that the woman and her friends would go away. She wanted to talk to Flynn, not this stranger.

The fair-haired young miss gave Augusta a quick once-over, then sniffed. "You can start by stepping away from my fiancé. And then you can keep your bloody hands off him."

Fiancé?

Augusta's gaze shot to Flynn, but he was slowly shaking his head. A look of horrified disbelief sat on his face. "I'm sorry. I think you might have the wrong person. I am not engaged to anyone."

"Come now, Viscount Cadnam. Or since we are engaged and shortly to be sharing a bed, can I call you Flynn?" replied the woman. She turned to her friends, and they both nodded. As she turned back, a grin of expectation slyly spread across her lips.

A wave of nausea hit Augusta, and she swayed on her feet.

This was some strange nightmare. One she hoped she would soon wake from.

Flynn cleared his throat. "This is not the least bit amusing. I would suggest you and your friends should take your leave. You are disturbing the peace and this young lady." He nodded in Augusta's direction.

The smile disappeared from the other woman's face. "But we are engaged to be married. As far as I can see, the only person who should be leaving is her." She pointed a gloved finger at Augusta. "Lord Cadnam, I won't stand for you to be bedding any courtesans. Get rid of that woman, or my papa will be hearing about it."

Augusta blinked out of her stupor. Had the woman really just accused her of being a whore? "I am Lady Augusta Kembal. My father is the Duke of Mowbray. How dare you?"

"I don't care if you are the bloody Queen of Sheba. Stay away from my intended, or else you might find yourself receiving an unpleasant visit from one of my father's employees."

It wasn't every day that a young noblewoman taking a casual stroll in Hyde Park was accused of being a courtesan, but the threat of bodily harm was a step too far. Augusta moved forward, ready to have harsh words with the unwelcome interloper. Flynn put a hand up and held her back.

For a long moment, he simply stared at the girl in the pale green ensemble. Flynn's silence had a gnawing sense of unease settling over Augusta's heart.

"When did we become betrothed?" he asked.

She batted her eyelashes at him and grinned. It was the smile of a victor. After slipping off her white leather glove, she gently waved her left hand in Flynn's face. A pearl and ruby cluster sat on her ring finger.

"You silly, wonderful man. How could you forget such a momentous day so soon? But not to worry. Papa received our special marriage license from you yesterday, so all we need to do now is set the date."

Augusta stood rooted to the spot, as Flynn's supposed fiancée brandished her betrothal ring at him.

"I... I," stammered Flynn.

The woman had his mother's ring on her finger. And if she had got that, there was every chance that she wasn't lying about the special license. His father had gone ahead and done what he said he would do; he had secured Flynn a wife.

Augusta's gaze burned into the back of his head. She would want answers. And he had none to give. None that would see her looking at this in any favorable light.

"Do you recognize that ring?" asked Augusta.

Flynn's heart sank to his boots. *That* ring had belonged to his mother. *That* ring had been kept secure in the top drawer of his dresser. *That* ring was meant for his future wife. For Augusta. Now some stranger had possession of it.

There was no point in denying the jewel. "Yes. It belonged to the Countess of Bramshaw, my late mother. It was left to me in her will. It should be in my room at Bramshaw House," he ground out.

He had been so close to breaking free, and now this...

His father had stolen the most precious thing Flynn had left of his mother. A priceless memento. And he had given it to some stranger. Anger burned bright in his mind. Rage coursed through his veins.

Flynn's brain worked feverishly, trying to find the right words. But there was nothing he could say in the face of his father's dark treachery. While he had been busy making plans to build a new life, the earl had been working to ensure that his son stayed chained to his past. Marriage to this woman was the ultimate checkmate.

The rustle of Augusta's skirts spoke loud in the tense air. She held out a hand to the other woman. "May I offer you my sincere congratulations. I hope you and Viscount Cadnam have many happy years together."

To Flynn's stunned dismay, the two women shook hands, after which Augusta turned and silently walked away.

"Well, that put her in her place," observed one of the other young women.

He went to follow Augusta, chase her down, but a hand gripped tightly to his coat sleeve. Flynn attempted to shake it off but found himself dragged back to his supposed fiancée.

"Don't be trying to embarrass me now, my love. Just remember it's my papa's money which is going to clear all your father's debts. You get to keep a roof over your head. Well, our heads once we are married, and in exchange I am going to be Viscountess Cadnam. It's a pretty sweet business deal in anyone's opinion."

"I have no idea who you are, and I don't even wish to know your name. But if you continue to hold onto my coat for a second longer, you are going to discover that even gentlemen have their limits," he bit back.

The moment his future bride let go of him, Flynn set off after Augusta. He had to try and explain things to her, let her know that no matter what his father did, he wouldn't go through with the marriage.

And I must get my mother's ring back.

Flynn caught up with Augusta just as she reached the spot where Lady Victoria and the footman were waiting. He skidded to a halt on the loose gravel. "Augusta, please."

To the day he died, Flynn would never forget Augusta's shattered face as she turned to him with tearful eyes and whispered, "Was this the big secret? The thing that made you change your mind and suddenly start making plans for us."

"No. I have no idea who she is or how she came to have my mother's ring. Augusta, you have to believe me. My father said he had found a wife for me, but I didn't think he would go ahead and arrange the wedding. I..." He struggled for air. His whole life was unraveling in front of him.

"I do believe you, Flynn. But it would appear that the earl has once again been that one step ahead of you. He has arranged your betrothal and your marriage. And if a special license does indeed exist, you might just have to go through with the wedding."

Her lovely face was the heartbreaking picture of broken dreams and lost hope.

No. He wasn't going to be forced into marrying a stranger. Or lose Augusta.

He pulled her into his arms and kissed her, ignoring the cries of anger from his new fiancée. This was the only woman he was ever going to hold in his arms. The only woman in his life, now and forever.

"I am going to go home and confront my father. He cannot make me take this woman as my wife. I told you I had made plans. My uncle Charles is going to lend me money. Friends have offered paid work. Yes, I know that part is ridiculous considering my family and title, but I will do whatever I have to in order to make you mine."

He held her close, while Augusta sobbed into his chest. Her anguish stirred the beast within him. Rage fired his blood to boiling point. No man would ever stand in the way of their love.

"You are mine, Augusta, and I will not rest until I can call you, my wife."

She clung to him. "I love you, Flynn. We deserve a life together. He cannot be allowed to win. Not this time."

He lifted her face, and their gazes met. Augusta's eyes were red, but the glint of determination still shone in them.

"I love you too, Augusta. I'm going to sort this out and then come for you. Wait for me, please."

"Yes."

Flynn let go of Augusta and marched back to where the other woman and her friend stood. He held out his hand. "Give me the ring."

She went to protest, but he stepped closer. "Go and tell your father that he should hold on to his money and cancel any plans for a wedding celebration. Earl Bramshaw has no sway over me or whom I marry."

The woman slipped the ring off her finger and handed it to him. "This is not the last you will hear from my family. Rest assured that you will pay for this, Lord Cadnam."

Flynn raced back to where Augusta stood. He pressed the ring into the palm of her hand. "This is yours, and it always will be, Augusta, my love. I am going home to pack my things, and then I shall come and speak to your father. I promise that you and I shall be engaged before the end of this day."

"I love you," whispered Augusta.

He bent and kissed her once more, then a determined Flynn headed for the gates of Hyde Park.

His destination—Bramshaw House and the long overdue showdown with his father.

Chapter Thirteen

✦

Flynn's fisted hands bashed the knocker hard against the front door of Bramshaw House. He didn't give a damn about the passersby who grumbled about there being no need for such uncivilized force. That gentleman likely had a key to the door of his own home.

I am not going to cave to his demands. I would rather die on my feet than live on my knees for another single day.

When the head butler finally opened the door, Flynn brushed past him. "Where is Lord Bramshaw?"

He got a slow looking up and down for his troubles. The expression on the butler's face was an all too familiar one. It spoke of him trying to decide just how big an explosion was about to go off and where best he should be when it happened. Flynn couldn't blame the man. He had been standing in the wrong place too many times himself and suffered for it.

"His lordship is in his study. But I don't think he wishes to be disturbed," offered the butler.

Flynn paused. No one needed to explain what those words really meant. They were Bramshaw House staff code for 'The earl is deep in his cups, and if you know what is best, then you will go back out the front door.'

But Flynn wasn't in the mood for hearing any sort of caution; he was done with taking a step back. Reaching his father's study, he didn't bother to knock. He pushed open the door, smashing it against the wall.

The earl, who was seated behind his desk, whisky glass in hand, shot out of his chair. His eyes were glazed, but he was steady on his feet. He set the glass down with a violent thud. Dark amber liquid spilled across the wooden top, stopped only by scattered papers which began to soak the whisky up.

"What the devil are you doing?" bellowed the earl.

Flynn's gaze went to where his father's cane usually sat. The earl had a special one for use in this room. The book-shelf-lined walls absorbed more sound than other parts of the house, so the cane was thick. His son's cries of pain never escaped the earl's study.

Anger tensed Flynn's body. He didn't care that his brain was screaming in warning that he should flee. "You sold me into marriage. To some woman who just accosted me in the middle of Hyde Park. And who called Lady Augusta Kembal a whore!"

The earl busied himself with picking up the sodden papers and heaping them into a pile. "Yes, well Lily is a bit rough around the edges, I will grant you that. And she will take a bit of training to get her up to some sort of social standing. But once you have bedded her, I am sure she will come to heel."

With one eye on the cane, Flynn stepped closer. He was ready to snatch the weapon up and toss it into the fire if his father made the slightest move toward it. "I am not marrying her. I am going to marry Augusta. And how dare you steal into my room and take my mother's ring?"

Earl Bramshaw's eyes narrowed. "How dare I? You will

marry this girl, or you will be out on the street. That ring was a cheap trinket that your bitch of a mother only wore to vex me. She refused to wear the betrothal ring I gave her."

That had Flynn hesitating for a moment. His mother had loved that ring, said it was her most precious possession other than her son.

It probably meant more to her than any jewel you could have offered.

He had never stood up to his father before today. But over the past few days, Flynn Cadnam had finally grown a spine. "I am not marrying Lily. If you want to save your fortune, then marry her yourself."

That was a sobering thought. If his father did remarry and managed to sire another son, it could make things difficult for him. A second son would stand behind Flynn in the line of succession for the title, but who knew what mischief the earl could make for Flynn in the meantime.

The earl began to cough, his thick neck and rounded cheeks turning a deep red. He gripped the edge of the desk while his lungs demanded more air. Flynn stood impassively watching. Any other dutiful son would offer to pat the earl's back, but not him. There wasn't a single day when he didn't silently wish that his father would breathe his last. No son should wish his father dead, but Flynn often did.

"I married once, never again. Women are wicked creatures. They steal men's hearts and set them to flame," growled the earl.

"You have to cancel the special license. I am not going through with the wedding, no matter what you say or do," replied Flynn.

He took a deep breath, doing his best to steady his rapidly fraying nerves. So many nights he had imagined standing up to the earl and challenging his father's tyranny, vanquishing him with his clever words. But the courage of his dreams wasn't the same as the truth of reality. His father didn't cave in an instant.

"No? Well, here is your choice, my lad." Earl Bramshaw moved back behind his desk, his hand settling on the grip of the top drawer. He opened it and took out a knife. Flynn's gaze locked on the short, deadly blade. He had seen his father use it to cut meat from the bones for his dogs. In that capacity it was an everyday hunting knife, but in this moment, it transformed into something else.

A threat. A warning. A weapon.

His father's large fingers closed over the knife, and raising it, he began to twirl it round his fingers. For a nobleman, he had far too much skill with handling such a sharp, brutal weapon. "Your choice, Viscount Cadnam, is this," he sneered. "Either marry the chit and in doing so settle my debts, or I will cut you out of my life for good."

That last remark was delivered as he lifted the knife and plunged it deep into the pile of wet papers. It made a sickening sound, and Flynn was reminded of being a young boy and watching the Bramshaw Hall farmhands as they carved up a fresh kill from the estate's livestock. His stomach churned.

Get a grip. He is just trying to intimidate you.

His father's words didn't hold the same power they normally did. He didn't cower or beg. Flynn straightened his back. For the first time in his life, he held his father's disapproving eye.

I will not live under his violent hand a minute longer.

"So be it. I will go and pack my things. I swear that after I depart this house today, I won't set foot back inside while you still draw a mortal breath. The next time I walk through the front door will be when I am Earl Bramshaw." Flynn bowed to his father, then turned for the door.

Today he would take his meager belongings and leave. He

would go straight to Mowbray House and speak to the Duke of Mowbray. As long as he and Augusta were together, nothing else mattered.

From behind him came a bellow of fiery anger and unrestrained rage. Blinding pain shot through Flynn's back, and he dropped to his knees. Wincing through a haze of searing agony, he caught sight of the earl as he stepped in front of Flynn and raised the knife for a second time.

"You will never leave this house alive," roared his father.

Blackness descended, and Flynn knew no more.

Chapter Fourteen

Augusta had sat up late into the night, watching out the window of her bedroom, waiting, looking for any sign of Flynn. Victoria had stayed up with her until the early hours, but when she had eventually fallen asleep, her face pressed against the glass, Augusta had told her to go to bed. Until Flynn arrived, there was nothing either of them could do.

The following morning, a bleary-eyed Augusta took her place at the breakfast table. She struggled through several cups of tea. When the Mowbray House head butler brought in the morning mail, she sat up in her chair, eager to see if a note had been sent from Bramshaw House. Gideon received several letters, but there was nothing for her. No news from Flynn.

Not a word. Flynn, don't fail me. Not now. Please.

While Coco and Richard happily exchanged details of their respective plans for the day, Augusta glanced at Victoria. The sad smile her sister offered from across the table had her swallowing down a lump of dread.

He said he was going home to pack and then come here. Where can he be?

Her mind was running at a furious pace. Had Flynn done as her dark fears whispered and caved to his father's demands? Was the man she loved right this very minute standing in front of a priest and saying his wedding vows to another woman? That horrid thought had Augusta pushing her untouched plate of food away.

What will I do if that is what has happened?

"Are you coming shopping with us this morning, Augusta?" asked Coco.

Augusta envied Coco for her happy ignorant bliss. Her sister hadn't a care in the world past where her next pretty bonnet came from. "I don't think so, Coco. I'm not feeling the best this morning."

Gideon cleared his throat. "Are you ill, Augusta? You look quite pale and drawn. I can't say walking in Hyde Park late on a chilly day is the wisest of things to be undertaking. You seemed quite distracted when you got home yesterday."

Trust her brother to cut to the chase. Gideon had never shared her opinion that getting out and going for a long walk was beneficial to one's health. Unlike Flynn, he was far more inclined to take the carriage.

Flynn.

Where are you?

Not knowing was slowly killing her. He had said he was going home to confront his father. If he'd had it out with the earl, he should at least have sent word by now.

Apart from Victoria, no one else at the table had the slightest clue as to Augusta's distress. And with everyone still in the dark regarding the nature of her and Flynn's relationship, it was near impossible for her to raise the subject of the viscount without also raising suspicions.

"I hope you will be feeling well enough to go out tonight.

I've heard the party at Lord and Lady Browne's is being catered for by a hot new French chef. He is rumored to be one of the best pastry chefs in all of Europe. They paid a fortune to bring him over for the next six months and are planning a series of special banquets for the coming season," said Victoria.

Augusta couldn't care less about the wonders of French cooking. She scowled at her sister. Why was she being so thoughtless?

"Which means Viscount Cadnam will probably make an early appearance at the party. I've seen him attack a plate of pastries like a ravenous beast," added Victoria, nodding at Gideon.

The marquis chuckled. "Yes, Flynn loves his sweet pies and cakes. I will make sure to remain at a safe distance when he enters the supper room tonight."

Augusta gave silent thanks to her sister. Of course, Victoria hadn't forgotten her worry over Flynn. While waxing lyrically about the French chef, Victoria had neatly posed the question of whether the viscount was expected to make an appearance at the party tonight. Gideon had now confirmed it.

Tonight. If he doesn't send word before then, at least I will be able to speak to him later. But he promised he would come here yesterday. Something is wrong—I can feel it.

Augusta set her napkin aside and rose from the table. "If I am to be feeling well enough to venture out this evening, then perhaps it might be a good idea for me to go back to bed and get some sleep. Excuse me."

"I will come with you," said Victoria, pushing back her own chair.

Lady Coco let out a sigh of disappointment. "Isn't anyone coming shopping with me today?"

The two eldest Kembal girls exchanged a knowing look.

They might well be worried about Flynn, but they also had to keep up appearances. If both Victoria and Augusta cried off on the trip with Coco, the duchess would surely find out. Then she would come asking questions. Augusta hadn't a clue what to say to anything her mother might ask.

Especially not when it came to Flynn and the possibility of him having gone off to marry some stranger in order to settle his father's debts.

He promised he would confront the earl.

"I will come with you, Coco, but could we perhaps leave a little later? I would rather be certain that Augusta is on the mend before I leave her," replied Victoria.

"I'm sure some sleep will do me the world of good," added Augusta.

Her chances of actually falling asleep were slim, but if she retired to her room then at least she could go back to watching the window and waiting for Flynn to arrive. She glanced at the ring which sat on her right hand. He had given it to her, along with his promise to speak to her father. She wanted nothing more than to be able to wear it on her left hand, along with a wedding band.

I have to trust in him. He will come.

Chapter Fifteen

❦

M*id-February 1817*

Augusta had established a new routine. Every morning after rising and dressing, she would make her way to the breakfast room and scour the newspapers. The marriages section was her main interest.

But three weeks after she had last seen Flynn, there was still no sign of him, nor of him having married the mystery girl from Hyde Park. He may well be the head of a dysfunctional family, but even Earl Bramshaw would have made certain to place his son's marriage notice in *The Times*.

Across the table from her, Victoria closed up the *Gazette* and shook her head. "Not in here." She tapped her finger on the other pile of newspapers. "Nothing. Not even mention of an engagement. I am beginning to think you might want to go and check the official records and see if the special license has been used."

It was tempting, but it would mean having to acknowledge that Flynn had once and finally, utterly failed her. Augusta had lost more than enough sleep already. She couldn't keep punishing herself.

Not knowing left her with at least some sense of hopefulness. A foolish notion though it was, but it kept her heart from completely breaking in two. She clung to that glimmer of possible good fortune like it was a lifeline.

"I am not at the point of having lost all sense of self-respect," replied Augusta.

That was a lie she kept telling herself in the vain hope that it might hold a modicum of truth. The reality was that she was long past begging for word of Flynn.

But if he hasn't married, then where is he? What if something has happened to Flynn, and no one is looking for him?

Deep down she feared that if Flynn had met with an accident or even worse, his father wouldn't likely go in search of his son. Which left only his friends to come to his aid. Gideon was Flynn's best friend.

"I might ask Gideon if he is expecting to see Flynn this evening," said Augusta. She had made discreet inquiries with her brother over the past few weeks, but Gideon had been oddly evasive as to the whereabouts of his friend.

"You must know that Gideon is eventually going to put two and two together if you keep asking about Flynn. Let me check on his plans for this evening. I can drop the subject of Viscount Cadnam into the conversation at some point," suggested Victoria.

Gideon was far from dull-witted, and it was only a matter of time before he would pointedly ask why both his sisters were so interested in his best friend. At present, neither Augusta nor Victoria could furnish him with a clear answer.

"I was thinking you might mention a new restaurant to Gideon and suggest he take Flynn out to dine there." Everyone knew that Flynn loved his food. "And if he agrees, then you could also ask that he invite us as well. What do you think?"

Victoria bit down on her bottom lip. She was normally up for most things, but there was a definite sense of hesitancy about her. "I think you need to talk to Gideon. Have an honest conversation about you and Flynn. If you don't want to mention that the two of you have shared a romance, then perhaps just let him know that you and the viscount had a disagreement. You are old friends, so it makes sense that you would wish to make amends."

"But I don't—"

Augusta's reply was cut short by the unexpected arrival of their mother into the breakfast room. She and Victoria exchanged a questioning glance as the Duchess of Mowbray took a seat and beckoned a footman over, requesting fresh tea and two boiled eggs.

What is going on with her and Papa?

The duke and duchess had always shared breakfast in their private suite. Even on the mornings when they were at war with one another, they declared a ceasefire over food. Their mother being at the family breakfast table was an unsettling sight.

The duchess greeted her daughters with a cheerful grin. "Good morning, Augusta. Good morning, Victoria. Where is Coco? Don't tell me she is still abed at this hour."

As far as Augusta and Victoria were concerned, it went without saying that Lady Coco Kembal wasn't in her room. If she stayed true to form, she was still out with her wild friends roughing it in a crowded tavern somewhere in the mean streets of east London. And she had been there all night. Not that they were going to tell any of that to their mother.

Coco might be the youngest of the Kembal offspring, not long out of the schoolroom, but she was also the most headstrong. And out of control. Her sisters were forever having to cover her tracks and hide her close scrapes with scandal.

"When I saw Coco last night, she was leaving the library with a heavy book and said she planned to sit up and read until the early hours. It makes sense that she would probably be trying to catch up on sleep this morning," said Victoria.

Augusta gave a mere nod to her sister's lie and added, "I shall go and check on her after breakfast."

A cup of tea was placed in front of Lady Anne, and she took a sip. When an uncomfortable silence descended, Augusta went back to her eggs and salmon. She wasn't particularly hungry, but if she kept stuffing food into her mouth, her mother would find it difficult to undertake any serious interrogation of her daughters and their plans for the day.

Victoria finished up her coffee, then rose from the table with a polite, "Please excuse me. I have some matters which need my attention."

Lady Victoria had recently declared that the usual offerings at the Mowbray House breakfast table were a waste of her finely tuned palate. She made a point of avoiding the plain fare of toast and eggs.

Augusta suspected that her sister would be shortly stealing out the front door and making her way over to the local German bakery, where she would avail herself of some freshly baked sourdough bread, topped with lashings of salted butter.

I wonder which footman will win the prize of accompanying her today.

Her maid had shared the gossip from below stairs that being able to shadow Lady Victoria when she visited the bakery was a task fiercely contested by the young footmen of Mowbray House. A generous serving of butter on a slice of thick, hot bread was a strong lure for any young man, especially when it was paid for by a duke's daughter.

But Augusta had more pressing concerns this morning. She had to get Victoria to speak to Gideon. Dabbing at her lips with her napkin, she also excused herself, then hurried after her sister.

To her relief, Victoria was not only still outside in the hallway, but she was also talking to their brother. As Augusta approached, Gideon turned to her. The expression of deep concern on his face had her slowing her steps.

"I was just saying to Victoria that I am beginning to have serious concerns about Flynn. I'm not sure if you have noticed, but he hasn't been at any social functions over the past few weeks. He appears to have gone missing. I am worried about him," said Gideon.

His words sent a spear of dread coursing down Augusta's spine. If Gideon was concerned about Flynn, then she had good cause to be afraid.

"When did you last see him?" asked Victoria.

Thank you, Victoria.

Gideon frowned. "To be honest, not for a little while. The last time was the week we went to the theatre with him. I've been busy working with Papa on the estate accounts and deciding what to do about that patch of land near the top field at Mowbray Park. What with various appointments and letters to the ducal bankers, I simply haven't had the time to be out in the evening and socializing."

"How do you know he has gone missing then?" asked Augusta.

While it was a logical question, and one that hopefully wouldn't raise any suspicions in her brother's mind, she was determined to get some answers. Her concern was growing stronger by the day.

"Well, Richard was meant to meet him for their regular monthly roast pork supper earlier in the week, but Flynn didn't show. According to Richard, over the past three years

Flynn has never once missed that night. And, of course, we all know that when it comes to food, Viscount Cadnam is always at the head of the line. That was the first inkling I had that something might be amiss."

Augusta hated it when people spoke about Flynn like that, as if he was some hungry beast who was never satisfied. Gideon might well have meant it as a mere comment, but it still had her clenching her fingers into balls.

"Then, when I was at White's club late yesterday, I happened to mention Flynn, and one of the footmen noted that he hadn't been in at all over the past few weeks."

A chill of dread gripped her. Had Flynn gone somewhere outside of London to get married? It would be the perfect explanation for his sudden disappearance. And why news of it may not have been printed in the London newspapers.

What if his father sent him away to stop him from marrying me? I wouldn't put it past Earl Bramshaw to do such a thing. Anything to control his son's life.

He had said he was going to confront his father and have the betrothal called off, but Flynn's continued silence and unexplained absence spoke of a very different outcome from his meeting with the earl.

"What are you going to do? I mean, are you planning on calling in at Bramshaw House to find out where Flynn is?" asked Victoria.

If a medal for sisterly loyalty could be struck, Lady Victoria Kembal would have been its first recipient. She was asking all the questions that Augusta herself wanted to pose but was too afraid to ask.

I feel awful about all this. Oh, Flynn, where are you?

Doing her best not to appear too anxious, Augusta gave a supportive nod in her sister's direction. "Yes, it makes sense to see if he is alright. Perhaps he has come down with a cold or something. You never know, he might be staying at home to rest and recuperate."

Gideon slowly shook his head. "No, I don't think that is what has happened. Flynn has the constitution of an ox. He has barely been sick a single day in his life. Something else has occurred."

Her brother's words added to her growing fears. What if Flynn had gone home and confronted his father, and things hadn't gone well? That he had been forced to finally accept the truth of his sire's financial mess and do what had to be done in order to save the Cadnam name and estate? If that was the case, then more than likely Earl Bramshaw would have quickly bundled his son and the young woman from Hyde Park into a coach and sent them to his estate in Southampton.

Even as she and her siblings discussed his fate, Flynn could very well be waking up this morning with his new bride sleeping in his arms.

Please, Lord, not that. I couldn't bear to see him with another woman. Flynn is mine.

Augusta screwed her eyes shut as panic welled up inside her. She dared not break down in front of her brother. Turning, she headed for the stairs. "Excuse me, I don't think my breakfast has agreed with my stomach."

With Victoria following close on her heels, Augusta dashed upstairs. She had barely made it to their room before the tears overcame her. She collapsed to her knees and sobbed. Flynn was missing, and the only logical explanation was that he had left town and gone back to his family estate in order to marry the woman they had encountered in the park. A woman he didn't know. A woman he had not wanted as his wife.

"What am I going to do?" she cried, getting to her feet, and throwing herself into the comforting arms of her sister.

They had been so close to finally seizing their happily ever after. But Flynn's spiteful father couldn't even let him have that—he was determined to control his son's life, from the coin in his purse to the woman who shared his bed. A woman who would never be her.

No matter what Gideon discovered, the hard and cruel truth was that she was going to have to find a way to move on with her life. A life she couldn't share with Flynn. Her hopes and dreams of them being together were gone forever. Crushed into dust, along with her heart.

Chapter Sixteen

❦

E arly March 1817
The front steps of Bramshaw House

"Do you think this is a good idea? I mean, what will people think if they see you standing on the doorstep of Bramshaw House in the middle of the day?"

Augusta ignored her sister's concerns. She wasn't in the mood to listen to anyone who had a different opinion to hers about why she was knocking on Earl Bramshaw's door.

"What else am I to do, Victoria? I can't just sit at home and wonder what happened to Flynn. I have to know."

She had waited long enough. Gideon had shared with her the developments in the ongoing search for Flynn, but the details had been few and far between. He, like the rest of London, had little to go on. With Earl Bramshaw still not cooperating with anyone who requested details of Flynn, there had been no real progress in weeks.

Coming to Flynn's home and demanding answers seemed the only logical thing left for her to do. It may well transpire to be a fool's errand, but it was something. Sitting at home worrying over what had happened and where the man she loved might be was slowly driving Augusta mad.

The Mowbray House footman who had accompanied them stood a respectful distance away at the bottom of the steps, but he was under strict instructions to leap into action should anything untoward happen to either of the Kembal sisters. The extra coin in his pocket would buy his silence, but it wouldn't save him if Augusta or Victoria came to harm on his watch.

After taking the front door knocker firmly in hand, Augusta gave it a hard rap. She waited for a minute or two, then tried again. It was only after the fourth knock that the door finally swung open.

On the other side stood a surly old man who looked Augusta slowly up and down. She sensed he would love to tell her to clear off, but from the manner of her dress and the footman who lurked nearby, only an idiot would choose that course of action.

"Yes," he snapped.

She straightened her spine and, after taking a deep, courage-gathering breath, addressed the butler. "I wish to speak to Earl Bramshaw. I am a friend of his son."

The butler slowly shook his head. "If you have come asking where the viscount is, you are wasting your time. His lordship has nothing to say on the matter."

Augusta moved forward, placing her foot strategically in the doorway. Her actions were clear in their unspoken intent. She wasn't going to leave until she got some answers.

"Wait here," said the butler. He returned a few minutes later with a huffing, snorting Earl Bramshaw close on his heels. Flynn's father took one look at Augusta and turned up his nose. "When did it become socially acceptable for the young women of noble families to come knocking on the door of good homes without an invitation? Does your mother know you are here? What would she say?"

She took the time to run her gaze disapprovingly over the bulk that was Flynn's father, silently letting him know how little she thought of him and his so-called manners. "Who says I wasn't invited? I am looking for Viscount Cadnam. You remember him, don't you? Your son? The one no one has seen for many weeks." It took a great deal of effort not to add a touch of snark to her voice. Augusta let her words do what they needed.

She slipped off her glove and made a deliberate show of her right hand. The gold and ruby betrothal ring glistened in the morning sun. She tracked the earl's gaze, enjoying the flash of anger which crossed his face at the sight of the jewel.

He loomed over her, meeting her eyes. His were cold and hard, utterly lacking in emotion. How many times had Flynn stared into those icy pools of hatred and wished this man was not his sire?

"And as for my mother, I can assure you that her opinion of me is far more favorable than the one she holds of you, Lord Bramshaw."

If he was going to be rude, she was well with her rights to be uncommonly crass with him in return.

Flynn, wherever you are, take this as a blow struck on your behalf.

The curl of Earl Bramshaw's lip was enough to let her know that he was not the least interested in what she had to say. She did note that his gaze fixed on the ring more than once, and she could just imagine him wondering how she had come by it. And how he could get it back.

"Rude, impertinent young miss. My son's life is his own. And I keep my own counsel. Now I would suggest that you and the rest of your family should do the same and learn to mind your own bloody business. Don't come here again," snapped the earl. He pointed at where her slipper rested on the threshold. "Move your foot."

"Where is Flynn? Where is your son and heir?" she demanded.

A huge greyhound ambled up alongside the earl, and he turned his withering gaze from Augusta to the dog. He bent and gave the animal a pat.

With a sigh, he righted himself. "Maybe you should be asking yourself that question, Lady Augusta. If Flynn gave you that ring, he must have had plans to offer you marriage. Considering that it is not on your left-hand tells me that he realized what a poor bet you were, and that is why he ran away. Now remove yourself from my front step. When this door closes, both of your feet had better be on the other side of it."

Augusta had just enough time to pull her leg back before the door was slammed shut in her face. She stared at the knocker for a moment. Should she try again?

Victoria's hand rested lightly on her shoulder. "I don't think he is interested in speaking to you. Nor, for that matter, anyone else."

She hadn't expected a warm welcome at Bramshaw House. It was well known throughout London society that the earl didn't offer tea and toast to anyone who had the misfortune to call at his home.

But whether he realized it or not, the earl had given Augusta one vital piece of information and it was more than she had hoped to gain from this visit to Flynn's home. "He might think he has sent me away with nothing more than a flea in my ear, but he said Flynn had run away."

Victoria followed her down the front steps and into the street. "What is so important about that?"

Augusta stopped and met her sister's enquiring gaze. "Because it means Flynn isn't with that girl. If he was, don't you think the earl would have made a point of telling me? He had to have finally known that Flynn wanted to marry me, and I can't see Earl Bramshaw passing up the opportunity to inflict pain when it so easily presents itself. If his son is married, he would have told me. Didn't you see the way he looked at the ring? He was angry."

This was the best piece of hope she had received since Flynn's disappearance. The first sign that he may have decided to run away from home rather than be forced to marry a stranger. And if that was the case, she and the viscount still had a chance for their happily ever after.

"I just wish Flynn would get in touch. Even a short note would be better than nothing."

Victoria took hold of her hand. "It is a good piece of news. But please don't get your expectations up. Not yet. The fact that Flynn hasn't written to you or even Gideon is a major cause for concern. I worry that he might not be in a position to send word."

Augusta shook her head, stubbornly refusing to consider what might lay beyond her sister's words. She didn't want to hear any of it. She was desperate to cling to hope. "You are right, of course. But I am still going to take this to Gideon. He needs to know what the earl said to me. That as far as he is concerned his son is alive but is somewhere in hiding."

As they made their way over to the waiting landau, Augusta quietly absorbed the news. According to his father, Flynn wasn't yet married. Her sense of relief over hearing this from the earl was mixed with her fear over the viscount's continued silence. What could have possibly happened after he had left Hyde Park that afternoon to make him flee and go to ground? And was Flynn safe?

Taking a seat in the Mowbray town carriage, she glanced up at the windows of Bramshaw House and whispered,

"What did you do to him? Why is Flynn so afraid that he won't dare come home?"

She turned to Victoria. "I am not letting this rest—not until I have some answers. Flynn has to be somewhere. And I fear he is on his own and possibly in grave danger."

What if he is injured and in the hands of people who won't let him leave?

If the viscount was in hiding, there was every chance he had little to no means of support. His friends were unable to help him. And he lived in fear of his father. Of the earl and his evil vengeance.

If only I could get to him.

Chapter Seventeen

The Star
Tuesday, April 29, 1817

The case of the missing viscount
Inquiries are continuing as to the whereabouts of the son of Earl
Bramshaw. Our readers will recall that this newspaper first made
mention of Viscount Cadnam's disappearance in late March. Earl
Bramshaw has apparently made it known that his son's business is no
concern of others. The Star has it on good authority that senior
members of London society are now pressing for a formal
investigation into the young nobleman's continued absence from the
company of his friends.

After paying the newsboy, Augusta folded up the paper and stuffed it into the deepest pocket of her warm woolen coat. She then crossed back over Bruton Street and began the short walk home to Berkeley Square and Mowbray House.

Flynn had now been missing for almost twelve weeks. Despite Gideon's inquiries and those of Flynn's uncle, Charles Cadnam, no sign of him had been found. Every day she scoured the papers from cover to cover for any hint of news.

In the weeks following her first visit to Bramshaw House, she and Victoria had twice knocked on Earl Bramshaw's door, but each time the door had been answered, it had been swiftly closed in her face. The earl wouldn't deign to speak to her, and her numerous letters to him were swiftly returned unopened.

Her concerns over Flynn having married the woman from Hyde Park had long been replaced by the gnawing fear that something terrible had befallen the viscount. His father's refusal to put paid to the rumors surrounding his son's disappearance only served to add to her worries.

Gideon had taken it upon himself to journey to the Cadnam family estate, Bramshaw Hall, in Southampton but had returned to London both dejected and empty-handed. No one at the earl's estate had seen Viscount Cadnam since the day he had left in his father's coach, some ten years previously.

Augusta had always suspected that things were bad between the earl and his son, but it had never crossed her mind that Flynn had been effectively banned from his family's country home. And with his father holding tightly onto the purse strings, the man she loved had to all intents and purposes been kept a prisoner in London, only allowed to leave when it suited the earl.

And now he had disappeared, leaving not a trace.

Rumors of Flynn having met foul play continued to swirl about town, but with Earl Bramshaw's steadfast reluctance to assist with inquiries both formal and informal, the search had ground to a halt.

"And that is exactly what he wanted," muttered Augusta.

She had taken to buying the newspaper from a local seller first thing each morning rather than reading the one which had been delivered to Mowbray House. Clipping pieces from the paper took time, and she didn't want to have to explain her actions to anyone other than Victoria.

Her sister greeted her inside the foyer of their home a short while later. As Augusta bade a quick thank you to the footman who had accompanied her, Victoria hurriedly waved her over. "Thank heavens. Where have you been?"

"To get the newspaper. Why, what's happened?"

Victoria took her gently by the arm and drew her into the nearest sitting room, closing the door behind them. "You might want to sit down for this. I am afraid it's not good news."

Over the past months, Augusta had tried to prepare herself for the possibility of receiving the worst news when it came to Flynn. But her private imaginings were nothing compared to the bone-deep dread she was now experiencing.

"Gideon and Papa have just returned from Bramshaw House. Apparently, Earl Bramshaw is now claiming that Flynn has been..."

Augusta was certain that her own heart had suddenly stopped beating. "Please, Victoria. Flynn has been what?"

Don't say it. Don't say it. I beg of you.

"He has been done away with. One of the Bramshaw House footmen also disappeared on the night that Flynn went missing. Late yesterday, his father informed the authorities that he believes this man is responsible for the death of Viscount Cadnam. The earl didn't have an explanation for what might have happened to Flynn's body."

"I see," whispered Augusta as her emotions shut down. She gripped hold of her sister's arm, afraid that if she didn't, she might well collapse.

Her world stopped. The man she loved was dead.

No. No. He can't be. He said he would come back and that we would be married.

"Oh, V, you heard him that day in the park. Flynn promised we would be together. Him being dead is impossible. He wouldn't do this to us. He wouldn't leave me. What am I going to do? This is beyond terrible," she sobbed.

It wasn't just terrible—it was the end of all hope. The final, bitter end to everything. For many weeks she had resolutely held onto a tiny sliver of hope. That a miracle would occur, and Flynn would reappear in her life. Good would triumph over evil, and they would find a way to be together. With this latest news, it seemed that her prayers were not going to be answered.

Flynn was gone, and he wasn't ever coming back.

Chapter Eighteen

✥

The Star
Friday, July 10, 1817

An inquest into the disappearance of Viscount Flynn Cadnam was informed that on the night he went missing, a member of Earl Bramshaw's household staff had been dismissed for poor conduct. In a written submission, the earl stated that earlier on the night in question, his son and the missing servant had been heard exchanging harsh words. Unfortunately, without a body, the authorities are limited with regard to opening a criminal investigation.

No corpse, no crime. Augusta folded the newspaper up and set it aside on the breakfast table. She wasn't going to bother with cutting out the article. Flynn had been missing for over five months, so there seemed little point. From the way his father had behaved at the hearing, it was clear he had accepted his son's death.

And moved on. The heartless blackguard.

Her gaze settled on the letter sitting on the table which had come with the morning's mail. It was from her friend Serafina in Rome, marked with the stamp of her family's shipping company, de Luca Shipping.

Serafina's letter was a small bright point in Augusta's otherwise dark existence. She picked up the missive and stared at it. Turning it over, she gently smiled at the pretty hand-drawn pictures of flowers on the back. Serafina was always one for decorating her correspondence.

"Is that a letter from Serafina?" asked the duchess from her seat at the head of the table.

Her mother no longer just ate breakfast with her children —she had also taken to sharing the supper table. Augusta's concerns about the fate of Flynn had been recently surpassed by her worries over the state of her parent's marriage. Of the long silence that continued to exist between the Duke and Duchess of Mowbray.

Having grown up with two passionate parents, who fought constantly, this change in their behavior was disconcerting. There were days when Augusta would gladly have endured the screaming and yelling that had been the hallmark of her upbringing. Anything other than the void which her mother and father appeared to have fallen into over the past months.

She picked up the letter from her friend, passed it to Victoria, who handed it to their mother. There was nothing particularly private in Serafina's correspondence. Her carefully crafted words of English covered the usual topics of the weather and fashion. Along with the constant invitation for Augusta to come and visit her in Rome.

The duchess snapped open the wax seal of the missive but didn't give it back to Augusta. She spent the next few minutes humming softly to herself while she read Serafina's letter.

When she was finished, she folded it back up and set it on the table.

"Serafina does write a lovely letter. And it was particularly nice of her to pen a quick hello to Gideon at the bottom of the third page. I am sure he will greatly appreciate her kind regards. I have a suspicion that he took a bit of a shining to Serafina during her time with us last year," said Lady Anne.

Augusta and Victoria exchanged disappointed glances. They had failed in their attempts to play matchmaker with their brother and the beautiful Serafina de Luca during her visit to London the previous year. The marquis had never treated their houseguest any different to that of being just a friend. If Gideon had taken a shining to Serafina, he hadn't acted upon it. He had stood alongside Augusta on the dockside as the ship which took her friend back to Italy had sailed away.

What a clod. Any other man would have snapped Serafina up and made her his wife.

It was slowly becoming clear to her that the Kembal siblings were somehow cursed when it came to finding love. Or when they did indeed find it, it was cruelly snatched away from them.

Grief was a heavy burden, especially when she had to keep much of it to herself. Victoria had been her one touchstone of support. There were still those surreal moments, when she was out walking the streets of London, that Augusta would suddenly stop, having thought she had caught a glimpse of Flynn out of the corner of her eye. Her heart would skip a beat, and her pulse would begin to race as desperate expectation took hold.

But every time she looked closer, she realized she was mistaken. Her broken heart was finding it hard to let go.

"And Serafina asked when you are coming to Rome," noted the duchess.

Augusta picked up her toast and took a bite. It was cold, but at least the crunch of bread in her mouth let her know she was still alive. Mourning Flynn had taken her through various stages of pain and denial. This latest phase had her wallowing in the dark depths of depression. Of wondering if she would ever be happy again.

Time is meant to heal the heart, but I don't think I shall ever be over the loss of him.

Serafina's invitation to visit hadn't ever been more than a postscript in her letters. Augusta had written much the same in her regular replies, asking her friend to return to London someday.

"Yes, she is generous with her offer," she replied absent-mindedly.

"We should go."

It took a second or two for her mother's words to filter through Augusta's early morning haze. She snapped to attention, her gaze going straight to her mother. She mustn't have heard Lady Anne correctly.

"What? I mean, I beg your pardon?" The note of confusion clear in her voice.

The duchess rose from her seat and came around to where Augusta sat. "We should go to Rome. You and me. We women are condemned to live such small lives. I think it's high time we went to see the world. Well, Rome at least. Think of it as our own small version of the gentleman's grand European tour."

Most days simply getting out of bed was a struggle for Augusta, so the thought of getting on board a ship and sailing all the way to Italy was something she hadn't ever seriously considered. It seemed an impossibility.

Lady Anne bent and took hold of her hand. "I am sure that soon you will find a lovely nobleman to marry. He will wish you to settle down and give him a family. I am just saying that you owe it to yourself to have lived a little before then. Let's go and visit Serafina. Be brave, my dear girl."

She lifted her head and met her mother's gaze. Excitement danced in the duchess's eyes.

I can't believe she is serious about this.

The way her mother held her hand so tightly, it was clear that she was indeed earnest in her plea for them to leave England and travel to Rome.

"Well, truth be told, I have always wanted to see Palazzo Lazio. The way Serafina talked about it and how she described the magnificent artwork and sculptures was quite appealing," replied Augusta.

Were they really having this conversation?

"And Rome. The eternal city. The ancient Colosseum, Saint Peter's Basilica, and all those other wonderful sights. Come, Augusta, we must do this. I promise you won't regret coming with me," pleaded her mother.

What would the rest of the family think of the two of them sailing all the way to Italy? And what about the duke? Her parents had never spent more than a night or two separately in her entire life. How would her father cope with spending months apart from his wife?

A flurry of questions raced through her mind.

"I don't know. It's just such a long way. And what if we get there and I hate it?"

The duchess brushed her other hand over Augusta's cheek. "But what if you love it?"

It would be easy to say no. To stay in London and continue to grieve. But the thought of Flynn and the things that he wouldn't ever get to do settled in Augusta's mind.

I owe it to his memory to travel where he would have loved to have gone but didn't get the chance. To honor him.

"Alright, let's go to Rome. When do you think we should leave?"

SASHA COTTMAN

Lady Anne rose. She glanced around the breakfast room for a moment. From the deep furrow in her brow, her mother appeared to be giving Augusta's question about possible departure dates a long hard consideration.

"How soon could you pack? I mean, if we can secure passage in the next few weeks, would you be ready to sail?"

In a matter of minutes, the notion of going to Italy had gone from a mere flight of fancy to becoming something very real.

Augusta turned to Victoria. "What do you think?"

"It might do you good to take a long trip. See some new sights and freshen your soul," said Victoria.

She had always wanted to see Rome, but now that the offer to travel was laid before her, Augusta hesitated. "It's six weeks to reach Civitavecchia. I remember that because Serafina said the long sea voyage was boring at times."

Six weeks to Italy, then six weeks home. In between they would have to spend at least a month in Rome to make it worth their while. "When would we be back in London?"

The duchess rubbed her hands together. "Well, if we could find a ship to take us before the end of July, we could be in Rome by sometime in September. With all things running in our favor, you would be back in England well before Christmas."

"Don't you mean we?" corrected Augusta.

"Yes, of course, I meant we," said her mother, following a short pause.

Augusta picked up the letter from Serafina. She still hadn't read it, but she could imagine what it said. Lots of stories about the places and people that were in her friend's life. Places and people that Augusta would get to know if she took the chance and got on board a boat.

"What do you think Papa will say when we tell him we are planning to go to Rome? Will he want to come with us?"

She suspected that the duke might not think it such a wonderful idea. Her father wasn't one for travel. He loved London and Mowbray Park. This was the man who refused to travel to Strathmore Castle in Scotland, her mother's family seat, because he considered it too far to go. The notion of spending months away from home wouldn't likely be something Clifford Kembal would leap at with any sense of joy.

"I am going to enquire about when we could sail for Rome. As to what your father says, I don't really care. This is not his adventure. It is yours and mine," replied the duchess.

"I could come with you," said Victoria.

Their mother shook her head. "No. I need you to stay here and keep your brothers in order."

"What about Coco?" asked Augusta.

At the mention of the youngest Kembal offspring, the duchess raised her gaze to the ceiling. "Your father needs to bring her into line. I have tried and failed. Repeatedly. That girl is going to get herself into serious trouble someday. While I am out of England, it will present him with the perfect opportunity to do something to curb her wild ways."

Victoria studied her toast with great interest. Augusta opened Serafina's letter and ran her eyes over it. Neither of them was going to dare to ask the duchess as to how much she knew about their younger sister's nocturnal habits. Augusta had a horrible suspicion that little of it had gone unnoticed.

Serafina's missive was full of its usual color and interest. One of her younger sisters had recently received her first holy communion, and there had been a huge party at Palazzo Lazio to celebrate. Augusta had lost count as to how many siblings her friend had, but there were quite a few.

"Apparently, Rome was very warm when she wrote this letter, and Serafina said they were expecting a long, hot summer. Or at least a better one than last year."

The thought of walking the streets of Rome with Serafina while enjoying long sunny days was a strong lure. Italy might well do her a power of good. To be in a new city, and not surrounded by the things which constantly reminded her of Flynn, may be just what she needed.

Rome could be the place where she finally saw the light which would bring her out of the long dark tunnel of grief. Augusta had nothing to lose. She had already lost the one thing that truly mattered.

"I shall start making arrangements," said the duchess, quickly heading for the door.

With their mother gone, Victoria came to sit beside Augusta. "You have to do this, G. Get out of London, and go see the world. Or at least some of it. I promise that if any news comes of Flynn, I shall write to you immediately."

If, as his father had claimed, Viscount Cadnam was dead, there would be nothing of any real note for Victoria to impart. A body which they could give a decent burial to was the most she could now hope for when it came to Flynn. Not knowing what had happened to him still hurt, but she was slowly, surely coming to accept that he was gone.

"Alright. I will go with Mama. She says we will be back before Christmas, so I won't be away that long."

Chapter Nineteen

❦

Early December 1817
Palazzo Lazio, Rome

Serafina de Luca appeared in the doorway of Augusta's room. From the dark blue cloak draped around her shoulders and the gloves on her hands, it was clear she was ready to go out.

Rising from her chair, Augusta picked up her reticule and dusty pink cloak. "What are our plans for today?"

It was a little game that she and her friend played most mornings. Augusta would ask, and Serafina would give her a grand pronouncement as to where and with whom they would be visiting.

"I was thinking we could go and visit Saint Peter's this morning. The papal mass will be starting early, after which we can wander back across Ponte Sant'Angelo and then find somewhere to eat."

Augusta stifled a grin. Serafina de Luca was nothing if not predictable. It was Wednesday, and they had a well-established tradition. Take the bridge over the River Tiber to the Vatican and on their way back, they would find a restaurant where they could sit and share a big bowl of pasta and a bottle of wine. Then they would amble slowly through the shops of Via del Corso, letting their lunch settle before heading home to Palazzo Lazio and enjoying a late afternoon nap in one of the many sitting rooms of the Duke of Lazio's family home.

It was a home, but in reality, it was a palace. Bigger than any that Augusta had seen before undertaking the long sea voyage to Rome. The butter-colored walls of Palazzo Lazio, with their white-bordered windows, fitted in with the rest of the local streetscape. But it was the ornate interior that set it aside from most other private residences.

There were plenty of other wealthy and powerful families in Rome, but Augusta was yet to find one whose home matched that of Palazzo Lazio. Even the private rooms of the Vatican, where Serafina was afforded special access due to family ties, were set in their place by the opulent foyer of the de Luca residence.

The two friends made their way down the stairs and toward the front door. As with every time she walked through the main gallery, Augusta's footsteps slowed. Her gaze lifted as she took in the gilt-edged ceiling with its painted blue sky, white clouds, and golden cherubs. Heaven, in all its glory, hung overhead.

"Come now, G, you have been here for nearly three months. How can you still find the roof a source of wonder?" observed Serafina.

She had lived in the palace her whole life, so it was no surprise she didn't find the décor as fascinating as Augusta, who simply chortled at her friend's remark. "Yes, well you know what my home looks like, and fine though it is, it's nothing like this place."

Home.

That single word pulled Augusta up short. She and her mother should have sailed for home by now. Their original departure date of late October had come and gone, yet the duchess had not given the slightest indication that she was ready to book them passage to take them back to England.

Serafina seized Augusta by the arm and dragged her toward the front door. The pair of bodyguards who were waiting either side of the entrance fell in behind them.

Stepping out into Via della Pilotta, Augusta stopped. For a bliss-filled moment she stood, eyes closed with her face raised to the Roman sun. It blessed her skin with warm good morning kisses. She sighed. "This is why people come to this city and never leave."

But leave she must eventually do. Return home to London and her family. To a future different from the one she thought had been set for her. To a life without Flynn.

When she opened her eyes, she discovered Serafina quietly studying her. Her Italian friend could, unfortunately, read her mind and mood all too well. During her time in Rome, Augusta had turned to Serafina for comfort, for counsel as she finally came to terms with the loss of her beloved viscount.

"You look like you need a day of laughter, or at least one with smiles," said Serafina.

The dark-haired beauty with deep brown eyes always seemed to know what Augusta needed. She also knew how to draw her out of the dark corners where her grief still sat, waiting to embrace Augusta whenever her heart whispered its pain.

"I dreamed of Flynn again last night."

"Was it a good dream, or a sad one?" asked Serafina, brushing a hand gently over Augusta's cheek. At times like these, her friend was a godsend.

Every thought of him was filled with sadness, of the sense of loss. But worse was simply not knowing what had happened to him. Victoria's letters from home had given Augusta the occasional update on the search for Flynn, but with it nearing eleven months since he had disappeared, her hopes of ever discovering the truth had slowly faded.

"I dreamed that he happened to walk into a restaurant where I was dining. He took the chair opposite mine and helped himself to some of my pasta. I just watched, and then he smiled at me and spoke. *"I love this food, but I love you more."*

Augusta drew in a ragged breath. There were times when she wished he didn't appear to her, then others when she feared she would forget what he looked like. Even worse would be losing the memory of his voice. Of his words of love, spoken only to her.

"He was always looking for food."

What she would give to be able to spend one more hour with him, to tell him how much she missed him. How empty her life had become.

I would give him a plate of pasta twenty feet high just to have that chance.

Serafina slipped her arm around Augusta's waist and gave her a hug. "I only met him the one time when I was in London, but he seemed like a really nice man. I am so sorry, G."

Augusta rummaged in her reticule for a handkerchief. She wiped her face, then took a deep breath. Regret was something that would always haunt her steps. But there was nothing she could do. Tears wouldn't bring Flynn back.

"Come on. Let's walk. I love nothing better than trudging through the streets of Rome and across the river to the Vatican. It helps to clear my head."

That was only a half-truth. Augusta liked to walk everywhere because the pounding of her leather-soled boots on the hard cobblestones of the ancient streets was the best way to drown out the constant beat of despair in her heart.

Chapter Twenty

The Morning Herald
12th December 1817

*Your Herald correspondent has been informed that the ship which
arrived at London Docks from Italy on Tuesday the 9th of December
was lacking two expected passengers.*
*The Duchess of Mowbray and her daughter Lady Augusta Kembal
are rumored to still be in Rome. In other news, the Duke of Mowbray
and his family have suddenly dropped out of social circulation and are
not accepting callers at Mowbray House.*
*The senior matrons of the haut ton are rumored to be asking why.
What could have happened to keep the duke and duchess apart for so
long, dear reader?*

Chapter Twenty-One

✦❧✦

E *arly March 1818*
  Rome

Flynn's right hand moved like lightning. While his gaze remained fixed firmly on the fruit stall across the marketplace, his fingers went to work. The apple was in his grasp and hidden inside his coat pocket in under a second. The Rome fruit vendor had no idea what had just happened.

He turned and made a deliberate show of being genuinely surprised to find himself standing in front of a market stall. The bustling Piazza della Rotonda was full of them, but the well-honed act still worked like magic.

Pointing at the same barrel of apples from which he had just pilfered his breakfast, Flynn asked smoothly in Italian, "How much?"

The stall holder gave him a price, and he scoffed at it. He was still waving his left hand in the air as he walked away, his right digging into his pocket for the apple.

One day, if he managed to have more than two small coins

to his name, he would repay all the merchants he had stolen from. Or at least the ones in Rome. He dared not venture back to Florence, where the locals would surely remember the scruffy Englishman who had passed through their city and helped himself to their wares.

His morals had long ago reconciled any misgivings he might have for petty thievery. It was either that or starve.

But Rome was different. It had a long-held tradition of street beggars and pickpockets. He privately enjoyed watching the skillful borseggiatori as they helped themselves to the purses of tourists and locals alike. There was a certain artistry about the way they worked. One which he knew he could never emulate.

Stealing small scraps of food was his forte, and more than once he had managed to talk his way out of trouble by playing the role of the bumbling English tourist. Shaking his head while exclaiming, "I thought they were complimentary," had held him in good stead.

But living rough under one of Rome's stone bridges was slowly taking its toll. He may have recovered most of his health following his father's knife attack, but Flynn feared what a few more months of an Italian winter might bring. And whether he would survive.

I can't die here. I have to find a way home. This is not my destiny.

The days were cold, and the nights long. His overcoat was well past providing much warmth. He hadn't yet resorted to begging, but the time was coming when he may well have to set his pride aside and hold out his hand for money.

He'd heard a lot more English accents since arriving in Rome. Tourists visiting the eternal city and wishing to see the sights gave him some hope. Yesterday he had earned a few welcome coins by showing some visitors around the Pantheon, the ancient Roman temple which was now a church. They had been more than pleased to avail themselves of a guide who not only spoke fluent English but who also had a good command of Italian.

Not that Flynn had any choice in being here and having to learn the language. He was doing everything he could just in order to survive.

From what he had been able to piece together, after attacking him, the earl had paid someone to dump Flynn on board the first available ship sailing out of London. It had been his good fortune that the captain of the vessel had had a change of heart and decided that he and the crew would try to save their captive's life. With Earl Bramshaw having missed vital nerves and organs in his attack, loss of blood was the major problem that Flynn had been forced to overcome.

He had spent weeks in the tiny cabin of the ship fighting for survival, and was still weak when the ship finally docked in Pisa, northern Italy. A local monastery had taken him in and seen him restored to health.

But charity could only last so long, and Flynn had eventually found himself living on the streets and surviving purely by his wits. It had taken him close to eight months to make his way the two hundred and twenty odd miles south to the city of Rome. His wounds and the lack of money had made the journey long and, at times, precarious.

While in Florence, his attempts to borrow money through a major international trading bank had been met with a polite but firm no. No one wanted to believe that the ragged beggar was, in fact, a penniless English noble. He couldn't blame them. The whole story sounded preposterous.

He took a bite of the apple, and his empty belly gave thanks. He was still chewing the first bite when a hand landed on his shoulder. Flynn whirled round. In one swift move, he had shoved the apple back into his pocket while at the same time dropping the sharp blade he kept hidden in his coat sleeve into his fingers. He readied himself for a fight.

"Oh, sorry. I didn't mean to startle you."

His gaze landed on a well-dressed gentleman. Flynn quickly sized the man up.

Decently cut suit—not the finest tailor but still not bad. If his rounded cheeks are anything to go by, he eats both regular and hearty meals.

Good clothes. A stout form. Those two things meant that the gentleman who spoke perfect English had money.

Better not slash him with my knife.

The blade joined the apple as Flynn painted a smile on his lips. "Good morning to you, sir. May I be of assistance?"

One of the first lessons he had learned on the street was that manners went a long way. As did having a concealed weapon.

The man shyly offered Flynn his hand, but Flynn shook his head, refusing to take it. Just because the gentleman appeared harmless, didn't mean he could be trusted. Another lesson he had learned the hard way on the road to Rome.

"I mean you no harm, my friend."

There was a degree of nervousness about this stranger, and Flynn guessed that he wasn't used to approaching strangers in the street.

"What do you want?"

"Forgive me for intruding, but I have noticed you wandering about the market place most mornings. At first, I thought you were a local, but earlier I overheard you speaking to some of the English tourists who are staying at the Albergo del Sole." He pointed toward the hotel at the other end of the square. "From your voice and mannerisms, I would suggest you are a well-bred gentleman, one possibly down on his luck."

Soon after arriving in Rome, Flynn had picked up on the fact that many English visitors stayed in accommodation close to the Piazza della Rotonda. Having been away from home for so long, there were times he simply hung around the entrance to the Pantheon just to hear a familiar accent.

Loneliness was a cold friend.

Flynn's senses remained on edge. If this man thought he was going to turn Flynn into the local authorities, he was in for the devil of a fight. He hadn't survived the agony of a knife wound, kidnapping, and weeks at death's door only to succumb to the hangman's noose far from home.

Flynn's hand dipped into his pocket, and he made ready to use the knife. If push did come to shove, he was ready to defend himself. The other man's gaze followed to where Flynn's hand sat out of sight, and he took a wary half-step back. "My name is Michael Cooper. I work with the local Anglican church mission here in Rome. There is no need to be afraid, my good chap. I thought, and pardon me if it is not the case, that you looked like a fellow who might be in need of some Christian charity. As I said, down on your luck."

Flynn's head tilted forward as he let out a dry laugh. Down on his luck. From where he stood, he didn't have any luck. He had used it all up in surviving his father's attempt to kill him, and then making it to Rome. "Yes, one could say that I am living a hard life. One which I have only recently become accustomed to, but one which I intend to put behind me some day."

Please offer me some money. I could do with a plate of hot food. Did he say he was with the Church of England?

"I didn't know there was an Anglican church here in Rome," said Flynn, more than a little perplexed.

Rome was the center of the Catholic faith, so a protestant church being situated here was a touch odd.

Michael shifted on his feet.

Bless you. You really aren't good at accosting strangers in the street, are you?

Flynn found it refreshing and a touch sweet to encounter

someone so open and naïve like Michael Cooper after all this time. Apart from the priests at the monastery in Pisa, it was rare for him to meet people in the street who regarded him as nothing more than a likely beggar.

"We don't have a church building per se, but we have a meeting room. Sundays, we hold services, and when we are able to find a visiting minister, we invite them to conduct a full mass," explained Michael.

It had been a long time since Flynn had set foot inside an Anglican church. He had become quite comfortable with Catholic ones, since it was often a good place to find a charitable feed. "Your church mission sounds wonderful. But what does that have to do with me, Mister Cooper?"

Michael's face lit up, and he smiled. "How about I take you somewhere and buy you a hot meal? Then we talk, after which you can decide whether you would like to take me up on my offer."

Flynn's eyes narrowed. He had received enough unpleasant approaches from men over the past few months to know that well-mannered conduct and appearances didn't always match with sordid demands. "I am not in the business of selling my body," he ground out.

The smile disappeared as a look of shock surfaced on Michael's face. "Oh, no! I didn't mean that sort of offer. I mean... I wanted to talk to you about giving you a place to live."

"What did you say?" Surely, he had misheard this stranger. A lump formed in his throat. It had been a long time since anyone had been kind to him. A place to live. This was more than Flynn had ever dared dream he might find.

"It's not much, just a room off our meeting place, and you would need to help out with things. But from the look of you, sir, I would suggest that you are living a rough life."

Any moment now, Flynn was going to break down in the

middle of the bustling market. He let go of the knife and pulling his hand out of his coat pocket, held it out to his newfound friend. "It is an honor to meet you, Michael Cooper. I am Flynn."

"Just Flynn?"

This man might be who he said he was, but trust wasn't something that came easily for Viscount Cadnam. Not after the past year of having endured a life of hell. For all he knew, his father might have discovered that he was still alive and be on the hunt for him. And if that was the case, and Earl Bramshaw had unfinished business, the last thing his son should be doing was giving his full name freely to any stranger who he happened to meet. Especially ones who spoke perfect English.

I have survived this long; I am not going to let him win.

There was also the question of Lily and her family. Her father might well wish to seek retribution for Flynn not having married his daughter. Or worse, send someone to drag him on board a ship and take him back to England, where a wedding service and an eager bride awaited his arrival.

For the time being it was better that no one knew that Viscount Flynn Cadnam was still alive.

As he gave Michael his best smile, Flynn leaned in. "Yes, just Flynn."

Chapter Twenty-Two

The Morning Herald
March 21st, 1818

Where is the Duchess of Mowbray?

*Rumors of her grace having abandoned her duties as a wife and
duchess have been circulating since just before Christmas. Now it
appears, dear reader, that certain members of the Kembal family,
including the Marquis of Holwell, have retired to the family estate,
Mowbray Park. It is not known when they are expected to return to
London.*
The mystery deepens.

Chapter Twenty-Three

E aster Sunday, 22nd March 1818
  Rome

If he lived to one hundred, Flynn Cadnam would never again take for granted the pure and simple joy of clean, hot water. After dipping his hands into the basin, he splashed the luxurious liquid over his face. When the ripples in the water cleared, he glanced down, grinning at his reflection in the bowl. A neatly shaved face, framed by straggly, long brown locks, smiled back at him.

"I really ought to do something about my hair," he mused.

There was a barber's shop situated close to the meeting hall which the congregation of All Saints used for their church, but he was reluctant to spend his valuable coin on indulging in a haircut. The scissors which he used to trim the flowers adorning the two large vases on the altar table each Sunday would have to suffice to bring his unruly locks under control.

His appearance might still be a little rough around the

edges, but it was a vast improvement on how he had looked the day, some three weeks earlier, when Michael Cooper had met him in central Rome. Hot tears pricked at his eyes whenever he thought about the moment Michael had offered him not only friendship but a safe and warm place in which to live.

He had existed on the edge so long that it was only after he had moved into the makeshift Anglican church that the precariousness of his previous life had finally dawned on him. He had been mere weeks away from either arrest, death, or both.

Lifting his head, Flynn took in the clearer view which the small mirror hanging on the wall above the basin afforded him. His cheeks were sunken. Even three weeks of steady meals couldn't quite undo the damage of the past year. But he was determined not to go home until he looked like his old self again. He couldn't face Augusta in this condition.

Augusta. What did she suppose had happened to him? Did she think him dead?

Knowing my father, he would have told some cock and bull story about me frequenting houses of ill repute and having been murdered in one of them.

He took comfort in knowing that without a body, the earl would likely have to wait the full seven years before making an application to the court to have his son declared legally dead. Charles Cadnam, followed by his son Christopher, would become his father's heir. No matter whether his uncle or cousin eventually inherited the title, the line of Earls of Bramshaw would continue.

The fact that Flynn was not only alive but that he fully intended making it back to England would come as a rather nasty shock to his father. When his not-dead son turned up on the doorstep of Bramshaw House, the earl would find it a terrible inconvenience.

And hopefully you will have to face the consequences of your villainy.

"You didn't count on the kindness of strangers, did you?" he whispered.

The men on board the boat, who had been paid to smuggle the badly injured Flynn out of England, had decided that they couldn't bring themselves to toss the wounded viscount into the sea. Instead, they had sewn him up as best they could and eventually dumped him at a monastery near Pisa. Far from home, and far enough away from anyone who might come looking for him. The chances of Flynn making it safely back to England were remote.

But the past weeks had seen a vast improvement in his situation. He now had a warm, safe bed. And he had made a couple of friends. In his pocket were a few coins, enough to make sure that his belly was full by the time he went to sleep most nights.

A local café owner and his wife had taken Flynn under their wing and extended him credit when necessary. And when he was particularly low in funds, they had graciously allowed him to work off his food and wine scrubbing pots and cleaning tables.

As a future earl, it was a long way from where he should be, but if the past year had gifted anything to Flynn, it was a deep sense of gratitude for the smallest of blessings. Despite his father's best endeavors, he was still alive. He had mostly recovered from his injuries, and his life had taken a turn for the better.

I have hope.

His thoughts drifted to the letter he had written to Augusta, explaining what had happened to him and why he had disappeared. He had caved to his desires and decided it was worth the risk to write to her. In his note, he had instructed Augusta to keep his whereabouts a secret.

And if someone else did discover that he was alive and decide to visit mischief upon him, Flynn was recovered enough from his wounds that he felt ready to face any potential threats which might happen to come his way.

Last week, he had passed the precious missive onto a tourist who was heading back to England. With luck, Augusta would have it within the next month. And if she penned him a quick reply, it could possibly reach him by no later than June.

Who knows, I might be home by then and be able to surprise her in person.

It had been over a year since he had last seen Augusta. His vow to confront his father, then come and claim her, had gone unfulfilled.

Many nights he had lain awake and wondered what was happening in London. What Augusta was doing. What lies his father had told the world.

Had she given up on him and found someone else? Their parting that day in Hyde Park had been one of hurried promises and tenuous hope. Who was to say that long before his letter finally arrived, she had decided to move on? She might well have married someone else.

I couldn't blame her if she has. I've been gone for so long. Me being dead is the obvious answer to the question of my disappearance. I just hope that wherever she is, Augusta is happy.

He didn't want to consider what his reappearance in England might do to her. He just wanted to see Augusta, even if it was merely as polite friends.

Postage to England was prohibitively expensive for a man struggling to feed himself. It had only been after his arrival at All Saints that Flynn had finally been able to get access to pen, paper, and the all-important means to send an urgent letter home.

Pushing aside the thin cream-colored curtain which separated his small sleeping quarters from the rest of the meeting room, he stepped out into the empty space. The morning sun, which filtered through the upper window, gave the room a little light, but without the warmth of a fireplace, the makeshift chapel was always chilly.

He considered the minor shortcomings of his new accommodation to be a blessing in disguise. It would help him not to get too comfortable. He wanted to follow the letter home, to find Augusta.

"A boat fare home won't come cheap, but I can't stay in Rome forever."

The letter to Augusta had included a polite request for money, but he wasn't going to pin all his hopes on her being able to send him funds. Michael had been making enquiries about helping Flynn to secure paid employment.

Flynn's grasp of the Italian language had progressed from a mere smattering of words to being able to conduct a sensible conversation with most people he met. His fluency in English and a decent grasp of French was an added bonus in Rome. He had the perfect set of skills to be able to work as both a guide for visiting tourists as well as a liaison with the locals.

His second, less pleasant reason for wanting to get to London was his father. He was ready to face down the earl, but he wasn't yet settled on how that encounter might well look. Did he bring criminal charges against his sire? But with it having been over a year since the violent incident at Bramshaw House, the chances of him being able to present enough evidence to secure a guilty verdict were, at best, slim.

Earl Bramshaw had likely greased enough palms in London to ensure that if anyone attempted to press charges against him over the disappearance of his son, they would find it a near impossibility to have the matter brought before the House of Lords. Squabbling noble families were nothing new.

As far as Flynn was concerned, he would much rather that his father paid him handsomely for his silence. A happy life with Augusta far away from the earl was all he desired.

I have to get home.

Picking up his patched-up coat and the scarf which Michael had generously gifted to him, Flynn headed for the front door and down the stairs. Once out in the street, he made his way past the ruins of Emperor Trajan's Column and the Forum. His destination this morning, Saint Peter's square and the papal blessing for Easter Sunday.

Easter in Rome was ridiculously busy. All week, people had been bustling to and fro in the crowded city streets. Everyone was making preparations for today. Easter Sunday was a day for church services, followed by large family gatherings. For faith and feasts. Flynn envied his fellow citizens of Rome for their joy and hope.

His own plans were a little less grand, but still meaningful. He was going to join with the hundreds of pilgrims who flocked to the Vatican today. On Good Friday, he had walked over to the nearby Colosseum and stood outside waiting with the faithful while Pope Pius VII was inside saying a prayer at each of the fourteen stations of the cross designated around the ancient stone arena.

Experiencing the holiest of days in the eternal city was a once-in-a-lifetime opportunity, and he wasn't going to miss any of it. He had been gifted a second chance at life, and Flynn Cadnam intended to live this new existence to the fullest. At least as far as his poor purse would allow.

Reaching the church of Santa Maria de Loreto, with its large brick and marble dome, he stopped and crossed over to Via della Pilotta. He made his way north, glancing at the ornate doors of Palazzo Lazio as he passed it by. The heavily armed guards who stood outside put paid to any thoughts he might have of calling in to see Augusta's friend, Serafina de Luca. He doubted she would remember him from her short time in England, but he made a mental note to leave a letter with the guards before he left for home.

Chapter Twenty-Four

T*he same morning.*
    Palazzo Lazio, Rome

"What is going on? And why are we not sailing for home?" demanded Augusta. She stood, hands on hips, and glared down at her mother. She wasn't normally one for speaking so plainly to the duchess, but lately it seemed the only way to get through to her was to be blunt to the point of rudeness.

"Nothing is going on. I thought you were enjoying your stay in Rome," replied Lady Anne.

She was. Rome was wonderful. But it wasn't home. They had been gone from England for nigh on eight months. What had started out as a bit of an adventure, with the private hope of it being a way for her to deal with her grief over the loss of Flynn, had now become somewhat akin to a long war campaign. One which didn't seem close to coming to an end any time soon.

I want to go home.

"Rome is magnificent, it exceeds everything I have ever

read about it, but it is not my home. I want to see Papa. I miss my brothers and sisters. Don't you also want to see our family again?"

Augusta gritted her teeth as the duchess let out a tired sigh and rose from her chair by the sitting room window. Anyone would think she was asking too much of her mother.

"It's Easter, Augusta, my dear. Go and enjoy yourself. Rome is full of people from all over the world. Find them and make new friends."

She was tempted to throw up her hands in disgust, but Augusta was fast discovering that her mother's temper lacked somewhat of its usual balance. Lady Anne had developed an unfortunate habit of flinging what could only be described as a tantrum whenever her daughter questioned her actions.

"If you are bored with Rome, don't forget we are off to visit Tivoli this coming week. I am sure that the change of scenery will do you the world of good. My friend, Signore Arosio has been most generous in inviting us to stay with him at his villa. And I hear the ancient ruins are particularly fine," added the duchess, with a dismissive wave of her hand.

This is ridiculous. Anyone would think I was asking the impossible.

While they were out walking near the River Tiber late yesterday afternoon, Serafina had raised the issue of their long-overdue departure. Her friend's question had concentrated Augusta's mind ever since.

Why are you and the duchess still in Rome?

She didn't have an answer to that thorny question, or at least not one to which she wanted to give voice. The longer she remained in a state of denial, the better. But the time was surely coming, and soon, when Serafina's mother, Donna Francesca, would make it plain that her guests had overstayed their welcome.

It was late March. Her mother had promised they would

be home in time for Christmas. What the Kembal family were making of their extended absence Augusta didn't wish to consider.

She had diligently written to Victoria every week since their arrival at Palazzo Lazio. And in the earlier part of their stay, her sister's letters had arrived frequently from England. But since Christmas, she had received no word from her beloved sibling. Not even a quick note to wish her a happy new year.

They must have gone to Strathmore Castle for Hogmanay and not returned to London until later in January. I am sure that is the reason for Victoria's correspondence being delayed.

She missed her connection to her family at home. The longer she heard nothing from her siblings, the heavier the silence settled in her heart. It was almost like experiencing a second form of grief.

I want to go home. I want my father, and my brothers and sisters.

Augusta didn't wish to go to Tivoli. She wanted to remain in Rome and be here when Victoria's long-expected letters finally arrived. She couldn't be bothered mustering any interest in the prospect of visiting yet another set of ancient ruins; she'd had more than her fill of temples, churches, and relics. Tivoli might be wonderful, but it held little appeal.

"I would appreciate you giving me some sort of indicative date for when you plan for us to set sail. If you are unable to do that, then perhaps I should write to Papa and ask him to come and fetch me?"

The word *unwilling* sat on the edge of her tongue, but Augusta held it at bay. She was carefully trying to draw her mother out, to get the duchess to tell her the real reason why they were still in Rome. And why she wasn't making any moves to leave.

I know you and Papa had a falling out, but you can't stay mad with him forever.

Her mother's eyes narrowed, and a flush of red appeared on her cheeks. Augusta flinched as Lady Anne wagged a finger in her face. "Don't you dare threaten me, young lady. I am your mother, and I will be the one who decides when we leave for home. Now run along before I lose my temper. I am sure Serafina is waiting for you."

Hands clenched into fists, Augusta did a quick turn about face and marched out of the sitting room. As she headed back to her own bedroom, she was left to ponder her mother's sudden show of temper. Her words had struck a nerve with the duchess, and for the life of her, she couldn't figure out why.

She met Serafina downstairs in the foyer. The moment their gazes met, her friend drew Augusta to one side. "What's wrong? You seem upset?"

Augusta glanced over at the guards standing either side of the door. She had been told that they couldn't speak a word of English, but over the months that she had been living at Palazzo Lazio, she had begun to have her doubts. There were times when she had said something to either her mother or Serafina in English, and she could have sworn the guards were not only listening, but they understood her every word.

"It's nothing. Mama is just in one of her moods. Again."

Serafina gave a brief nod. Like everyone else in the palace, she had borne witness to the Duchess of Mowbray and her various moods. Between Lady Anne and Serafina's own mother, Donna Francesca, the two women had a stranglehold on displays of haughty outrage.

"Are you sure?" pressed Serafina.

Her friend knew her all too well. Days when Augusta's worry and grief over Viscount Cadnam were at their worst, she was the one who sought to offer comfort. The afternoons where the two of them sat quietly reading in one of the palace's sunlit rooms were precious—they helped keep her grief at bay. When the time came that she and Lady Anne did finally leave for England, Serafina would be the one thing Augusta would miss the most.

"Yes, just a little disagreement with my mother. Nothing to worry about. Are we still heading to the Easter sermon at Saint Peter's?"

"Of course. Then we are going to find some food and wine, and while away the rest of the day until the fireworks this evening," replied Serafina. As her gaze drifted to the bodyguards who were standing waiting, a sly smile crept to her lips. "I had a private word with them earlier, and after I made the offer of a small bribe, they said they would be willing to accidentally lose us later in the afternoon."

Not long after she and the duchess had arrived in Rome, Augusta's mother had agreed to let her daughter wander the streets of Rome with her friend, just as long as they had the armed palace bodyguards following them. The halberd-bearing guards provided a similar protection service to the one that the Mowbray House footmen did in London, but to Augusta's disappointment, they refused to carry packages or open doors. And while it was good to have the protection of the guards whenever they were out in the city, their constant presence was stifling at times.

In the cool Easter morning sunshine, Augusta wrapped her hooded cloak around her shoulders and tied it at her throat. It would take them close to an hour to make their way up Via della Pilotta and cross over the River Tiber via the Ponte Sant'Angelo bridge, but once they joined the throng of Easter pilgrims, the respectful head covering would be essential.

She might not be Catholic, but in the city which stood at the center of the Roman Catholic world, she was more than willing to observe the Easter religious customs.

The bodyguards remained at a respectful distance, waiting

while the two young women made ready to leave. Augusta was grateful that Serafina took great care to make sure her protectors were well out of earshot whenever the two of them wished to share a private conversation.

"How are you this morning? I mean, after yesterday's news," asked Augusta.

Serafina shrugged. "I don't actually know how I feel. Discovering that I am to be married off to a much older man came as quite a shock. But the fact that my mother opposes the union is probably what worries me the most. Donna Francesca has stood silent while my father arranged other marriages for my older siblings. I have never heard her use the language she did with him yesterday as I left my father's office."

Serafina was shortly to be betrothed to one of her father's business connections, a man old enough to be her grandfather. Donna Francesca was apparently not happy with this arrangement. Rumors of the heated argument between the contessa and Enzo de Luca had spread rapidly through Palazzo Lazio yesterday.

"What a fine pair we two make. Your mother standing up to your father, while mine seems determined to avoid going home to see my papa," replied Augusta.

"Things are changing. And I fear not for the better. Both our lives seem destined for great upheaval in the near future," sighed Serafina. Augusta noted the dark rings under her friend's eyes but held back from making mention of them. It was clear Serafina hadn't slept well last night.

Can you blame her? The man she is going to marry is ancient.

Unlike Serafina, she would be granted a say in whom she eventually wed. Augusta glanced at the ring on her right hand. It was the ring Flynn had gifted to her just before he raced out of Hyde Park and embarked on his mission to confront his father. The small gold and ruby band had once held the promise of a happy future, of a life with the viscount. Her fingertip skimmed over the delicate gem.

Oh, Flynn. You would have loved Rome.

She really ought to stop wearing it but hadn't yet found the courage to do so. She'd promised herself that the day she left to go home to England, she would take it off her finger and put it somewhere safe. Treasure it as a memory of him. Of a life lost far too young.

The shuffle of feet followed by the not-so-subtle tapping of the dull end of halberds on cobbled paving had them both turning in the direction of the Palazzo Lazio bodyguards. They were getting impatient.

Serafina's fingers brushed the ring as she softly laid her hand over Augusta's. Her friend knew the painful story behind the jewel.

"We had better go, Augusta. Rome is going to be a crush of people, and it will take time to make our way over to Saint Peter's. I don't want to get on the bad side of the bodyguards today. Not when they have agreed to conveniently turn the other way, just as we run off to meet up with our friends for this evening."

Augusta nodded.

I will miss you terribly when it comes time for me to leave for England.

Serafina was right. Time wasn't standing still. Soon they would be separated. Serafina would be married, while she would return to London and her family. To her own uncertain future.

Chapter Twenty-Five

I t wasn't long after they had left Palazzo Lazio that the girls found themselves swept up and carried along in a crush of people. Augusta and Serafina joined hands as the crowd moved as one. If they lost each other now, it would take them hours to reconnect.

The ancient Ponte Sant'Angelo was the only way to cross the River Tiber in this part of Rome, and everyone seemed to be headed toward it.

Serafina grinned as Augusta raised her eyebrows. "Sunday morning at Easter and every Roman and pilgrim is out on the street. And they are all going to the same place, Saint Peter's square at the Vatican."

Their bodyguards drew closer, politely shoving other people out of the way if they got anywhere near Serafina. The de Luca family was well known in Rome, and its immense wealth was not a secret. It wouldn't take much for someone to attempt to kidnap Serafina and hold her to ransom. The sharp halberds and swords which the guards displayed were meant as strong deterrents to anyone foolish enough to try.

Augusta had never experienced anything like Easter Sunday in Rome. London was a city of order and carriages, whereas this was something entirely new—a wave of devout worshippers sharing the excitement of spending the day as one, celebrating the rebirth of Christ.

I could almost get used to this, to the passion of these people.

Her gaze traced over the crowd. Without thought, she slipped into a familiar habit. Something she had been doing for the better part of a year.

Searching. Seeking for the signs of a familiar face. For him.

In Rome, her heart didn't quite skip a beat as often as it did when she had done the same thing in the streets of London. All around her was a sea of jet-black manes. If she slipped the hood of her cloak from her head, her brown hair would stand out in the crowd.

Continuing to look for Flynn was a fool's errand; he was dead. But her heart still spoke of its deep longing to see him once more. Just one last time.

There were moments when Augusta realized what she had been doing and tried to stop herself, but her heart had always had its way. No doubt, in time it would eventually heal, and the pain lessen. But she sensed she would always be searching for his face in the crowd.

A flash of light brown hair caught her eye, and she snapped to attention. Through a gap in the multitude of people, she could just make out the figure of a man. He had his back turned to her.

His coat was grubby, and his hair had been badly cut. Whoever this poor pilgrim was, he certainly couldn't afford more than the basics in life.

Turn around, let me see your face.

A large body moved between her and the man she had been observing. The flash of a sharp sword had Augusta coming to a sudden and violent halt. The people who had been following her, now crashed into her back, and a good deal of swearing and cursing reached her ears.

"Sorry! Scusi!" she exclaimed.

She glanced at Serafina standing beside her, but her friend's attention was focused on the bodyguard in front of them. He had a street urchin by the scruff of his neck and was violently shaking the young boy. Augusta caught a few words, then, to her surprise, the pickpocket handed over a small purse. It was Serafina's.

"How on earth did he get hold of that?" she muttered.

"They are professional thieves. Even with our armed bodyguards standing so close, they managed to get under my cloak and relieve me of my money. I hadn't realized what had happened until our guard grabbed hold of him," replied Serafina. Augusta caught the note of shock mixed with a tinge of admiration in her friend's voice. The borseggiatori certainly knew their illicit trade.

The pickpocket put on a tearful show, and Augusta's heart went out to him. From what she understood, thieves, petty or not, didn't tend to receive kind treatment in Rome. In London, the boy would have been dragged to the nearest water pump and received the punishment of a ducking, with his head held under water for a lengthy period. From the look of fear on the boy's face, she suspected he was in for a similarly unpleasant experience this morning.

"Couldn't we just let him go?" she gently pleaded.

Serafina gave a brief shake of her head. "That is not how things are done here. I will ask the guards not to turn him over to the authorities, but the rest of it is out of my hands. He has not stolen from me; rather, he has offended my family."

She spoke a few brief words to the guard, which Augusta did not quite catch. The man seemed to consider them before loosening his hold on the boy, but he didn't let him go. Augusta suspected the lad was in for some sort of corporal punishment.

"At least he will get to go home tonight," said Serafina.

The guard and the pickpocket disappeared into the crowd. When the man returned a short time later, he gave Serafina a nod but said nothing. He fell in behind them, and from her friend's stony silence, Augusta concluded that the matter was now considered closed.

At the bridge, all the various streams of pilgrims merged into one. Augusta and Serafina linked arms and walked in step with one another. It was slow going. A low chant rose through the gathering. It took Augusta a moment or two to realize that it wasn't a chant; it was a song. As more people began to join in, the song grew in volume.

"It's Victimae paschali laudes, the Easter sequence. It's part of the official Easter liturgies. They are singing in Latin, which is probably why you don't understand the words," explained Serafina.

Augusta didn't understand them, but she could feel them. Sense the joy and reverence of the crowd. There was an undercurrent of anticipation that had tears pricking her eyes. Easter at home had never been this powerful.

Then again, I haven't been at the center of the Catholic world before. This is quite emotional. I really am going to weep.

Serafina leaned in and gave Augusta one of her knowing smiles. "Don't be surprised if you spend a good deal of today feeling emotional. Rome at Easter tends to have that effect on people, especially those coming here for the first time."

"Oh good, that is a comfort. I was beginning to worry that I was on the verge of becoming hysterical." She let out a strangled laugh. "With the way my mother is behaving at the moment, is it any wonder I am familiar with that particular Latin word?"

They shuffled over the bridge, along with hundreds of other people, slowly making their way to Saint Peter's Square. This wasn't Augusta's first visit to what was widely considered the greatest church in all of Christendom, but her previous trips had been in the comfort of a carriage and without being stuck in the middle of the Easter crush.

The sense of energy which hung in the air—this was more than a simple church going. It was a celebration of unity and faith. It stirred her blood.

This has to be the most emotional and interesting day of my entire stay in Rome.

Reaching the large plaza, the crowd of pilgrims spread out, and Augusta was finally able to let go of Serafina without the fear of losing her in the milling throng. She rolled her shoulders back and stretched out her arms. "That's much better. I hope it won't be such a squeeze on the way home."

"No, it won't. Come on. We should make our way closer to the front and find our seats," replied Serafina.

Serafina led the way past rows and rows of pilgrims. Some people had brought their own chairs, while most others either stood or knelt to pray. The de Luca family had their own private seating in a special roped-off area to the left of the main steps leading up into Saint Peter's Basilica.

The enormous plaza was an interesting palette of red, white, and gold. Swiss guards in their red and gold striped tunics moved across the front of the red-carpeted entrance. The Pope's window, at which she had already seen him appear each time during her previous visits, was draped in a crimson curtain. A large red and white banner hung over its balcony. Priests and senior members of the clergy were all clad in robes of red and white. They stood out in contrast to the hundreds of pilgrims who were mostly dressed in somber, respectful black.

With the Easter mass scheduled to last over two hours,

Augusta was more than grateful that she could look forward to the comfort of a seat. Reaching the de Luca family section, Serafina went to greet several relatives while Augusta paid her respects to the head of the de Luca family. She curtseyed to Serafina's uncle, Lorenzo de Luca, the Duke of Lazio.

Her gaze slid over the various people seated around them. Most of the extended de Luca family members that she knew had gathered here this morning, but to her consternation, the Duchess of Mowbray was nowhere to be seen.

She and her mother had been guests of the de Luca family for many months, and Lady Anne should have been here. Leaning in to Serafina, she whispered, "I am so sorry that Mama has not made the pilgrimage this morning. She isn't herself at the moment."

Serafina waved her concerns away. "I just spoke to Donna Francesca, and your mother kindly offered to keep company with one of my elderly aunts who is too frail to come and sit out here in the chilly wind. They are waiting in the carriage near the Sacramento Fountain and will receive the Easter blessing from one of the cardinals once the main service is over."

Augusta sighed with relief. Her mother hadn't embarrassed the family.

I really ought to think the better of Mama, but at the moment she is so unpredictable.

A reflective Augusta followed Serafina to where they had been allocated their seats. A servant appeared and handed both young women woolen blankets. She was warm from walking with the mass of pilgrims, but it wasn't long before Augusta found the need to drape the cover over her knees. She huddled deeper into her cloak as the March winds whipped through the plaza.

The hum of the crowd settled to a hush as Pope Pius VII

slowly made his way out the front of Saint Peter's and to the crimson-draped dais.

~

Flynn stood shoulder to shoulder with the other pilgrims some three hundred yards from where the Pope offered his Easter blessing. It was the closest he was able to get.

Has every person in Italy undertaken the journey to be here today?

Even if they hadn't, it certainly felt like it.

He had made the crossing over the river via the Ponte Sant'Angelo this morning along with hundreds of other members of Rome's faithful, enjoying the camaraderie and songs of faith. At school, Flynn had excelled at Latin, so he was able to sing along. Life was so much more enjoyable when you had food in your belly and a safe place to sleep. But the pickpockets who had rifled through his tattered coat, and there were more than a few of them who did, still found his pockets empty of coins.

He had made a solemn vow that before he eventually left Rome, he would give Michael Cooper the details of each market stall that he had stolen from with the request to see the proper funds handed over. This country had given him back his life, and he owed it to himself and his future heirs not to leave owing any debt which could be easily repaid.

After an hour of the Easter mass, Flynn retreated to the rear of the plaza and sat down. His knife wound had healed, but the long months of hunger and living rough still took their toll. He could stand for a reasonable length of time, but he found he tired easily.

As soon as the mass was over, he would make his way home to the chapel and take a long afternoon nap. All Saints had an evening Easter mass scheduled, after which he intended to head out and enjoy the late festivities and fireworks.

When the tiny figure of the Pope finally moved back inside Saint Peter's, he was followed by the long procession of red-and-white-clad clergy. The mass was over, and a restlessness quickly rose through the crowd.

Flynn took that as his cue to leave.

Chapter Twenty-Six

The walls of the café began to sway in her vision. Augusta was certain it wasn't her. But after six glasses of strong red wine, she couldn't swear to that being the truth.

Across the table from her, Serafina's brows furrowed. "Are you alright, Augusta? I think perhaps it is time we went home."

She gave a half-nod in response, then thought the better of it. It wasn't the room which was unsteady. "Yes, I think that might be a wise idea. As soon as we return to the palace, I shall head up to my room and go to bed. But first, I am going to finish my wine."

Serafina moved the glass out of Augusta's reach. "You forget. We are expected at supper this evening. If you arrive in your current state, then both of our mothers are going to be angry. Perhaps a cup of strong coffee might help."

Augusta huffed in frustration. She had planned to finish her wine, but her dizzy head made its protests loud and clear.

Pushing back her chair, she quickly rose to her feet. Her fingers gripped the edge of the table as she hurriedly attempted to steady herself.

Oh. I really have had a few too many glasses of wine.

"Let's forget about the coffee and go back to Palazzo Lazio. I would like to hide out and rest for a little while. As soon as my head clears, we can make our way to the supper room."

Serafina pursed her lips. Her friend was clearly not so sure about Augusta's ability to shake off the effects of the wine. "Alright, but I think we should avoid coming in the front door and sneak in through one of the side gates in the garden. If the palace guards see you, they will definitely tell my mother that you are... how do you English phrase it... under the weather."

Victoria had gifted Serafina an English phrasebook when she was in London, and her Italian friend loved to play with the various idioms that amused her. Under the weather was Serafina's favorite this week.

Leaving the café, they joined the busy crowd in the street outside. Serafina stopped and pulled up the hood of her cloak. It wouldn't do for them to be seen in public without Serafina's bodyguards. Augusta attempted to do the same with her own cloak but struggled.

The cool night air hit her with its full force, and the effects of the alcohol went straight to her head. She swayed unsteadily on her feet. She was beginning to regret having drunk the last few glasses of strong northern Italian wine.

Serafina took her by the arm. "Come on. It's not far to walk home. One foot in front of the other and we shall have you safely back at Palazzo Lazio. But we might need to rethink our plans to join my family for supper. I can't see you being sober any time soon."

Augusta did as she was told, concentrating her efforts on making it back to the de Luca home in one piece, while at the same time trying to avoid running into other people. It wasn't easy. Her head felt light, but her feet weighed a hundredweight.

Once inside the palace grounds, they quickly made their way across the lawn and in through a servants' entrance. Serafina's maid Maria Volpe was waiting for them as they stepped through the door of their favorite sitting room. She gave a *tsk* of annoyance to Serafina, then turned to Augusta. "Lady Augusta, your brother is here. He is sharing the evening meal with the de Luca family, but I don't think your mother is happy with his arrival."

Serafina and Augusta exchanged surprised glances.

My brother?

Augusta took hold of Maria's hand. "Which brother?"

"The Marquis of Holwell. He arrived at the palace with Count Nico a few hours ago. Apparently, he sailed into Civitavecchia early this morning, and your cousin found him in the waiting room of the shipping office."

Gideon was in Rome.

Augusta started for the door, but Serafina stopped her. "No, you can't go—not in your current state," said her friend, overruling her plans.

Instead, coffee was ordered, and Augusta was made to sit in one of the overstuffed chairs.

I know Serafina is right, but I want to see Gideon.

The surprise at hearing the news of her brother's unexpected arrival had Augusta sobering up somewhat, but as her head began to clear, her stomach turned. A disappointed Augusta finally had to concede that she wasn't in any condition to see Gideon this evening and allowed Serafina to escort her back to her room.

"A peaceful night's sleep is what you need. If Gideon has just arrived, he is not going anywhere until the two of you have been reunited, G," offered Serafina. "Get some rest, and I shall see you in the morning."

"I suppose you are right. He won't be happy with me if he thinks I am drunk."

After Serafina had left, Augusta closed her bedroom door and readied herself as best she could for bed. She still couldn't believe the news that Gideon was here in Rome. His arrival could mean many things, but she had a horrible suspicion he would have only made the long sea voyage because he had been sent to deliver bad news.

I just hope I don't have a hangover in the morning. I have a feeling that tomorrow is going to be a long trying day.

~

"I still can't believe this is happening," said Augusta the following morning as she and Gideon walked the well-manicured grounds of Lazio Palace. The duchess had made herself scarce not long after her eldest son had arrived at the door of the sitting room where the two Kembal women were sitting eating breakfast. She hadn't been in the room when Gideon broke the news of the Duke and Duchess of Mowbray separating.

A grim-faced Gideon nodded. "I'm really sorry to be the bearer of such bad news, G. Papa wants me to bring you home as soon as possible."

The notion that her mother had left her father was, of course, ridiculous, but it also brought everything Lady Anne had done over the past few months into clear and horrible focus. It both saddened Augusta and made her bitter. Her own mother had lied to her.

Augusta stared at him, unable to understand why he was so calm about this disaster. "Why aren't you a mess over this?"

He sighed. "I am, believe me, but I have known for some months. You shouldn't have been the last member of the

Kembal family to find out. It's not fair that you have been kept deliberately in the dark. I intend to take Mama to task over that piece of duplicity."

Augusta was also going to have harsh words with their mother. This betrayal of trust went beyond a simple evasion of the truth. It broke the bond of family unity.

Mama and Papa living separate lives. This is dreadful.

A different expression now appeared on Gideon's face. It was the look of someone in great distress. She had seen that same look all too many times when she had stared at herself in the mirror. It spoke of the struggle of coming to terms with loss.

"Gideon?"

"I talked to Serafina in the early hours of this morning. I am shocked that they are going to marry her off to some old man," he said, drawing in a shaky breath.

"Yes, it's an awful situation. It seems a day for receiving terrible news. Speaking of horrible news, can I ask if there is anything new regarding Viscount Cadnam?" She had accepted that her secret lover was dead, but Augusta still wanted to hear any possible update on his fate.

"I'm afraid not. When I left London, the earl was still sticking firmly to his story about Flynn having met a terrible fate at the hands of one of the servants. Of course, few people believe that lie, but it's left the authorities and the rest of the Cadnam family with nowhere to go," replied Gideon.

Augusta nodded. She hadn't honestly been expecting any new developments in the case of the absent viscount. Flynn had been missing for over a year. Any trail which might have led to his whereabouts would have long gone cold.

I ought to tell Gideon about Flynn and myself. About what his friend really meant to me. But he seems quite upset over Serafina marrying Signore Magri. Perhaps this isn't the right time to be bringing this up with him.

Her love was lost, but Gideon was here, and so was Serafina. Her brother seemed genuinely distressed at the news of Serafina's impending marriage.

Could it be that he has finally seen the light and come to realize that he does care for her?

What if his visit to Rome was an unexpected second chance for Gideon and Serafina to make a future together? It would certainly go a long way to easing the hurt of her own private loss. It would also mean not having to say goodbye to her dear friend.

Perhaps I can help. I should help. I can't leave it up to Gideon to do it on his own.

"You look like you have lost a good deal of weight on the sea voyage, Gideon. Were you ill?"

"Yes, I was awfully unwell for most of the journey. Count Nico de Luca has given me the name of a tailor in the city. I was thinking I might go and visit the shop this morning." He glanced at his trousers which hung low on his hips. "I look and feel like a young boy attempting to wear his father's clothes. I'm not sure how long we will be here in Rome, but I don't want to be getting about dressed so poorly."

A smile crept to Augusta's lips. "Especially not in front of Serafina."

Gideon's eyes narrowed. "Don't. Please don't do anything to play matchmaker. I remember you and Victoria trying that game when Serafina was in London, and you didn't succeed."

Augusta took a firm grip on her brother's arm. "Yes, but that was over a year and a half ago. You are not going to stand there and tell me that you are prepared to let Serafina marry one of her father's business connections. A man who is old enough to be her grandfather. A man who will expect Serafina to share his bed." She didn't hold back on the desperate plea in her voice. He had to understand what was at risk.

I want to see someone happy. To know that love can triumph over heartache.

Her brother flinched at those last words, and Augusta's fevered hopes flared to life. Gideon might be doing his best to act disinterested, but it was clear that he cared for Serafina. As far as she was concerned, he just needed a good hard push to do something about his feelings.

His hand settled gently over hers, and he gave a tired sigh. "G, I have just arrived in Rome after having endured the worst six weeks of my life. Please grant me a day or two to find my feet before you start berating me over what Serafina and I may or may not share."

Augusta shook her head. She could understand her brother being exhausted after having been so terribly ill, but at the same time, she couldn't simply stand by and watch him suffer the sort of heartbreak she had endured with the loss of Flynn.

There is hope for these two, and I won't stay silent. Not if I can do something to help.

"Serafina's betrothal is due to be announced next week, Gideon. If you feel one ounce of anything for her, you have to understand that you don't have the luxury of time to decide what to do."

Her brother had a real chance to change both his and her friend's fate. She owed it to Flynn's memory to do whatever she could to assist another couple in finding their way to happiness. If she could help to save Serafina from a loveless political union, one which was designed purely to further Enzo de Luca's grasping ambitions, then at least her own pain of the past year would have amounted to something.

Our happily ever after was stolen from us, but you can claim yours.

Much as Gideon didn't like her meddling, Augusta was determined that when the time came for them to get on board the ship to go home, Serafina would be going with them.

~

By the time they eventually did make it to the tailor shop on Via del Corso, Augusta was firmly set on her mission. Gideon was going to marry Serafina, and that was that. They had spent the morning at the Colosseum, where due to Serafina's quick thinking, they were able to outwit the de Luca body-guards and enter the ancient arena unaccompanied.

Her own efforts in feigning sore feet then allowed her brother and friend to snatch a few precious minutes alone. Time during which they had apparently come to some sort of agreement about their future. When a grim-faced Gideon took Augusta to task over her efforts, she gave him her solemn word that she would cease and desist from any other attempts at playing Cupid.

But she was far from done.

Gideon is clueless when it comes to women. If I let him dictate how things are to go, he will still be trying to make up his mind as Serafina walks up the aisle and marries the odious Signore Giovanni Magri.

She could play subtly when it was needed. Someday, hope-fully very soon, her brother would be thanking her for the small things she had done to ensure he had made Serafina his marchioness.

After the Colosseum, they headed to Via del Corso and the tailor's shop which Count Nico de Luca had suggested to Gideon. While Serafina assisted her brother with choosing the right fabrics for his new waistcoats, a delighted but watchful Augusta kept her distance.

Hidden behind a rack of linen shirts, watching while the two tentative sweethearts worked their way through a pile of fabric swatches, Augusta sensed a shift in the relationship between Gideon and Serafina. A budding connection that hadn't been there before.

When Gideon picked up a pale blue piece of fabric and offered it to Serafina, she simply smiled at him, shook her head, and placed it back on the table saying, "No, it would wash you out too much, Gideon. You are a man who can wear stronger colors."

Emotion clogged Augusta's throat as she witnessed the loving exchange. When their hands brushed against one another, and the touch lingered, it was all Augusta could do not to break down and sob with grief.

It was impossible to ever resent them this moment, but it was still so heartbreakingly painful to watch. To know that she and Flynn would never have the chance to share the simple pleasure of shopping for clothes. Augusta gripped tight to the ring on her hand—the only thing she had left of her lost love.

Augusta was still fighting to maintain her composure when Serafina finally handed Gideon over into the care of the tailor and his staff. Her friend grinned at the men as they fussed over the marquis. While Gideon stood arms and legs akimbo, the tailor and his team set to work taking his measurements. They spoke in rapid-fire Italian. Augusta could understand quite a bit of what they were saying, but from the expression on her brother's face, it was evident that he didn't have a clue as to what was being said about him or his choice of clothes.

When she met Augusta's gaze, the happiness slipped from Serafina's face. She glanced at Augusta's hands. At the ring. She softly sighed.

"How about you and I go to the drapers shop and let Gideon finish being measured for his new wardrobe?" she offered.

A grateful Augusta forced a smile to her lips. Serafina was the one person other than Victoria who fully understood what the past year had been like for her, of what she had lost.

She waved to Gideon. "While you get measured for your new clothes, Serafina and I are going to visit the drapery a few doors up the street. She wants to look at ribbons and bonnets. We won't be too long. After we come back, we can go and find some food. I, for one, am starving."

At times, it was hard to put on a brave face, but she was determined not to cry in front of her brother. If she did, he would likely think it was on account of the breakdown of their parent's marriage.

He would be wrong. She was yet to process that shocking piece of news, still in a state of denial over the lies her mother had spun. Until she spoke to the duchess and heard the truth from her own lips, Augusta was prepared to cling to the hope that the letter Lady Anne had sent to her husband had just been yet another tantrum in a long melodramatic list of them.

Serafina ushered her quickly out of the shop and up the street. Once they were inside the draper's shop, she didn't stop to look at the ribbons or bonnets. Instead, she towed Augusta to the very back of the store. When they were out of earshot of the other customers, she brushed a hand on Augusta's cheek. "Are you alright? You look about ready to cry?"

The social mask which Augusta had worn for the better part of a year now slipped into place. It was either that, or breaking down and sobbing her heart out all over the fine Venetian lace. "I am alright. I'm just a little emotional after having watched you and Gideon. Please tell me my brother realizes how close he stands to losing any chance he might have of a future with you. And that you won't let him do such a foolish thing? Please, Serafina. I beg of you."

Her friend gave a small nod in response. "Gideon

certainly seems more in earnest than he was when he and I met in the garden late last night. I don't know what you might have said to him this morning before we left Palazzo Lazio, but whatever it was, it seems to have spurred him into action."

Good. He had been paying attention.

Augusta moved away and began to examine a nearby rack of ribbons. Serafina followed. She sensed her friend had more she wished to say, but Augusta had heard enough. "It's alright, Serafina. I understand I should leave things alone. As we were leaving the Colosseum, Gideon cautioned me not to attempt to meddle any further."

"Thank you," replied Serafina. "I know you mean well, and I expect your brother understands that too, but this is a delicate situation. My father is set on me marrying Signore Magri, and it is going to take more than just a few polite words from Gideon to change his mind. Besides, things are only just becoming clear between your brother and me. No one should be making assumptions about what feelings we might have for one another."

You don't really expect me to believe that do you? I know you have a soft spot for Gideon, and he was more than a little interested in seeing you this morning. And I saw the two of you kiss when you thought you were out of sight at the Colosseum.

Augusta held her hands up in surrender. She had been officially warned off from interfering with Gideon and Serafina's budding romance. "I shall hold my tongue. But I warn you, if it looks like you are not going to be accompanying us back to England, then all bets are off. I swear if you end up being wed to that old man, all of Rome will hear my displeasure."

A pretty blue bonnet caught her eye, and she took that as a good sign to change the topic of conversation. "I thought you wanted to look at hats. What do you think of this one?"

Serafina glanced at it, then shrugged her shoulders. "I

have two others very similar to it." She pointed at a cream capote bonnet. "That would be lovely for the summer. I could buy some green ribbons and have them stitched around the front of the bonnet. Then I might put a couple of matching ribbons on the back, where they could drape nicely. I saw a few scoop-shaped hats like it when I was in London. What do you think?"

Her beautiful, raven-haired friend could wear anything and make it look stunning. "That would be lovely. Let's finish up here and then head back to Gideon. I am famished. If I don't see a large plate of pasta in the next half an hour, I am positive I shall faint dead away."

"Are you sure you are alright, G? Your brother will understand if you want to go home."

Serafina was being her usual kind self, thinking of others. It was lovely, and she appreciated her friend's sentiments. But to Augusta's way of thinking, it was also completely ridiculous.

You need to be thinking of yourself, and my idiot brother. Not worrying about me.

Augusta pondered her options. "I think it would be nice of us to take Gideon to our favorite restaurant and introduce him to the joys of Roman pasta. Food, then home."

Gideon was more than likely exhausted from his trip, and in dire need of sleep. But if she was going to make sure that he and Serafina were to become a couple, Augusta wasn't going to waste a single opportunity when the two of them could be spending time together.

My brother can sleep all the way home to England. Just as long as Serafina is in his arms when he does.

Chapter Twenty-Seven

※◎※

S erafina purchased the cream capote bonnet, while Augusta absentmindedly chose a red hat which was the exact same color as the one she had bought only a few weeks ago. Her thoughts were elsewhere. Hat boxes in hand, they left the drapers and headed back down the street toward the tailors.

They had barely put a foot in the front door when Gideon rushed over to greet them. His brows were knitted in confusion, but a mystified grin sat on his face. It was a most peculiar sight. Augusta and Serafina exchanged equally mystified looks.

"Gideon, what's wrong?" asked Augusta.

Unshed tears shone in his eyes. "You will never guess who I just met. Viscount Cadnam. Flynn is alive and living in Rome."

Flynn. Flynn is alive. Alive. But . . . but how? That's impossible!

She heard the words and kept repeating them in her head. They didn't make any sense. Flynn was dead, so how could he be here in Rome?

Her mind had to be playing tricks. It was either that, or

she had truly gone mad. It had been an emotional day. Full of life-changing revelations, which challenged her sanity. But this latest piece of news was too fantastical to accept. A loud ringing in her ears, along with a sudden wave of light-headedness, had Augusta swaying unsteadily on her feet.

It was all too much for her to take. Augusta let out a strangled cry of distress, and her eyes rolled back in her head. Her packages tumbled to the floor. Her knees buckled from under her, and she collapsed. It was only the quick intervention of Gideon which saved her from crashing to the ground.

Flynn was alive.

Chapter Twenty-Eight

F lynn couldn't believe his change in luck. He had thought
the gods were finally smiling upon him when Michael
offered him a place to live. Stumbling across Gideon in the
tailor's shop had been beyond his wildest dreams. Finding
someone he actually knew had come as such a shock that
instead of immediately embracing his best friend, he had
made a foolish quip about not having the money to buy new
clothes.

Gideon was in Rome.

And so was Augusta.

Augusta is here. And she will now know that I am alive.

He let out a shuddering sigh. Whatever pain she had felt
for him over the past year would finally be at an end.

This truly was the city of miracles. The thought that the
woman he loved was not only in Italy but staying at Palazzo
Lazio, a mere hundred yards or so away from where he lived,
had Flynn fighting back tears long before he reached his
rooms at All Saints.

A glance at his weathered attire validated his hasty decision not to wait for Augusta to return to the tailor's shop.

Her memories of him would be vastly different to how he appeared now. Everything about him spoke of suffering and hardship.

I couldn't have her seeing me like this, it would be cruel to both of us.

His anxiety over what Augusta might think when she did see him battled with his desperate need to be reunited with her. To hold her in his arms and tell her that the nightmare was finally over. They were both safe, and despite his wicked endeavors, Earl Bramshaw hadn't won.

But he couldn't bring himself to do it. Couldn't bear to see her reaction to his current tattered state of dress and unkempt appearance. He wanted her love, not her pity. More than once this week he had been mistaken for a beggar in the street and offered alms. Pride had seen him refuse the kindness of strangers.

And yet only a matter of weeks ago you would have gladly accepted the coins.

His life had taken a turn for the better. Good fortune had him wondering if he should pinch himself.

When he reached the end of Via del Corso, Flynn eschewed his normal route home by way of the piazza. Instead, his feet moved in another direction. They had him walking up the wide stone steps of the domed church of Santa Maria di Loreto and in through the front door.

Flynn wasn't a religious man by nature, but he was possessed with the strong urge to give prayers of gratitude for this recent run of miracles. Someone somewhere was finally watching over him.

After settling into a pew, Flynn dropped to his knees and bowed his head. He closed his eyes as the hope he had thought lost forever filled his heart once more. There was no man in the world more humble than him as he whispered, "Thank you."

When Augusta came round, she found a worried-looking Gideon staring down at her. The expression of deep consternation which sat on his face had her clutching at his arm.

"What happened?" she asked, more than a little alarmed.

"You fainted. I caught you just as you fell."

Light and sound rushed in, and to her dismay she realized she was lying on the floor of the tailor's shop. "Oh, dear Lord, help me up."

Her brother, aided by Serafina, assisted Augusta gently to her feet. She swayed. Her woozy head had her clutching for Gideon's arm. A chair was hastily produced from the back of the room, and her knees held up just long enough for them to get her seated on it.

While Serafina spoke to the tailor, Gideon knelt in front of Augusta and took her hands in his, saying, "Are you alright? You didn't half give me a fright."

Nausea rolled through her body. She hadn't ever fainted before, and it was a confronting experience.

And to think I have harshly judged all those women who get the vapors at parties.

For a moment, she couldn't recall the last few minutes. Her memories were of being in the hat shop with Serafina and then leaving to head back to the tailor's to meet up with Gideon. She was certain her mind had been focused on pasta. After that, things had all turned to black.

What could have possibly happened to make her faint?

A glass of water was pressed into her hand, and Augusta took a long drink. One of the many things she loved about Rome was the fact that the water was clean and fit to drink. She nursed it for a moment, then downed another mouthful. For some unknown reason, her mouth was dry, and her throat parched.

A concerned-looking Serafina returned to where Augusta sat. "The tailor has kindly offered us the use of his personal carriage to take you home. He is most concerned about you, Augusta, as are we."

"Grazie, siete molto gentili."

Augusta managed to summon a small smile for the owner of the shop, who stood nearby wringing his weathered hands.

"I will be fine. I'm just feeling a touch unwell."

She wasn't going to admit that she now remembered the reason for her sudden collapse.

Flynn. Gideon said he was alive and had been in the tailor's shop.

But that's impossible. Flynn is dead. I must have imagined it.

Augusta turned to her brother. "I swear you said something about having met Flynn. It came as such a shock that my body and mind simply couldn't comprehend. That's why I think I fainted. Flynn is dead. I thought I had accepted that, but clearly, I haven't."

A teary-eyed Gideon slowly nodded and replied in a voice thick with emotion, "You heard right, Augusta. Flynn is here in Rome. I can't believe it either, but beyond all hope, my friend is alive."

Serafina brushed a hand over Augusta's arm. A silent acknowledgment of her understanding of her friend's reaction to hearing the news that Viscount Cadnam was not dead.

I didn't think it was possible to faint from shock, but that's what must have happened. Flynn is alive.

"Flynn is alive." She spoke the words aloud, still unsure as to whether she believed them or not. "Flynn is alive. He is here in Rome. But... but how?"

Augusta took a few more sips of the water, then handed the glass back to her brother. "Thank you. I think I am feeling a little better. Perhaps I could try to stand. It's my fault for not having finished my breakfast."

She didn't want to tell Gideon the truth of why she had collapsed. That the news of Flynn being alive had shaken her entire world to its core.

One of the other shop staff arrived, and after a few brief words were exchanged between him and his employer, the tailor beckoned for the de Luca party to follow him.

Gideon kept a firm arm around her waist as he helped Augusta out to the rear of the tailor's shop and into the narrow laneway which ran along the back. A small carriage stood waiting.

Augusta was helped on board, and after several more expressions of deep regret were offered by the tailor, she, Gideon, and Serafina headed for home. During the short journey back to Palazzo Lazio, Augusta sat silent. She was still taking it all in.

I am not dreaming. I am fully awake. And this is really happening.

The hopes which had died now sprang to life once more. Her lips kept moving as she silently repeated the same words over and over. Flynn is alive. Flynn is alive.

Reaching the palace, Gideon ignored her protests and carried Augusta inside and up to her room. The duchess was immediately summoned. When her mother arrived, Augusta finally gave up the fight and let Lady Anne fuss over her.

"What did you do to her?" her mother growled at Gideon. "I expect this is all your fault."

To his credit, her brother held his tongue. Augusta had a horrible feeling he was biding his time, waiting for the right moment when he would have an all-out row with the duchess. From the whispers of the servants, the storm clouds of war had been brewing between them from the moment the Marquis of Holwell had arrived the previous evening.

"It's not Gideon's fault. I should have had more food at breakfast."

~

Returning to his home at All Saints, Flynn quickly put pen to paper. He sent a note to Gideon informing him of his address, then walked the short distance over to Palazzo Lazio and offered it to the heavily armed guard who stood at the front door. It took a few attempts to get the man to accept the letter, but when Flynn finally made mention of the Duchess of Mowbray, his missive was snatched dismissively out of his hands and spirited away. He stifled a grin at the thought of the opinion the servants at Palazzo Lazio must hold of the fearsome Lady Anne. From his own experience of Gideon's mother, it was a fool who made the mistake of attempting to cross her.

Letter delivered, Flynn turned and headed for home once more. There was a spring in his step, something he couldn't recall having had in a very long time. Augusta was the reason. She was also the reason for the smile on his face.

I can't believe she is in Rome and has been here all this time.

While he had been slowly finding his way to Rome, the woman he loved was, unbeknownst to him, already in the city. Their meeting had to have been written in the stars. Fated.

If only I had been able to arrive here all those months ago. We could have been together and back in England. Married.

He consoled himself with the knowledge that he couldn't possibly have made it to Rome any earlier. His wounds and lack of money had dogged his every step. He'd walked much of the way, gratefully accepting the kind offers of strangers who did allow him to travel with them for parts of the journey.

While his heart had been begging for him to ask for Lady Augusta Kembal when he delivered the note, Flynn was still too ashamed of both his appearance and his shabby attire to make such a request. He'd had a year in which to imagine what their reunion might look like, and his hope-filled dreams hadn't included her seeing him in this current disheveled state.

I want to look like the man she loves.

If he appeared as a ragged beggar to her sight, how could he possibly ask her to marry him? A mixture of joy and sadness swirled within.

It was wonderful that Augusta was in Rome, and he would soon see her, but his happiness was dulled by the fear of what she would say when she finally did see him. And even if his appearance didn't have her holding back her joy, he worried what she would say. There had to be a thousand questions which she needed him to answer. The first being what had happened to him that fateful afternoon after they had parted in Hyde Park.

At the end of Via della Pilotta, Flynn turned and looked back at the entrance to Palazzo Lazio. On the corner of the busy street, he made a vow.

"I have to tell her everything," he muttered.

If he was going to attempt to salvage their future, it was time Augusta knew everything about him. Of the life he had been forced to live before his disappearance. And what potential threat his father might still pose to their future.

But first he had to speak to Gideon. To understand what else had been going on in the world during his absence. Only then would he feel ready to share the truth with Augusta. Including why he had lied to her about his father's refusal to allow them to marry.

His private shame would finally step into the light, and when it did, he could only pray that Augusta loved him enough to take her place alongside him.

Chapter Twenty-Nine

A gentle tap came on Augusta's bedroom door not long after Lady Anne finally left to allow her to get some well-deserved sleep. A figure entered the darkened room, then quietly closed the door behind them. "Are you still awake?" whispered Serafina.

"Yes, I was beginning to think Mama would never leave. I had to feign falling asleep twice before she finally took the hint."

Augusta lit a candle while her friend took up a seat on the end of her bed.

The glow from the flame revealed a deeply worried Serafina. "You gave us all an awful scare in the shop this afternoon. Poor Gideon didn't know what to do with himself, or you."

Poor Gideon.

She could sympathize with him. Her brother wasn't used to the females of his family fainting. The Kembal girls were all of robust health.

They had also been raised not to employ underhanded tactics such as pretending to swoon when they wanted to get their own way. The duchess considered that sort of behavior to be well beneath their social station. She had made it clear to Augusta, Victoria, and Coco that the daughters of the Duke of Mowbray were not the kind of girls to ever play games, especially when it came to men.

"I can't believe I fainted either, but when Gideon mentioned Flynn, everything suddenly spun out of control. The next thing I knew, I was lying in my brother's arms on the floor in the middle of the tailor's shop."

At some point she would have to return to the shop and apologize to the owner. She had given the tailor and his team a terrible fright.

There was some comfort in having been out of the public eye when she fainted for the first time. And she was, fortunately, hundreds of miles away from London. Hopefully, the *haut ton* would never find out.

Serafina scooted along the bed and when she reached where Augusta sat, took hold of her hand. "Flynn is alive. This is wonderful, glorious news. I told you—they don't call Rome the city of miracles for nothing." She leaned in close. "I hear from the palace servants that Gideon received a note from Viscount Cadnam a little while ago. Aren't you keen to know where he is staying? To see him again?" The grin on her friend's face was one of barely restrained delight.

Augusta's heart had not stopped racing from the moment she had heard the words from her brother's lips. Flynn. Alive.

Serafina was right; her miracle had been granted. What happened now was, however, a mystery.

"To be honest, I am still dealing with the news that Flynn is alive. I had given up hope long ago, so this has come as quite a shock. As you say, wonderful, but still a huge life-changing piece of news."

She had managed to hold her tears at bay while the duchess had fussed over her, but Augusta was powerless as a new wave of emotion welled up inside. Tears snaked their way down her cheeks. It was a relief to finally have them fall. And to know that they were no longer tears of grief.

If Gideon knew where Flynn was staying, it wouldn't take much to get that information out of him. Her brother was still in the dark about matters between Augusta and Flynn, so he had no reason to withhold such things from her. As far as he was concerned, Flynn was simply a family friend, and his sister would be like everyone else in the Kembal family— relieved to know that he was alive and well.

Augusta would speak to her brother in the morning, then find a way to meet with Flynn in private. The rest of the Kembal family didn't need to know the depth of the connection between her and the viscount.

After more than a year apart, who was to say that things between them hadn't changed? She wanted to tread carefully, to test the waters with Flynn. He must have known that she and Serafina were close by the tailor's, yet he hadn't waited for her. Doubt crept into her heart.

What if things have changed? What if he has found someone else?

Serafina handed Augusta a handkerchief. "Are you alright? Do you wish to be left alone?"

"No. I would rather talk to someone. I have spent far too much time alone with my thoughts of Flynn. Did anything else happen after we returned home? I mean, between you and my brother."

There was no point in attempting to be subtle about matters. She wanted to know if Gideon and Serafina had had the chance to talk. To further their relationship and possible understanding.

"Unfortunately, no. But have received news from my mother that she and I are to pay a visit to Signore Magri at his house tomorrow. Apparently, we are to make a close inspection of my future home and decide if there are things which might need changing. There is also going to be a cele-bratory supper there tomorrow night, attended by members of my family, and a number of other select guests. Things are moving forward at a fast rate," said Serafina.

In all the confusion and angst of this afternoon and evening, Augusta had momentarily forgotten about Serafina and her impending marriage. The thought of it pulled Augusta's own emotional state into sharp perspective.

The discovery that Flynn was indeed still amongst the living gave her a sense of hope. But for Serafina, an arranged, loveless marriage meant the end of all hope.

"Would you like me to accompany you when you visit Signore Magri's home?" Any sort of support she could give would sadly be only of a moral kind, but it was better than nothing.

"No, thank you. Donna Francesca is adamant that she and I go alone. I am not sure what my mother has planned, but I have a sneaking suspicion that, as far as she is concerned, this impending betrothal is not what the French would call a *fait accompli*. She is behaving most oddly. If she plans to do anything to undermine my father and stop this marriage, then I must do exactly what she says."

If Serafina could find her own miracle and avoid having to marry the man her father had chosen, that would be...

Beyond a bloody miracle. I fear Enzo is going to have his way, no matter what his wife or daughter do.

Gideon had to find the courage to step up and offer to make Serafina his wife. As far as Augusta was concerned, he had wasted the perfect opportunity to do just that when Serafina was in London. But here in Rome, with Enzo de Luca firmly set on pushing ahead with the arranged union, Augusta sensed things were more than a little complicated.

She brushed her thumb over Serafina's hand. "Do you think there is any real chance that my brother would speak to your father? I know Gideon kissed you this morning when we were at the Colosseum." Tears still worked their way down Augusta's face, and she prayed her reddened cheeks were not clear in the pale light. "He did ask me not to play Cupid, but when I think of what lies ahead for you, I can't help but hope he can see that he has to act, and soon."

The sound of movement outside her room had them both falling silent. The guards regularly patrolled the halls and galleries of Palazzo Lazio, and Augusta was well aware that they had a tendency to listen at doors.

"You have enough to deal with, Augusta. Don't worry about me. Your main concerns should be about Viscount Cadnam," replied Serafina after the footsteps had faded away.

If only that were true. There was far more to contend with both here and back home in England. Flynn was just another piece in a complex puzzle, one which Augusta was yet to put together.

"Gideon is taking me back to England with him. Papa has placed me under his guardianship. Mama is likely to be staying on here in Rome. Alone. It is not yet public knowledge, but she has decided to separate from my father."

The thought of her family breaking apart was just too awful to consider. But if Serafina could find a way to make that journey home with Gideon, her marrying into the Kembal family would at least be a balm for the pain of them losing the duchess.

I still can't believe Mama won't be coming home with us. What on earth must have happened between her and Papa for things to come this? I can't see either of them being happy ever again.

It was all so unfair. Just as she was being given a possible second chance at happiness, everyone else was about to have theirs ripped away.

Augusta lay with her head against Serafina's shoulder as her friend wrapped a comforting arm around her. "I should be the one offering you solace, not the other way around. Oh, Serafina, I hope you can find a way out of this horrible mess. You deserve to find happiness. We both do."

She couldn't think of which was worse, the thought of her losing Flynn forever or Serafina being forced to marry a stranger when the man whom she loved was so close at hand. Suffering the heartbreak of grief over the past year had taught her some of the cold hard truths of life.

If only I could save Serafina from what I have been through.

Drawing out of Serafina's embrace, Augusta wiped at her face. "I don't care what anyone says—there is still hope for you to be happy. I know it is a matter of mere days until the betrothal ceremony, but we have to do everything we can in order to stop it. Gideon doesn't want me involved, but if I can speak to Flynn, then perhaps he can talk sense to my brother."

Gideon had always listened to Flynn, and Augusta suspected he was the keeper of many of his friend's private confidences. There had to be aspects of his old life that the viscount had never shared with her. Things to which only Gideon was privy.

If there was one person who could help give the marquis a hard shove in the right direction, and have her brother finally claim his future duchess, it was Flynn. "I am going to find out where Viscount Cadnam is, and then I am going to go and speak to him. If he can come back from the dead, I am sure he can work a miracle or two."

Chapter Thirty

T*he following evening*

Augusta could have sworn the day was the longest in her life. She had endured a frightful row with her mother before the duchess finally left for Tivoli with her gentleman friend, Signore Arosio.

Serafina had been unavailable, having spent most of the day with her mother; firstly on the visit to Signore Magri's house and then later, getting ready for the pre-betrothal celebrations which were being held at her future home this evening. What Augusta had assumed was going to be a small private affair was apparently nothing of the sort and many of Rome's elite were expected to be in attendance. Enzo de Luca was determined to make his mark on Roman society.

Even Gideon didn't have time for Augusta. He had left Palazzo Lazio early in the morning and gone to a fencing academy with Serafina's brother, Matteo, and didn't return until it was almost time for them to leave for the private party.

Left to her own devices, Augusta had done what all well-bred young ladies of her acquaintance would consider the right thing to do. She had broken into Gideon's room, searched for the missive from Flynn, and upon finding the note, had stolen it.

She now knew where her beloved was staying, but since she was obliged to attend the party at the Magri house, Augusta was forced to wait until late at night to finally go in search of Flynn.

"All Saints' Chapel." The letter contained an address near Trajan's column. "I didn't even know there was a Church of England chapel in Rome," she muttered.

It was odd to think that they had walked right by the chapel only yesterday on their way to the Colosseum. Even stranger to know that Flynn was living close by Trajan's Column, which was but a short walk from Palazzo Lazio. His home was close enough for Augusta to have decided on risking a late-night ramble as soon as she could steal out of the palace.

We have been living only a matter of a hundred yards or so from one another.

The gathering at Signore Magri's modest home had been tedious, to say the least. Serafina had been forced to spend the evening close to her mother, while Augusta had spent much of her time observing Gideon and silently wishing she could strangle her brother for not having offered for her friend when he'd had the chance in England.

A feigned headache had seen Gideon and Augusta accompany Serafina home early from the supper. While Gideon and Serafina stole a rare private moment together behind the closed door of Augusta's bedroom, she kept watch in the hallway outside.

Augusta was on the lookout for both the palace body-guards and any other de Luca family members who may also have happened to come home from the party. The last thing any of them needed was for the de Luca family to discover that the Marquis of Holwell was spending time alone with Serafina, and that he intended to make her his wife.

If he knows what's good for him, he will be planning to marry Serafina.

Augusta was busy concerning herself with what she would say to Flynn when they were reunited, when footsteps from the nearby gallery roused her from her musings. Serafina's new maid Anna, appeared at the top of the stairs and began to signal to her.

Someone must be coming.

She knocked hurriedly on her bedroom door, then waited for an answer. After a gruff "Come," came from within, she opened the door. Her brother and best friend were standing barely an inch apart from one another.

"Anna is at the top of the stairs, waving her arms about frantically. I am sorry, but I think your time is up. Some more members of the family must have followed us home. Serafina, you should go to your room."

Serafina hurried away, leaving Gideon and Augusta to quickly take up their positions in a pair of chairs near the window. When Enzo and Francesca de Luca appeared in the doorway a few moments later, they were greeted with the sight of the Kembal siblings sitting at the table chatting about their plans to return home to England.

Augusta turned to the contessa. "I see you are home. I helped Serafina to bed a short while ago. Her headache hasn't improved. Hopefully, she will get some sleep. Will you look in on her?"

Donna Francesca met her gaze but offered no reaction to what Augusta suspected she knew was a lie. Instead, the contessa turned and snapped at her husband. "I told you Serafina was ill. I don't know why you didn't believe me. We didn't need to leave the party in such a hurry. Now, kindly get out of my way while I go and check on our daughter."

Enzo grumbled a half-apology. He didn't say goodnight to either Augusta or Gideon. It was clear he was angry at having been spoken to in such a haughty manner by his wife.

Gideon rose from his chair and closed the door. "He is not happy. I am determined to press ahead with courting Serafina and securing her hand in marriage. But knowing how suspicious Enzo de Luca is, Serafina and I have agreed that we will need to tread very carefully over the next day or two."

Serafina's maid Maria had suddenly been replaced earlier that day and Augusta had an inkling that it was Donna Francesca's way of making certain that her husband didn't get wind of anything. "Yes. Enzo seems definitely wary of everyone and everything at the moment."

"I am going to steal Serafina out of the palace early tomorrow, I want to spend time with her so she and I can talk. Do you perhaps have a piece of paper on which I can write her a note?"

Augusta nodded. "Speaking of notes, I should give this back to you." She handed Gideon the letter from Flynn. His brows knitted together in obvious confusion, to which she explained, "It fell out of your pocket."

He took the paper. "I suppose since my clothes are so big on me, I didn't notice when it happened. Thank you, Augusta."

Tonight was a night of lies upon lies. But if it meant being able to see Flynn, she was prepared to suffer the possible consequences.

Movement outside in the hallway had Gideon putting his ear to the door. "The de Lucas have gone. If I can write a short note, I can slip it under Serafina's door as I leave."

Her brother quickly penned his letter, then bade Augusta a good night. He kissed her on the cheek. "If anyone is looking for me tomorrow, could you please tell them I have gone to see Viscount Cadnam. I intend to spend as much of the day as I can with Serafina, but I don't want her family to know."

Augusta gave a brief nod. This was the news she was hoping to hear from him. That he was finally taking action and refusing to see her friend married off to a stranger. When she met his gaze, there was a definite glint of something in his eye.

"What's wrong?"

Gideon shook his head. "I didn't fully grasp the depth of Enzo de Luca's ambition until tonight. I now understand that Signore Magri not only has a mistress living under his roof, but that they share a number of children together. Serafina apparently became aware of this during the visit she and Donna Francesca paid to the Magri house earlier today. I can only pray that Serafina's mother will not stand for such a grave insult to be made against her daughter without doing something about it."

She hadn't had an opportunity to speak to Serafina and find out what had transpired during her and Donna Francesca's visit to Signore Magri's home earlier that morning, and this shocking piece of news filled Augusta with regret.

Oh Serafina, you poor girl. I can't begin to imagine how terrible it must have been for you to visit your future home only to discover that the man you are meant to marry already has a family.

Enzo marrying his daughter off to a man who had a secret unofficial wife came as no surprise, but the thought that Donna Francesca might actually seek to scupper her husband's plans was exactly what Augusta had been praying for. But she wasn't leaving it to chance.

"I don't care what the contessa does. Just you make sure that you do something which involves you and Serafina becoming husband and wife," replied Augusta.

"Leave it to me."

Augusta waited until silence had once more settled in the hallway outside her bedroom. With the rest of the de Luca family having now returned from the supper at Signore Magri's home and retired to their rooms, she was confident in taking the risk of sneaking out through the garden and down the steep path which led to the street at the bottom of the hill behind Palazzo Lazio.

It would, of course, be far easier to go out the front door, but the guards were sure to stop her. Or worse, send for Gideon. She didn't want to be having any sort of conversation with her brother about Flynn. Not until after she had seen the viscount. And certainly not until she knew where their relationship now stood.

After changing into a plain blue gown, Augusta replaced her evening slippers with her sensible leather walking boots. At this late hour, the more inconspicuous she was out on the streets of Rome, the better. A well-dressed, unaccompanied young lady would surely draw attention.

Snatching up her woolen cloak, Augusta wrapped it around herself and slipped the hood over her head. She fiddled under her cloak, searching for the silver chain on which her locket watch hung. When she finally did manage to pull it out from under the front of her gown, Augusta noted the time.

It was a little before eleven. "Perfect," she whispered.

For a brief moment, she considered stopping by Serafina's room and letting her know where she was going but decided against it. This was something she had to do for herself. An opportunity to go and claim the future she had thought she had lost. But until she'd had the chance to see Flynn and talk to him in private, she didn't want to share any of it with anyone else. Time may have changed things between her and her lover, so she wanted to be sure of where she stood with Flynn. If he still loved her.

Slipping out of her room, Augusta crossed quickly over to a small alcove. There she hid in the darkness, waiting, listening for any sign of approaching footsteps. Her heart was racing at a furious pace. This was a dangerous and reckless thing she was doing. But she was determined to go through with it.

I have to see Flynn.

The routine of the guards in Palazzo Lazio was so regimented that a person could have set their watch by it. It was a blessing in disguise. This precision timing meant Augusta had but a few minutes to make her way out of the main house before the shift change happened at eleven o'clock. If she left it any later, the new guards would be making a full sweep of the house, and she wouldn't be able to make her escape without running the risk of being caught. As a guest at the palace, she was under the protection of the de Luca family, as well as their well-trained army of private guards.

After the day she had already had, the last thing Augusta needed was to find herself having to explain why she was wandering the halls dressed in such a manner. It wouldn't take much for the guards to realize she was attempting to sneak out. With Serafina having already cautioned Augusta that the night guards were less pliable than the ones who patrolled the palace during the day, she was at pains to avoid them.

From the alcove, Augusta made her way to the nearest set of stairs. Moving as quickly and as quietly as possible, she headed down to the ground floor and out into the garden.

The palace was surrounded by high stone walls, and while they offered a good deal of privacy and protection, they were still not enough to keep the occasional unwanted visitor out. Which meant that the guards also patrolled the gardens at night. Augusta was well aware that they were under strict instructions to challenge anyone, including family and guests, who they found wandering the grounds in the dark.

The trees at the edge of the garden afforded a degree of cover, and she wasted no time in making a quick dash across the lawn toward them.

On as light a foot as she could manage in her walking boots, Augusta raced to the garden gate. From her skirt pocket she withdrew the key Serafina had given her not long after she'd arrived at the palace.

"Make sure you keep this safe and secret. If my parents ever discovered that I had a key to the rear gate, they would have the whole wall bricked up. And I would never forgive you."

Glancing over her shoulder one last time, Augusta slipped the key into the ornate lock. A sigh escaped her lips as the key turned, and a soft *click* whispered into the night air.

She was through the gate and had it closed within seconds. Pausing, she listened once more, praying that the noise of the gate being opened hadn't traveled across the grass and been heard by the guards. To her relief, a welcome silence still hung over the garden.

"Thank God," she muttered.

Locking the gate behind her, Augusta made her way to the hillside path. Her destination—the nearby All Saints' Chapel and the man she loved. Viscount Flynn Cadnam.

Chapter Thirty-One

B y the time she finally arrived at the bottom of the narrow set of stairs which led up to the front door of the chapel, Augusta's hands were trembling. In her haste, she had missed the doorway in the dark and been forced to retrace her steps. Panic threatened.

With her heart pounding hard in her chest, her greatest fear was that she was going to faint once more. She dreaded suffering the indignity of being found by some stranger while lying in an unconscious state in the street. That would be the ultimate humiliation. Not to mention extremely dangerous.

She stopped and took a slow, deep breath, but it did little to calm her racing heart and mind. On the walk over from Palazzo Lazio, Augusta had considered what her first words to Flynn might be, but nothing seemed quite right.

The long descent down the hill hadn't helped. In the dark, she'd had to go slow and make sure not to lose her footing. By the time she reached the street far below and then made her way around to the piazza, Augusta was a barely held-together bundle of rapidly fraying nerves.

What did you say to the man who you had loved, lost, and buried in your heart?

"This is Flynn. It shouldn't matter what I say."

But it did.

Her feet touched the edge of the first step, and she slowly made the climb. For each footfall, her heart was thumping. Flynn. Flynn. Flynn. Being this close to something she had dreamed of, had prayed for, seemed almost unbelievable.

Halfway up the stairs, Augusta stopped. Her heart was beating so fiercely in her chest she feared she might collapse before she could make it to the top.

When she finally did make it to the small landing at the head of the stairs, she found herself standing in front of a dark brown door. A notice on the nearby wall read.

All Saints' Chapel
Daily Mattins
Sunday Holy Communion with visiting Church of England ministers

Augusta scowled. It didn't look much like a church. Or not the kind of one she was used to visiting.

What did Gideon say? It's a meeting hall, not a proper chapel. I don't care, just as long as he is here.

Her hand shook as she rapped lightly on the door. From the other side came the unmistakable thud of boots on a wooden floor. Augusta was quickly losing the fight against the rising tide of tears.

When the door finally opened, a miraculous sight appeared. A tall, ruggedly handsome man with cool blue eyes. She barely managed a tiny "Flynn," before her vision blurred, and she broke into shuddering sobs.

~

"Augusta," he whispered. Her name left his lips like a prayer. Flynn swept Augusta gently up into his arms, wrapping her in his embrace. For the longest time, he simply held her. No words had ever been written which could convey what this moment meant to him. He was rendered speechless. The sheer magnitude of this impossible, wonderous reunion would have failed even the great bard himself to put to prose.

Augusta.

The long nights when he had lain close to death's door and thought of her came flooding back in a heated rush. It robbed Flynn of everything but the deepest, most humble sense of gratitude for having been gifted this day. For having survived long enough to finally see her again. To hold the woman he loved in his arms.

Augusta.

When she finally drew back, Augusta lifted her head to meet his gaze. The hood of her cloak fell away, and as it did Flynn could have sworn that his heart stopped beating.

She reached up and pulled on the pale blue ribbon which held up her hair. Unfettered by pins or ties, her long brown locks fell in a stunning cascade over her shoulders. Flynn gasped at the sight. She'd always known how much he adored her hair.

His fingers itched to run wildly through her long tresses. There was nothing better in the world than when this woman was in his arms, and his hands were in her hair.

"You let your hair down, just how I like it," he croaked in a tight voice.

"Flynn," she whispered and gave him a shy smile. Tears ran down her cheeks.

His heart began to beat once more.

He brushed a hand over her face, then bent and kissed a

tear from her right cheek. Then he did the same to the other cheek. His lips were a benediction for her teary smile.

Augusta's smile had always meant the world to him. The memory of it was sometimes the only thing he'd had to bring him comfort during the long, tortuous days of the past year.

It had been the thought of Augusta and their love which had given him hope on those cold, dark nights when the only place he'd had to lay his head was a soft Teucrium bush under a bridge as he huddled into his thin coat and tried to stay warm.

Words might well have failed him, but they had always been able to speak to one another in other ways. Flynn bent his head and placed a soft, tender kiss on Augusta's lips. He prayed he still had the right to kiss her, because if he didn't, he would surely die.

She had thought to ask if he was a ghost, but the way that he held her firmly in his arms told her all she ached to know. Flynn Cadnam was very much alive.

The warmth of his lips shattered any foolish notion that this might simply be an illusion of her grief-stricken mind. When his hand drifted lower and cupped her rear, pulling her hard against his firm body, all remaining doubt fled.

Flynn. God, I have missed this, missed your touch.

When his manhood pressed into her stomach, heat pooled between her legs. She had thought desire had died with the loss of Flynn, but now that he was here, and more than obviously alive, her body roared back to life. Hunger burned within.

He deepened the kiss, his tongue dancing over hers, capturing and claiming what had always been his, what she had never wanted to give to any other man. Augusta clutched at Flynn's coat, desperate to never let him go.

They had both suffered, endured a year of unbearable pain while separated. She wanted this kiss to last for eternity.

When he finally drew away, almost breaking the kiss, she refused to let him go. Her mouth eagerly chased after his, and she silently exalted when Flynn came back, and his lips crashed over hers once more.

The whole world could stop, and she wouldn't care—just as long as they were here, and this embrace never ended.

But eventually it did, and slowly, reluctantly, she let him pull away. Her hands remain gripped tightly to the folds of his coat. He might be releasing her from the kiss, but she had no intention of letting her hold on him slacken.

"G. You are here... in Rome. I can't believe it."

"What I can't believe is that you are standing here, hale and hearty. I thought you were dead. So does everyone in Londonincluding your father."

She hated making mention of Earl Bramshaw, but Flynn had to know what his sire had said, and what little he had done to find his son. The happy grin which had been sitting on Flynn's face disappeared in an instant. Her heart threatened to break as tears welled in his eyes.

She didn't yet know what he had been through over the past while, but she could imagine it must have been something terrible.

Her gaze took in his pale, washed-out face—the hollowed cheeks. The dark circles under his eyes. Flynn had aged dramatically since last she had seen him. His bright youth was gone, stolen from him.

Augusta wanted nothing more than to weep the world down for him, to rail against the injustice of things. But she could sense that wasn't what Flynn needed from her. He wanted her light, her affection.

And that is what you shall have. All of it.

"I'm sorry, G. So bloody sorry you have had to suffer all this time, thinking that I was dead. If I could have arranged to send word earlier, I would have; as it is, the letter I did manage to finally send to you is still somewhere on the high seas. It will beat you back to England. As for my father, I don't give a damn what he has told the world about me. My misfortune was all of his doing."

"So, the earl knows you are alive?"

She had always thought Earl Bramshaw was a cold-hearted man, and she would never forget his spiteful response to her calling at his door asking about Flynn, but she had never imagined he would ever seek to actually harm his son.

Flynn sighed. "I don't know what he knows of my fate. What I am certain of is that he knew full well I was still alive when I left Bramshaw House, but he had put plans in place to make sure that I was dead well before anyone came looking for me. Even now, I am unsure as to what he might do if he did discover the truth about me, and where I am."

Augusta's fingers fell from Flynn's coat, and her hand went to her mouth. This was beyond horrific. Earl Bramshaw had tried to kill his own son.

"Flynn—" Her next question was cut off by his lips meeting hers once more. She didn't fight it, accepting that the last thing he wished to discuss right now was his villainous sire.

She relaxed into the tender offer of his mouth, sighing as her heart rejoiced in this glorious reunion. There would come a time when Flynn would tell her what had happened to him that day after he left the park, but tonight was for them. For the rebirth of their love.

He broke the kiss but continued to brush soft butterfly kisses over her lips as he spoke. "I love you. I have never stopped thinking about you. You have to know that my every waking moment has been caught up in wondering where you were and what you were doing," he said. Flynn's gaze dropped to the floor, and he shifted uneasily on his feet. "I must confess there were times when I drove myself to the point of madness worrying that you had found someone else. That you had given up on me and married another."

She had threatened to do that very thing not long before Flynn disappeared. Augusta could well understand his reasoning.

Placing her hand over his, she nodded at the ring which sat on her finger. His mother's ring. "I have worn this every day from the day you gave it to me." She swallowed deeply, not wishing to tell him the rest but knowing she owed him the truth. "I would be lying if I didn't tell you that I planned to take it off before I returned to England."

Her bottom lip quivered. She had lost all hope of ever seeing him alive. And while it had made perfect sense, her decision to set aside the promise ring smacked of betrayal. She had failed him.

"I'm sorry, Flynn. I feel terrible about giving up on you, but you should know that I was going to try and move on with my life. Can you ever find it in your heart to forgive me?"

"Ssh," he whispered, giving her another kiss. "There is nothing to forgive. You were not to know I was still alive. No one did. I haven't even told the few friends I have here in Rome the truth of my identity."

"Why haven't you told them?"

"Because if there is one thing the past year has taught me, is that it is unwise to fully trust people. You and Gideon are, of course, excluded from that rule."

The moment of silence which followed had Augusta finally taking in her surroundings. When she'd walked through the door, her whole focus had been solely on Flynn, and she hadn't noted the room. Taking a small step back, but still holding onto his coat, her gaze tracked around the small, sparsely furnished room.

"So, this is All Saints' Church?"

"No, it's a meeting room where we hold services. There is a small British community here in Rome, mostly centered in the area around the Spanish Steps. It's been growing, so they have to keep finding new places to house the chapel. I expect in time they will seek to build a proper church."

Augusta nodded. "Yes, during my time here, I have met a few people who live in what they call the English ghetto. I just didn't know they had established an Anglican ministry here. If I had, Mama and I would have come."

And I would have found you sooner.

The whole time she and the duchess had been in Rome, they had attended Sunday mass with the de Lucas. Their hosts, who had close ties to the Holy See, had decided that it was better for them to attend some sort of Christian religious service rather than none at all.

Flynn took her by the hand and led Augusta in a slow walk about the room. Apart from what appeared to be some sort of musical instrument in the corner, along with a couple of scattered tables and a few empty vases, there wasn't much else.

She turned to him, an off-the-cuff remark sat ready on her lips. But as her gaze locked on him, the quip died. Augusta's knees began to buckle under her, and she staggered forward in a desperate effort to avoid crashing to the floor.

"Flynn. Oh, Flynn," she sobbed.

Just the sight of him standing there, casually chatting about the meeting room had brought her undone. He was broken, damaged, but he was here. He was alive. All her prayers had been answered. And it was suddenly all too much for her to bear.

Strong arms wrapped around her shoulders, holding her upright. "Augusta, my love. It's going to be alright. I promise. This nightmare will soon be over. We will go home, and have that life together. And I swear no one will ever tear us apart again."

She rested her head against the front of his greatcoat, doing her best not to cry all over it. "They won't, because I will never let you out of my sight again, Flynn Cadnam."

His chest rose and fell as a deep chuckle escaped his lips. "I pity the first person who tries."

I have missed that laugh. That smile.

Augusta softly sighed, after which a gentle peace fell over the room. Held in Flynn's embrace, she made a silent vow. From this day forth, no one and nothing would separate them. And when they finally returned to England, she was going to do everything in her power to make sure that Earl Bramshaw paid a heavy price for his treachery.

Chapter Thirty-Two

❦

A little while later, they adjourned to a nearby café. To Augusta's surprise, it was not only still open at this late hour, but it was also packed with customers all eating and drinking.

Flynn gave the owner a cheery wave as they stepped through the door, and he led Augusta toward a table at the back. The proprietor of the café waved back, offering Augusta a polite bow. It was clear the viscount was somewhat of a regular. His friends were their friends.

Augusta glanced around at all the customers busily tucking into large bowls of hot pasta. Her stomach rumbled. She hadn't eaten much at the supper at Signore Magri's home, having been more concerned with Serafina and how she was handling things.

"Where have all these people come from? It's the middle of the night," she remarked. The café was an energetic hubbub of laughter and chatter.

Flynn pointed back toward the street. "Late worshippers at the nearby churches. That domed church across the road is

Santa Maria di Loreto if you didn't already know. It's a very popular place of worship in this part of the city."

Augusta shook her head. This wasn't an area that she and Serafina tended to frequent all that often. They had a set routine most days, and it usually involved stepping out of Palazzo Lazio and heading toward the shops and cafés in Via del Corso and along the River Tiber. When they had visited the Colosseum with Gideon yesterday, they had passed by this café, but she hadn't taken any notice.

I have been blind to so much of the hidden joy of this city. Wrapped up in my own thoughts and only seeing what others have pointed out to me.

Soon after they sat, two large bowls of pasta were placed on the table in front of them. Augusta smiled as she recognized Serafina's favorite meal. "Ah, Rome's greatest pasta dish, Cacio e Pepe. I will miss this when we go home. Serafina makes a point of eating it at least every other day."

"I love the simple blend of cheese and pepper," replied Flynn.

When the owner of the café brought them both coffee, Flynn dug his hand into his coat pocket and handed the man some coins. *"Per te, amico mio."*

The man accepted the money with a smile. He pointed at Flynn's greatcoat, and Flynn nodded. *"Sì, è un cappotto migliore dell'altro."*

Augusta sat back in her seat and stared at Flynn's coat. Her eyes narrowed. The coat was strangely familiar. Then the penny finally dropped. "Did Gideon give you that?"

"Yes, your brother did. And he also gave me a generous amount of money, along with the promise that he would fund my ticket home to England." His gaze dropped to his bowl, and Augusta sensed he was both relieved and humbled by Gideon's gift.

Flynn picked up his fork and with skilled precision

quickly wrapped the strands of cheesy sauce-coated pasta around it. He smiled at it as he brought it to his mouth.

The mere thought of how much Flynn must have suffered over the past year had Augusta lowering her head. She feared she would burst into tears in the café and make a fool of herself. God bless kindhearted Gideon. He must have seen Flynn was in need and immediately offered his help. As always, her brother was generous to a fault.

Thank god Gideon came to Rome.

There was every chance that without Gideon and their rather fortuitous visit to the tailor yesterday, she might never have found Flynn while in Rome. Ignorant of just how close he was to where she was staying, she would have got on the boat back to England.

And without Gideon's money, Flynn may never have made it home.

"I don't want to think what might have happened if you hadn't visited the tailor's shop. We may have all passed like ships in the night." Emotion weighed heavy in her voice.

Flynn reached across the table and took Augusta by the hand. "But we did find each other. And while I know this is all a bit too much to take in... because I know it is for me, there is one simple truth. Augusta, my love, we are here. You and I have got our miracle. Let's enjoy this moment in the knowledge that we have many more moments like this one to come." His eyes shone with love and hope. It was a beautiful thing to behold, and it had her blinking hard.

He was always looking on the bright side of things. In the long months that he had been missing, she had given thought to the way Flynn had always behaved. In the painful days of grief, it had occurred to her that his happy disposition had probably been a means to protect himself from the world. A way to force down the painful humiliation he had lived with on a daily basis as the Vagabond Viscount.

She owed it to him to share his positivity. They had been given this wonderful second chance; she should grab it with both hands and push all thoughts of regrets away.

And now he would be coming home with them.

He grinned at her. "I think this coat looks better on me than it does your brother. I can say that because he can't take it back."

"What did you do for a coat before now?" she asked.

Flynn played with his fork and spaghetti, twirling the thin pasta around. He nodded at Augusta's untouched plate. "Eat it before it goes cold. You don't want to leave any as the owner's wife might take offense."

Her eyes went wide, and she turned to peer over her shoulder. Behind the small counter stood a buxom, dark-haired woman. She wore the same no-nonsense expression that the duchess did whenever she was holding court. It spoke of not tolerating fools.

Fearful of disappointing the café owner, Augusta set to her enormous bowl of glossy pasta with unrestrained enthusiasm. It was good. Really good. She considered it better than what the master chef at Palazzo Lazio regularly served up, not that she ever planned to mention it to anyone. The servants at the palace had been especially kind to her during her long stay, so any form of criticism would be ungracious on her part.

Flynn brushed his hand over the soft wool of his finely cut greatcoat. "I do have a coat. It was given to me by one of the priests at a monastery in Pisa. I spent some time there recovering from—" His voice faltered for a moment. "My travels."

Augusta wanted to ask about what had happened to him but sensed that now wasn't the right time. And if the way Flynn spoke in brief snatches of information was anything to go by, he was also reluctant to go into matters at this juncture.

Leave it be. In time, the truth will come. Enjoy this meal. And that the man who you love is alive.

"This garment is, of course, a far superior one. Whoever had owned my other coat before it came into my possession had subjected it to the rough of the Italian countryside. The back of it was more patches and repairs than actual coat. Even my skillful repairs wouldn't have seen it last another northern winter."

He brushed his hand over the top of his hair. "And this coat goes nicely with my new haircut and freshly shaven face. To be honest, I feel like a man reborn. Before Gideon gave me this along with a princely sum of money, I looked more like a beggar than an English noble."

His words had August dropping her fork on her plate. It made a loud clattering noise, and heads at several of the nearby tables turned in her direction.

"What's wrong?"

Augusta leaned forward. "Did you attend the Easter Sunday service at Saint Peter's?"

His brows furrowed in obvious confusion. "Yes, I did. Why do you ask?"

The man she had seen in the tattered coat and scruffy hair. Could it have been Flynn? She had been a matter of a yard or so away from him, and she hadn't had a clue. "On Easter Sunday morning, Serafina and I walked over Ponte Sant'Angelo with all the other pilgrims. I was searching the crowd for you, like I have done every day since you disappeared. On the way, I spotted a man with long brown hair wearing a coat which had seen better days. I didn't get a look at his face, but from where I was, he looked like a beggar. Could that have been you?"

Flynn nodded. "I walked over the bridge in the morning, along with hundreds of other pilgrims. Considering that I had long scraggy hair until late yesterday, and wore my old coat, I would say there is a very good chance that it was me. You can understand why I was so pleased when Gideon gave me his spare coat. He is also arranging to have some new clothes made for me at the tailors. So I look respectable. Presentable to polite society."

His words stuck fast in her mind. "Is that why you didn't wait for me to come back to the shop yesterday? You were afraid of how you looked?"

When Flynn wouldn't meet her eyes, Augusta set her fork down. "Oh, my love. I don't care what you look like—I care that you are alive. You could come back dressed in rags, and it wouldn't matter."

"Forgive me," he whispered.

"You have nothing to apologize for, Flynn. You never have."

As long as he lived, Flynn would never forget the look on the tailor's face when he arrived at the shop late that afternoon and asked to have a new suit, and some shirts made. The man had been ready to show him the door, but the sight of the handful of coins which Gideon had given Flynn, along with him mentioning the Marquis of Holwell by name, quickly had the tailor having a change of heart.

Tonight, Flynn was wearing one of Gideon's old shirts, which considering the size difference between them, meant it hung loosely off every part of his torso apart from his shoulders. But he didn't mind. The shirt was clean and had no holes or tears in it. For the first time in a very long time, he almost looked respectable. He was still a mere shadow of his former self, but today he had enjoyed the simple pleasure of being out on the streets of Rome and not having people stare or whisper as he passed them by.

Gratitude was the one gift he did value from the past year. Flynn was grateful for every small blessing. Every new day was one more than he had expected to live after the nightmare of his voyage to Italy.

And now he was seated in his favorite café enjoying a late-night supper with the woman he loved.

Late night? It's well past midnight.

He cleared his throat and chose his words carefully. If he knew anything about Augusta, it was that she hated being treated like a child. Or worse, a young woman in need of constant protection. "Who knows you are here? I mean, did you tell Serafina you were coming to see me?"

She wouldn't have told Gideon because her brother would not have permitted her to come alone. Then again, his friend must have given her the address of the chapel, so they may have come to some sort of understanding. Perhaps he had walked her over here and left her at the bottom of the steps leading up to the chapel.

"I pilfered your note from Gideon's room when he was with you and Serafina's brother, Matteo, at the fencing academy this morning. Actually yesterday morning, since it must be tomorrow by now. I left the palace after we returned from the supper at Signore Magri's house. He is the man Serafina is supposed to be marrying."

The heated contempt which dripped from Augusta's lips as she said the name of the man her friend was going to wed informed Flynn as to what she thought of the impending nuptials.

She leaned closer, and Flynn followed suit.

"If you can get Gideon to stop being all noble and actually go and fight for her, Serafina might well be coming back to England with us. But in answer to your previous question, I slipped out of the palace unnoticed."

"Gideon wouldn't be happy to know what you have done. Or that you are here unaccompanied."

Augusta shrugged. "I've been in Rome since last year—there are a good many things I have done which he would be unhappy to hear about. Not that I intend to tell him."

He caught the familiar glint of defiance in her eyes. It should have made him angry to know she had taken such a risk in sneaking out of the palace to come and find him. He couldn't find it in himself. "You are a willful young woman, Lady Augusta Kembal. I should put you over my knee and spank you. But I have a feeling you might like it."

When she blinked slowly and murmured, "I love you," a jolt of lust shot through him.

I have missed you. Missed our secret rendezvous. Missed my lips on your naked skin.

After picking up his cup of black coffee, Flynn took a long, considered sip. His imagination was playing out a naked, naughty moment where a heated, needy Augusta was laid out before him, begging him to take her in hand.

"I love you too," he said, clearing his throat. "Now, what about Serafina and Gideon?"

He remembered Matteo de Luca's sister Serafina from her stay at Mowbray House in September of the year before he disappeared. She was a stunning beauty, one whom he suspected had quickly stolen his friend Gideon's heart. But Gideon being Gideon likely hadn't realized the truth until it was too late. The marquis might be an intelligent person, but when it came to women, he could be a touch blind.

But time could change a man. Flynn knew that truth only too well. He had become someone over the past year he never thought he would be. Liar. Thief.

"As I recall, when Serafina stayed at your home, Gideon was worried that you and Victoria were busy playing matchmaker. What tells you that he has changed his mind about her?"

A knowing smile spread across Augusta's lips. "The evidence of my own eyes. On Monday morning, when we went to visit the Colosseum, I saw my brother kissing Serafina. And just a short while ago, he was busy penning a note to her to meet him at daybreak so they can spend the day together in the city."

Gosh. He really is serious about her. About bloody time.

"Won't her family have something to say about Gideon trying to marry their daughter? I mean, this arranged union must come with powerful favors for Serafina's father. Or money at least."

Money might not have been the main reason. From what he had heard, the de Lucas were one of the richest families in Rome. Enzo de Luca and his constant political maneuverings was the stuff of legends. Flynn couldn't imagine Enzo giving up any sort of advantage merely to let one of his daughters marry an English nobleman. Especially one who would take her out of the country.

"I am hoping my brother finds a way to force Enzo's hand. If you get my meaning." Augusta pushed her unfinished bowl of pasta away. "That was wonderful, but I cannot possibly eat all that food, especially not at this hour. I promise to let the café owner know how much I appreciated it."

Flynn took one look at the bowl and picked it up. He added the leftovers to his own meal. "These people have been more than kind to me—any food left behind would be an insult to them. If you finish your coffee, we shall call it even. Then I shall walk you home."

Chapter Thirty-Three

❦

Augusta had no intention of going back to Palazzo Lazio —not until she was good and ready. Instead, she had other plans.

With Gideon expected to be out of the palace at first light, and her mother still visiting the rural estate of her gentleman friend in Tivoli, there was no one who would come looking for her after breakfast. She intended to use that to her advantage.

Flynn managed to empty his bowl then, after he had pressed more coins into the palm of the grateful café owner, he took hold of Augusta's hand, and they walked out into the street. His strides grew long, and she quickly deduced Flynn was in a hurry to get her back home and to the safety of her bedroom before anyone noticed she was missing.

No. I have a different place I am going to sleep tonight.

Silently congratulating herself for having worn her thick-soled boots, Augusta dug her heels into the cobbled footpath and tugged back hard on Flynn's hand.

He kept going for a half step more before he stopped and turned round. "What are you doing?"

"You think to take me home, but I am not going back to the palace. Not tonight."

His brows furrowed at her words, and she could just imagine how he was taking in this change in plans. Not well, if the expression of confusion on his face was any indication. "If you are not going back to Palazzo Lazio, then where am I taking you?"

They were standing at the entrance which led up to All Saints' Chapel. Augusta pointed toward the stairs. "You are taking me home. To your home. I have spent over a year without you in my life, Flynn Cadnam. I am not wasting another day wondering what it would be like to share your bed. To know you."

Flynn's mouth dropped open. There was a clear moment of indecision on his part, and Augusta speculated that he was imagining what Gideon might do to him if he ever found out about this evening.

She was preparing her arguments, ready to press her demands for them to become one, when to her relief, Flynn finally nodded. "Yes. It's been too long. And you should have been in my arms the day I last saw you."

He shifted his hold on her hand and brought it to his lips. A soft, tender kiss was placed on each one of her fingers, the last being the one where the ring sat. "But just so we are clear. If you climb those stairs with me, you are agreeing to be my wife. To spend the rest of your life with me, bear my children." His voice turned gravelly. "To be my countess when the time comes. And to wear that ring on your left hand."

The middle of a darkened street in Rome hadn't been on her list of places where she imagined Flynn might propose, but tonight it was perfect. They would be forever bound together from this moment on.

"And I am going to stand alongside you when you

confront your villain of a father when we return to England," she added.

He slowly shook his head. "I don't know what will happen with the earl when I get back to London. But let's not talk about him anymore. I have done my best over the past year not to think about my sire, and he is the last thing I wish to discuss tonight. Right this minute, you are the only thing I care about, Augusta."

The pain in his voice when he mentioned his father cut deep into Augusta's heart. Tonight, she would give herself to the man she loved, but come the morning, she was going to start asking questions.

If they were to share a future together, she had to know everything that had befallen Flynn and not just over the past year. She wanted to know why Earl Bramshaw had been so cruel to his son.

And why he hated Flynn so much that he would try to kill him.

Chapter Thirty-Four

Upstairs in the meeting room, Flynn locked the door behind them. He grabbed a chair and jammed it under the door handle. Augusta raised an eyebrow at this, and he quickly explained, "We can't have any of the church community suddenly deciding to pay a visit early tomorrow morning. I don't think I could talk my way out of that embarrassment."

Augusta laughed. "Yes, there couldn't be too many ways to explain why you have a duke's daughter in your bed."

It hadn't occurred to her that others might have a key to the meeting hall. This was Flynn's home, but it was a temporary one. He was here due to the charity of the English community in Rome.

"Michael Cooper is really the only one who might call in outside of the Sunday and evening services. He lives a long way up past the Spanish Steps and so wouldn't make the trip at night. He has been kind and respected my privacy since I came to stay, so I would hate for him to think I have abused his trust. At the moment, he still thinks I am just an Englishman down on his luck. He doesn't know I am Viscount Cadnam."

"I should like to meet him, to thank him for his kindness, before we leave for home. It means that you might have to tell him the truth of who you are."

She wanted to know a little of the life Flynn had led during his time in Rome.

"Yes, it would be good for you and Michael to become acquainted. And I promise I shall tell him who I am. He is going to ask questions when he sees me with my new clothes and haircut."

A moment of awkward silence fell between them. Before Flynn's untimely disappearance, they had shared a number of intimate encounters at parties and balls in London, but those moments had only seen them take things so far. Much further than the strictures of society deemed was sufficient grounds for Flynn to have made an offer for Augusta's hand. Not enough that she was completely ruined.

Tonight, she intended that they would take that next step together. There would be no going back. No shying away from meeting with her father once they returned home.

But Gideon has custody of me while I am in Rome.

She unclipped her cloak and dropped it onto a nearby chair. The thought of her brother and what he might have to say about tonight's developments had her making a snap decision.

While lying to Flynn minutes before they were to finally become one wasn't her greatest moment, Augusta decided it was unfair to hand yet another problem to Gideon. He already had more than his fair share to deal with when it came to the situation with Serafina.

She would wait until after they were safely back in England to tell her brother the truth of what had happened between her and Flynn in Rome.

"Could we pretend for tonight?" she asked.

He wrapped his arms about her waist and drew her close. "What do you mean?"

Augusta let out a sigh. "I mean, let's pretend we are who we were going to be after you went home and packed your things that day. You can play the role of the Flynn Cadnam who walked out of Hyde Park and then came to see my father and asked for my hand in marriage. While I will be the naïve young miss who, after waiting patiently for you, gladly accepted your proposal of marriage."

It was a fiction. Neither of them were the same people. Time and grief had irretrievably changed their souls.

But not our hearts.

"Or am I being foolish in thinking we could do that?"

He bent his head and kissed her lightly on the lips. "Tonight, my love, I am going to give you everything your heart desires, and if that includes creating a world of our own, then so be it. I love you, Augusta. If it were in my powers to take back our old future, I would. But I can't. What I can do, however, is live this night with you and give you the promise that when we wake, it will be as one."

"I love you too, Flynn. No matter if you had been lost to me forever, I would never have stopped loving you."

The small alcove where Flynn had his bed and stored his meager things lay behind a faded pale cream curtain. Augusta's heart was racing at a fast clip as he led her across the floor and to this private space. Her blood was heated, her skin flush with desire. Lust, and a small dash of nerves, coursed through her body.

I have missed your touch. Your warm kiss. The brush of your fingers. Oh, Flynn.

Flynn took off his greatcoat, then shrugged out of his

jacket. Augusta bit on her bottom lip as she took in the state of his clothing. The jacket was torn and frayed, as were Flynn's trousers. With Gideon's money, he would soon have new clothes, but it pained her to know that there was a definite disparity between their manner of dress.

His gaze settled on her pale blue gown. It was one of her simplest of gowns, but it still stood in sharp contrast to Flynn's poor attire. She lifted her skirts and showed him her practical brown leather boots, hoping it would help him feel less uncomfortable.

"This is the plainest gown I own, and I am wearing my sturdy boots, but I still feel overdressed in your company. And I hate feeling that way."

Her heart skipped a beat as Flynn smiled at her. "And here was me thinking you looked nothing short of magnificent. Augusta, my love, you couldn't ever make me feel uncomfortable. Right at this moment, all I feel is an overwhelming sense of happiness." The smile turned wicked, and she caught a glint of mischief in his eye. "And hunger."

He stepped forward and laid his hands on the front of her dress. "You don't have to do this tonight. I don't want you feeling any sort of obligation. We can wait until we are back in England and married. If you want to simply cuddle tonight, I will understand."

His touch sent a shiver coursing down her spine. "I know. You have never made me do anything that I wasn't willing to do, and I love you for being that sort of man. Which means I am fully aware of what I am asking for when I say... Viscount Flynn Cadnam, love of my life, would you please strip me naked and take me to your bed? Make me yours. Claim me tonight, and forever."

Chapter Thirty-Five

To her relief, Flynn quickly gave up his honorable protests. His lips were on hers, claiming them with a deep kiss which sent thrills racing down her spine. Clever fingers soon set to work on the laces of her gown.

When the last of her garments hit the floor, leaving Augusta standing clad only in her stockings and boots, Flynn dropped to his knees. She closed her eyes as his warm hands settled on her hips and drew her closer to him.

"Oh god, I have missed this. Missed the way you touch my skin," she murmured.

His tongue parted the soft folds of her sex. Augusta settled her hand on the top of Flynn's head, taking hold of his hair. He groaned as she gave his locks a gentle, encouraging tug.

He licked and teased her sensitive bud, sending shock-waves of pleasure through her core. Augusta's head slumped forward as she sucked in short, desperate breaths. In the quiet of the meeting room, her sobs, and gentle pleas for him to give her more echoed off the walls. If All Saints was meant to be a place of worship, Flynn was doing his best to offer her his own form of benediction.

Flynn may have been missing for more than a year and a half, and she had little idea of what had happened to him during that time, but he certainly hadn't lost any of his touch when it came to the task of pleasuring her body. He took command with all the skill and intimate knowledge of a man who possessed a crystal-clear memory.

"Flynn," she pleaded.

In their previous stolen liaisons, this had usually been the signal for him to slip his thumb into her wet heat and bring Augusta to a crashing climax. Tonight, however, when she spoke Flynn's name, it was her spoken consent for him to take things that one step further. For them to finally become one.

He sat back on his haunches and glanced up at her. Augusta was sure that she had made her position plain, but the look on his face was still one of uncertainty.

Such a noble man. I think I might be unworthy of you.

She would spend the rest of her life trying to be everything to him. Augusta nodded. "Yes."

Flynn got to his feet and, taking her hands in his, met her eyes. "I vow to be yours from this night on. Till death do us part. I love you, Augusta Kembal."

"I love you, Flynn Cadnam, and very soon I intend to be your wife." She reached for his cravat and slipped it free. His shirt came next. Her fingers went for the buttons on the folds of his trousers, but Flynn took hold of her wrist, bringing the motion to a halt.

"How about you go and make yourself comfortable on our bed," he suggested.

Our bed. She had never shared a bed with anyone else before. The thought of being naked with this man and in his arms had her swallowing deeply.

His gaze dropped to her boots, and a chuckle escaped his lips. "Though you may want to take those off."

Augusta laughed. "I'd forgotten about them."

Being this close to him always tended to muddle her brain. She hadn't the slightest idea how she was going to manage him once they were married. Spending a good deal of time in the bedroom was the only thing which made any sort of sense.

I can't wait.

While Flynn rid himself of the vestiges of his clothes, Augusta set about unlacing her boots. Out of the corner of her eye, she caught him hiding his own badly worn footwear under his shirt. She turned her head. He was embarrassed about the state of his dress, but still too proud to say anything.

She climbed onto the bed. It wasn't much of a bed—more a narrow cot. The thought of how they were going to fit on it crossed her mind. Then she remembered her mother's talk. How the birds and bees worked. The one the duchess had apparently given to every one of her daughters on the day when their courses first arrived.

Man on top is the traditional way.

From overhead conversations in the garden between her brothers, she knew there were other ways. But knowing Flynn, he would stick to convention. At least for their first time.

He crossed the floor to the bed, slowly shaking his head. "What are you thinking about, my love? I ask because you have your thinking line showing deep between your eyes."

"Nothing and everything," she murmured. Her gaze was fixed on his naked form. On the outline of his waist. She had seen him partly naked before, so the novelty of his hard, erect manhood pointing at her was less than if it had been the first time.

What did capture and hold her attention, however, were the scars. The red, angry scars which slashed across his chest. Augusta sucked in a deep breath. Anger and a sense of profound sadness tore at her. "Oh, Flynn, what did they do to you?" she said in a voice barely above a whisper.

He glanced at his chest, then back to her. "I am here, and I am alive." He bent and kissed her. Soft. Tender. Then deeper, hungrier. As their lips joined, tongues tangling, she forced away all the thoughts which threatened to scramble her mind, giving herself up to Flynn's loving embrace. His kiss carried a silent message. He didn't want to talk about the past —he just wanted to forge their future. Tonight.

Augusta shuffled over into the middle of the bed and lay down. Flynn climbed on and straddled her. She couldn't ignore his erection any longer. It was long, large, and much bigger than she remembered.

Then again, she hadn't ever seen it fully in the light. They had always met in darkened rooms, gardens, and on the odd occasion, a dimly lit orangery.

The firm flesh of his manhood sat heavy on her belly, all but begging her to touch it. Augusta wrapped her fingers around the long length and began to stroke. "I have missed you, Flynn, but I have also missed being friends with this," she purred.

Flynn gave a dirty chuckle in response to her sultry tease. "He has missed you too. The poor chap has suffered without any real attention for far too long." He paused, and she sensed his hesitation. This was a moment from which there could be no return.

"Come to me, my love. Claim what I have longed to give you."

He gave a nod of acceptance, and Augusta shifted, making room for Flynn between her legs. Her intention was clear. She released her hold on his erection and lay back as he positioned the head of his cock at her entrance, and he slowly pushed in.

As their gazes met, she reveled in the desire which shone brightly in his eyes. They were together in the moment, now and forever.

"I hope this won't hurt—"

Augusta silenced Flynn's statement with her lips. She didn't want to hear any words of reassurance or regret.

I want to feel.

There was no pain, not even a pinch. Just a glorious sense of being filled. Of knowing that Flynn was here, and they were finally joined together as one. Nothing would ever take this beautiful connection with her man away from her.

Caught up in the moment, Augusta raised her arms above her head. Her breasts moved to and fro as Flynn slowly stroked her sex. The expression of enrapture which sat on his face telling her just how much he appreciated her doing this, that it was all for him.

He shifted, taking one of her tight, hardened nipples between his lips. Pleasure rocked through her core. She had always thought there was nothing better than having Flynn feast on her breasts but having him lavish his attention on them at the same time as his hard erection rubbed against her sensitive bud had her world shifting on its axis.

This was heaven.

"Flynn," she whimpered.

He gave her a low growl of manly desire in return, then picked up the pace. His thick cock stroked her sex, and with each thrust, the tension built.

When she thought she couldn't take it any longer, Augusta shattered into a thousand shards of light.

A second later, Flynn stilled above her. "Augusta," he whispered.

The near-empty room echoed with their sighs and gasps as they both struggled to catch their breaths.

A short time later, he finally stirred, raising himself up and sitting back on the end of the bed. There wasn't room for Flynn to lay down beside her on the narrow cot.

As her body began to rapidly cool, Augusta shivered. Flynn shook his head and climbed off the bed. He held a hand out to her. "Come, my love." On shaky legs, Augusta rose and came to him.

They stripped the blanket from the bed and wrapped it around them. It didn't help much—she continued to shiver.

"I am sorry. There isn't any heating in here. I often sleep in my clothes," said Flynn.

Augusta clung to him for warmth, but quickly gave it up as a lost cause. She drew out of Flynn's arms and, gathering up her gown and cloak, hurriedly dressed. Flynn did likewise.

Once they were fully clothed, he pulled her back into his embrace and kissed her again. "Is that better, my sweet?"

She smiled up at him. "Yes, being warm is good. Being with you is even better. You know, I don't think I could ever tire of just seeing you. I could happily sit and watch you for hours, though I expect I might have to pinch myself a few times just to remind myself that you are really alive. Feel free to keep kissing me."

I love you touching me.

"I am indeed still one of the living, but there were times when I wasn't sure if I was in the mortal world or if I was on the cusp of crossing over. On the boat out from England, I think it was touch and go for several days."

Augusta kept her arms wrapped about Flynn's waist. She didn't want to spoil this wonderful moment. Didn't want to let him go. This first time together was special. It should have happened long ago.

But she had to know some of what had transpired

between the afternoon when Flynn had walked out of Hyde Park and today, even if it was just a little piece of what she suspected was a large and complicated story.

"What did your father do?"

There was no point in pretending otherwise. It was obvious that the earl had played a part in his son's disappearance. He had made a solid enough effort to obstruct the investigation into Flynn's fate.

"You must have seen the scar on my shoulder," he replied. Augusta nodded. "Well, there is another one on my back. They are where my father stabbed me. Where my sire tried to end my life."

Augusta gasped. "No!"

"While I was unconscious, he had me carried to the docks and stowed on board a boat which sailed from London late that evening. When I finally did regain consciousness, we were somewhere off the coast of Portugal."

Augusta shook her head in disbelief. How could anyone do that to Flynn, let alone his father? And why?

"The crew was meant to throw me overboard, but they had a change of heart. We hit a huge storm, and apparently, being superstitious sailors, they decided it was a sign from the gods. A warning that they shouldn't do the evil that they had planned. They kept me alive but then realized they couldn't release me too close to home just in case I set the authorities on them."

"So, they brought you all the way to Italy? Where you didn't speak the language, and you didn't know a soul. And then they abandoned you?"

The sailors might well have chosen the lesser of two evils, but they had still done a terrible thing. Sentenced Flynn to a life far from home and with little hope of finding his way back.

He nodded. "They handed me over to the priests at a

monastery close to Pisa. I spent many months there recovering from my wounds. Eventually, I left because of an outbreak of typhus which was spreading through the city. They said I would stand a better chance of survival if I took to the road."

"Which is when you decided to head to Rome?"

"No, I spent a long time in the city of Florence. I lived on the streets, stole food from market vendors to survive, and eventually lost count of the times I barely escaped from being arrested for petty theft. I would still be there but for a chance meeting with a group of traveling musicians. They took me in, and I played the violin for them when they stopped at towns along the long road south. I got a hot meal and the occasional coin for my efforts. I had hoped to travel all the way with them, but I took ill in the town of Fabro, and we parted company. When I was well again, I continued on foot alone. I only arrived in Rome a few weeks ago."

All this time she had been in Rome, Flynn had been trying to make his way to the city. "I wish I had known where you were. I can't believe you have suffered all this time when I could have helped."

Her not knowing that Flynn was still alive didn't help to alleviate Augusta's guilt. She would forever feel a sense of shame that, while she had been living the life of luxury at Palazzo Lazio, the man she loved had been homeless.

"And what now? Will you return to England and face your father?"

Flynn slowly shook his head. "I don't know. So much has happened in the past few days. The only thing of which I am sure is you and me. And for the moment, that is more than enough."

Chapter Thirty-Six

❦

They had sat hand in hand on the banks of the River Tiber and watched the sunrise. A simple pleasure that Augusta was grateful to be able to share with Flynn. A moment she would always treasure.

"A new day. A new beginning," said Flynn as the sun rose over the horizon and bathed the city in its golden light.

A short while later they took the steep path back up the hill to the garden gate, which led into Palazzo Lazio. Augusta slipped the key into the lock. Their plans for the day included her freshening up and changing her clothes before sneaking back out to meet with Flynn in the city a little later in the morning. While they would be parted for only a matter of hours, she was reluctant to let him go.

"The boot maker on Via della Pace at eleven o'clock, don't forget," said Augusta. She was going to buy Flynn a new pair of boots. He couldn't possibly go home to England with the ones he was currently wearing. When her fiancé stepped off the boat, she was determined that he was going to not only feel at his best, but he would also look the part of an English nobleman. The first person who dared mention the words vagabond viscount was going to feel the sharp end of her tongue.

Flynn grinned at her. "I won't forget. We can do the same as Gideon and Serafina and spend the day together. Just the two of us. And I could certainly do with a new pair of boots. I can feel the cobblestones under my toes when I walk in these." He gifted Augusta a final kiss before letting her go.

She slipped in through the gate and closed it behind her. The garden was fortunately clear of servants. Augusta hurried across the lawn and up the nearest set of steps. Once inside, she headed directly for her bedroom. When her maid, who was waiting in the hallway, greeted her with a raised eyebrow, a flustered Augusta pressed a generous pile of coins into her palm and whispered, *"Per il vostro silenzio."*

She hated to think how much extra coin the servants of the palace made each day by accepting bribes from the de Luca family and their guests. But if her maid kept her lips sealed, as far as Augusta was concerned, it was money well spent.

Chapter Thirty-Seven

A ugusta might well have been able to buy her maid's
silence, but no amount of money could undo the mess
that Gideon dropped the Kembal family into the following
day.

After a wonderful day spent with Flynn shopping and
exploring the city, an exhausted Augusta had retired to her
room at Palazzo Lazio and fallen asleep the second her head
hit the pillow. She was still sound asleep when in the early
hours of the next morning, a loud knock came on her
bedroom door. When she opened it, two palace servants,
bearing her travel trunk, marched straight in.

A bleary-eyed Augusta was seated on the edge of her
mattress, trying to stir from her deep slumber as the servants
frantically tossed all her clothes and belongings into her
luggage. When her maid appeared, Augusta posed the
obvious question. "What is going on?"

Her harried-looking maid simply shook her head and
replied. "You are leaving."

At the sound of more footsteps in the hallway, Augusta
turned her attention to the door. As she did, a fully dressed

Duchess of Mowbray swept into the room. Her mother, who had returned early from her trip to Tivoli, appeared ready to do murder. She took one look at her daughter and huffed. "Hurry, you need to find a warm gown. I am not sure how long Enzo de Luca has given us, but I would hate for you to still be in a partial state of undress when he throws us out into the street."

Oh, dear Lord, what has Mama done now? Have the de Lucas finally lost patience with her?

It was the obvious answer as to why they were suddenly leaving the palace in the middle of the night. Augusta narrowed her eyes at the duchess. "I don't understand. Will someone please tell me what this is all about?"

Lady Anne glanced at the servants, then hurried over to where Augusta sat. She bent and whispered in her daughter's ear, "Gideon and Serafina have apparently lain with one another tonight. I expect your brother thought it would be the best way to get Enzo to agree to the two of them marrying. Instead, the stubborn count has thrown Gideon out, and we are to shortly follow suit."

Oh, Gideon. You finally tried to force Enzo into agreeing to let you marry his daughter. And it didn't work. Now things are going to be terrible for Serafina.

Her brother had made a bold move, which had apparently backfired on both him, Serafina, and his family. But if Gideon was already somewhere out on the streets of Rome, then it fell to her to go and find Serafina.

I have to do something. This cannot be the end of them. Not now.

Augusta rose from the bed, taking two steps toward the door. She had to talk to Serafina. Her mother took her firmly by the arm and pulled her back. "If you think to go and speak to Serafina, you are wasting your time. She has been locked in her room. No one is permitted near her. I spoke to Donna

Francesca, and she informed me that the wedding between Serafina and Signore Magri is going to be brought forward."

"Oh, no." This was an unmitigated disaster. All Augusta's hopes for a happily ever after for Gideon and Serafina lay in tatters.

"It's still hours until the dawn—where are we to go? Enzo can't seriously expect us to wait outside in Via della Pilotta until someone comes to collect us," added Augusta.

The duchess snatched up a gown from the top of the pile in Augusta's trunk and pressed it into her hands. "Gideon has gone to stay with Viscount Cadnam, who I understand resides close by. Now get dressed. We have to be ready when he hopefully sends word as to where that is."

A still half-asleep Augusta quickly dressed and threw on her cloak. She had just finished lacing up her boots when two palace footmen appeared at the door. Behind them stood Flynn.

Their gazes met, and in response to her smile of relief, he shook his head. Now was not the time to reveal their long-secret relationship to her family.

"Ah, Flynn. It is good to see you," said the duchess. She embraced the viscount. "I can't believe you are alive—it is such a wonder. I'm just sorry that our meeting has to be under the current circumstances. Augusta, come say hello to the viscount."

Augusta gave Flynn a brief hug—it befitted their official relationship. It was nothing like what they had shared the night at the chapel.

"I have come to show the servants where to carry your luggage. I live close by, so Enzo de Luca has mustered an army of servants to lug your things the short distance. I'm afraid that you are to go on foot," he explained.

Lady Anne huffed at the obvious insult to her noble

SASHA COTTMAN

status. "Well then, let us take our leave of this place. I know when I am not welcome."

Augusta followed in her wake. She had always suspected that when the Duchess of Mowbray finally left Palazzo Lazio that it would be under a cloud. She hadn't ever imagined it would be as a result of Gideon taking Serafina to his bed.

Gideon had played his hand, and he had lost. She could only pray he had a backup plan.

Eloping might be a good idea, dear brother.

250

Chapter Thirty-Eight

Shortly after their arrival at Flynn's modest accommodations, it was decided that the hotel Albergo del Sole in the Piazza della Rotonda was the best place for the Kembal family's next home. It was centrally located, safe, clean, and full of English tourists.

At such an ungodly hour, Augusta didn't particularly care where she slept. She just wanted a comfortable bed and somewhere to think. It had been a long day, followed by a sleep-interrupted, drama-filled night. She was exhausted.

Gideon and Flynn quickly organized for them to take three separate suites. Her brother frowned at Augusta's insistence that she have her own room rather than share with their mother. Fortunately for Augusta, he wasn't in any sort of position to argue with her demands. It was his actions which had landed them in this pickle in the first place.

"I am so sorry for all this," offered a contrite Gideon.

Augusta wrapped her arms around her brother and gave him a reassuring hug. "I am glad you finally did something about Serafina—I just hadn't expected you would go that far."

When she drew back, she caught the beet-red glow of Gideon's cheeks.

Anyone would think an unmarried miss would have no clue as to what happens in the marriage bed. You would be shocked to hear the talk in the ladies' retiring room at parties.

"Are you planning to elope with her? If you do, you must know that the guards change at eleven o'clock both during the day and at night. I have a key for the garden gate, which leads down to the street below the palace."

Gideon's brows furrowed, and she could just imagine what he was thinking. Wondering how she knew all these things and why she had a key.

"I am going to try and get some sleep. I can't think straight when I am overtired. In the morning, Flynn and I are going to discuss our options." He glanced at Augusta's travel trunk, which sat in the corner of her room. "Can I ask that you don't unpack? If Serafina and I do try and elope, you and Mama might need to leave here at short notice. Flynn will, of course, assist, and he has offered to accompany you back to England just in case Serafina and I have to find somewhere to hide. I promised Papa I would bring you home, and I won't fail him."

Gideon sadly didn't mention the duchess in that sentence. It was clear that things between him and Lady Anne were still at a stalemate. The only good piece of news was that their mother had taken Gideon's side in the aftermath of the recent unexpected event.

Perhaps there is still a chance for them to come to some sort of agreement. I don't want to go home and leave her here.

Augusta was still angry with her mother, and more than a little confused over the duchess's decision to remain in Rome. The thought of going back to London, and the Kembal family never being whole ever again filled her with heartbreaking sadness. One form of grief had been replaced by another.

She was tired and wanted nothing more than this nightmare to be over. For Gideon and Serafina to be wed, and for all of them, including Lady Anne, to sail home together.

But the night's proceedings had not been so kind. Shortly before they departed from All Saints, a pensive Matteo de Luca had appeared bearing a letter from his father. Enzo had decided that the de Luca family had suffered a grave insult to their honor, and Gideon was going to have to fight Matteo in a duel to the death.

I know Enzo de Luca is angry about what happened between Gideon and his daughter, but this is insane. Why can't he just let them marry? No one has to die.

Her brother was a marquis, and one day would be the Duke of Mowbray. The Kembals were rich, they were well connected. But it clearly wasn't enough.

We are not Catholic, nor are we members of Rome's elite. Serafina's father obviously doesn't see any gain for him in allowing this marriage.

When Gideon turned to leave, Augusta reached for his arm, drawing him back. "Gideon. Please just worry about you and Serafina. And about doing whatever it takes to avoid fighting Matteo. He is a skilled swordsman, and you don't stand a chance against him. I don't care what you have to do or who you have to bribe to make this right, but you must take Serafina and flee Rome as soon as you can. Flynn and I will deal with any other problems."

She was a stubborn woman, and from the expression on his face, she could tell that Gideon had immediately taken her words to heart.

"Of course, I will do what I can. In return, I ask that you stay well away from things. I don't want you hurt. This is a dangerous situation. You need to hold back any romantic notions you might have of Cupid coming to the rescue. Serafina's father is not a man to be crossed. He values her bride price and will do everything in his power to make sure his daughter is married to the man of his choosing. And from the way he raged against Serafina and me being together, I can tell you he would be more than happy to see me dead."

After Gideon left, Augusta paced the floor of her private suite. She was still contemplating what she would do if her brother wasn't able to rescue Serafina when a gentle knock came at her door. When she opened it, Flynn stepped across the threshold and quickly closed the door behind him.

Her resolve faltered. Augusta threw her arms around Flynn and cried, "Oh, what are we to do? I can't bear the thought of Gideon fighting Matteo in a duel."

He held her for a moment, his silence doing nothing to help calm her already frayed nerves.

"I am trying to figure out a possible solution to the problem of Gideon and Serafina getting married. As for Matteo, I doubt very much that he will fight your brother. Not unless his father is holding his sword hand. Enzo is the only one who is outraged about what happened tonight. I saw Donna Francesca when I arrived at the palace earlier, and I got the distinct impression that she was quite relieved that Serafina had defied Enzo and slept with Gideon."

With Gideon having taken Serafina's virginity, the contessa had a new and powerful bargaining chip. Signore Magri wouldn't likely view a tainted bride too favorably. It would only take the right word in the right ear, and the wedding would be called off.

The weight of Donna Francesca's support for Gideon and Serafina was an unexpected but welcome piece of news. And of course, no matter how good he was with a sword, she wouldn't be happy for her eldest son to be fighting in a deadly duel.

"I know Serafina's mother was against her marrying

Signore Magri. According to the palace servants, she and Enzo have had several terrible fights over it."

Flynn nodded, and for the first time this night, hope flared in Augusta's heart.

"Do you have a plan?" she asked.

"I'm not entirely sure of how things work here in Rome, so I am going to go and pay a visit to my friend Michael Cooper. He has lived here for some time. Hopefully, he will have a good idea about what we can do to get your brother and Serafina legally married."

Augusta had been hoping Flynn was going to stay and perhaps share her bed. Her insistence on her own room had been more about them, than staying away from the duchess.

At the moment, however, the matter of Gideon and Serafina's wedding was, of course, the higher priority. But if they could solve that thorny problem, then there would be plenty of time for her and Flynn.

She offered him her lips, and he bent and kissed her. When he finally drew back, she caught the look of determination on his face. "It's an ungodly hour, but I need to go and see if I can rouse Michael. If time allows, I will come back here before the morning, and we can spend a little while together. In the meantime, try and get some sleep Augusta."

There was a glint of hunger in his eye.

"Do what needs to be done, Flynn. Soon all your nights will belong to me."

Chapter Thirty-Nine

Augusta's lips were still humming with the warmth of Flynn's kisses when she stepped out of her room late that morning. She was too caught up in her private thoughts to notice the duchess until it was too late. Her mother fixed her with a haughty glare. "You look like the cat which has caught a tasty mouse."

That's not all I got, but we digress.

"A few hours of sleep has done wonders for me. I was going to go and check on Gideon. See if he had any news," Augusta replied.

She was quite prepared to lie to her mother. If Lady Anne felt it was acceptable to bend the truth about why they were still in Rome, then she was well within her rights to do the same.

The hard edges on her mother's face softened. "I saw him just now. He told me that Flynn has discovered that a Church of English minister and his family are staying at the hotel. If Gideon can arrange to smuggle Serafina out of Palazzo Lazio, they can be married today. The priest will officiate at the wedding. When he returns to England, the minister will take the paperwork back with him and register their marriage with your Uncle Hugh."

It paid to have a member of the family who was the Bishop of London. Lord Hugh Radley was Lady Anne's brother, and the perfect person to make sure that the nuptials between the future Duke of Mowbray and Serafina de Luca were legal in the eyes of the Church of England. It ensured that their children would be legitimate and their eldest son able to one day inherit his father's title.

Augusta feigned her surprise. She had already heard most of this from Flynn, who had returned to the hotel after seeing his friend Michael Cooper. Word of him having located an English priest in the hotel was an additional piece of welcome news.

The only major hurdle left to overcome was possibly the biggest. How to get Serafina out of the palace?

The duchess moved closer and held out her hand. "You and I should talk."

Augusta took one look at her mother's tentative peace offering and shook her head. "No."

"But you will be leaving for England shortly. We can't part on bad terms."

She had no intention of making this easy for her mother. If the duchess was going to abandon her family and remain in Rome, then as far as Augusta was concerned, she deserved to know what her eldest daughter thought of her decision. "You lied to me. You kept me here under false pretenses. Any right that you might have once thought you held to tell me what to say and do is long gone, your grace. If you are going to stay here in Rome, I have no interest in offering you a sweet farewell. You can go to the devil for all I care."

Brushing past her clearly shocked mother, Augusta headed for the stairs. Being kind and thoughtful toward the duchess had got her nowhere. Perhaps some cold, hard truths might help Lady Anne to see sense. To make her get on board that ship.

You need to understand what refusing to come home with us will cost you and our family.

~

Late that evening, with Augusta's secret key hidden in his coat pocket, Flynn made his way up the steep path to the garden gate at the rear of Palazzo Lazio. He was on a mission of utmost importance. And deadly danger. Kidnapping a noblewoman wasn't something he had ever done before, and he wasn't entirely sure he could pull it off.

He was close to the final bend in the long winding track when the unmistakable sound of a metal gate being swung open reached his ears. There was little chance of finding a place to hide. A nearby tree was his only hope. He had barely made it to the tree before the whisper of female voices cut through the silence.

"What will I do if Gideon doesn't come for me?"

Flynn grinned at that. His friend was head over heels in love. Nothing would stop him from marrying Serafina.

He moved out from behind the tree and onto the path, making his way toward the two women. A tall figure stepped in front of Serafina. The moon's light glinted on a sharp stiletto blade.

"I would rather not die today if that's alright with you. I have a friend's wedding to attend to very shortly, and he has asked me to be the best man."

"Who are you?" challenged Donna Francesca. She slashed the air with the blade in a brave attempt to intimidate him.

Flynn snorted in frustration. He had seen the contessa when he was helping Augusta and her mother leave the palace the previous day, but they hadn't actually spoken. Apparently,

Donna Francesca only stabbed those to whom she had been formally introduced.

"Viscount Cadnam. He is Gideon's friend," said Serafina.

"I am here to kidnap you. Though I can't begin to tell you how relieved I am that you decided to start your kidnapping before I got here. I wasn't looking forward to breaking into the palace."

The contessa sheathed her weapon, but not before she gave him an odd disapproving glare. Clearly, Donna Francesca didn't care for Flynn's flippant remarks.

"Please excuse my nerves, ladies. This has been a particularly trying day, and it is far from over."

They moved quickly down the path and into the nearby street. A grim-faced Flynn led the way, his gaze constantly darting from left to right, checking for danger. Anyone who sought to waylay him tonight was going to be met with deadly force.

Reaching All Saints' Chapel, Serafina raced across the room to Gideon and threw herself into his arms. As they embraced, Flynn finally allowed himself the luxury of sighing with relief. His part in the dangerous endeavor was over.

He turned to Augusta, giving her a hopeful smile. She grinned back at him and mouthed, 'Well done.'

Father Morris, the vacationing English priest they had found at the hotel, called the gathering to order.

"Dearly beloved, we are gathered here in the sight of God..."

Chapter Forty

T*he following morning*
    Palazzo Lazio

Enzo de Luca was livid, but he wasn't a fool. Once it became apparent that not only had Serafina and Gideon been married by a priest, but that through Donna Francesca's family connections they had secured a papal dispensation recognizing their marriage under Catholic law, there was little he could do. He had lost.

Augusta caught the perplexed look on Enzo's face as both his eldest son, Matteo, and his wife, Donna Francesca, stood behind the newlyweds in public support of their union. When the Duke of Lazio himself then added his blessing to the marriage, the fight seemed to go out of Enzo.

The moment he shook hands with Gideon, Augusta's shoulders sagged with relief. It was over. Her brother wasn't going to have to fight Matteo to the death. Nor would he and Serafina have to elope.

Flynn put a comforting arm around her. "We did it. Do you know, I think I am starting to get the hang of this miracle business?"

She buried her face in the folds of his jacket, not caring who saw them embrace. This was a day for tears and celebration. Her best friend had just married her foolish brother. Serafina would be coming back to London with them.

"Your mother and the contessa look deep in conversation. I expect they have much to discuss," said Flynn.

Augusta turned, taking in the duchess and Donna Francesca's exchange. "I wonder what Serafina's mother will say when she discovers that she won't be handing her daughter into the care of Lady Anne."

"The de Lucas don't know your mother is staying on in Rome?"

She found herself resenting the judgment which laced Flynn's question. While he had no right, especially when his father was an unashamed villain who had tried to murder him, she could well understand his confusion. The duchess was keeping her future plans to herself.

I can't imagine the horrible rumors I am going to have to deal with when I get home.

The matrons of the *ton* were going to be beside themselves with vicious glee when news of the Duchess and Duke of Mowbray formally separating became widely known. She would be married and settled with Flynn, but her sisters Victoria and Coco were still on the marriage market. The scandal would impact their chances of making solid matches. Of finding love.

Flynn brushed a hand down her back then released her. As their gazes met, he slowly shook his head. "I am sorry. I didn't mean for it to sound the way it did. I meant it more of a question as to whether the duchess has perhaps had second thoughts. She might now that Gideon and Serafina are married."

Augusta had a horrid suspicion that her mother had stubbornly painted herself into a corner, and it was her pride which was the main thing keeping her here. Not that Lady Anne would ever admit to such a thing.

"No, Mama is keeping her own counsel. Which is why I think she won't move back into Palazzo Lazio even if invited by the de Lucas. I think Gideon and Serafina might, just to help smooth things over. Mama will likely stay at the hotel until she decides on permanent lodgings."

It was hard to speak of her mother carving out a life away from the rest of the Kembal family, but Augusta was slowly coming to terms with this change in her life.

Flynn bent and spoke softly so only Augusta could hear. "G, can we go back to the hotel soon? There is something important I wish to discuss with you. Actually, it's a few things, but we cannot talk here."

She hesitated. It would appear odd if she and Flynn left the gathering. The event itself had transformed from what was meant to be a bloody duel to that of an open exchange of diplomacy. And now wedding congratulations.

Flynn turned and nodded toward the priest, Father Morris, who had accompanied the party this morning. He had confirmed that he had indeed married the Marquis of Holwell and Signorina Serafina de Luca the previous evening. At Flynn's signal, Father Morris made his excuses and hurried over.

"Father Morris, I am going to take Lady Augusta back to the Albergo del Sole. I was wondering if you would like to accompany us. I am sure your family will be waiting for you at the hotel."

A soft smile appeared on the priest's face. "Thank you. I

was wondering how I was going to find my way. Everyone here seems busy with making amends, and I thought it might be rude to ask. Thank heavens it all appears to have worked out for the best. I must confess I was worried there for a moment."

So was I, but sanity has prevailed.

They slipped quietly out of the reception room and made their way to the front door of the palace. Considering how unceremoniously she had been forced to leave only a day earlier, Augusta wasn't certain about the protocols of farewell, so she didn't bother to say goodbye. Truth be told, she was still angry over the way she and her family had been treated. Enzo had thrown them out into the street like unwelcome beggars.

And now he is family. But at least he won't be in London any time soon.

Once they were outside in Via della Pilotta, Flynn took Augusta by the hand. "Let's walk. It's only a short way. I feel the need to stretch my legs." He turned to Father Morris. "You don't mind walking do you, Father? We can give you the guided tour of this area on our way back if you like."

At the hotel, Augusta headed toward the stairs. She stopped when Flynn didn't make a move in the same direction, rather he remained with Father Morris in the foyer. "Aren't you coming with me?" she asked.

"In a moment. I need to speak to Father Morris. I promise I won't be long. Then you and I can talk."

Augusta's gaze went from Flynn to the priest. Her brows knitted together, and he could just imagine what she was thinking. What possible reason would Flynn have for talking to Father Morris? Gideon and Serafina were married, and there was nothing left for him to do.

He watched her go, then turned to Father Morris. "You have done the Marquis of Holwell a great service this day. I was wondering if I could call upon you to do the same for me."

Chapter Forty-One

Augusta threw herself onto the bed. Arms stretched out on the coverlet, she sighed up at the ceiling with unrestrained relief. "Thank you, Lord."

The past day had been trying to say the least. The butterflies in her stomach were still bouncing around. She hadn't bothered with food, afraid that she wouldn't be able to keep it down. Throwing up all over the polished marble of Palazzo Lazio would have been the final humiliation.

She glanced at the door, silently wishing that Flynn would hurry up. A laugh escaped her lips as a knock came at that very moment, and the door opened.

"I was just hoping you would appear, and here you are," she said, rising to sit up.

He stopped mid-stride, and his head dropped. "I lost count of the nights I lay and wished to have you beside me. And I expect you did the same. It's still a little strange to think that we can now do that, and our wishes will be heard."

Her gaze never left his as Augusta crossed the floor and came to Flynn. There were moments when she feared that if she dared look away, he might suddenly disappear.

Flynn wrapped his arms around her, whispering, "I love you, G. Life without you has been near impossible. You are the only thing which kept me sane through the darkest of days."

He pressed a kiss to her forehead, and Augusta closed her eyes. This was perfect. If she could hold this moment in time. Keep it under a glass and hope it never faded.

"What did you need to speak to Father Morris about?"

"Us." Flynn took a step back, then went down on bended knee. "I know we have both been through a terrible time, and there were days when hope seemed lost. But I have always held onto the promise of this day. When I could finally ask you to be my wife. Augusta, I love you. Will you do me the greatest honor and marry me?"

Augusta sucked in a deep breath and summoned up the only word she needed. "Yes."

A grinning Flynn got to his feet and swept Augusta up in his arms. He smothered her with kisses and tender words of hope. "I love you." "From this day." "Always."

The last vestiges of her grief fell to the floor. She was reborn. "I love you, Flynn. My life was shattered when you disappeared. And the day I thought I had truly lost you was the worst of my life. So, I am telling you here, and now, you'd better live to a ripe old age, Flynn Cadnam, because I don't intend going through that pain again—not until I am ready for the grave."

His lips were on hers. Soft and tender. Full of the promise of a long life together.

"Will you marry me today? Father Morris has said he will perform a marriage service for us."

"Yes. Let's not waste another minute."

Flynn held Augusta's hands in his and took in a deep breath. "But before we say our vows, I need to beg an indulgence from you."

"What sort of indulgence?" Augusta didn't like the sound of that, not the least bit.

"When we go back to England, I am not going to use my father's courtesy title. I will be plain Mister Flynn Cadnam. Nor will I set foot in Bramshaw House, other than to collect my things. I am going to have to work to support us."

"So that is the favor you ask. That I don't become Viscountess Cadnam. I have no issue with that—it sends a very public message as to how badly your father has treated you."

When Flynn shook his head, a sense of dread gripped Augusta. What else was he going to ask of her? And were their pending nuptials dependent on her answer?

"Count Nico de Luca has offered to train me in the shipping business. When I return to London, I will be taking up a position with de Luca Shipping. It means I will have to remain here in Rome for the next few months to learn from him. But I want you to go home with Gideon."

"No! Why? I... I don't understand," she pleaded.

Rejection stabbed at her. Flynn wanted them to marry, but he also wanted to put her on a boat back to England. Without him.

He pointed to the bed. "Can we sit for a minute? I want to explain why, so that you see things through my eyes."

Augusta's bottom lip trembled. Her big romantic moment was fast turning into disappointment. Flynn didn't want her to stay with him in Rome.

With reluctance, she did as he asked. He deserved to have her listen to his reasons. Compromise was the first rule of marriage she was determined to learn. Her union with Flynn was not going to be the fire and brimstone of her parents' marriage. Seated on the coverlet, she slipped her fingers into his and waited.

"I have spent the past year or more living through hell.

Most days, I hadn't a clue as to when I would eat my next mouthful of food, let alone a hot meal. I have stolen, lied, and fought to survive. Now that I have the means to experience Rome as it should be done, I want to do that. But for some of that time, at least, I need to do it on my own. Can you understand that?"

Augusta shrugged. "Not entirely."

He raised her hand to his lips and kissed her fingertips. "I also need a little time to work through some things. Not only to decide what to do about my father, but also to set us up financially. To make sure everything is ready so I can support us. I want to be able to focus as much of my attention as I can on working with the de Luca's. On studying the shipping business."

Since their sweet reunion, Augusta had been making plans in her mind for the day when together they would set foot on board the boat back to England.

"How long will you stay in Rome?" She dreaded his answer, fearing it would be many months, but no matter how painful it might be, she needed the certainty of knowing when she would see Flynn again.

"I spoke to Count Nico about shipping timetables. De Luca ships sail regularly from Civitavecchia. The day you are due to arrive in London will be the day I step onto a ship bound for England. I will be with you by the end of July. I know this sounds selfish, and I expect from your point of view it is, but I am asking you to grant me this boon. To give me the time to find my feet so I can come to you ready to be the best husband I can be. And to make sure that we always have a roof over our heads."

Was it selfish of Flynn to want to remain in Rome a little longer? No. But she could admit to a sense of sadness over his need to do it on his own.

"You are the most unselfish person I know, Flynn. And I

will never fully understand what you have been through. Yes, I will agree to your request, but in return, could you grant me that during whatever time you can spare before I leave, I am permitted to show you my favorite parts of the city?"

It would be good for them to have some shared memories of Rome to look back on in the years to come. To be able to tell their children about the time their parents spent together in the eternal city.

"Of course. I don't expect Serafina's parents will allow Gideon to steal her away in the next few days. And your brother will likely be at great pains to mend family relationships and have them on firmer ground before he departs."

The mention of her brother had Augusta pondering Flynn's chances of success of getting Gideon's agreement to him remaining in Rome without her. Without his wife.

Slim to none would be my guess.

If she was going to support Flynn, then some hard choices were going to fall at her feet. "You said Father Morris can marry us today, so why don't we do that now? Let's go and find him and ask him to come with us to All Saints."

Flynn rose from the bed. "Alright. But don't you want to wait until Gideon and your mother can attend?"

"No. I don't want any of my family knowing. Not until you arrive in London." Augusta got to her feet. "You have your reasons for wishing to spend a little more time in Rome, while I have mine for not telling my family."

She held up one finger. "One. If Gideon knows we are married, he will force you to come home with us. That won't help with your plans for de Luca Shipping and our future financial situation. Two. If my mother knows, then it will give her one less reason to come home. I can let it slip at some point that you and I might marry when we are back in England. Hopefully, the prospect of missing the wedding of her eldest daughter might help to get the duchess to change her mind."

Augusta added a third finger to the two already raised. "And truth be told, I don't want Mama at our wedding. She has lied to me. She has abandoned our family. And at the moment, I can't stand the idea of being in the same room as her, let alone having her witness our marriage."

She had finally given a voice to her pain. To the deep sense of betrayal she felt over her mother's decision to leave.

"Are you sure? This is not something you can take back. The duchess will eventually find out."

Augusta bit down on her bottom lip, nodding as she did. There was a degree of spite in her decision, and she hated herself for allowing it, but at the same time, she couldn't deny it.

"When you get back to London, we will tell my father about our marriage. Until then, only you, me, and the people who are witnesses to our vows will know that we are man and wife."

Her mother would be hundreds of miles away when she eventually discovered the truth of Augusta's deception. The duchess might finally come to realize the cost of what she had done. Of how deeply she had hurt her daughter.

Chapter Forty-Two

"I don't normally get to marry two couples in a week, let alone two nobles. I have to say this is quite an honor."

Augusta glanced at her hands, where they were joined with Flynn's. To the ring which now sat on her left hand. He was her husband. They were married. And while she would agree not to use the title Viscountess Cadnam, in her heart that was who she was—she was his wife. Someday, she would be his countess, and the whole of London would know.

Today, however, only Father Morris, the owner of the nearby café and his wife, along with Michael Cooper, knew that Augusta and Flynn were married. She had wanted it this way. In time, when Flynn returned to England, they would tell the duke of their happy news. They would have a formal celebration. Notices would be published in the newspaper.

And Earl Bramshaw would finally realize that Flynn and his new bride were forever out of his reach.

After adjourning to the café, where they shared a glass of wine with their wedding guests, the Cadnam's returned to the hotel. In the privacy of Augusta's room, Flynn drew her into his embrace. "My wife. I can't believe we are here. At last. It feels like we have journeyed around the world and back again."

"I think to hell and back is probably closer to what we have both been through. But yes... husband."

She wouldn't ever tire of saying that word. Flynn was hers. To have and to hold.

"Are you certain that you don't want to tell the rest of your family that we are now married? I will understand if you have a change of heart," he offered.

Augusta's head was still shaking as she reached for the first button on Flynn's trousers. She didn't want to think of her family or anyone else. The only thought on her mind was of getting her husband naked and into her bed.

Our bed.

Fortunately for her, Flynn was an intelligent man. He stopped talking and kissed her. She happily sighed into his mouth; longing and lust coursed through her body. When her husband pushed the top of her gown down, Augusta groaned.

To her delight, he didn't linger to admire his handiwork. Instead, his nimble fingers were on the front laces of her short stays, which soon found their way to the floor.

Only then did Flynn pause.

He appeared to be in two minds as to what he should do next. Which piece of clothing should hit the elegant woolen rug. Augusta reached for the second of Flynn's buttons, but he beat her to it. His hard erection popped free as the placket fell open. She licked her lips at the sight.

When Flynn brushed his hand over the front of her thin slip, Augusta's nipples peaked. He hummed with satisfaction.

"I have long dreamt of this moment. And while we may have already shared our bodies a number of times over the past two days, this coupling will be our first time as husband and wife."

Hunger burned in his eyes, along with a glint of wicked intent.

"What would you have me do, husband? I am yours to command."

A deep, dirty chuckle was his first response, followed by the words which had a shiver of lust coursing down Augusta's spine. "It pleases me that you see it that way because, from this day forth, you will do as I tell you when we are in the bedroom. Here, I am master."

Augusta thrilled at his words. A powerful Flynn was a gorgeous, manly thing. And he was all hers.

He lifted her thin muslin shift over her head and dropped it to the floor. Augusta reached for her stockings. "Tsk. Did I tell you to take them off?" he admonished.

A grin tugged at her lips. She loved teasing him. "No, master, you did not."

"Hands by your side until I tell you otherwise."

Her core throbbed with aching need. "Flynn," she murmured.

He drew close, cupping her sex in the palm of his hand. She whimpered when he slipped his thumb deep into her heat and began to stroke. When he bent his head and took her erect nipple into his mouth, nipping it with his teeth before drawing back hard, Augusta saw stars.

His strokes and rough attention to her breasts quickly drew her wetness to the surface. She closed her eyes, luxuri-ating in the sensual embrace—crying out when he shifted and thrust two fingers deep into her sex, then let his thumb work its way around her sensitive bud.

Divine.

There was no other word to describe what he was doing to her.

Flynn released her nipple and righted himself. "On the

bed, wife, kneeling facing the wall. Hands in front of you, legs spread."

She did as he instructed. It was thrilling to hear him speak to her in such a wicked and firm way. Augusta was still trying to figure out how this was actually going to work when a fully clothed Flynn came and stood behind her. Wrapping an arm around her hips, he drew her back to the edge of the bed, then pushed her legs farther open with his knee.

Augusta whimpered as Flynn's cock parted the moist folds of her sex, and he took command of her body. The heady delight of knowing he was still dressed in his suit while she was completely naked soon had her demanding that he take her hard. To stake his claim.

The rough abrasion of his woolen trousers against her bare ass had her sobbing with need. "Flynn."

He rode her without mercy; all the while Augusta begged for more. For his mastery. When the pace of their coupling drew to fever pitch, he slammed into her one last time, then stilled.

The scent of sex still hung heavy in the air as Flynn gently rolled Augusta over onto her back and pulled her once more to the edge of the bed. He knelt before her, with one of her legs on either side of his head resting on his shoulders. The first touch of his lips and tongue sent her eyes rolling back in her head.

"Flynn," she sobbed.

"Wife, take your pleasure," he growled.

Augusta did as she was told.

Chapter Forty-Three

The time had come to say goodbye. The past weeks in Rome had been a blur. The de Lucas had thrown several extravagant parties to celebrate the marriage of Serafina and the future Duke of Mowbray.

Enzo de Luca was at pains to note that Gideon would one day be a duke whenever anyone happened to mention his new son-in-law. He was also keen to discuss future shipping contracts and forging new trading links via the English family connection.

Augusta kept her own counsel as to what she thought of Serafina's father, but she was grateful that the chances of her having to set eyes on Enzo de Luca again after today were slim. She doubted she would ever forgive him for trying to sell his daughter into a loveless union with a man who already had a family. Or for throwing the Kembal family out into the street.

The newlyweds had spent the days following their wedding back at Palazzo Lazio, leaving Augusta and her mother to reside at the hotel. The Duchess of Mowbray had in turn invested many hours with Donna Francesca shopping and packing a number of large trunks for Serafina to take with her on the sea voyage to her new home in England. From what Augusta had gathered, her mother was still keeping the news of her extended stay in Rome a closely guarded secret.

It was her choice, and the rest of the English contingent were content to keep the duchess's decision to themselves. When the de Lucas discovered the truth, Augusta, Gideon, and Serafina would be on their way home. Lady Anne was going to be living her own life, far from her blood family. As far as Augusta was concerned, there was nothing more which could be done to change her mother's mind.

Flynn had taken up his new post with de Luca Shipping, which meant that nights were often the only time Augusta and he got to see one another. Their marriage was yet another tightly kept secret. She was tempted to tell Serafina but decided that would only put her sister-in-law in a difficult situation, and it wasn't fair to ask her to lie to her new husband.

Her own husband had, with the hotel management conveniently turning a blind eye, quickly mastered the back stairs of the Albergo del Sole. Flynn spent every night with Augusta before slipping out just after dawn to head back to All Saints' Chapel, where he still helped out. And still officially resided.

Augusta considered her stack of packed and ready travel trunks through a sheen of tears. This morning was her last day in Italy. Tonight, she and her brother and his wife would be on board a boat and headed home. Her mother and husband would remain in Rome.

Coming to stand behind her, Flynn wrapped his arms around Augusta and whispered in her ear, "You promised to be strong today. But it's alright if you give in to the tears. Just don't let them take you down."

She silently nodded, fighting her emotions. Her heart and

head were a sorry mess. This day had always been coming, but now that it was here, she was at a loss as to what to do with herself. Leaving Flynn and her mother weighed heavily on Augusta's heart. Flynn would soon join her in London, but the duchess might possibly never come home. Today may well be the last time they would ever speak.

Before the coach left in an hour or so, Augusta planned to go and say her final farewells to her mother. Last night, they had all attended a farewell dinner at Palazzo Lazio.

Turning in Flynn's arms, Augusta kissed her husband. "Six weeks. You promise that in six weeks you will be on board a ship. You will return home to me. If you are a day late, I will come and find you."

His warm embrace held a promise, which was matched with his words. "I am coming home to you. The moment you set foot ashore in England is the day I will be stepping onto a boat at the port of Civitavecchia."

Their lips met once more in a long, lingering kiss. His touch bringing back memories of being woken by Flynn in the early hours of the morning and her husband making love to her. In the afterglow of their joining, they had curled up together. While Flynn slept, Augusta had watched the dawn as it broke through into a golden Rome sky. She hadn't wanted to waste a minute of being in his arms. Sleep would find her when she was settled on the boat.

Time had slowly, but inevitably ticked down. Flynn would soon have to leave. His own final goodbyes had been made yesterday, with the reassurance to Gideon that he would soon return to England.

"I love you. Stay strong, and I will see you very soon."

"I love you too."

He kissed her one last time, and then he was gone.

Chapter Forty-Four

Augusta fought her tears for as long as she could, but when the cross on the top of Saint Peter's Basilica disappeared from view, and Serafina let out a cry of anguish, she buried her face in her hands and wept. She was leaving Rome. Leaving Flynn. Leaving her mother behind.

I shouldn't have been so horrible to her these past few weeks.

She had let her anger dictate her actions, and now as she sat in the coach headed north toward the port of Civitavecchia, regret rushed in. The worry that she may never see the duchess again sat heavy in her heart.

Gideon reached across the carriage and gave Augusta a pat on the hand. "We did all we could to get Mama to come home. I gave her the box of love letters which Papa had written. I talked to her. And right to the very end, I pleaded with her to make the trip back to England. There is nothing more any of us could have done."

Augusta closed her eyes. She had been cold and hard toward her mother. Had her own behavior acted to under-mine all Gideon's good work? How could she possibly face her father if she was the reason why Lady Anne didn't come back.

"I just wish Mama could have, for once, put her stubborn pride aside. Now she will be all alone," sighed Augusta. At this moment, she hated herself for being far too much her own mother's daughter. If there was one fault in their personalities that all the Kembal females seemed to share, it was the inability to get out of their own way.

The pain of losing her mother only served to make her pain over leaving Flynn behind worse. Three months from now, she would see her husband again.

But will I ever see Mama?

The rest of the trip was spent mostly in silence. Gideon and Serafina sat hand in hand, occasionally whispering words of love and comfort.

Her brother had come out of his long trip to Rome with a wife. Serafina was now the future Duchess of Mowbray. The family line would continue. But the duchess wouldn't see her grandchildren when they inevitably arrived. Augusta caught the expression of sadness on Gideon's face whenever he turned and gazed out the window.

In the early evening, the coach drew up alongside the dock at Civitavecchia. The sight of the ship, which was to take them back to England, had Augusta screwing her eyes closed and bowing her head. She had longed to go home and see her family but had never imagined it would be under these circumstances.

Their luggage was taken on board. Gideon and Serafina stood together on the dockside. Every so often, Gideon would place a tender kiss on his wife's forehead and murmur something to her. Love shone in his eyes, along with a fierce glint of protection. They would do well together.

I wish Flynn was here. I miss him already.

Augusta's gaze kept darting back to the road. Her heart had not learned to stop seeking Flynn.

My husband will come home soon. Take comfort. He needs this time.

With the last of the travel trunks loaded, Serafina held out her hand, and a grateful Augusta took it. "Come, sister. It is time we sailed for home."

They walked up the gangplank together, followed by Gideon. On board the boat, Augusta headed toward her cabin. She wasn't sure if she had the strength to stand and watch as the ship drew away from the dockside. There was every chance she would dissolve into a flood of tears.

Augusta was halfway across the deck when a shout rang out from the crew, and she turned. Her gaze landed on her mother. Gideon was helping the duchess down from the gangplank.

Oh. Thank god. Thank god.

Her feet began to move toward Lady Anne. She couldn't imagine how hard this moment must be for her mother. She was setting out on the journey home, unsure of her welcome back in London. But if the duchess could swallow her pride, then so could her daughter.

"Mama," she whispered.

As Gideon and Serafina took up a spot on the deck, the gangplank was lifted. The duchess came to stand on the other side of her son. Augusta sucked in a deep breath and moved to her mother's side. She brushed her fingers against Lady Anne's in a silent gesture of gratitude and support. The duchess turned and gave her a hopeful smile.

Maybe there still is a chance for our family to be together again. Thank heavens Mama is coming home with us.

The boat gave a lurch as it drew away from the dockside, and Augusta clenched her left hand into a fist. Her right hand was raised. She waved in the direction of Rome. Six weeks from now, her husband was due to make the same journey and sail for home.

"I am holding you to every single one of your promises, Flynn Cadnam. Don't let me down," she whispered into the wind.

The duchess had already moved away, and Augusta went to follow. This final moment of farewell was for Gideon and Serafina to share in private.

Serafina reached out once more to Augusta. "He will come; I know he will. Flynn loves you," she said.

A weeping Augusta nodded, then walked away.

Hopefully, her sister-in-law would forgive her when she finally learned the truth of what had happened between Flynn and herself in Rome.

Chapter Forty-Five

The Morning Herald
Wednesday, June 17, 1818

Seen disembarking from a ship which arrived in London early yesterday morning were the following persons of note. The Duchess of Mowbray, her daughter Lady Augusta Kembal, and most surprisingly, the Marquis of Holwell, along with an Italian lady. It would appear that London society had been tricked into thinking that Lord Gideon Kembal had retired to the Mowbray ducal estate, when in fact, he had slipped out of England and sailed to Rome. Word has it that the young lady who accompanied the marquis is his new wife.

Dear reader, your correspondent is eagerly anticipating what London society will make of these latest developments in the ongoing Mowbray Scandal.

Augusta lay in her bed listening while Victoria read out loud from the gossip column of the newspaper. Gideon's hopeful plans for the Kembals to slip quietly into London unnoticed had all come to naught.

Not that she particularly cared either way. She was far more interested in the fact that their father had not only raced with great haste downstairs the moment he heard his wife was waiting in the travel coach in the mews, but that he had apparently thrown her over his shoulder and carried her up to their private apartment. No one had seen either of them since.

The case containing the duke's love letters had clearly done the trick.

Augusta and her mother had taken the opportunity to talk during the long sea voyage home, but things between them were still strained. She hadn't told the duchess about the wedding, nor that she and Flynn had become lovers. Until her husband returned, Augusta was determined to keep those things secret.

Late last evening, Gideon had received a private note from their father, the details of which had been shared with the rest of the family and servants. It stated simply that the duchess was home and resting from her long sea voyage. This was the official line that the Kembal family was to go with if anyone asked.

Unofficially, the Kembal siblings had been informed that their parents were going to be spending much of the rest of the week in the ducal suite, discussing matters. As a married woman, Augusta now had a pretty good idea what those discussions would involve.

"Are you coming down for breakfast? You didn't eat much at supper last night?" asked Victoria.

Food. Urgh.

The mere thought of it turned Augusta's stomach.

On the voyage home, Gideon had suffered terribly from seasickness whenever they left port. The poor boy. Serafina had spent many nights nursing her husband through bouts of extreme nausea.

In the privacy of her cabin, Augusta had endured her own delicate stomach. Coupled with sensitive nipples, and two missed monthly courses, she suspected her reasons for having been under the weather were not due to any tempest of the sea.

If she was pregnant, how long could she keep it a secret?

No one knew she and Flynn were married. And until he arrived, she didn't want to say anything to anyone.

Except perhaps his uncle. Charles Cadnam.

"I have somewhere I need to be this morning, so breakfast will have to, unfortunately, wait. Perhaps you, Coco, and I could go and find a nice cake shop later in the day," offered Augusta.

She wanted to be with her sisters. She hadn't realized how much she had missed them until a tearful Victoria had embraced her yesterday morning. And when Augusta had sought out Coco, her younger sister had been an uncharacteristic sobbing mess.

At times, it felt like forever since she and the duchess had left London—almost another life that she had lived. Rome was so far away, and not just in distance.

Augusta was painfully aware of the cost to the other members of her family of what had happened in the intervening months. The lines of sadness which sat etched on Victoria's brow told a tale of a difficult time after their mother's letter had reached London.

I am not the only one Mama is going to have to seek forgiveness from.

Victoria left in search of sustenance, while Augusta struggled out of bed. The morning sickness was less severe on dry land, but it still held sway at this hour of the day. She rang for her maid, quickly dressed, then took the Mowbray House carriage to Mortimer Street. It was time for her to pay a visit to Flynn's uncle.

Charles Cadnam greeted her with a smile wider than the ocean. In his hand, he held the letter Flynn had sent home with Augusta and which she'd had couriered to him as soon as the boat docked. The other letter, the one Flynn had written to her, and which had beaten Augusta back to England, had sadly remained unopened on her dresser. Only now was Flynn's uncle discovering that his nephew was still alive.

He brandished the note. "This is the most excellent—the most wonderful piece of news. I am still pinching myself over it."

Augusta grinned at him. "I promised Flynn I would send it as soon as we arrived. He was worried for you. Over the pain you must have suffered this past year and a half."

Charles Cadnam rang the bell, and a servant soon appeared at the door of the drawing room. "Tea and some light refreshments please," he said. The footman bowed and quickly disappeared.

"Please have a seat, Lady Augusta. I've barely slept, hoping that someone would come to see me. In truth, I am a little surprised that it is you. I was expecting your brother or your father."

Augusta took up a spot on a bright yellow sofa. It didn't do much for her tender head and stomach, but she did her best not to focus her gaze on the fabric.

She cleared her throat and made ready to give the speech

she had spent long weeks at sea practicing. Flynn was trusting her to speak on his behalf, and she was not going to fail him. "Flynn is alive, he is well, and as of today, on his way home. He wanted to spend some time in Rome with friends, which is why he is not here."

No. That didn't sound right. It made Flynn sound like he didn't care enough to return to England. Which couldn't be further from the truth.

Just tell him everything. Let it all come into the light.

"Let me start again. Flynn is alive, but no thanks to his father. The earl tried to murder him. Then he had his son kidnapped and taken far from home, where I suspect he hoped Flynn would die. He didn't."

Charles, who had taken a seat in the matching sofa opposite to the one in which Augusta sat, flinched. "I suspected that my brother had a hand in Flynn's disappearance. But I didn't think he would go that far." He nodded at Augusta. "Please do go on, Lady Augusta."

She had known the truth of Flynn's disappearance for some time, but even now it was still difficult to put Earl Bramshaw's villainy into words. "As he states in his letter, after finally recovering from his knife wounds, Flynn lived rough on the streets of Italy. He eventually made it to Rome, where we had the good fortune to meet."

Augusta paused. She was determined to get the next part right. "Without knowing that I was in Rome, Flynn sent a letter home to me. If things had gone differently, you would have known that he was alive some two months ago. On Flynn's behalf, I must beg your forgiveness for the unfortunate delay."

Tears glistened in Charles Cadnam's eyes, and his hands trembled. His grief must have been as bad as hers. "Foolish boy, how could he think he would ever need to beg for my forgiveness. But what I don't understand is why this is being kept a secret. I want to shout it from the rooftops. Let the whole world know that Flynn is alive."

She swallowed deeply as her own tears threatened. "Flynn said you would probably say that. He doesn't want the earl knowing he is alive until he returns to England. My husband doesn't trust Earl Bramshaw not to send someone to Rome to finish the job that he started. That's why we have kept things secret."

There, I have said it.

"Your husband?" murmured Charles.

Augusta nodded. "We agreed to keep that piece of news a secret between the two of us but seeing you in person has made me realize how terribly selfish it would be not to tell you. Flynn and I were married in Rome. But please don't tell anyone until he returns. My family doesn't as yet know."

Charles rose from his chair and embraced her. "He always wanted to marry you, but he was afraid of what his father would do." He sighed. "My brother is an evil man. He has made Flynn's life a misery."

During long nights sitting and talking at the hotel in Rome, Flynn had told her the truth of the vile abuse his father had subjected him to over the years. Of how his humiliation had gone much further than just withholding money. That family honor had been why he had kept secret the truth of the earl's violent nature. Flynn had paid a heavy price for his silence.

"I know all about Earl Bramshaw. So many things I didn't understand before now make horrible sense. Which is why we must keep all of this a closely guarded secret until Flynn returns."

The footman reappeared carrying a tray with a teapot, cups, and a small platter of freshly made sandwiches. He set them on an occasional table, which he placed in the space between the sofas, then took his leave. Augusta politely refused the food, opting instead for a small cup of sweet tea to help calm her stomach.

They settled back in their seats. There was more she had to say. Her promise to Flynn was that she would make certain his uncle had a complete understanding of matters before his nephew returned home.

"Flynn and I will find somewhere to live. He is adamant he will not go back to Bramshaw House while his father is still alive. The de Luca family, whose daughter, Serafina, my brother has just made his wife, have offered Flynn paid employment. At the moment, they are training him in Rome, after which he will take on the role of a London representative for the de Luca shipping company. We will not be using either the Viscount or Viscountess Cadnam titles."

Charles closed his eyes and slowly shook his head. "I can't believe my family has come to this, that my brother would hate his heir this much. Flynn has been punished for the crime of simply having been born."

When he opened his eyes once more, Augusta noted the odd look on Charles Cadnam's face, one which she couldn't quite decipher. It was there and gone in an instant. She would've loved to have asked him what it meant but sensed he wouldn't give her a clear answer.

She rose from her seat. "I am still weary from the boat trip, so please excuse me for making my visit here a short one —I need sleep. I'll come and visit again before Flynn returns home."

Charles got to his feet and took her hands in his, his gaze dropping to the ring on Augusta's finger. He drew in a ragged breath. "I cannot begin to tell you how much it means to me to see that ring once again on the hand of the future Countess Bramshaw. I gave it to Flynn's mother before she married the earl."

His words spoke of a private pain. Some day she might

ask him to elaborate, but as with many things of late, now didn't seem the right time.

"Flynn gave it to me the day he went missing. He said it was the most precious thing he owned."

Flynn's uncle wiped a tear from his eye then hugged Augusta. "I am overjoyed that my nephew is alive and that you are together. Until yesterday, I didn't believe in miracles. Now I think I do."

She smiled at him. "I have spent quite some time in Rome, and I no longer have any doubt that miracles are real. Flynn is my miracle."

Augusta left the Cadnam family home and headed back to Mowbray House. On the way, she offered her own prayer of gratitude for the gift of her husband, and the child she carried.

But today was a day for confessing delicate truths. She was going home to speak to her parents and tell them what she and Flynn meant to one another, and that they were married. The news of the baby she would keep to herself until she could tell Flynn in person.

Chapter Forty-Six

The second his feet touched English soil, Flynn let out a little cheer. He punched the air.

"I made it." On the long voyage from Italy, he had done some calculations. By the time he did arrive home, he would have been away well over five hundred days. A long time in anyone's reckoning, especially when the absence had not been planned.

First thing on his long list of things to do was to go and find Augusta. To hold his wife and tell her that things were finally going to be alright. The long nightmare was almost over.

He carried a large travel bag—a gift from Matteo de Luca. It was full of fine linen shirts and exquisitely tailored Italian suits. Thoughts of his new wardrobe put a smile on his face. No one would ever again call him the Vagabond Viscount. He was now the epitome of finely dressed nobility.

Where he would sleep tonight was also high on his list of priorities. If Augusta had kept their marriage a secret, he wouldn't be able to stay at Mowbray House. His own home, Bramshaw House, was out of the question. The last time he had set foot in the front door, his sire had tried to murder him.

After walking from the dockside and onto the Ratcliffe Highway, he hailed a hack. "Number five, Mortimer Street, please. Actually, no, change of plans. Mowbray House, Berkeley Square."

He had intended to go to Charles Cadnam's house, but he couldn't wait to see Augusta. If things had gone according to plan, his uncle would know he was alive and on his way home. A short delay in being reunited with his family couldn't be avoided.

When the butler at Mowbray House opened the door, Flynn could have sworn the man had tears in his eyes. "Lord Cadnam. Welcome back."

Flynn barely had time to set his travel bag down in the foyer before he was swept up in a bear-hug-like embrace. "You made it. About bloody time," said Gideon, with barely restrained glee.

"It's good to be home. I can't believe how long I have been away. But if you don't release me from this hug, I might expire on the spot."

That would make his long sea voyage a terrible waste.

"Viscount Cadnam. As I live and breathe."

Flynn's gaze landed on Clifford Kembal, the Duke of Mowbray. His father-in-law. The duke made his way to the bottom of the stairs and came to embrace him. And while his hug was less crushing than Gideon's, his gaze when they broke apart was deep and searching. He wrapped an arm around Flynn's shoulder. "You and I have much to discuss, young man."

Gideon followed in their wake as the duke guided Flynn up to the next floor of Mowbray House. Reaching the door of his private study, he turned to his son. "Be a good lad and fetch your mother and Augusta. I know Serafina is out in town this morning, but this cannot wait."

Flynn was ushered into the room and handed a generous glass of whisky. Suddenly possessed with the worry that he might be in need of a large shot of alcohol, he downed it quickly.

To his growing concern, the duke took the glass, refilled it, then handed it back, saying, "Just keep going until your nerves are feeling numb."

He took the seat he was offered and waited. Years of dealing with his father had taught him that it was wise to hold his tongue. Speak only when spoken to; that mantra had saved him from more than one beating.

As silence fell, Flynn's heart kicked up a notch. He might not be in Earl Bramshaw's study, but old habits die hard. It took all his willpower not to start looking for any sign of a hard wooden cane. At least there were no greyhounds lounging by the fire.

"Well, I suppose congratulations are in order, Viscount Cadnam. Welcome to the family."

He looked up and was genuinely shocked to discover that the duke was grinning from ear to ear.

A relieved Flynn didn't quite know where to look. "Thank you, your grace. I wasn't expecting whisky and kind words."

Still smiling like the cat who had got the cream, Clifford Kembal dropped into the chair next to Flynn's. When he met his gaze, the duke softly laughed. "If you had secretly married my daughter before you disappeared, you probably wouldn't have received such a warm welcome. But this past year has taught me a lot of harsh lessons. Family is the most important thing for any of us, and something which I will never take for granted ever again."

Flynn raised his glass to his lips. When Gideon had been in Rome, he had made mention of his father's emotional response upon hearing the news that his wife wasn't coming home. The duke had apparently been shattered. He had been unaware that the duchess was deeply unhappy and had made the decision to live apart from him.

If only his own father would welcome him with such warmth.

"Now, I expect you are thinking that I wish to discuss the payment of Augusta's dowry. I do. But firstly, I think we need to come up with a plan to keep any and all of that money out of your father's grubby hands. If Earl Bramshaw gets wind of this marriage, he will be on my doorstep within the hour."

More relief flooded Flynn, who nodded his agreement. He was relieved because the Duke of Mowbray not only seemed to have the right measure of the earl, but that he was also firm in his intent of not handing over the dowry while there was even the remotest possibility of Flynn's father being able to access it. Having a caring family made him feel less alone. The Duke of Mowbray was a powerful man; his support would carry weight within London society.

"We had thought to keep the news of our marriage a secret from everyone for as long as we could. Or at least until I returned home. Of course, it is now inevitable that people will find out. And that is a good thing. Augusta deserves to be recognized as my wife."

His wife must have had her reasons for not waiting until his arrival to tell her family. He trusted Augusta, and her judgement.

"Agreed. My daughter does have the right to be known as Viscountess Cadnam, but I understand if the two of you decide not to use the courtesy titles. Have you given any thought as to what you might say to the earl when you see him?" asked Clifford.

A dry laugh escaped Flynn's lips. There were a great many things he could say to his murderous sire. Few of which were fit to speak aloud. "I am going to go to Bramshaw House later today and retrieve what little possessions I own. Hopefully, the old swine hasn't burned them. But as for Augusta and myself, I will make it plain to the earl that if he attempts to come near me and mine, I will let the authorities know what he did. That he stabbed me and then paid a group of strangers to toss me overboard from a ship far out to sea. The only reason why I am still alive is because those men had a change of heart in the middle of a storm."

Before leaving Rome, Flynn had visited the Trevi Fountain and tossed a handful of coins into the water as payment to the god Oceanus. It was the ancient deity, whose statue graced the center of the ornate fountain, who the kidnappers had blamed for the mighty tempest which they had encountered in the Northern Atlantic. They had not been willing to further incur the god's wrath by murdering a badly injured English nobleman.

Fear had saved him from a watery grave. It was also the weapon he intended to yield against his father. He might find it hard to get a charge of attempted murder to stick, but he doubted Earl Bramshaw would dare to risk having his son make such vile allegations against him.

He cleared his throat and steadied his nerves. "I have accepted paid employment with the de Luca Shipping Company here in London. I intend to provide for my wife and family as best as I can under the circumstances."

The notion that those circumstances might go on for a good number of years wasn't something he felt needed to be raised. The duke wasn't a fool—he would understand that his eldest daughter may have to live a financially restrained life for some time to come.

A few minutes later, the door opened, and the Duchess of Mowbray appeared. She smiled sweetly at her husband, then turned to Flynn. "Viscount Cadnam. About time."

Thoughts of a third stiff drink were dancing around Flynn's mind when the door opened once more and through it rushed Augusta. Gideon tracked in her wake, closing the door behind him.

Flynn and his wife took one look at each other, and all thoughts of playing this reunion cool went straight out the window. Augusta leaped into his arms, and Flynn wrapped her up in his embrace. "Augusta, my love. I have missed you."

She kissed him. Considering their audience, Flynn tried to make the kiss as chaste as possible, but it quickly became apparent that Augusta wasn't having any of it. His wife wanted his kiss, and she wouldn't take anything less than a full, deep locking of lips. Flynn gave in and let Augusta have her way.

"When the two of you are done," observed the duke.

Augusta eventually drew back from the kiss, but kept her arms wrapped about Flynn's waist. She turned to face her parents. The duke and duchess exchanged a knowing look.

These two seem to have settled their differences, thank heavens.

"Mama and Papa know that we are married. As do your uncle and aunt. I didn't think it fair to keep it from them. I'm sorry that goes against our agreed plans," said Augusta.

Now he understood why the duke had handed him several glasses of whisky. He was about to be interrogated as to why he had married Lady Augusta and not told her family when they were in Rome.

"What about my father?" The horrid thought that the earl knew and was waiting for him somewhere in the shadows had Flynn wishing he hadn't had that second drink.

Gideon cleared his throat. "Until today, few people outside of our family and that of your uncle knew for certain that you were, in fact, alive. Rumors have, of course, been circulating, but no one has given them any real credence. Especially since you have been missing for such a long time. Earl Bramshaw has remained silent on the subject."

Flynn sighed with relief. There was still much to do about the earl, but at least he was now safely back in London, where he had friends and family to help protect him from his wicked sire. As soon as he left here, he would be delivering letters to his solicitor—ones which would only be opened if something untoward were to happen to him. Letters which implicated Earl Bramshaw in the attempted murder of his son.

I will protect Augusta from that villain.

He met the duke's gaze. "I suppose it is a little late to be asking for your daughter's hand in marriage, but I would ask for your blessing. I love Augusta, and I will give her the best life I can."

He turned to Gideon. "I am sorry I lied to you in Rome. Augusta was under your protection, and it was a grave breach of trust for me to marry her without your knowledge or approval. We had our reasons, but again, I am sorry for the offense against you."

Gideon slowly nodded. "I can't say I was all that pleased when I heard that the pair of you had lied to not only me, but my wife and the duchess. Then again, at that time, I don't think any of us were behaving in accordance with social expectations. You are home and with your wife, Flynn. That is all that matters."

Augusta slipped her hand into Flynn's and gave his fingers an encouraging squeeze. She had been the one who'd had to deal with the issue of their secret wedding, so if she was fine with things, then so was he.

"What are your plans now?" asked the duke.

It was an obvious question, and one which demanded an answer. "I had planned to go and stay with my uncle for a time while I got things set up, but that was before this morning. Before I knew that Augusta and my marriage was no longer a secret."

He doubted the Kembals would be too happy if he continued with that original plan and lived in a separate household from his wife. From what Augusta and Gideon had told him when they were in Rome, the duke and duchess had been the subject of enough rumors already this year. The last thing anyone would want to see was Augusta's name being dragged into the mud.

"Good, then that settles things. You will move in here until you and Augusta decide on somewhere else to live. Gideon and Serafina have taken the other private apartment, but there are connecting rooms on the fourth floor which will serve as a suite for the two of you in the meantime," announced Lady Anne.

The Duke of Mowbray nodded his agreement. Clearly, the subject of where he and Augusta were going to live had been discussed and agreed upon prior to his arrival. Flynn bowed his head, grateful for the kind offer. "That is very generous. Thank you. Hopefully, we won't all be squeezed under your roof for too long, your grace. Once I get established with de Luca Shipping, I intend to look for a place for Augusta and myself to live."

His position was firm. They would set up their own home. Refuse to use his father's courtesy titles. And in doing so, make their opinion of Earl Bramshaw plain to all of London society.

Augusta squeezed his hand a second time. "Could Flynn and I be allowed some time alone? It's been eight weeks since we last saw one another."

The meaning behind her words was fortunately not lost on the others in the room. They were all married and therefore understood the need for a couple to have privacy.

The duchess stepped forward and placed a kiss on Flynn's

cheek. "Welcome to the family, Flynn. I think Augusta has chosen well."

He suffered the congratulations of Gideon and the duke, making a solemn promise to spend time with his father-in-law at his earliest convenience.

Flynn barely had time to wish his new family members a polite goodbye before Augusta dragged him out the door. They were down the hall, up the nearest set of stairs, and in the privacy of her room within a matter of minutes.

He took her into his arms and held her, breathing deeply, taking in the scent of the woman he loved. Eight long weeks without Augusta—how had he survived?

"Flynn," she whispered just before he lowered his lips to hers. As their tongues danced together, he made a silent vow. Never again would he ever be separated from her. Only death would see them part.

Chapter Forty-Seven

*

He wasn't meant to be here for another month. Augusta had steeled herself for four more weeks of longing. Her calendar was marked, noting the exact day when Flynn's ship was due to arrive in London. And yet here he was.

She couldn't be happier.

When they finally broke their long, love-filled kiss, Augusta stared into Flynn's perfect blue eyes. "Hello, husband. You are early."

He chuckled. "Hello wife. And yes, I know. I had planned to stay on in Rome as we agreed, but not long after you left, I shared a wine or two too many with Matteo and Count Nico. I confessed our secret wedding, after which they made it clear that I was going to be on the first boat back to England."

Oh, no. Flynn had lost his chance at spending time in Rome on his own terms. Augusta sighed. "I am sorry. I know you were looking forward to seeing more of the city."

Her husband shook his head. "I am not the least bit sorry. Seeing your beautiful, smiling face only confirms what my friends told me. That I was a silly man for wanting to remain in Rome and learn about the shipping business, while my wife went home. I have missed you terribly." He kissed her once more. Augusta loved how Flynn was always hungry for kisses.

"Besides. Once they understood my other reason for staying on in Rome, that I wanted to experience the city for myself, they arranged a whirlwind tour for me. I was taken on a private excursion of the Vatican by a cardinal and allowed to view the special art collection. Nico and Matteo pulled every string they had to make sure I spent the rest of my short stay seeing Rome. Even Serafina's father, stepped in and took me to places I would never have been able to visit on my own."

Enzo de Luca had offered Flynn special favors. Now that was a turn-up for the books. He had been dead set against his daughter marrying Gideon, so it was most unexpected that he would help one of Gideon's friends.

Augusta raised her eyebrows. "Now that is surprising."

"Once Enzo realized I was going to help with the shipping company here in London, he became quite friendly toward me. I have a better understanding of him as a result of our time together."

There was a lightness in his voice, a spark. Augusta couldn't remember a time when she had heard it. These weeks apart had changed Flynn, given him a degree of confidence she doubted he might have gained if he had come home with her.

She sensed he was ready to take on all that was waiting for him in England. The good and the bad.

But first, the good.

"How was your voyage home?" she asked, resting her hand over his heart.

"Fine. Well, considering how I got to Italy, it wouldn't have taken much for the return journey to be an improvement. The de Lucas made sure I was given an elegant cabin on board one of their best ships. They said it made sense for me to be able to give a firsthand account of the quality of their vessels for any potential customers. Speaking of journeys, how was your trip back to England?"

She lowered her head, then glanced up, offering him a soft, knowing smile. "With Mama's sudden arrival as we were about to depart, it was better than I had expected. Of course, poor Gideon was ill again, but Serafina nursed him through the worst." She paused, then added. "I was also unwell for some of the trip, but not due to seasickness."

Her hand dropped to her belly, and Flynn's gaze followed. He was silent for a moment, then he drew in a shaky breath. "Oh, G. My love, that is the most magnificent, the most precious news. You have made me the happiest man alive."

His fingers settled over hers, and he bent and kissed her gently on the forehead. "I am so glad I am here with you and our baby. Coming home early was the best thing. I promise we will never be parted again."

Flynn would make a wonderful papa, she was sure of it.

"Have you seen your uncle? I paid him a visit the day after we got home. He knows we are married."

"I came straight from the ship to here. To you. But yes, I will go and see him shortly. After that, I am going to Bramshaw House."

Dread settled heavily on Augusta's heart. This day had been coming, but she still couldn't imagine how hard it must be for Flynn.

"Are you going to confront your father?"

He shook his head. "I have put a lot of thought into things and decided he is not worth my time. I will go to his house, collect my belongings, then leave. An account of my life from the day he stabbed me until now has been written, and copies made. If the earl tries anything, those documents will be made public."

There was a knock at the door, and when Augusta opened it, the duchess stood on the threshold. She nodded to Flynn.

"I was wondering if I could steal Augusta away from you, Flynn. Now that you are here, we need to sort out accommodation for the two of you. And since your rooms will be your private suite, I thought it made sense for your wife to be making decisions about where things should go."

It was lovely to hear her mother speak to Flynn in such a warm manner. And for her to acknowledge their marriage. August slipped out of her husband's embrace. "I shall be with Mama while you go to visit your uncle. I am sure Charles will be delighted to see you."

"That sounds like a sensible plan, wife," replied Flynn. A happy smile sat on his face.

Augusta followed her mother. As she reached the door, she stopped and looked back. She had slept her last night in this room. From now on, it belonged solely to Victoria.

"I wonder how long before Matthew starts pressuring Victoria to give up the biggest bedroom," she muttered.

As far as she was concerned, if her brother had half a brain, he wouldn't bother. It would take more than his sweet persuasion to move Victoria and her growing library of cookbooks from the corner bedroom. The view from the window, which overlooked Berkeley Square was priceless.

Chapter Forty-Eight

"**M**y boy. My boy." In a morning full of welcome-home embraces, it was the hug which Flynn received from his uncle that was probably the most emotional. The last time he had seen Charles Cadnam weep was the day they buried the late Countess Bramshaw, Flynn's mother. That day, his tears had been ones of barely restrained grief. Today they were floods of joy.

His Aunt Erin and cousin, Christopher, were also effusive in their welcome. It took some time for the tears and hugs to finally subside.

Charles pressed a glass of whisky into Flynn's hand. His aunt disappeared, no doubt going to talk to the household cook and see what food could be quickly prepared for their unexpected guest.

Flynn took a seat on the bright yellow sofa next to his cousin. He smiled gently to himself. He doubted that anyone else in the world would own such a horrid, garishly hued pair of sofas. They were the ugliest of couches, but they also signaled that he was finally home.

"Augusta came to see me when she returned from Rome. I

am thrilled that the two of you are married. With her blue-blooded background, she will one day make an excellent Countess Bramshaw. As will you be a fine earl," said Charles.

Beside him, Christopher cleared his throat. "Speaking of earls. I think you should be made aware of how things have been since your untimely demise."

He glanced at his father, to which Charles replied, "Go ahead. Tell him all that you know."

Christopher nodded. "Your father has made it clear that he considers you dead. Over the past few months, he has taken to treating me like I am his heir. Offering gifts. Pressing money into my hand at every opportunity." He slowly shook his head as if in disbelief. Flynn could just imagine what his cousin thought of being courted by a man who, only a few years ago, had made threats against his person. Like himself, Christopher had also been a pawn in the battle between the two Cadnam brothers.

"He wanted me to move in with him at Bramshaw House. Couldn't understand why I said no. Every time I see him, he mentions that your room could be mine—I only have to say the word. Heartless, selfish knave."

A lesser man might succumb to such an offer, but Christopher was cut from the same cloth as his father. When his cousin spoke of Earl Bramshaw, his voice dripped with disdain.

"I am going to go to Bramshaw House this morning and collect what I can of my personal items. After that, I am done with my father. I won't set foot in that place again until he is cold in the ground," said Flynn.

"Let me come with you," offered Christopher. "He is keen for me to visit as often as I can, but you never know—he might not let you in. He has told the world you are dead, so you deciding to turn up on his doorstep and asking to come inside might be a tad inconvenient for the earl."

Christopher did have a valid point. And Flynn didn't have a key. He'd never had one. And if the servants of Bramshaw house thought him dead, they were unlikely to welcome him inside the house. If he came alone, there was every chance the door would be closed in his face.

It was with a good deal of reluctance that he accepted Christopher's offer of help. His cousin might well be family, but Flynn had long kept the shame of his life under his father's iron fist a closely guarded secret. Charles knew the details of various incidents, ones where Flynn had been forced to seek medical attention. Augusta had been told some things. But the truth was, no one knew the full extent of what and how Flynn had suffered over the years.

"Are you able to come with me this morning, Christopher? I would like this to be over and done with as soon as possible. Then I can go home to my wife."

And forget about my father.

Christopher rose from the sofa. "I shall get my coat. I have a personal interest in this sad and sorry state finally coming to an end. The sooner the earl knows you, his son and rightful heir is alive, the sooner he will stop badgering me. Flynn, I want you to be able to live your life as you so richly deserve, and that means never again suffering under his violent hand."

His cousin left the room.

Flynn got to his feet, and his uncle came to stand at his side. Charles put a hand on his shoulder. "Take care when you go to see my brother. I don't expect he planned for you to do a Lazarus and come back from the dead. Your reappearance will likely be problematic for him."

Life on the hard streets had taught Flynn some cold lessons. The first being that one should always be prepared for the worst. For enemies to suddenly appear out of the darkness. And for friends to turn false.

He patted the right side of his coat, checking that the short blade was where it should be, readily at hand. The knife had been a gift from Matteo, who, having seen the small weapon Flynn had been carrying for protection, had decided he was in need of a better, sharper one.

In his left jacket pocket lay the other knife. The one which had saved his life on more than one occasion. The new blade might be the more elegant weapon, but Flynn knew this knife like an old friend. An effective, deadly friend.

Besides, two lethal weapons are better than one.

"I will protect myself if my father seeks to finish his dirty work."

He was hoping that if the earl saw that he was accompanied by Christopher, he might stay his hand. But Flynn wasn't taking any chances.

Chapter Forty-Nine

H is reception at Bramshaw House was as he expected. The butler, who was at first shocked to his boots at seeing Flynn, quickly regained his composure and refused to let him in. It was only when Christopher put his boot in the door and offered a charming smile that the servant finally relented and stood aside.

"Thank you," said Flynn, marching inside and heading for the stairs. He didn't give a damn if the butler went in search of the earl. He didn't intend to linger in the house for a minute longer than was necessary.

Christopher went to follow, but Flynn stopped him. "If you go and speak to the earl, you might be able to buy me some precious time."

His cousin nodded and hastened after the butler.

Flynn reached his old bedroom and stepped inside. The door wasn't locked. The air in the room was dank and musty. From the look of things, the fire hadn't been lit in a long time. The jacket he had left on the bed, intending to mend a hole in the pocket, was exactly where he set it down a year and a half ago. Nothing had been touched.

It was as if his father had simply closed the door on his son's life and put it all in the past.

He paused for a moment, taking in the room. There was a thick layer of dust on the mantlepiece, and he dragged his finger through it. "Was this meant to be my tomb?" Without a body to bury, his old room had been left as a shrine. But this was a place at which no one had visited or prayed.

Stirring from his thoughts. Flynn hurried to the dresser. After pulling the drawer open, he snatched up a few books and an old, broken pocket watch. He silently cursed himself for not having thought to bring a satchel or bag. Not that there was much for him to carry.

He had just picked up his old journal from the side of his bed when the door crashed open.

"What the devil are you doing? Who are you! Thief! Robber! Fiend!" The earl stormed into the room. In the hallway lingered the dogs. They had the good sense not to follow their master.

Flynn rose to his full height. "My lord, I am here to collect a few meager possessions of mine. I won't be but a minute, and then I shall be out of your house. And your life." He still addressed his father in the same manner he always had, but he no longer feared his sire.

Their gazes met, and as they did, an evil grin appeared on the earl's lips. "This is my son's room. My son, Flynn, who was most cruelly murdered. Who are you to come into my house and try to steal from the dead?"

A tired sigh escaped Flynn. "You didn't succeed in killing me. I would suggest that you let me finish here. If you do, I shall try and forget that you are a foul beast."

The earl let out a roar and lunged for the fire poker. In one swift motion, he had picked it up and smashed Flynn across the chest. Flynn staggered back.

"My son is dead. You are an imposter. Die!"

In the past, Flynn would have yielded. Would have taken the beating. He'd had years of it. His father's thrashings. Berating. Abuse.

The earl was right about one thing—the night he had stabbed his son, the Flynn Cadnam of old had died. The man who now stood in his place was stronger. Braver. And not prepared to yield.

As Earl Bramshaw swung the poker a second time, Flynn caught it. He tore it from his father's grasp and tossed it behind him. It fell to the floor with a clatter. "Leave me be. As I said, I will be taking my things and going. If you let Christopher and I depart without further violence, this can all end here and now."

The words had barely left his lips before he caught the glint of a knife in his father's hand. The wicked villain planned to finish what he had started. "Oh, it will end here and now. I promise you that—you won't leave this room alive," bellowed the earl.

He leaped forward, slashing at Flynn's chest. The blow went wide, but not wide enough. It broke skin, and blood immediately stained the front of Flynn's shirt. Fiery pain exploded through him.

Shock had Flynn staggering back. He didn't have time to react before a second slash tore across his upper arm. If he didn't do something and quickly, he was going to die. The earl would win.

Rage born of years of abuse, humiliation, and violence roared to life. "No! I have everything to live for. A wife. And a child. You don't get to win," he ground out.

The earl shifted, drawing back his knife, moving in for the kill. "I won't fail this time. This time you will stay dead. And then I will come for your family. Every single one of them!"

Flynn had always been a good swordsman. The elegant hours with Matteo de Luca at the fencing academy in Rome had taught him a better technique, but the hungry, desperate days living rough had taught him how to survive. Those street-fighting skills rose to the fore. His fingers wrapped around the sharp weapon his Italian friend had gifted to him.

I will defend Augusta and our baby with my last breath if that is what it will take.

He lifted the knife and lunged. The flat blade pierced his father's chest and went deep. The earl dropped to his knees; his weapon fell from his fingers.

Flynn, clutching at his own wounds, bent in front of Earl Bramshaw. He met his father's eyes. They were full of fury and hatred. The earl's lips were moving, but all that came out of them was a horrid wheezing, and blood.

The light in the earl's eyes began to dim. He was dying.

"Why did you hate me? All I ever did to you was to be born your son. You blame me for being the reason why my mother detested you, why she couldn't bear to speak your name. But it wasn't me. It was you—you did that all on your own."

There came the sound of running feet. Then shouting. Christopher appeared in Flynn's line of sight. His cousin turned to the wide-eyed servant who had followed him. "Call for a physician."

"I don't think a doctor will help Lord Bramshaw," said Flynn.

"Not for him, for you."

Flynn's knees went from under him as he turned back and glanced at his father. He dropped to the floor. Christopher came and knelt beside Flynn, who waved him away. "Check on the earl, make sure he can't harm anyone else."

Christopher lifted his uncle up in his arms. A long, painful rattle rocked through Earl Bramshaw's chest, and then it all went silent.

His cousin quietly swore, then murmured, "Your father is dead."

Earl Bramshaw had lived a life of cruelty and violence, and now it had cost him his life.

Chapter Fifty

Augusta and her mother had been busy deciding how best to repurpose three adjoining rooms on the fourth floor of Mowbray House into a private suite of rooms. They had finally settled on which pieces of furniture would go where, when Augusta suddenly dismissed the servants who had been assisting them.

I have to set us back on an even keel. We cannot go on like this.

As soon as they were alone, she turned to her mother. From the unshed tears in Lady Anne's eyes, it seemed she wasn't the only one wishing things were better between them.

"We have to do something about this awful tension which exists between us. Find a way to be able to deal with one another."

The duchess promptly burst into tears, and mother and daughter quickly embraced. "I'm sorry I lied to you in Rome. I'm sorry I hurt you. I'm sorry for so many things, Augusta," sobbed Lady Anne.

Augusta hugged her. "And I'm sorry too. I was so angry with you over leaving Papa and all the lies that I couldn't stand to be in the same room as you. Those final weeks in Rome were terrible."

Giving voice to her pain brought it all back. But she had to tell her mother the truth of how she had felt. Why she had kept things from her. And still did.

"Is that why you didn't invite me to your wedding? To punish me."

Augusta winced at the painful accusation. She had stopped being angry with her mother, and was slowly finding her way to forgive, but nothing could change the past. Of what both women had done. "At first, I considered that keeping you in the dark about my marriage was a way to strike a blow against you. But I soon realized that was a foolish notion. How could I hurt you if you didn't know? I had thought that the idea of you missing out on me marrying and raising a family back in England might help to change your mind and make you get on board the boat. But you didn't say anything when Gideon and Serafina were married, so I decided you didn't really care."

"Of course, I cared. I was in a terrible frame of mind at that time. I knew I had been a fool, but I couldn't find a way to come home and save face. In the end, it was your father's love letters that made the choice for me. If he could still love me after all I had put him through, it would be utter madness for me to stay behind."

She hadn't understood what had happened between her parents. Gideon had made vague mention of matters, but nothing was clear. Now seemed as good a time as any to ask. "Why did you want to leave Papa?"

The duchess wiped at her face. "I thought he didn't love me anymore. That he had given up on us. We stopped fighting. I know it sounds silly, possibly even trite, but those rows have always been our way of expressing our passion, and when they ceased— it broke my heart."

Augusta had always thought her parents' marriage too fiery, but it hadn't ever occurred to her that without that grand emotion, her mother couldn't breathe. That she lived for her husband's love, and without it, she was lost.

"Oh, Mama," she sighed. After Flynn, loss was something she could well understand.

Things between the duke and duchess were still strained, but Augusta could sense her parents were slowly finding their way back to one another. As she crossed the downstairs foyer this morning, Augusta had spied them sharing a tender kiss and exchanging whispered sweet words of affection. The spark had returned to her father's eyes.

"Since we are having this conversation, may I ask why you didn't tell Gideon or Serafina about the wedding? I can understand why you would have excluded me, but not your brother. Or his new bride."

Augusta nodded. "Flynn and I agreed that if he knew of our wedding, Gideon would demand that my husband came home with me. And I didn't tell Serafina because it would have been unfair to ask her to keep it a secret."

"Which leads me to the next obvious question. Why didn't Flynn come home with us?"

That question had been something which had taken some time for Augusta to get her head around, but the long sea voyage home had granted her moments of reflection in which she finally was able to see things from Flynn's point of view.

"Matteo and Count Nico de Luca were teaching him about how their shipping company works so that he could take up a position with de Luca Shipping here in London." She paused for a moment, considering her next words carefully. "His other, more personal reason was that he wanted to experience the eternal city on his own terms. Having money in his pocket meant he could finally do that."

It had taken her some time to come to terms with Flynn's

request, but Augusta had finally made peace with it. The man she loved had suffered through a great deal—she could not have denied him that small boon.

We have a lifetime ahead in which to spend together.

"Before the people of the All Saints' congregation found him, Flynn was living hand to mouth. Did you know he walked most of the two hundred and seventy miles from Florence to Rome?"

The duchess slowly shook her head. "I had no idea. And what with all the drama surrounding Gideon and Serafina's wedding and then trying to smooth things over with her father, I didn't get the opportunity to spend a moment with Flynn."

"You also had some other pressing matters of your own that were demanding your attention." She took her mother gently by the hand. "I am glad you did focus on the most important matters, that you made the decision to come home. Now that Flynn is here, you can find the time to sit and talk to him. To understand what he has suffered."

Lady Anne had been through enough herself, and Augusta could well understand that she had been forced to swallow a good deal of pride and make the trip back to England. To not only return to her husband, but to face down the disapproving matrons of the *haut ton*.

"And you and I will also need to talk and make plans." A soft smile formed on Augusta's lips. "Because your first grandchild is on its way."

The duchess gasped. "A baby! Oh, Augusta. Oh, my darling, that is delightful news. I've wanted to be a grandmother for such a long time."

Relief coursed through Augusta. Finally, she had been able to share the news of her pregnancy with her mother. The long weeks of keeping it a secret had been exhausting.

She had suffered privately through the early months of

her pregnancy—first with sensitive breasts and backache, then the queasiness of morning sickness.

"Have you seen a doctor? I mean, to confirm that you are with child?" asked Lady Anne.

"No, I haven't. It's been hard enough keeping my marriage a secret, let alone a baby," replied Augusta.

"I shall send for the family physician at once. If you know when you last had your courses, he should be able to give you an indication of when your baby is due."

"That would be lovely. Thank you, Mama."

It would take time to repair their relationship. The past few months had seen lies and secrets told and kept by both mother and daughter. But if the duke could find it in his heart to forgive his wife for the pain she had caused him, it was only right that Augusta did the same.

This family has suffered enough over the past year. We deserve happiness.

She included her husband in that thought. Flynn had become part of the Kembal clan. The two of them were soon to become three, creating their own little branch of the greater Kembal and Radley family trees.

That thought pulled her up.

I'm a Cadnam now—a whole new family that I need to learn more about.

There were other people in Flynn's family aside from his odious father, and she owed it to her unborn child to become acquainted with them. To repair some of the damage that Earl Bramshaw had wrought.

Lady Anne pointed toward the door. "While we wait for the doctor, let's go and take a look in my dressing room. I kept some of my lovely gowns from when I was carrying Coco, and while they might be a tad out of fashion, I am sure we could get the modiste to remake them into something for you to wear."

Augusta glanced down at the top of her bodice. It was tight, and she suspected it wouldn't be too much longer before she wouldn't fit any of her clothes. "That would be lovely."

Searching through gowns that she could repurpose for her pregnancy would take her mind off the other issue which concentrated her thoughts, that of Flynn and how things were going at Bramshaw House. The sooner he returned, and she knew he was safe, the better.

Chapter Fifty-One

✿

S houting followed by the echo of boots on the staircase
had Lady Anne dropping the gown she held in her hands
and rushing for the door. Augusta followed her mother out of
the dressing room and into the hall.

Lord Stephen Kembal appeared at the top of the stairs
and caught Augusta's eye. "Flynn's been stabbed."

"No!" cried Augusta.

Not again. Not now. After everything they had been
through, fate couldn't be so cruel.

She dashed for the stairs. Reaching the bottom, she
stepped aside as her father, Gideon, and Christopher Cadnam
carried Flynn in through the front door. Her gaze went to her
husband, and for a brief moment, her heart skipped a beat.

Flynn glanced over at her and gave his wife a tentative
smile. "It's just a couple of flesh wounds—the bloody mess on
my shirt makes it seem worse than it is." He spoke through
gritted teeth, and it was clear he was in a great deal of pain.

*Please, Lord, don't take him from me. Not after all we have been
through.*

The men headed up the stairs.

To her relief, the doctor who had been summoned to confirm her pregnancy arrived at that minute. The duchess quickly instructed him to follow her as she made her way to the staircase.

Stephen came and put a comforting arm around his sister. "He's alive, G. That's a good start."

Augusta forced a tight smile to her lips. Her brother was right; Flynn was alive. And he was conscious. She had to hold onto those two good signs while praying that her husband was right about it only being a flesh wound.

"He was going to see his father this morning. To retrieve his things. What on earth must have happened?"

Upstairs, while the doctor worked stitching Flynn's wounded chest and arm, the others gathered out in the hallway. Augusta wanted to be with her husband, but Flynn had shooed her away, asking that the physician be allowed to work in peace.

"What the devil did Earl Bramshaw do? I am assuming this is his vile handiwork," demanded the duke.

Christopher Cadnam nodded. "We went to Bramshaw House to retrieve Flynn's things. His father attacked him. But unlike the first time the earl tried to murder my cousin, Flynn was armed. He defended himself."

He closed his eyes and gave a deep sigh. "Ronald Cadnam is dead. Flynn is now Earl Bramshaw."

The room began to spin, and Augusta clutched at the air. Her mind had only caught the words Flynn and dead.

Flynn. Dead. Not again.

Strong arms caught her.

It was a good few minutes before she was able to open her eyes. When she did, Augusta found herself lying on her sister Victoria's bed. Her mother was seated next to her. "Flynn, she is awake," announced the duchess.

"Are you alright, my love?" he asked. Augusta lifted her head and caught a glimpse of Flynn. Her husband was alive.

Oh, thank god.

He waved to her from across the room, where he lay on her bed. The doctor was busy wrapping a bandage around Flynn's chest, assisted by Stephen. Her father and Christopher were nowhere to be seen.

Lady Anne patted her daughter's hand. "Your father and Christopher have gone back to Bramshaw House. The authorities will need to be informed, and the body of the late earl seen to by a physician."

"I want to sit up," said Augusta. She slowly rose, aided by her mother.

On the other side of the room, Flynn was being propped up by a pile of pillows which had been stuffed behind his back. Apart from the pained expression on his face, he actually appeared to be alright. It was only when she caught a glimpse of his bloodied shirt on the floor that Augusta was reminded that he had been badly wounded. That she had nearly lost him a second time.

"There. Now you need to stay in bed for the next few days, Lord Bramshaw. No sudden movements, or the stitches won't take," said the doctor.

"Thank you. Yes, I understand about the stitches. Unfortunately, this is not my first knife wound," replied Flynn. He gave a half laugh, then winced. "And I won't be making any sudden movements, rest assured."

The Duchess and Lord Stephen accompanied the doctor out of the room. Augusta got slowly to her feet and made her way over to her husband. She stopped by the bedside. "I swear you have been sent to try me, Flynn Cadnam."

He offered her a grin. "I know, but I don't mean to. It just seems to happen."

Augusta pulled up a chair and sat. The day had started off

so bright and full of hope, now she had no idea what was to come next. "Christopher told us your father is dead."

Flynn sighed. "Yes. I have far too much to live for, so when it came down to it being a case of either him or me who died, the choice was obvious. He got a couple of blows in, including the blade that tore my brand-new shirt to shreds; damn him. I really liked that shirt."

She wanted so much to laugh at his jest, but this was all too close to the pain that she had endured in the months that she had thought Flynn dead. "You fought for your life. For our future. No one can blame you for what you did."

He reached out, and they joined hands.

"I told Mama about the baby. That's why the doctor arrived so quickly. He had already been called for me," she explained.

"Ah, now I understand. I couldn't figure out how he managed to get here so soon. I am pleased that he did. This cut might not have hit anything major, but blade and flesh still don't mix well."

Augusta bowed her head. She was already emotional with the baby, but Flynn's injuries made her want to cry her heart out. "What will happen now? I mean with your father's death. You are now Earl Bramshaw."

"I have no idea. This isn't the way I wanted things to end with him, but somehow, I sensed it was always going to happen. As for the title—it's the least of my concerns.

He wasn't dead, and that was a blessing he gave thanks for many times over during the next hours and into the following day. Flynn remained in Augusta's bed, while she slept in Victoria's. Her sister kindly decamped to Lady Coco's bedroom, where a second bed was hastily set up.

In the middle of the night, he woke to find Augusta seated on the chair beside the bed. Her head was in her arms, which were resting on the edge of the mattress. She was fast asleep. He thought to wake her and tell her to go back to bed, but seeing that she was breathing deeply in slumber, Flynn decided to let his wife be. She needed her sleep.

You have been through enough.

The morning brought the authorities, and questions. His Uncle Charles sat listening while Flynn went through his side of the story. Of what had happened from the moment he and Christopher had entered Bramshaw House, to the last few minutes when he had been carried out to the town carriage owned by the Duke of Mowbray.

There was a good deal of hums and furious notetaking on the part of the examiners. What he had assumed was a clear-cut case of self-defense clearly wasn't viewed in the same manner by those investigating the death of the late Earl Bramshaw. He could only hope the testimony from Christopher was viewed as solid.

As for the staff at Bramshaw House, their evidence may well prove crucial to his future. Where their loyalties lay was, however, a matter for conjecture. From what Flynn understood, they had remained silent during the inquiry over his disappearance, and he was worried that they might see this as the perfect opportunity to finally be rid of him. To have any evidence that might incriminate them in his assault and abduction buried once and for all.

I expect there are one or two of them who would do that in order to save themselves.

"Thank you, Lord Bramshaw. We will finish taking statements from the rest of the household staff at Bramshaw House this morning. Your cousin, Christopher Cadnam, has given his version of events. Now the matter will be handed to the courts to decide if there are sufficient grounds for you to answer any case over the death of your father," said the lead investigator, closing up his notebook and rising. He and his junior assistant left the room.

Charles took up the seat recently vacated by the investigator. "I can't believe they actually insisted on questioning you while you are injured," he huffed.

It was good to have people like his uncle on his side. Flynn was going through yet another of his life's misfortunes, but this time he wasn't alone. He wasn't at risk of being tossed into the sea, nor was he sleeping rough under a bridge.

"They have a job to do. Justice must not only be served but seen to be done." He reached out to his uncle. "Could I ask a favor? Would you please find Augusta and see how she is? I'm worried about her. She is with child."

A smiling but pensive Charles nodded. "Of course, I shall go and find Augusta. I am so relieved to know that you are going to recover. And a baby, gosh."

Flynn closed his eyes the minute Charles left the room. He intended to take a short nap, but when he opened his eyes, it was dark outside. He'd slept the afternoon away.

"Come in," he replied to the knock which came at the door. Augusta, the Duke and Duchess of Mowbray, Charles, and several other gentlemen all filed slowly into the room. There was a sense of doom in their every footstep.

"These gentlemen wish to speak to you," said the duke.

Flynn's gaze tracked Augusta's progress to the other side of the room. When the Duchess of Mowbray took hold of her hand, his heart sank. If this meeting was a mere formality, his wife and mother-in-law wouldn't be keeping their distance. He took a deep breath and faced the strangers. "Yes?"

A piece of paper was produced, and one of the men read from it. Flynn caught most of it. "On this day of our Lord." "Did feloniously, willfully."

The word which did land hard in his mind was *murder*.

Augusta let out a soul-piercing cry of anguish.

But Flynn couldn't go to her; instead, he was helped from the bed and to his feet. Then he was led out of the room and downstairs to a waiting carriage. No one from his family was allowed to come with him. The only blessing was that he was permitted to take an overcoat and a warm scarf.

The door of the carriage closed, and a shell-shocked Flynn turned to the man who had arrested him. "Where are you taking me?"

"Earl Bramshaw, you are to be tried for murder in the House of Lords by a jury of your peers. In the meantime, you will be taken by boat along the River Thames to the Tower of London and received through Traitors' Gate."

The Tower of London?

Flynn had heard of the right of privilege, where nobles could be excused for their crimes if they were found guilty in the English parliament, but he wasn't entirely clear on how it actually worked.

"So, what happens if I am found guilty? Do I have to go and live abroad? Or do I pay a substantial fine?" Not that he was guilty, but Flynn wanted to be fully aware of what punishment might lay ahead for him if things did go awry.

The arresting officer turned to his companion, who nodded. "I'm afraid that there are two offenses where the law of noble privilege do not apply. Treason is one. The other is murder. If you are found guilty of the murder of your father, then you, Earl Bramshaw, will hang."

Chapter Fifty-Two

"Quite a few famous people have been housed in the Tower of London," noted the guard. The gray-bearded, well-intended guard loved to play tour guide. He just didn't seem to appreciate that for Flynn and Augusta, this wasn't home. "This place has seen the best and the worst. Queen Elizabeth. Sir Walter Raleigh. Several of King Henry the Eighth's wives—"

"Yes, thank you. You certainly know your history of the Tower of London. Do you think perhaps my wife and I might have a moment's privacy?" asked Flynn.

He was being held in the Beauchamp Tower, which at least had some windows affording light. The rooms Flynn had been assigned were comfortable. Not the warmest, but they were far preferable to a prison cell. Having more than one room also meant that Augusta was able to come and stay.

Not that he had been in favor of her doing so, but his wife was stubborn. And he could confess to a degree of relief when he woke during the night to find her sleeping beside him.

The prison guard gave Flynn a knowing wink and took his leave. He left the door open, for which Flynn was most grateful.

They were still bound by the outer walls of the Tower of London but being able to enjoy the sunshine instead of sitting staring at dark stone walls was something Flynn welcomed. Walks around the castle grounds with Augusta helped to keep him sane.

While he was doing his best not to go mad, his wife was busy working on his defense.

"Now, I spoke to several people this morning while I was out," she began. Augusta hadn't been charged with any crime, so she could come and go as she pleased. As could the rest of his many visitors. Friends and family were a constant in his life, for which Flynn was grateful. He had never fully embraced the loneliness of his existence in Italy.

"I have employed the services of a special agent. He is making discreet enquiries as to the staff at Bramshaw House and what happened when you disappeared. Money was apparently exchanged with several parties."

Flynn scowled. "What has that to do with the charge of murder?"

Augusta shifted in her seat. It was now a month after the death of the earl, and her baby bump was beginning to show. If there were any justice in the world, his wife would be at home knitting baby booties, not dealing with his murder trial.

"Your defense counsel, who I also saw this morning and who is coming to visit later today, thinks that any evidence we can put together that might discredit the witnesses for the prosecution is worth chasing down. If the jury hears that the Bramshaw House servants were in on your kidnapping last year, then they won't place much faith in what might be said by those same people in court."

Augusta was like a dog with a bone; she wouldn't let go. Not until she had got what she wanted.

And she wants me, along with our baby, to live happily ever after.

She had always viewed her stubbornness as a character fault, but over the past weeks, Augusta had found that it was her strongest asset. Where other women might have given up and broken down in tears, she was determined to keep going. There had to be a way to save her husband.

When Flynn's defense counsel, along with her father, arrived later that day, she had a long list of questions ready.

"Has the prosecution given you a list of the witnesses they intend to call? Who are they, and what do they have to do with this case? Is there anyone else we should be calling? Are we going with a plea of manslaughter or not guilty?"

The lawyer cleared his throat. "I think we should be going with a plea of not guilty. I am going to press the case of self-defense. The earl attacked Flynn first."

Across the old wooden table, the Duke of Mowbray nodded his approval. "What happens if the jury finds Earl Bramshaw guilty of manslaughter?"

"Well, then he can claim the right of privilege, and they will have to release him."

A few heads were nodding at these words. Flynn's oddly did not.

"What's wrong with that outcome?" pressed Augusta.

He shook his head. "It means I will be free, but I will also be tainted forever as the man who killed his father and got away with it. I worry what this will do to our children in the future. And how much of a stain this will leave on the Cadnam name over the years."

Augusta's hands balled into fists. *And they say that I am stubborn.* "I don't care what people say, just as long as you walk free. No one gave a damn when your father treated you like dirt. No one stopped the earl from beating you. I will have firm, public words with anyone who wants to take issue with you winning this case."

"Thank you," whispered her husband.

Flynn's lawyer pulled out a folio of papers and opened it. "We have the official death report from the attending physician." He spread the papers out on the table. Included in them were several pages of drawings. Sketches of both the late earl and his injuries, as well as the one the investigators had made of Flynn and his wounds.

Unlike when Flynn had gone missing, these investigators had done a thorough job. Her finger tapped the drawing of her husband and the markings of his recent and old wounds. "How do we know which ones were inflicted by the earl's father?"

Flynn picked up the paper, nodded, then set it on the table in front of everyone. "There is a legend on the side of the page. The light lines marked on my body are from the original January 1817 attack and previous times. The dark lines are from this latest one. And the dotted lines... hmmm... they are from my time in Italy."

The room fell silent as they all took in the sketches of Flynn's body, and the scars and wounds which he bore. Augusta knew them all intimately, but it still had her gulping down tears.

"The late earl's wounds are, of course, fewer but clearer," observed the lawyer. He had been engaged by the Duke of Mowbray, and Augusta didn't want to guess how much money and favors her father had offered up in order to retain him. He was considered the best legal mind in the country. If anyone could get Flynn justice, it was Sir James Pence.

Sir James rose from the table and bowed to Augusta. "Countess Bramshaw, may I have a word with you in private?"

A mystified Augusta got to her feet and followed the defense lawyer to a corner out of earshot of her husband and father. She turned to face the table, just in time to see the duke ushering Flynn outside. "Perhaps now is a good time for us to take a stroll in the tower grounds," said her father.

Once they were alone, Sir James cleared his throat. "In my opinion, the evidence is evenly balanced. My concern is what the prosecution might present on the day. And whom they intend to call as witnesses. I have found witnesses to be unreliable. In this case, I wouldn't be the least bit surprised if some of the late earl's servants lie under oath."

This wasn't promising news. Not that Augusta hadn't been expecting to hear something bad. Nothing seemed to be going right. "What can we do?"

Sir James's gaze dropped to the stone flagging of the prison room. "Two things. One, make sure Lord Bramshaw goes over his written testimony, so that it can hold up under examination. I am hoping he won't have to give evidence, but we shall see. And two...."

He glanced at the door then leaned in. "Start making discreet inquiries as to ships sailing out of England on the day of the trial. You will also need to find people who can be bribed to snatch a prisoner in between leaving the House of Lords and coming back here. If the jury finds your husband guilty of murder, you must get him out of the country as fast as possible."

Blinking hard with shock, Augusta nodded her agreement. She was not going to lose Flynn a second time. If they had to flee England and go live in exile, it would be worth it.

"Of course, I cannot directly give you the details of anyone who may be willing to commit the crime of springing a prisoner, but who knows? I might just happen to accidentally drop a piece of paper on my way to the door. And as fate may have it, that piece of paper might contain the name of a gentleman who is skilled in dealing with situations that require a degree of brute force. I suggest you avail yourself of a large sum of money, preferably in guineas, just in case you need to engage his services. He will expect a substantial nonrefundable retainer." He cleared his throat. "Or so I would assume."

Sir James bowed and took his leave. When he reached the door, he stopped and rummaged violently in his pocket. He pulled out a handkerchief and wiped his face before continuing on his way. His footsteps were still echoing up the stone steps as Augusta scurried across the room and snatched up the piece of paper which had fallen from his coat onto the floor. She tucked it into the bodice of her gown.

"No one is hanging my husband."

Chapter Fifty-Three

She came to him in the quiet of the night, naked and hungry. Flynn closed his eyes as Augusta blessed his face with soft kisses. Her lips trailed down his neck, then to his chest. "Flynn," she whispered as she touched along the healing scars of his latest knife wounds. A hot tear seared his skin.

Flynn lay silent in the bed, sensing she needed the tactile sensation of skin on skin rather than speech. The night before his trial, he was prepared to give his wife anything. His all.

Her fingers drifted over his lower belly. He gasped as she took a firm grip of his erection and gave it a tug. This woman. His woman. She knew exactly how to touch him. How to give him what he desired. "Augusta." The word escaped his lips as she took him into her mouth and drew back.

His eyes opened, and he stared up at the heavy oak beams which crossed the roof overhead. Augusta set to her task with skill, lavishing her hot, soft lips and tongue over his sensitive flesh. There was nothing he could do but lay his hands on the sheets and accept her worship.

The tension within his body built. It would be so easy to just lie here and let his wife bring him to climax. But she deserved more. Augusta had always deserved more from him.

Flynn brushed his hand over her hair. "G, come to me," he commanded.

She continued to work him with her mouth, finally releasing him from the pleasure when he gripped her shoulder and spoke. "I need to see your face when you come. Please, my love."

Augusta crawled up the bed, straddling Flynn. He held her hips as she positioned herself over him, then sunk slowly down onto his cock. Their gasps echoed off the stone walls of the cell.

He touched his palm to the soft swell of her belly. To where their child, his child, lay deep within Augusta's womb. "You are so beautiful."

She rocked her hips back and forth, riding him. Flynn's hands settled on her breasts, cupping them. Augusta had always been a well-endowed woman, but with her pregnancy, she had grown even more bountiful. He pinched her nipples, and she let out a groan of need.

When Augusta's movements became more frantic, he gripped the top of her legs, urging her on. "Take what you need—let me give this to you."

She came with a sigh which went straight to his manhood, sending Flynn over the edge and into a deep well of pleasure.

"I love you... you are my life, G."

"I love you too, Flynn. No one will ever tear us apart again."

Chapter Fifty-Four

⚜

The Morning Herald
19th August 1818

Earl Bramshaw to be tried for murder.
It gives this correspondent no joy to report that the trial of the newly
minted Earl Bramshaw, formerly Viscount Cadnam, is to go ahead
today at the House of Lords. After hearing the various rumors which
have been circulating around London regarding the previous earl,
and his brutal treatment of his son, one can only pray, dear reader,
that justice is served.

F lynn would have much preferred to have gone by road for the journey from the Tower of London to Westminster, but he was overruled. There was a long history of tower prisoners being ferried back and forth along the River Thames, and that was especially true for nobles. When it came to the trial of peers of the realm, tradition was to be observed. He was to go to court as he had arrived, by boat.

Leaving the Tower of London, Augusta had protested, demanding that she be allowed to travel with her husband, but the guards and officials refused. Prisoners only. His wife was a picture of barely-held-together anguish as her father came and took her away.

Thank heavens for the understanding Duke of Mowbray. For a man who had been through his own trials of late, he hadn't hesitated to offer Flynn any and all forms of assistance when asked.

If things went badly today, he was going to need to call on his father-in-law one last time. To keep Augusta safe and help raise their child. A child Flynn would never know.

In the boat, he sat and observed the River Thames. The breeze rustling through his hair was a welcome change from the closed-in air of the Tower of London. Other vessels moving up and down the river provided a welcome distraction.

Please, Lord, let me never have to set foot in that place again.

At the end of their journey along the river, the boat drew in at the small dockside below the Palace of Westminster. Flynn was taken up a set of ancient stone steps and into the building. The guards from the Tower bowed as they handed him over to the court guards. "Lord Bramshaw."

"Thank you, gentlemen, you have been most kind to my wife and me. Please don't take this personally, but I hope never to see any of you ever again." If he was found guilty, he would be back in the Tower of London before nightfall.

He was led through a large, heavy oak door and along a narrow corridor. Flynn still found it hard to accept that he was the earl, and when people spoke to him, he kept looking over his shoulder, expecting to see his father.

But he is dead. At my hand.

Reaching the end of the walk, Flynn was ushered into a small antechamber and told to take a seat. He dropped onto a hard wooden bench and sat, head bowed. He threaded his fingers together, grateful that they hadn't clapped him in irons. That would have been the ultimate humiliation.

After a few minutes wait, a man dressed in a dark suit and wearing a long black judge's robe stepped into the room. A wave of nausea rolled over Flynn at the sight. While the man had a pleasant enough look about him, his manner of dress still reminded Flynn of the legendary Hanging Judge Jeffreys who had sentenced hundreds of so-called traitors to death following the English civil war.

That will not be my fate. They can't execute me.

That thought kept pulsing through his brain. He didn't want to consider what might happen if he was found guilty of murder. His life would be destroyed. And though his wife and unborn child would survive, they would be ruined.

"Earl Bramshaw. We haven't met before, but I am Earl Talbot. I will be acting as Lord High Steward for your trial. You are to be tried by a jury of twenty-three of your noble peers. To return a verdict of either guilty or not guilty only requires a simple majority of not less than twelve."

Flynn nodded. He had spoken with his father-in-law the previous afternoon, and the Duke of Mowbray had explained some of what was to happen. With an election having been recently held, parliament had been prorogued until the new year. The House of Lords was not in session. Flynn was to be spared the indignity of a trial before the full house.

"You will shortly be brought before me at the Lord High Steward's Court. I thought it only fair that you understand what is to happen today and how the case is to proceed," explained Lord Talbot.

"Thank you. I appreciate you coming to offer me your instruction. May I ask if, when I am before the court, will I be granted the opportunity to explain what happened?"

The door to the small chamber opened, and Augusta

walked in. She took one look at the black-robed judge, then Flynn and let out a sob of distress. To Flynn's relief, Clifford Kembal followed close on his daughter's heels.

The Duke of Mowbray put a comforting arm around Augusta and placed a kiss on her brow. "We must trust in English justice. Come now. Give your husband your best wishes, then let us go and find somewhere to sit."

Lord Talbot's gaze settled briefly on Augusta's pregnant belly. He shook his head, then quickly took his leave.

The agreement Flynn had struck with the duke was for Augusta not to sit through the whole court case, but rather for her to wait somewhere nearby. He didn't want his wife having to endure the retelling of the bloody violence which had taken place at Bramshaw House.

Flynn rose from his seat and took Augusta in his arms. "Augusta, my love, I need you to be brave for me. Can you do that?"

Her head was resting against his chest, and she gave the merest of nods. He doubted Augusta was capable of much more. He couldn't blame her. She had already lost him once before. He dared not imagine what was going through her mind now at the prospect of him being found guilty of murder.

Placing a finger under her chin, Flynn lifted Augusta's face, and she met his gaze. Her eyes glistened with unshed tears. Her lips were held tightly together. He bent and kissed her.

"I didn't survive that first attack and then all that time in Italy just to lose to my father now. We will prevail."

He wanted to tell her that was a promise, but he couldn't lie to his wife. Nothing was certain. Augusta was bravely trying to maintain her composure as her father led her from the room. The duke gave a nod at Flynn as he left.

A short time later, Flynn was taken into another room where the Gentleman Usher of the Black Rod brought him to the Bar. After some minor formalities, Earl Bramshaw was formally arraigned by the Clerk of the Parliaments on the indictment, charged with murder. When asked how he pleaded, Flynn answered in a clear and steady voice, "Not guilty."

Prior to leaving the Tower of London, he had been informed that there wasn't much evidence to be presented, and only a handful of witnesses were to be called. He and his father had been the only ones in the room at the time of the bloody encounter, and apart from Christopher and the butler, there were no other witnesses. The trial should be a mercifully short one.

With the charge now laid and read, he was shown to a chair and made to sit facing the jury.

To Flynn's right, another robed gentleman rose from his seat. His gaze settled on him. This was the man who had been chosen to act on behalf of the prosecution. What he had to say could very well change the course of Flynn's entire life.

What if I am found guilty? What will I do?

His meeting the hangman's noose would be the ultimate act of revenge from his late father. The earl reaching out to claim Flynn's life from beyond the grave.

To his relief, the prosecution first called his cousin. Christopher Cadnam gave a full and honest account of what had happened that morning. For a man who stood to benefit should Flynn hang, Christopher was an impressive and reliable witness.

Then came the Bramshaw House butler. Flynn shifted in his seat. This was a man who had taken particular delight in tormenting him over the years. The butler had clearly been shocked to find Flynn standing on the doorstep that morning.

If anyone had a reason to want to see Flynn out of the picture, it was him.

"Did you see the accused stab the victim?"

Flynn focused on the butler. From what he could recall, the man had been outside in the hallway, not entering the room until the earl was already dead.

The butler met his gaze, and Flynn's heart skipped into a fast, erratic beat. If the butler lied, this could well spell the end for him.

"I was in the hall. Mister Christopher Cadnam was the only one who entered the room. But I think by the time he did, the fight was already over."

The prosecutor cleared his throat. "So, the accused had already attacked the victim?"

Twisted words. Flynn bit down on his bottom lip. That was not what had happened. He was the victim, not the perpetrator.

"I don't know. All I know is that when I entered the room, the earl was lying in his nephew's arms. The viscount was also on the floor—he was bleeding from the chest and the arm. And there was a fire poker on the carpet just behind him."

The prosecution muttered something under his breath. This line of questioning was clearly not going as well as he had hoped. This witness wasn't handing him the winning blow.

"So, Viscount Cadnam had also struck his father with the poker?" Now he was fishing, looking for anything that could nail Flynn to the wall.

Flynn sat stony-faced, but all the while he was desperate to leap to his feet and cry, *"That's not what happened!"* His gaze shifted to his defense counsel, who gave a mere shake of his head. Their time would be coming.

The butler, to his credit, also shook his head. "No. If

anything, it would have been the earl who had hit his son. The poker, along with his cane, was one of the late Earl Bramshaw's favorite weapons of torture. He was a big man, and he beat his son at every opportunity."

A gasp of horror echoed in the room. The prosecution turned and wagged a finger at the jury. "That is not in evidence in this case. And, therefore, purely hearsay. You should disregard that last remark."

The judge nodded his agreement, but from the expressions on the faces of the jury, and the small smile on his lawyer's lips, Flynn could tell that the damage had been done. The butler had landed a heavy and decisive blow for the defense.

The prosecutor quickly dismissed the witness, then addressed the jury once more. "My Lords, ignoring the thoughts and opinions of witnesses, the simple indisputable fact is that the only person who was responsible for the death of Earl Bramshaw was his son and heir, Viscount Flynn Cadnam. The accused killed his father. You must find him guilty."

That pretty much sums it up. I was there, and I was the one who wielded the knife which killed my father. But as much as I wished him dead at times, I didn't murder him.

He glanced up at the judge. Lord Talbot wasn't paying attention to the prosecutions closing arguments. Instead, his gaze was fixed on something to the right of Flynn.

Flynn turned, and he let out a small gasp.

Moving to settle into a seat at the front of the public gallery was Augusta. To the right of her was the Duke of Mowbray, to her left, her uncle, Ewan Radley, the Duke of Strathmore. She was wearing a gown which did nothing to hide her pregnant belly.

When he tore his gaze away, Flynn caught sight of the jurors. To a man, they were all staring at Augusta. She didn't meet their enquiring looks, rather she sat, hands folded in her lap and stared at the floor. Her message was silent but powerful. She believed in her husband's innocence, and she would stand by him.

The judge and jury only stirred when the prosecutor spoke again. "The prosecution rests its case, your honor."

Sir James Pence rose to his feet. Flynn could sense he was eager to get on with the defense. To capitalize on Augusta's arrival and the show of support from two of the most powerful men in London. "My lords. The evidence is indisputable. Earl Bramshaw killed his father. What is in dispute, however, is the sequence of events. If it pleases the court, I would like to call Baron Halford to the stand."

Flynn's brows knitted together. Baron Henry Halford was the private physician of both King George and the Prince Regent. What had he to do with a murder trial?

A hum of whispers and words rippled through the room as the baron took a seat in front of the jury.

Sir James bowed his head. "Thank you for coming today."

The defense counsel picked up a piece of paper and handed it to the witness. Flynn caught a glimpse of one of the sketches Sir James had produced at the discussion they had held in his prison rooms.

"Could you please explain to the jury, in layman's terms, what this drawing is and what it means?" said Sir James.

Lord Halford nodded. "This is a post-mortem sketch of the body of the late Earl Bramshaw. On it is marked where the mortal knife wound was received. That part of the body is the lung."

Sir James nodded. "And what is the relevance of the lung in this matter?"

Flynn sat up in his chair and paid close attention. He hadn't heard any of this evidence before, so he didn't understand what it meant.

"The relevance of the lung is that once it is pierced, it collapses, and the victim struggles to breathe. From what the post-mortem tells us, the other lung of the late earl also collapsed at the same time. In layman's terms, it means that death is almost immediate."

Which was exactly how it happened. He was dying before he hit the floor.

Silence hung in the air. No one stirred. They were all on the edge of their seats, waiting to hear what came next.

Sir James turned to the jury. "So, Lord Halford, would that mean that the earl couldn't have attacked or stabbed his son once he had been stabbed?"

"Correct."

Flynn's lips began to move. His brain was filling in the gaps.

"Which means, according to the medical evidence, Earl Bramshaw would've had to have been the aggressor in this situation. To have attacked first."

Flynn shot a look at Augusta. Her eyes were closed, and she was sucking in deep breaths. Beside her, the Duke of Mowbray was slowly nodding.

"Yes. From the markings on the body and also the wounds on the current Earl Bramshaw, that is my considered opinion. The late earl attacked first, and then his son stabbed him. From my examination, I would suggest that it was an act of self-defense."

He didn't know where to look. He dared not chance another glance at Augusta. Flynn couldn't stand to watch if her hopes, which he guessed were soaring as high as his now were, came crashing down with an unfavorable verdict.

They had to find him not guilty. Or at the very worst guilty of manslaughter. His life had to finally be his to live.

He readied himself to be called as a witness. The truth

and nothing but the truth would come from his lips. And then he would wait for judgement.

"Thank you, Baron Halford. You may step down." Sir James bowed to the judge. "The defense rests its case."

And then he sat.

Wait, that's it? That's all he is going to say.

Flynn's brows knitted together. Perhaps he had got it wrong, and there was another part of the trial where he would get to speak. Things were happening far too quickly.

Lord Talbot leaned back in his chair and took a deep breath. "Well then, if that is all the evidence, and it is still early afternoon, I shall instruct the jury to retire and consider its verdict."

A perplexed Flynn was led back to the holding room. He had not been given the opportunity to speak in his own defense. It didn't sit well. He had spent his entire life being powerless against his father, and the one chance that he might've had to speak out against the earl had been taken away from him.

Sir James followed him into the room and took Flynn by the arm. "Lord Bramshaw, you appear a little confused. And I am guessing you want to know why I didn't put you on the stand. I didn't because the evidence from everyone, especially the doctor, was compelling, and I don't think you would have done yourself any favors by giving your side of the story."

"What do you mean?" he asked, his voice edged with frustration.

"I mean, people can become emotional and, at times, angry when they are given the opportunity to defend themselves. Your father, may he rest in peace, was not a good man. But a court of law is not the place for you to be finally telling the world of his evil deeds. If you walk free today, you will have plenty of time to settle scores."

The door of the holding room opened. Augusta, along

with her father and uncle, arrived. She was red-eyed, and her bottom lip quivered, but she was holding her tears at bay. For him.

Flynn and Augusta settled into a corner, holding hands. Augusta was silent. She looked wrung out. He couldn't imagine what sort of toll this trial was taking on her. At a time when she should be basking in the joy of impending motherhood and spending sweet afternoons wrapped up in his embrace, she was sitting in a courtroom while her beloved husband was on trial for his life.

Flynn bent and kissed her brow. It was hot and sweaty when it should have been cool. "My love. I am so sorry that I have put you through this," he murmured.

Augusta squeezed his hand and replied, "We are in this together, to the end. No matter what happens."

The door opened once more, and a court clerk poked his head inside and spoke to Sir James Pence. He, in turn, addressed Flynn. "The jury is back. I think we have a verdict."

"Is the fact that they are back within an hour a good or a bad sign?" asked the Duke of Mowbray.

Sir James shrugged. "One can never tell. And I don't make a habit of giving clients false hope when I cannot promise anything."

The guards came in, and Flynn got to his feet. He hugged Augusta one last time. "I shall see you soon, my love."

Back inside the courtroom, there were a good deal more people in the public gallery than had been there earlier in the morning. He spied Gideon and Serafina in the crowd.

Thank heavens they are here to support Augusta if this all goes wrong.

"Earl Bramshaw, please take a seat in front of the jury," ordered Earl Talbot.

Flynn made his way over to the chair which had been

placed in front of the jury. A simple majority would give a final, fateful verdict.

His heart was thumping hard in his chest. The next few minutes would define the rest of his life.

"My lord triers, is there a verdict?"

The jury nodded as one.

"On the count of murder, how many votes do you have for a verdict of guilty?"

Flynn closed his eyes. He didn't want to watch.

"None, my lord. And none for a verdict of manslaughter. We have agreed on a unanimous verdict of not guilty, the act of self-defense having been proven."

Chapter Fifty-Five

✦✦✦

"Not Guilty." Flynn covered his face with his hands and took in three deep, calming breaths. His mind was still trying to absorb and make sense of what the words 'not guilty' actually meant. It was only when he caught the cry of anguish from Augusta that he finally dropped his hands and looked to the public gallery.

His wife was wrapped up in her father's embrace. Her head was buried in the folds of the duke's jacket, while her whole body shook as great, heart-rending sobs tore through her.

A hand came to rest on his shoulder, and he turned to meet the gaze of his defense counsel. He numbly accepted Sir James's outstretched hand, muttering a weak, "Thank you."

Is this real?

The court erupted into applause and shouts of 'justice has been done.' The rowdy cheers were still echoing off the ancient wooden walls when the judge finally brought his gavel down on the oak bench. *Bang. Bang.* "Order. I will have order," he demanded.

Flynn would give the man anything he wanted, just as long as he could walk from the court a free man.

The room settled into near silence once more. Augusta was still weeping in her father's arms.

The judge cleared his throat. "Lord Bramshaw, you have been acquitted of the charge of murder by a jury of your peers." He motioned to the clerk. "Please arrange to have the earl's personal possessions returned to him. I don't expect he wishes to return to the Tower of London this afternoon."

I have no intention of ever setting foot through any gate which leads into the Tower of London again in this life or the next.

He had spent the better part of a month in the Beauchamp Tower, and as far as he was concerned, that was more than enough for several lifetimes.

"Lord Bramshaw, you are free to go."

Flynn's shoulders sagged with relief. It was over. He could leave the House of Lords a free man. Take his wife and go home.

It took a few minutes of paperwork and talking to his lawyer before Flynn finally bowed to the judge and the jury. He turned and headed for the door, determined not to spend one minute longer in the court than was necessary. He caught the eye of one of the guards and shook his head. He wasn't interested in stopping to discuss possible arrangements to have his things returned from the Tower of London. He just wanted to get out.

I need to breathe fresh air.

Augusta and the Duke of Mowbray were waiting outside in the hall, along with a good many of his friends and family by the time Flynn left the court. He caught sight of Charles and Christopher Cadnam. His teary-eyed uncle gave him a wave, to which he shyly smiled back. He bowed to his cousin, grateful for his honest testimony. He couldn't talk to them, as words were still a struggle.

His wife stepped into his arms, and as Flynn wrapped her up in his embrace, the rest of the gathering disappeared from his thoughts. Augusta, all that mattered was her and their unborn child. Flynn closed his eyes and let the knowledge that he was a free man wash over him.

I am free. For the first time in my life, I am actually free. I wish my mother was here to see this day.

The rest of the well-wishers politely kept their distance, and he was grateful that they did. He needed this moment. No one else in the room, apart from Augusta, knew what he had been through. What the death of the earl had really meant. The end of years of pain and misery.

There would be time for handshakes and happy congratulations, but now all he wanted was to hold the one person who had never stopped believing in him. Who had always fought for their future.

He brushed a kiss on the top of her hair, and Augusta looked up. Her beautiful face was tear-stained, but a smile sat on her lips. Lips he'd feared he might never be able to kiss again if things had not gone his way in court today.

"Not guilty. Those would have to be the two most wonderful words I have ever heard," she whispered.

Flynn silently nodded. It was all still sinking in. He expected that there would be some difficult days ahead. Taking over an entire estate and London house when he had been given no training or insight into its management would bring with it a new set of challenges.

If I can survive the past year and a half, I can do anything. As long as Augusta is by my side.

"Did you want to go and find somewhere to celebrate?" asked Augusta.

Flynn shook his head. He really ought to spend time with his many supporters, but he was emotionally wrung out, incapable of small talk. Not today. His friends and family would have to understand his need to be alone with Augusta, and for the reality of the verdict to sink in.

Slipping his arm about her waist, he turned so that they both faced the group which had gathered. What he had to say was on behalf of himself and Augusta. "Friends. Family. Today has been nothing short of surreal. As you no doubt must appreciate, it will take a little time for my wife and I to come to terms with the events of the past month. With that in mind, I must beg your indulgence in allowing us to spend the rest of today alone."

The Duke of Mowbray stepped forward. "Of course. And when you are ready to share your good fortune with us, my wife and I would be honored to have all of you good people to a special reception at Mowbray House."

He met his father-in-law's gaze and gave him a small smile. He owed a great deal to the duke for all that he had done. For his unwavering support. The first chance he got to speak to him in private, he would let Clifford know how grateful he was for everything.

Hand in hand, Flynn and Augusta made their way out of the Palace of Westminster and into the mid-August sunshine. "What do you think of nipping over to the Red Lion for a spot of food or a tankard of English ale?" suggested Augusta.

"That sounds wonderful. But I have somewhere else I want to go before I look to fill my belly. My solicitors. I want Bramshaw House on the market before the end of the day. If I can sell the house and settle my father's debts, then we can start a new life together."

She gave him a quizzical look, and Flynn guessed what his wife was thinking. He was now Earl Bramshaw, and he had every right to live in his family home. But the thought of never going back to the Tower of London had stirred another idea in his mind.

"I once swore I would never set foot in that place ever

again, and I should have kept that vow. Bramshaw House has been nothing but a place of abject misery and torture for me. Once we have sold it, we can buy another house."

His time in Europe and Rome had taught Flynn that he didn't need a large house. He had rattled around Matteo's private palace for weeks and never felt settled.

Augusta rubbed her hand gently over the small swell of her belly. It was a particular habit of hers that Flynn found endearing.

"We need a home of our own by the time this baby arrives. I love my mother dearly, but I don't want to be living under the same roof as her when I give birth."

Flynn chuckled softly. He could just imagine the duchess giving orders as to how her grandchild was to be nursed and raised. Augusta deserved her own home, a place where she could be the lady of the house. He rested his hand over hers and bent to kiss her. "I promise we will be settled in our new home long before then."

They had gone but a few feet more when Augusta stopped and turned to him. "I want us to go to Bramshaw House. While I never managed to make it inside whenever I called on the other Earl Bramshaw, today I want to be able to visit it with my Earl Bramshaw."

"What do you mean you called on him?"

"When you went missing, I made it my business to go and see your father. Victoria and I paid a number of visits to Bramshaw House. The earl and I exchanged unpleasant words."

Flynn bit back a grin. He could just imagine Augusta taking the fight to his father and not backing down.

"But that is none the matter. I want us to visit the house. If you feel you can't go inside, I shall understand."

He had survived a near-death experience, been kidnapped, and taken far from home, so it sounded foolish to think he might be afraid of an old house. The earl was gone.

Could he put his fear to one side and go with Augusta to see the house?

She gave him a soft, encouraging smile in response to his "Yes," and hand in hand they made their way out to the roadside, where Flynn hailed a hack. "Number seven, Cavendish Square, please."

He was going back to Bramshaw House, the mansion that held so many bitter, dark memories. A place that had never been home.

Chapter Fifty-Six

Augusta slipped the key in the lock and opened the front door of Bramshaw House. Earlier in the week, she'd been given the key by Christopher. Without her husband's knowledge, Countess Bramshaw had paid the Cadnam residence a visit.

It irked her that the late earl had seen fit to bestow upon Christopher Cadnam the means to enter Bramshaw House but spitefully not his own son. She doubted she would ever stop being angry with Flynn's father. Only time would possibly serve to lessen her boiling rage.

A scowling Flynn glanced at the key, his expression softening when she turned and handed it to him. "This is yours, Lord Bramshaw, from today until the last day that you leave this house. No one will ever make you wait outside in the street again."

Flynn ushered Augusta inside. Silence greeted them. During her first visit to the house, Augusta had paid all the staff and given them their immediate notice, informing them that their services were no longer required. Her reasons had been two-fold. If Flynn had been found guilty of his father's murder and they had been forced to flee the country, the house would have had to be urgently sold and the proceeds sent to them abroad.

Her second reason was now playing out. If Flynn came into the house and he didn't have to face the servants, he might feel a little different about things.

"Where is everyone?" he asked.

"I came here a few days ago and sacked them all. Paid them a severance and told them that if they ever dared speak of what had gone on this house during your father's lifetime, I would make certain that they never worked in a good house ever again. And then I would sue."

Her mother had given her that idea. The duchess had many years experience of dealing with loose-lipped servants. The threat of damaged reputations and poor job prospects usually did the trick.

"And the dogs?"

Augusta nodded. "At Mowbray House for the time being. The footmen have been taking them for daily walks. But we will need to decide on what is to happen with the dogs."

She might be able to work her magic and somehow convince Flynn to keep the house, but the greyhounds were likely a step too far. Having to see them every day would be a constant reminder of how he had been made to feel less than the late earl's pets.

"If you would indulge me for a short time, I have a few suggestions about Bramshaw House."

It wasn't as fancy a residence as Mowbray House, but it had the bones of a family home. The kitchens would need updating, along with new carpets and some minor repairs. Augusta had done some sums and decided she could make it work without bankrupting them.

He bent and kissed her cheek. "I have a lifetime of indulgence planned for you, my love. Lead on."

Over the next hour, they moved from room to room. Augusta giving Flynn her opinion as to what could be done and where. When they reached the door of his old bedroom, she stopped. "I think we could leave that room for another time."

Her husband had been through enough over the past month. Augusta was determined that this one room wasn't going to break the joy of today. She moved passed the door, heading toward the library at the end of the hall.

"I will catch up with you in a minute," he said.

Augusta sucked in a deep breath as Flynn disappeared through the doorway of his old room.

Every time he had sworn to never set foot in this place again, Flynn had proven himself wrong. He was sure the last time, had been the last time.

"And yet, here I am. Standing in my old bedroom."

His gaze went to the carpet, to the spot where the earl had died in Christopher's arms. Where he too had lain stricken on the floor, his chest ablaze with pain, his mind overwhelmed with anger and grief.

Today he felt none of those emotions, just a lingering sadness for what might have been and all the wasted years.

It would be so easy to turn on his heel, go downstairs, walk out the front door, and never return. To go to his solicitors and have the deeds of sale drawn up.

The spark in Augusta's eyes when she talked about the house. Of what it could be for them, and their children stayed his hand. Could this really be a family home once more? From what his uncle had told him, Bramshaw House had once been a happy place. It was now up to him to decide whether it would be such a home again.

No. It's G's and my decision. My wife is who will make wherever we live a home.

At the sound of her footsteps, Flynn turned. Augusta stood in the doorway; a pensive look sat on her face. She wanted this house, but he knew her well enough to know that if it caused him pain, his wife would give it up without a moment's hesitation.

He held out his hand to her. "If we stay here, I want this room stripped of everything. Every inch of wall and floor scrubbed. New carpet. New furnishings. And your agreement that it will never be used as a bedroom. I don't want any of our children sleeping in here."

It sounded petulant and small-minded, but he had to erase the past. This room had seen so much of his misery over the years, Flynn suspected his pain was imprinted deep within the plasterwork.

Augusta slipped her hand into his, rising up on her toes to plant a tender kiss on Flynn's lips. "Yes. I was thinking we could use this as a sewing room, a place in which to create good things. I've chosen some fabric for the windows. You only have to say the word, and I can order it."

Flynn stood on the edge of a momentous decision. Today had been a day of emotional upheaval with the trial and his release from prison. Much as he wished to say yes, he needed time. "Could we look at the Bramshaw estate finances first before we start ordering anything for the house? I have no idea as to their current state. We might well be penniless for all I know."

A blush of pink glowed on Augusta's cheeks. "Would you be angry with me if I told you I asked Papa and his steward to look over the books while you were in the Tower of London? The earldom isn't in as bad a financial condition as I thought. My father is prepared to make some minor changes to my dowry so we can clear the debts and then have a tidy sum left over. Less, of course, the sizeable, non-refundable bribe I had to pay in order to have your escape made ready."

"Escape?"

"You were going to be snatched on the way back to the Tower of London if the verdict didn't go our way. Serafina had arranged for a fast de Luca ship to be ready to spirit us out of England. We were going back to Rome."

He pulled Augusta into his embrace and kissed her soundly. She had always said they wouldn't ever be parted again, and his stubborn, wonderful wife had meant it.

I love this woman.

Chapter Fifty-Seven

A *month later*
Bramshaw House

"I am pleased that the two of you changed your mind about selling this place. I'm sure it will make a wonderful home for your children. I have many happy memories of here from my own childhood," said Charles.

The three of them were standing in the foyer of Bramshaw House. Servants and tradesmen were busy in every room. Slowly but surely, the house was being transformed. Gone was the drab color palette of grays and browns which the late earl had inflicted on the house. In its place were pale greens, blues, and summer cream. A fresh new look for a fresh start.

Augusta turned and nodded to her husband. "See, I knew it made sense not to rush into making a decision about selling the house."

Flynn raised his eyebrows and gave her a smile. Of course,

his wife was right. He was quickly discovering that when it came to matters of home and hearth, she was rarely wrong.

It had been a rash notion on his part, but he hadn't been thinking all too clearly in the minutes after he had been found not guilty of his father's murder. All Flynn had wanted to do at that moment was to sweep all traces of the late Earl Bramshaw from his life.

I am glad we kept the house.

"And what about the greyhounds—what's to happen with them?" asked Charles.

The decision over the fate of the overfed dogs had been a straightforward one. While some unkind people had suggested Flynn either sell the beasts or have them put down, he was adamant that any acts of cruelty had died along with his father.

"I have sent them to Southampton. They are going to spend the rest of their days living happily at the Bramshaw estate. There they will be taken on long walks every afternoon and allowed to be dogs once more."

He wasn't prepared to admit to his uncle that while he didn't wish ill of his father's pets, he also couldn't stand the idea of seeing them every day wandering the halls of Bramshaw House. They reminded him too much of the earl. Of the pain and suffering that he had endured at the hands of his sire.

Charles nodded his agreement. "That's probably the best place for them. My brother might have thought he was being a good master to those dogs, but they were not meant to be fat. A few months of them getting out and enjoying real exercise will see the two dogs restored to full health." He glanced over at Augusta and smiled. "And speaking of health, how are you, Countess Bramshaw?"

She slipped her hand into Flynn's and gave it a gentle

squeeze. "I am well, thank you, Uncle Charles. Tired most of the time, but otherwise in good spirits."

Flynn lowered his gaze to the floor, not wanting to meet his uncle's eye. The baby was only one reason why his wife had taken to enjoying naps in the afternoon. No one had ever told him how some expectant mothers were near insatiable. He was having a hard time keeping up with Augusta and her sexual demands.

~

Charles Cadnam waved his nephew and wife goodbye, then returned home to his own wife, who was waiting for him upstairs in their private sitting room. Erin rose from her chair and came to his side. She smiled up at him as he wrapped his arms around her.

"Do I take it from the smile on your face that your visit went well?"

Her husband nodded. "Yes, the house looks wonderful, and Flynn has done exceedingly well in choosing Augusta. She is already settling into the role of Countess Bramshaw."

Erin sighed. "Thank heavens that whole nightmare is finally over. And you are right, my love. He did select the perfect girl. Augusta is a fine young woman, and I am relieved to know that the title is once more in safe hands. And that Christopher is no longer under the sway of his uncle. I feared in time our son would succumb to Ronald's temptation, and he would be lost to us."

What his own late father would have made of his brother's terrible treatment of Flynn, Charles couldn't begin to imagine. The Cadnam's had once been a happy and close-knit family, and he hoped that with the recent changes, it might well be a loving one again.

Erin kissed her husband, then drew out of his embrace. "I

had better go and talk to cook about this evening's supper. Do you know if Christopher will be home to join us?"

Charles nodded. "Yes, he mentioned he would be. I think the events of the last month or so have given him pause."

His uncle had been grooming Christopher to take over as Earl Bramshaw, but with the return of Flynn, his life had reached an unexpected fork in the road. It would take time for him to figure out his own future. Charles intended to be there for his son.

As he would be for his firstborn son.

After Erin had left the room, closing the door behind her, Charles crossed the floor to the small rosewood nightstand which sat under the window. He unlocked the top drawer and took out a piece of folded yellowed paper.

The Morning Herald
June 12, 1791

One has to wonder, dear reader, as to what has transpired at Bramshaw House over the past few weeks. For several months now, the Honorable Charles Cadnam has been seen in the company of Lady Alice Henn, and it was noted from their happy disposition that they made quite the handsome couple. Yet, one reads in the Times yesterday morning that it is the older Cadnam brother, Earl Bramshaw, whom Lady Alice is now set to marry.

The paper might have aged, but the pain and anger still burned brightly. His brother had stolen the woman he loved. Valuing the connection of a noble title, Lady Alice's father had ignored her heartbroken wishes and forced her to marry the earl. With his victory against Charles complete, Earl Bramshaw had then treated his new bride most cruelly.

Following the birth of their only child, Flynn, both the countess and her son had been banished to the Bramshaw estate near Southampton. Never to return to London.

Charles read the note one last time, then did something he had always promised himself he would do—he threw it into the flames of the nearby fire. As he stood and watched it turn to ash, a soft smile crept to his lips.

"You might have wanted Christopher to eventually become Earl Bramshaw. Assumed you could take my son and mold him into being someone bitter and twisted just like you. But I would have killed you myself, and gone to the gallows a happy man, rather than standing idly by while you stole yet another of my sons from me."

Epilogue

The Morning Herald
Social Pages

*A party full of laughter and wonderful food was held at Bramshaw
House last week. The Earl and Countess Bramshaw shared the
evening with close friends and family.*

*The Bishop of London, Lord Hugh Radley, the countess's uncle, gave a
blessing to the newlyweds, who our readers will recall were married
in Rome earlier this year. More than one guest was overheard to
mention how handsome and happy the new Earl Bramshaw appeared
as he paid special attention to his expectant wife.*

*Dear readers, it makes your correspondent's heart sing to know that
the former Vagabond Viscount is a happily married man, and his
clothes now match his elevated status. He makes a particularly fine
specimen of the English nobleman.*

Augusta smiled as she read that last sentence. It was wonderful to know that the rest of London's high society no longer considered her husband to be someone open to such public scorn. Flynn had suffered long enough with that horrid moniker.

She was about to set the newspaper down and get on with the rest of her breakfast when her eye caught the letter to the editor section. Her pulse quickened as she took in the all-too-familiar words. "They have published one of Victoria's letters to the editor."

Across the table, Flynn's mouth opened in a small 'O' of surprise. She handed him the paper and sat watching the expression on her husband's face as he read her sister's hastily penned tirade.

A letter to the editor
My good man, I wish to take issue with your choice of food critic. As displayed in his weekly column, the fool is clearly lacking when it comes to the fundamentals of the culinary arts. This reader is forced to endure his bumbling words of praise for both restaurants and chefs who have no business offering their wares to unsuspecting customers. One would think that in a city the size of London, you would be able to find someone with a better understanding of what is good food, and what is most certainly not.
Your continually dissatisfied reader.

Flynn glanced up from the newspaper. He burst out laughing. "Oh, my Lord, this is priceless. Your sister doesn't hold back on giving her opinion, but to actually see it published in a major newspaper is beyond brilliant. What will your mother say?"

A grinning Augusta shook her head. "Poor man, he has no idea what he is up against." She genuinely pitied the food critic for *The Morning Herald*. Victoria had set her sights on taking the man down, and she suspected this was only the first volley in the bloody war her sister intended to wage. And win.

"I can only hope Mama doesn't read it. She has certainly taken a dim view of *The Morning Herald* since the scandal over her, and Papa was reported so heavily by them."

The Duchess of Mowbray had initially been quiet on the social front since her return to England, but over the past few weeks she had started getting out more, and when she did, Lady Anne hadn't held back on confronting anyone who dared to offer their opinion as to the reason behind her extended stay in Rome.

Her parents were reunited and back to their battling best. Coco and Victoria were keeping Augusta abreast of all the current rows their parents were conducting. And of the long periods the duke and duchess were spending sequestered in their private apartments while they made up. All was right once more in the Kembal family.

"Did you see what they wrote about us? And especially you."

Flynn folded up the paper, then rose from his seat. He came around to where Augusta sat and knelt beside her chair. "Handsome and happy. I'm not sure about the first, but I am certain of the second. And it is all down to you, Augusta, my love."

A smiling Augusta accepted his tender flurry of kisses.

For once the newspaper had it right. Flynn was no longer the Vagabond Viscount. Her wonderful husband was Earl Bramshaw. Together, they had a bright future ahead of them.

Taking his hand, she placed it gently on her pregnant belly.

"It's been a long journey, Flynn, but you are home at last."

I hope you enjoyed Flynn and Augusta's story. Please visit my website for details of my other books, including print and audio editions.

Sasha Cottman Website
www.sashacottman.com

Author's Notes

It is, from beginning to end, a tissue of bombast, silliness, and absurdity.
The curtain fell amid the hisses and groans of a great majority of the House.

This is the actual review of the play *The Humorous Lieutenant* which appeared in the London Star on Monday, January 20, 1817. Apparently, it was a play which had previously failed, and had undergone a major rewrite. The new version of the play opened and closed on the same night. Flynn's so called friend had clearly heard the rumors and decided that his Saturday evening was better spent elsewhere.
Spare a thought for the playwrights, the review of their terrible play still lives on some two hundred years later.

All Saints' church in Rome is situated at number 153 Via del Babuino, close to the Spanish Steps.
https://www.allsaintsrome.org/

Join the VIP readers for your FREE book

Regency London's wild child is about to meet her match...

If Lady Cecily Norris' parents are ashamed of her, they only have themselves to blame.

As a young girl, she was sent to live at a country estate along with other unwanted children of the *ton*. Her upbringing could only be described as unconventional and haphazard.

Cecily has now become a young woman both beautiful and wild at heart. Returning to London, she is determined to set her own rules for how she lives her life. As far as she is concerned, the *ton* and all its expectations for how a young unmarried woman should behave, can all go hang.

But she cannot fully escape her future, and her dismayed parents demand that she make a suitable and sensible marriage.

When Lord Thomas Rosemount trips over Cecily in a dark garden, he falls hard. His heart quickly follows.

In Thomas, Cecily encounters a man very different from those that she has lived with all her life. He is reliable, sensible, and dare she say a little boring?

But Thomas offers her something that she has never known before. A home and a future with someone who loves her.

Thomas knows it will take more than pretty words and a kind heart to win Cecily's hand, and he will have to look deep inside himself to discover whether he is truly the man who can tame a Wild English Rose.

Scan the QR Code to join the VIP readers and receive your FREE copy of A Wild English Rose.

Also by Sasha Cottman

SERIES

The Duke of Strathmore
The Noble Lords
Rogues of the Road
London Lords

For other releases and international editions please visit
www.sashacottman.com

The Duke of Strathmore

Letter from a Rake

An Unsuitable Match

The Duke's Daughter

A Scottish Duke for Christmas

My Gentleman Spy

Lord of Mischief

The Ice Queen

Two of a Kind

A Lady's Heart Deceived

All is Fair in Love

Tempted by the English Marquis

The Vagabond Viscount

Duke of Strathmore Novellas

Mistletoe and Kisses

A Wild English Rose

The Noble Lords

Love Lessons for the Viscount

A Lord with Wicked Intentions

A Scandalous Rogue for Lady Eliza

Unexpected Duke

The Noble Lords Boxed Set

Rogues of the Road

Rogue for Hire

Stolen by the Rogue

When a Rogue Falls

The Rogue and the Jewel

King of Rogues

London Lords

Devoted to the Spanish Duke

Promised to the Swedish Prince

An Italian Count for Christmas

Wedded to the Welsh Baron

Bound to the Belgian Count

About the Author

USA Today bestselling author Sasha Cottman was born in
England, but raised in Australia. Having her heart in two
places has created a love for travel, which at last count was to
over 55 countries. A travel guide is always on her pile of new
books to read.

Sasha's novels are set around the Regency period in England,
Scotland, and Europe. Her books are centred on the themes
of love, honor, and family. Visit her website at www.
sashacottman.com

For international editions of novels, please visit
www.sashacottman.com

Lightning Source UK Ltd.
Milton Keynes UK
UKHW040946160223
417122UK00002B/441